THE FLORAL ARRANGEMENT

ELIZABETH LULY

ISBN 978-0-6455808-7-7 (paperback)

ISBN 978-0-6455808-6-0 (ebook)

Red Tractor Farm

Sapphire Springs

CHAPTER ONE

OLIVIA

THIS IS A BAD IDEA.

Heart thudding, I peered through the door adorned with rainbow flags. A group of people sat by a table near the window, looking like they'd stepped out of a queer clothing ad: flannel shirts, button-ups, piercings, tats, and stylish hairstyles.

I looked down at my tan coat, floral jumpsuit, and brown boots. *Oh dear.* I should come back later, once I'd had a chance to buy a whole new wardrobe and visit a hairdresser. Or not at all. The whole thing was stupid.

Someone cleared their throat behind me. "Are you going in?"

My stomach somersaulted. I sucked in a deep breath to steady myself. *Olivia, you've been planning this for weeks. Just do it. The clock is ticking. You'll regret it if you don't.*

"Do you need help opening the door?" The woman's voice, smooth and calm, gave nothing away. She was either genuinely concerned about my door-opening abilities, or she was just getting impatient.

"No. Sorry." I pushed the door open, keeping my head

facing forward in case the sight of her weakened my resolve to go through with my plan.

Inside, the smell of stale alcohol and the low hum of chatter hit me. Now that I was actually doing this, a buzz of excitement mixed with my nerves, sending my stomach swirling. Trying to exude confidence, I walked with purpose to the bar. I passed the five stylish patrons at the window. To my disappointment, they didn't look up. Another group of people were gathered around the pool table, laughing. A few couples were seated at the bar. I didn't recognize anyone. *Thank god.* Sure, my hometown, Sapphire Springs, might be over thirty minutes away, but Pryde was the only queer bar in the Hudson Valley south of Poughkeepsie—at least the only one I knew that did "Sapphic Saturdays."

I chose a bar stool away from the couples and clambered onto the high leather seat. Losing my balance, my butt slipped on the smooth surface. I grabbed the dark wooden counter to steady myself just in time and exhaled. Falling on my ass was *not* part of my plan.

Okay. What now? In my fantasies, a hot queer woman would approach me and strike up a conversation, but now I was here, that prospect seemed less likely. Everyone in the bar was engrossed with their lovers or friends.

Someone slid onto the bar stool two seats down from me. My heartbeat quickened. They were alone. Perhaps waiting for someone? I swallowed, unable to make eye contact. I needed a few minutes to regain my composure before attempting to start up a conversation with a stranger.

I picked up a drinks menu from the counter and stared at it intently, taking nothing in. Sweat pricked under my arms. Fumbling, I unbuttoned my coat and pulled it off. *Now, what to do with it?* I ran my hand under the bar, smiling when it hit a hook. I bent down and draped my coat over it. The coat fell onto the ground. Sighing, I clambered off the stool, bending down to place it more carefully over the hook. At least since no one was paying me any attention, there was no one to witness my butt sticking in the air.

As I went to stand, my head smashed against the counter. Pain tore through my skull. I took a deep breath, readying myself to climb back onto the stool. I stopped still as my gaze fell on the woman who'd taken a seat near me.

I noticed her clothes first. She'd also missed the dress code. A tailored, navy-blue suit flattered her slim, tall frame. Her jacket was open, and underneath was a white business shirt, unbuttoned part-way down her chest. A hint of cleavage was just visible.

My gaze wandered up, taking in her full lips, high cheekbones, and short blond hair, which was parted on her left side and flopped across her forehead above her piercing blue eyes—piercing blue eyes that were staring directly at me.

Shit. Stop gawking Liv.

She was exactly the sort of woman who'd always turned my head. Androgynous. Older than me. Self-assured. But was it sexual attraction I felt, or just a platonic appreciation for a beautiful woman? I usually hated suits—almost all of my encounters with them had been extremely negative— but somehow I didn't mind this one. In fact, I might have even liked the suit. On her.

Her intense eyes narrowed.

Heat flushed my cheeks. Fuck. She'd clearly caught me ogling at her and wasn't pleased.

"Are you okay?" she asked, raising an eyebrow.

Oh god. I recognized that voice. This striking woman

was the person who'd witnessed me hesitating outside the bar only minutes earlier.

"Um, yes, sorry," I mumbled. I couldn't exactly tell her I'd been mesmerized by her androgynous beauty.

"Why are you apologizing? You hit your head, not mine. Or are you concussed?" she asked.

Thank god. She'd been asking if my head was okay, not calling me out for staring at her. Except—my cheeks flamed even hotter—she must have witnessed me fumbling around under the counter with my butt in the air.

"Oh, no. I'm fine, thanks." I ran my fingers through my hair and then focused my efforts on getting back on the stool without slipping off again.

"I'm not usually this clumsy. It must just be nerves," I babbled, wincing as the words left my mouth. *Very smooth, Olivia.*

"Nerves? Are you waiting for a date?" She raised an eyebrow again, her voice silky.

"No..." I said, my mouth dry. I'd bet my best peonies that it hadn't taken watching Michelle Pfeiffer slinking around on the screen as Catwoman as a wide-eyed four-teen-year-old for her to start questioning her sexuality—and another seventeen years to get around to actually exploring it. She'd probably been born knowing her sexual orientation.

To my relief, the woman didn't press me further. Instead, she waved down the butch bartender. "I'll have a double Woodford Reserve, neat, thank you."

The bartender nodded and turned to me. "And anything for you?"

"Um." I grabbed the menu, picking the first thing my eyes fell upon. "A negroni, thanks."

"Good choice." The woman tilted her head, her eyes lingering on me. "Are you from around here?"

Huh. I hadn't expected her to keep up the conversation, especially given how lackluster my contributions had been so far. Perhaps she felt sorry for me?

"Um, fairly close." I wanted to protect my anonymity for the time being. "You?"

She shook her head. "I live in Manhattan. I'm just here visiting my parents and needed... to get out of the house."

I grimaced. I'd had to move back in with my parents a few times in my twenties, and as much as I loved them, I'd found it a struggle not having my own space. Thank god those days were behind me.

The bartender placed my negroni in front of me, the red liquid lapping against the rim of the glass. "Would you like to start a tab?"

"No, that's okay. I'll settle this one now." My wallet was in my coat pocket, so I bent down to unhook my coat, one hand clutching the counter for stability.

"This one's on me."

I straightened up just as the woman handed over a fancy-looking Amex to the bartender. "No, that's okay–"

"To avoid any further head injuries," the woman said. "I don't think Brenda wants to have to fill out an incident report."

"Brenda?" I frowned.

The woman nodded toward the bartender, who was swiping the Amex at the other end of the bar. "Her name is Brenda."

"Ah. Do you come here often?" I cringed. Could I sound any more clichéd?

"No, just when I'm visiting my parents and need to get my mother off my back. She'll stop bothering me for the rest of the weekend now that I've made an appearance at a queer bar."

I took a sip of my drink and stared at the woman. I couldn't quite imagine her having a mother who harassed her into going to a queer bar.

"She's very eager for me to move here, settle down and have kids." The woman pursed her mouth.

"Ah, so you're here looking for a wife?" I asked, a teasing tone to my voice. I twisted on my seat to face her more fully, surprised by my growing comfort.

"Are you volunteering?" She raised an eyebrow, the corner of her mouth curving up.

I laughed. "I think we should get to know each other first a little, don't you?" Either this woman's company was putting me at ease, or the negroni was. Possibly both.

"Probably," she said. "But before you start planning our wedding, I should let you know it's only my parents who want me to find a wife. I'm happily single."

"Damn! I'd already chosen a color scheme," I said, pouting.

"My bad." The woman grimaced and took a swig of her whiskey.

I tilted my head. "So you just make an appearance here to appease your mom and then head home?"

She nodded. "I usually nurse a drink at the bar while I do some work and then wait until it's safe for me to drive home again."

"That sounds like fun," I said, the corners of my mouth twitching. "But not tonight?"

Had she changed her usual anti-social routine to speak to me? I edged slightly closer to her on my seat. Over the scent of stale booze and greasy food, I caught a hint of cedar. Was that her? I resisted the urge to lean in farther to find out.

The woman's blue eyes flickered for a moment, and then she smirked. "No, not tonight. After witnessing your head injury, for medical reasons I thought it was best to strike up a conversation with you, to ensure you remained lucid."

I snorted. While she was clearly joking, was she a doctor? My gaze dropped to her hands, taking in her long, slender fingers and short, unpolished nails. She wasn't a manual laborer, that was for sure. An image of those fingers lightly trailing down my back flickered into my mind, sending a shiver down my spine. I blinked. Straight women wouldn't have these types of thoughts, would they?

Brenda returned, handing the Amex back to its owner. Her elegant index finger and thumb clamped down on her credit card, then she slid it into a pocket on her phone case.

Stop gawking at her fingers, Liv. She's going to think you're a creep.

As she snapped the case shut, I caught a glimpse of a photo of a young blond girl who bore more than a passing resemblance to her. Was it her daughter? Maybe she was divorced, and that was why she was so anti-marriage.

"Thank you." I smiled. "I'll get the next one."

"Fine. As long as I can hand you your coat." While her delivery was deadpan, there was a twinkle in the woman's eye. She shifted her body so she was facing me, and the scent of cedar grew stronger. *So it is her.*

"We'll see. You might be falling off your chair soon too." I grinned and nodded at her glass which contained a very generous pour of whiskey. "I'm Olivia, by the way."

"Roz," she replied, then raised her glass, those intense blue eyes focused directly on mine. "Cheers."

Roz's soft, full lips pressed against the glass, and a flicker of heat licked my core. *Oh god.* That definitely did not feel platonic.

"Cheers!" I said, taking a larger-than-intended gulp of my negroni.

As the alcohol warmed my throat, I glanced around the room again. Roz was clearly being polite, probably having taken pity on me after witnessing my ineptitude. While she was intriguing and attractive, was her presence scaring off potential suitors who might actually be interested in me? I resisted the urge to chuckle at my own thoughts. *Other suitors? This isn't the 1800s, Liv.* My scan of the room didn't identify any eligible options in any event.

A ringtone brought my attention back to Roz. She whipped a phone out of her pocket and glowered at it.

"Is everything okay?" I asked.

"Yes, just work," Roz replied, pursing her lips.

"On a Saturday night?" I frowned.

"Yes, unfortunately, in my line of work I'm on call twenty-four seven. I was in a video conference earlier today, trying to resolve something. It appears things have unraveled again." Roz slipped off the bar stool. "I need to take this. Wait for me."

She turned and strode out of the bar.

Her words rang in my ears. *Wait for me.* Usually, I'd bristle at someone giving me directions like that, especially in her clipped tone, but instead my neck tingled.

I gazed after her, my eyes lingering on her firm-looking butt encased in navy suit pants that looked like they'd been tailored especially for her. They probably were. Everything about Roz screamed expensive.

Roz wasn't giving me doctor vibes anymore. Now it was more like political-fixer or ruthless-CEO energy. Something told me I wouldn't want to go up against this woman in a work context.

"First date?"

I jumped in my seat, turning to find Brenda, the bartender, smiling at me over the counter.

Heat warmed my face. "Um, no. We don't know each other."

"You will soon if you two keep up with that flirting," Brenda said, her smile even wider. "It's very cute—not that I'm eavesdropping or anything."

I stared. *Flirting?* We hadn't been flirting. Had we? I ran through our interactions in my head. I certainly found her interesting... and attractive, possibly in a sexual way. Shit. Had it been that obvious?

Had Roz been flirting with *me?* There had been a definite note of teasing to her voice. She'd said she was happily single, but perhaps she was looking for something more casual. Or just playing with me.

My pulse jumped as the door to the bar opened, and Roz stepped inside, striding over to me. A shiver of nervous anticipation rushed down my spine.

I twisted my body to face Roz as she sat down. "Is everything alri—*shit!*"

As I turned, my elbow collided with my negroni, sending it skidding across the smooth wood of the bar at an alarming speed. My chest clenched. I shot out my hand to try to stop it, but I wasn't fast enough. It flew off the counter, splashing over Roz's shirt and pants before landing in her crotch.

"Shit, shit, shit! I'm so sorry."

Roz's previously white shirt clung to her small breasts and flat stomach, stained a reddish brown. The outline of her bra was visible underneath. *Oh god, I think it's soaked her bra as well.*

I blinked.

Stop staring at her chest and do something, Olivia.

I grabbed the napkin Brenda had served with my drink. I reached out, almost patting Roz's chest directly before I came to my senses and handed it to her instead.

Roz, who had frozen for a moment, took the napkin and began to dab herself.

"I'm so, so sorry," I repeated.

She pursed her lips. "I'll chalk that up to the head injury."

"I usually have a spare t-shirt in the car, just in case I get dirty while I'm working. I'll go grab it."

"Dirty while you're working?" Roz raised an eyebrow. Was there something slightly suggestive in the way "dirty" had rolled off her tongue? "But yes, if you have a spare t-shirt, that would be appreciated." She stared down at her soaked torso.

"Okay, I'll be back in a moment." I slipped off the bar stool.

Roz placed the napkin on the bar. "I'll head to the restroom to clean myself up."

I jogged outside to my car parked on the dark street, breathing out a sigh of relief as I opened the trunk and spotted my t-shirt poking out of a bag in the corner. I pulled it out of the bag and gave it a sniff. Thankfully, all I could smell was the faint scent of laundry detergent.

I pushed open the door of the bar to find Roz's seat still empty, so I headed for the restroom. There I found her standing in front of the mirror, shirtless, patting a half white, half brown-splattered bra with paper towels. I took in her toned, pale upper body and the curves of her breasts. My heart stuttered. Okay, surely that wasn't the reaction of a straight woman. Heat rushed to my cheeks.

"Um, here's the shirt," I said, trying to avert my eyes while throwing her the top. It was a shocking throw, and it was only thanks to Roz's quick reflexes that she caught it before it landed in the overflowing trashcan behind her. Roz shook out the t-shirt and inspected it, her eyebrows shooting up.

A twinge of defensiveness needled my chest. "Sorry. I don't keep any formal shirts in my car." Or anywhere else, for that matter.

"Are you serious?" Roz continued staring at the shirt.

I frowned. It wasn't as fancy as her negroni-splattered shirt, but surely it was fine as a temporary solution.

Roz held the t-shirt out so I could see the front.

Oh.

Heat warmed my cheeks. "Oops, sorry. I forgot it said that."

The words *I wet my plants* over a pot of flowers seemed twice as big tonight. It was perfect for me to wear around Sapphire Springs as the local florist, but perhaps it wasn't quite as funny when you'd just had a drink spilled on your chest and crotch, especially not when you were a bit fancy like Roz.

"I'd offer you my jumpsuit, but I think it would give you a wedgie," I said, gesturing toward Roz's extra few inches of height.

Roz pressed her lips together. "This will have to do."

"Well, at least you're not trying to pick anyone up tonight. And if you wanted, you could tell your mom a hot woman at the bar gave it to you. That might get her off your back for a while." I slammed my mouth shut. I hadn't thought through just how flirtatious that would sound.

"A hot woman?" Roz smirked.

"Well..." I dug my teeth into my lower lip.

We gazed at each other. Was it my imagination, or were her eyes smoldering?

Heat sparked low in my belly.

There was absolutely nothing platonic about that sensation.

Roz's tongue slipped out, wetting her red, full lips. I watched, transfixed. It was only as my tongue slid back into my mouth, my lips now moist, that I realized I'd mirrored her movements.

My heart thudded.

Was I reading this situation right? Were we about to—

Roz tossed the t-shirt on the restroom counter and stepped forward, her stunning, lean, shirtless body now only a foot from mine.

Oh god, I think this is actually happening.

Adrenaline rushed through me as Roz took another step toward me, now so close I could feel her soft, warm, whiskey-scented breath on my face and smell the hint of cedar I'd detected at the bar.

I swallowed.

"I think you're very hot, Olivia," Roz murmured, her voice low, "despite your terrible taste in t-shirts."

The fine hairs on the back of my neck prickled.

I leaned forward, my nerves overcome by a bolt of desire for the woman in front of me.

My whole body quivered as we gazed into each other's eyes, our heads moving closer in unison, as though a magnetic force was at work.

Oh shit. There was no doubt about it. This was sexual attraction alright. And on a completely different level to anything I'd experienced.

Our lips met, and my mind tipped off a ledge.

Our tongues tangled as our hands grabbed at each other's bodies, hers on my butt and waist, mine on her upper back and neck. I was breathless, dizzy, completely into it. Hunger roared through me. This kiss was unlike any other.

Suddenly, my back was against the wall, Roz's thigh pressing between my legs, sending a delicious pressure to the place that needed it most. *Oh god.* The need to be as close as humanly possible to this woman was all consuming. Nothing else mattered. I moaned.

An image of Roz tearing off my clothes, falling to her knees and satisfying my desires with those long, elegant fingers shot into my head, and I moaned even louder. Yes, we were in a public place, but I didn't care. In fact, the thought of being discovered sent a small, surprising thrill of excitement shooting down my spine.

As if conjured by my fantasies, a creaking noise stilled our bodies and sent my eyelids shooting up.

The door to the restroom had opened, and a woman stood in its frame, her eyes widening as she took us in. Despite my earlier thoughts, I didn't want to make anyone uncomfortable. I dropped my hands, and Roz stepped back.

"Sorry," said the woman as she edged into a toilet stall, averting her gaze. "Don't mind me."

"Perhaps we should continue this somewhere more private," Roz murmured, swiping my t-shirt off the counter. "If you're okay with this just being a one-night thing?"

"Yes," I said, ignoring the urge to grin wildly and pinch myself. This gorgeous, sophisticated older woman wanted to sleep with *me*?

Roz pulled my shirt over her head. Even though I was

still buzzing from the kiss and from Roz's invitation, I had to hold back a laugh.

Roz looked in the mirror and frowned. Her refined, sophisticated vibe was seriously undermined by the unfortunate pun.

The woman who'd interrupted our kiss exited the toilet stall, quickly washed her hands, and left.

I readjusted my jumpsuit, which had gotten out of alignment. "You're more than welcome to come to my place, unless you'd rather parade me in front of your mom at your parents' house."

Roz snorted. "As appealing as that sounds, your place is preferable—assuming you don't live with *your* parents."

I allowed myself to grin. "Nope, I live alone."

"Your place it is, then."

My stomach flipped. Only an hour ago, I wasn't even sure whether I was interested in women. Now, I'd just had the best kiss of my life and was about to take an extremely hot woman back to my apartment.

"I might just use the restroom before we head off. I'll meet you out there?" I didn't need to pee, but I wanted a minute to take stock.

Roz nodded and left the restroom.

I sat on the toilet seat, my mind racing. This evening was going better than my wildest dreams. Roz was perfect: attractive, older, more experienced, and only available for a one-night stand. I'd have a single, hopefully mind-blowing night with her, and then she'd go back to Manhattan. My worries about whether it was ethical to try to meet people to work out my sexuality didn't apply here. There was no risk of leading anyone on or having them feel like I was "using them" with a mutually agreed upon one-night stand. In the —now admittedly unlikely—event I reached the conclusion

I was straight after all, no feelings would be hurt. And if I was terrible in bed, I'd never have to see her again.

I exited the stall and washed my hands. Staring at my brown eyes in the mirror, I took a deep breath. "You can do this."

I skipped back out to the bar then stopped.

My coat still hung where I'd left it, but Roz, her phone, and her jacket were nowhere to be seen.

I frowned. We hadn't spoken about how we'd get to my place. Perhaps she'd just gone to get some things out of her car so I could drive us to my apartment and then drop her back here tomorrow.

At the bar, I looked around for Brenda, but she had disappeared. In her place was a brunette drying glasses.

"Excuse me, have you seen a tall woman with short blond hair, wearing a t-shirt that says *I wet my plants*, by any chance?"

The woman chuckled. "No, sorry. I definitely would've remembered that t-shirt if I'd seen it."

"Thanks. Could I get a Diet Coke?" With a tightness in my chest, I slid onto my bar stool to wait.

Each time the door to the bar opened, my head shot up. With every stranger that came through, I deflated more. Had I completely misunderstood the situation? I didn't see how I could have. Roz had very clearly proposed a one-night stand. So why had she left without a word? If she'd changed her mind, she could have at least had the decency to tell me. My grip tightened around my glass.

After another ten minutes, I stood and gathered my belongings.

Roz had vanished. And she'd stolen my t-shirt.

CHAPTER TWO

OLIVIA

SIX MONTHS LATER

I STEPPED BACK from the colorful window display, admiring the arrangement of tulips, crocuses and hyacinths and inhaled a deep breath of sweetly scented air. Warmth rushed over my body. Sometimes I couldn't believe how lucky I was to spend my days surrounded by gorgeous flowers and earn enough from it that I didn't need to worry where my next rent payment for the shop and my apartment above it was coming from. It had taken a lot of time, effort, and heartbreak along the way to get to this point, but it had all been worth it.

My phone buzzed in my apron pocket, and I pulled it out. Jenny.

I answered, smiling, as I walked back to the storage room to retrieve some more greenery for the display.

"Hello! How did the wedding go on Saturday?"

"It was great, and the flowers were a hit. I had tons of guests ask about them."

"Oh, that's a relief." I beamed. The bride had been

skeptical when I explained that, because I only stocked locally and sustainably grown flowers, we couldn't provide the Vendela roses she wanted, as they would need to be flown in from Ecuador or Colombia. But she'd seemed happy enough when I'd shown her what I could provide—ranunculus, anemones, and hyacinths grown at Red Tractor Farm, along with gorgeous dried flowers.

"I've got another couple who are interested in dropping by to talk to you about flowers for their wedding. Will you be around Friday afternoon?"

"I'm free any time after one." I paused to grab my planner and a pen from my workbench and wrote a reminder to myself.

It was serendipitous that my sister Blake's wife, Jenny, had become an event planner after she'd moved back to Sapphire Springs and that we got on so well. It was probably time I started giving her a commission for all the extra business she sent my way. Holding the phone between my ear and my shoulder, I continued to the back of the store. I pushed open the door to the storage room, cool air sending goosebumps down my arms, and plucked out five sprigs of fern.

"Great. They've booked Prue's vineyard for the venue. I'll email you their initial thoughts about color schemes. Oh, and by the way, Yuri and Mike were at the wedding on Saturday, and Yuri is pregnant!"

"Oh, that's amazing," I said, exiting the storage room and closing the door firmly behind me. "I've been wondering how they were doing and hoping we'd hear some good news."

"Me too."

The reminder of Yuri and Mike's flower-planning session tugged at my chest. They'd received the news right here, at the counter just in front of me, that their latest round of IVF had been unsuccessful. Yuri's face had crumpled, Mike enveloping her in a bear hug as he wiped his eyes on the back of his hand.

"Well, I'd better get back to work," Jenny said, breaking me out of my thoughts. "Are you still coming Thursday night?"

"Yes, I'm looking forward to it! See you then." I hung up and walked back toward the window display, clutching the ferns. Yuri and Mike had started trying before their wedding date due to Yuri's "advanced maternal age." She was only thirty-six.

I carefully added the ferns to the flower arrangements next to the window and then stood back to check they looked balanced.

If I was going to have kids, I needed to get a move on—if I wasn't already too late. Realistically, I probably had to allow for at least one year to find a partner and two years to make sure we were compatible before it would be reasonable to consider having kids with them. That would bring me to thirty-four. But what if I met some duds on the way, wasted a year, or more, in a relationship only to discover we didn't work? That would bring me to thirty-five, thirty-six... possibly even older if it happened more than once before I found the right person. My chest tightened. Maybe I should look into egg freezing again. But last time I'd investigated it, it was prohibitively expensive. Sapphire Blooms was going well, but not *that* well.

I shook myself. The best option was just to throw myself into dating again. It was a numbers game, and I needed to play the game to have any chance of winning. Heaviness settled in my stomach.

I walked back to my workbench, where I selected a

round glass vase and began preparing the flower arrangement Mr. Livanidis had ordered for his wife's birthday.

I sighed. Maybe there'd be someone eligible at the pub on Thursday, although it was doubtful. My mind skipped over all the failed possibilities I'd found there. Will, the local handyman who was nice enough, but things had fizzled out after a couple of months. Henry, the friendly tour guide, who was full of fun facts about Sapphire Springs. Unfortunately, the chemistry between us was severely lacking. Drew, the handsome New York banker visiting for the weekend, who'd looked perfect on paper, except he lived in New York and, as it turned out, was married—a fact I hadn't discovered until two months into our semi-long-distance relationship. After my string of business failures, I'd been distrustful of men in suits. That experience with Drew had only cemented my dislike. And then there was the fact that corporate America was destroying the environment. At the rate they were going, if I did have kids, there'd be nothing left for them anyway. I scanned the bucket of tulips next to me and selected a handful. I'd made an exception to my no-suits rule for Roz, and look how that turned out.

Sure, my visit to Pryde had confirmed my attraction to women, but it was a stark reminder of how painful and undermining dating could be. Ghosting, mixed messages, lies, and even, in Roz's case, theft.

The memory of Roz's soft lips on my mouth, her toned lean body pressed against mine, and that amused glint dancing in her eyes filled my mind. I scrunched my eyes, willing the image to fade away. It had been six months—far too long to be dwelling on the striking woman who'd disappeared with my t-shirt.

I stabbed a red tulip into the vase. I couldn't let these bad experiences discourage me.

The doorbell jingled.

"Flower delivery!" Jim Wardell called, walking backward pulling a cart of flowers. A cowboy hat sat on top of short gray hair that framed his wrinkled brown face. As usual, he was wearing mud-spattered boots and blue overalls covered in dirt.

Grinning, I hurried over to help him. "Thanks Jim. Why are you doing the delivery today?" Maybe the farmhands were tied up.

Jim's smile faltered as he unloaded a bucket of daffodils.

"Is everything okay?" I took the bucket from him.

"We're selling the farm." Jim shuffled his feet, ducking his head.

I froze.

"Selling?" The word came out as a squeak. "To who?"

"We're not sure yet." He handed me another bucket, overflowing with lavender crocuses. "We knew we'd have to sell at some point—Penny and I are getting on in age, and none of the kids want to take over—but we'd been putting it off. Then Samadhi Resorts approached us out of the blue with a generous offer, and it felt like a sign that it was time. We'd rather sell to someone who'll keep the farm running, so we're putting it on the market to see if we get any other takers." He gripped the handle of the trolley. "But if that falls through, we'll sell to Samadhi."

My stomach plummeted. Samadhi Resorts would bulldoze everything. The petting zoo, the pumpkin patch, the corn maze, the orchards and strawberry fields, and most importantly, the flowers.

A montage of memories of Red Tractor Farm spun through my head. As a child: picking pumpkins and bumping along on the hayride in fall, devouring juicy straw-berries in the strawberry fields during summer, and eating fresh fluffy donuts and apple fritters at the café all year round. My first job as a teenager: serving customers at the café over the summer break. The day Jim had asked if any of the café staff could give him a hand in the flower field, and I'd volunteered, starting my love affair with flowers.

I let go of the bucket too soon, and it banged on the counter.

"I'm sorry, Liv. I know how much you love the farm. Hopefully, we'll get some other offers."

My throat clenched. "I can help more with the flowers if that would lighten your load." It was a ridiculous thing to say. Jim was in his seventies, and the flowers were only a small part of Red Tractor Farm's business. No amount of help from me would make much of a dent in his overall workload.

"Thanks, Liv. I'm sorry. I know this is going to make things difficult for you." His eyes misted over.

"That's okay." I swallowed, reaching out and squeezing his hand. "I really appreciate everything you've done for me."

Jim swiped his eyes with his hand and then twisted around to pick up another box.

"If the deal with Samadhi goes ahead, when will it all happen?" I asked, my chest tightening. If Red Tractor Farm was bought by Samadhi Resorts, I'd lose my only supplier. There were other flower farms in the Hudson Valley, but they were established businesses with their own clientele. It was highly unlikely they were going to accommodate my needs the way Jim did. And as far as I knew, none of them had a greenhouse that sustainably grew flowers over the winter season. *Shit.*

"We're going to put it on the market for three weeks, but if there are no other takers, we'll have no choice but to sell to them. We can't risk losing their interest if another option doesn't come up." He pressed his lips together. "There'll likely be some time before the sale closes, but we'll need to spend that time shutting down operations, including the flower farm."

The corners of my lips wobbled. *Get it together, Olivia. Don't make this harder for Jim than it already is.* Jim leaned in and patted my shoulder.

"I'm sorry, Liv. If that happens, I'll try to keep the flowers going for as long as possible to give you time to find another supplier. But I think, at the most, it'll be two months."

Tears welled in my eyes. *Two months.*

I had two months—if I was lucky—to find a new supplier or lose my home and my beloved flower shop I'd worked so hard to establish. I blinked furiously. I couldn't let that happen. Not again. I'd do whatever it took to make sure of it.

CHAPTER THREE

ROZ

"TELL them the merger will only be successful if they're willing to streamline, consolidate, and restructure, and that means layoffs," I barked into my phone at a junior partner as I strode across the floor toward my corner office. "If they don't have the stomach for firing people, they shouldn't move ahead." I nodded at Sofia, who sat at the desk outside my office, stabbed my phone with my finger to hang up, and then swung open the door.

I frowned. An enormous vase of flowers sat in front of the window, which showcased expansive views of Bryant Park from the thirty-fifth floor. I walked over, my nose wrinkling at the sickly, cloying scent. I grabbed the card and opened it, stepping away. A note from James. *Good luck, Roslyn.* I gritted my teeth. What a dick. He knew I hated flowers. And no one called me Roslyn. For some preposterous reason, the idiot clearly thought he had some chance of getting the promotion.

I strode to my desk and pressed the button on my phone.

"Sofia, what are these flowers doing in my office? Get them out of here, now." I threw the card in the trashcan.

"Sorry, Roz. They must have been delivered while I was on the phone with Jess."

"Jessica? What did she want?" My pulse spiked. With only weeks until Adam's official retirement, it was about time he shared the results of the senior partners' vote. As managing partner of the New York office, with an impressive client base that included some of the world's largest tech, energy, and pharmaceutical companies, I was the obvious choice to be Adam's successor.

"Adam wants to speak with you this morning. The only time you were both free was nine-thirty. I've put it in your calendar."

I glanced at my phone. It was 9:05 a.m. Plenty of time for me to finish ripping a report one of my consultants had prepared for another project about clean energy to shreds. I stretched my fingers.

"Yes, that's fine." I dropped the phone onto my desk, my gaze falling on the photo of Lottie and Matt next to it, and I paused. I'd give them a call over dinner. Lottie had no clue what I did, but she'd become bizarrely fixated on my promotion after overhearing Matt and me talking about it. I smiled. I'd finally have good news to share with her tonight.

The door opened, and Sofia rushed in to remove the flowers. Her eyes lingered on them as she left.

"Thanks, Sofia," I said as I straightened the photo. "Feel free to keep them if you'd like."

That should make up for me snapping at her—not that Sofia took my curt manner personally anymore. But she deserved the flowers.

I sat at the desk, whipped out the clean energy report and my favorite red pen from my briefcase, and got to work.

After making quick work of the report, I made my way across the floor to Adam's office, arriving with three minutes to spare. A few offices down, one of the assistants watered a potted plant. The memory of Olivia and her ridiculous t-shirt came flooding back. I clenched my jaw. It had been six months. I should just throw it in the trash and move on. But the evening had stuck in my mind. Olivia's dark shiny hair and intelligent eyes, the rapport we'd shared, the way she'd looked at me, desire clear in her eyes, that kiss. And then... nothing.

What had gotten into me that night? It was like I'd been transported back to my pre-Sadie days, when I'd flirted with gorgeous women, dating some and falling into bed with others. It had felt good, being desired and desiring in return, but I knew from experience that it didn't always end well. Especially with desire that strong.

I pressed my lips together. That night was an anomaly that would not happen again. Anyway, I wouldn't have time for dating once I was promoted.

"Did you get your flowers, Roslyn?"

Gritting my teeth, I looked up. James was sitting on Jessica's desk, smirking. Jessica, sitting behind him, rolled her eyes. I fought the urge to do the same. *Be civil, Roz.*

He must have flown in from London to hear the results of the vote. While he was the only other contender for the role, he was a weak one. The insufferably pompous Brit's financials were nowhere near as good as mine, and his vision for Saunders & Company was effectively the status quo, whereas my focus was ensuring our relevance well into the twenty-first century. There was no real contest. I almost felt sorry for him. *Almost.*

"I got them." I studied the cuff of my right shirt sleeve.

"Excellent." James slid off the desk, ran his hand

through his salt-and-pepper hair and adjusted his tie. "Well, I'd better leave you to it. All the best."

I wanted to rub that damn smirk off his face, but instead, I nodded. "You too." He wouldn't be smiling when I got the job.

He sauntered off, and I approached Jessica's desk. "I take it James hasn't met with Adam yet?"

She glanced at her screen. "No. He's meeting him at ten."

Adam must have decided to give me the good news first before letting James down gently.

Jessica's eyes flicked up, gazing over my shoulder. I turned just as Adam stepped out, tall and impeccably dressed, with teeth and hair that looked whiter than white against the tan he'd acquired from spending weekends at his house in the Hamptons. He ushered me into his office.

Excitement vibrated through me. This was it. Since joining Saunders & Company at twenty-three, I'd dedicated my life to climbing its rungs. Each time I'd reached one milestone, I'd firmly set my sights on the next one: the youngest person to be made partner at the firm, the first female managing partner of the New York office, the firm's top earner three years in a row. Now, here I was, finally about to reach the pinnacle of everything I'd worked for. How would it feel to be global managing partner? There wasn't anywhere to go from there.

I followed Adam into his office, which was almost identical to mine but on the other corner of the building with a slightly more attractive view of Bryant Park.

"Take a seat, Roz," he said, sitting behind his large mahogany desk and gesturing at the chair opposite him. "How are you doing?"

"Good, thank you. How are you?" I plastered a smile on my face.

"Excellent, excellent." He glanced out the window. "Great weather. Might go golfing this weekend if it keeps up."

I nodded, tapping my foot on the floor. Couldn't he get to the point? We needed to discuss practical matters. It would make sense for me to start taking over the role immediately. I had so many plans for the firm: expanding our global footprint into Asia; building up our sustainability and environmental, social, and governance practices; and overhauling our diversity, equity, and inclusion strategy, to name a few. I was confident that under my leadership, Saunders & Company could become the top management consulting firm in the world.

Adam refocused his attention back on me. "So, as you know, the senior partners met last night to vote on the global managing partner position."

"Yes." I straightened in my seat, taking in a deep breath. While inwardly I'd be doing a happy dance, I had to remain composed when Adam broke the news. I had a reputation to maintain.

"You have made an amazing contribution to the firm and are one of our most valued partners." Adam leaned forward, pressing his lips together.

I smiled. This was it.

He cleared his throat and looked me straight in the eye. "But the senior partners decided that James is the best fit for the global managing partner role."

"What?" I blinked, my mouth dry. Surely I had misheard.

"I'm sorry, Roz. You'll continue to head up the New York office, of course. And you're still young. Maybe by the time James retires, things will have changed and you'll get the votes."

"Things will have changed?" I spluttered.

"You know what I mean, Roz." His gaze pierced me. He was smart enough not to say anything else or risk a lawsuit.

My chest tightened, and my vision blurred. I knew exactly what he meant. While Saunders & Company had overhauled its hiring practices over the past few years in an effort to employ more diverse employees, senior management in the firm was still dominated by white, cis, hetero, married men with kids. I'd convinced myself that they'd look beyond my age, gender, sexual orientation, and marital status and put the future of the firm first. But clearly they'd decided James, in his fifties with a wife, three kids, and fancy private school background, was what the firm needed.

I took a deep breath, trying to stop my body from shaking. I'd devoted my whole life to this fucking company, only to get bumped out by some mediocre guy?

Well, screw them.

"I'm not hanging around here in the hope that the partners become less bigoted and James kicks the bucket before he runs Saunders & Company into the ground. And I'm sure as hell not going to keep working my ass off, bringing in profits for everyone else to enjoy." I fixed Adam with a steely gaze. "Take this as my resignation."

With that, I turned and strode out the door, slamming it behind me.

I STEPPED out of the building and took a breath of early spring air. I'd instructed Sofia to have all my personal effects boxed and sent to my Upper East Side apartment and cancel my meetings or send someone else to attend in my place. My direct reports were preparing draft handover notes to be provided to the partners who picked up my work. I'd review them at home before I officially switched off for good. Under the terms of my contract, I was meant to give more notice, but I wasn't going to hang around at Saunders & Company for a protracted transition period. I'd given them enough. They could sue me if they wanted to, but I knew they wouldn't. They didn't like having their dirty laundry aired in public, and I wouldn't bat an eyelash at making a counterclaim for discrimination if they tried.

My blood boiled, but I willed myself to calm down. *It's not worth it, Roz. You need to let it go. They don't deserve you.*

With the cool air in my lungs, I looked around, taking in my surroundings. Across 42nd Street, the London plane trees that lined Bryant Park were still leafless, but the sky was a gorgeous blue, and the sun shone on the mix of early twentieth century buildings and modern soaring glass skyscrapers that surrounded the park. Despite working across from Bryant Park for the past nineteen years, I rarely stepped foot in it. Too busy working. Now I had all the time in the world.

Feeling slightly giddy at my newfound freedom, I crossed the street, picking up my pace at the end to avoid being hit by a yellow taxi. Taking the steps two at a time, I entered the park. Vibrant green grass covered the center where the ice rink had stood only a few months earlier. I wandered down a path lined with plane trees and green shrubs until I reached the small green waffle stand.

"A latte, thanks," I said to the young man behind the counter as the sweet, buttery scent of waffles flooded over me. If I hadn't had my usual breakfast of toast and scrambled eggs already, I might have been tempted.

Coffee in hand, I sat on one of Bryant Park's iconic green chairs in the sun, turning it so my back faced a patch of yellow and white tulips. I'd had more than enough flowers already today. I shut my eyes, soaking in the sun, listening to the birds chirping, the horns of impatient cars and the hum of people chatting at nearby tables.

It was pleasant, but it wasn't long before restlessness rolled over me. I couldn't just sit around here all day. I needed to do something.

But what?

The latte swirled in my stomach. I was a quick thinker, but rash was not my style. Yet this morning's decision—possibly one of the most momentous of my life—had been made on the spur of the moment. I'd spent my entire career at Saunders & Company. Without it, I had no purpose, no goal, nothing to work toward. I didn't regret it, though. Staying there, reporting to James, was completely untenable.

I sucked in a breath. Strictly speaking, I didn't need to work again. I'd been a partner since twenty-eight, invested wisely, and lived relatively frugally. But an early retirement was never part of my plan. I liked working too much.

You don't need to work it all out now. Take some time. Try to relax a little.

I pulled out my phone, my thumb hovering over the icon for my work email. Thirteen new emails. It was tempting to check them, to fire off a few responses and make sure all my matters were still in order.

Do not click on it, Roz. They're not your matters any longer.

I sighed and moved my thumb to my text messages

instead. One new message from Matt. I opened it. It was a selfie of my seven-year-old niece, Lottie, sitting next to my brother on their couch. They were covered in a blanket, both wearing hoodies and broad smiles on their faces. Accompanying the photo was some text.

> Sick day today, so I'm introducing Lottie to Back to the Future.

I grinned. Those two didn't have any trouble relaxing. *That must be nice.*

> Once you've finished, I'm available for a call if you'd like. I'm not at work.

> Not working?! Are you OK?

My thumb hovered over the screen. The news would travel fast once I told Matt. But I might as well rip the Band-Aid off.

> I resigned.

My phone lit up with an incoming video call.

I sighed and accepted it, steeling myself.

Matt's face appeared, his brow furrowed. "What happened?"

"I didn't get the promotion, so I decided I'd had enough." No point in telling Matt that it was almost certainly because Saunders & Company's leadership were sexist homophobes. He might get riled up and threaten to drive into Manhattan with his construction buddies and give them a talking-to. Not that Matt would hurt a fly, but as a burly six-foot-two builder, he could be intimidating when he wanted to be.

A small blond head popped into view, and my face softened. Lottie's hoodie was now pulled down, revealing large blue eyes wide with concern.

"You didn't get the promotion?" she asked.

A pang of guilt stabbed my chest. The last thing I wanted was to cause Lottie any more heartache.

"I'm afraid not," I said.

She frowned, and then her face brightened. "Can you come see us if you're not working?"

"You know, maybe I will," I said. "I haven't worked out what to do yet." The thought clamped itself around my chest, but I focused my attention on Lottie. "How are you feeling?"

"Sick," Lottie said, emitting a not-very-convincing cough. Matt rolled his eyes, and I held back a chuckle.

"Did you hear about Red Tractor Farm?" Lottie asked, her face falling again.

I frowned. "No, what about it?"

"It's closing down." The corners of Lottie's mouth trembled.

What? My chest constricted.

"We don't know for sure, sweetie," Matt said, gazing down at Lottie and stroking her head. He looked up and grimaced. "The Wardells are selling the farm. They're getting older and finding it all to be a bit too much. And none of their children want to take it over."

"But surely someone would buy it and keep it going? I mean, it's been a Hudson Valley institution for generations."

Our visits to Red Tractor Farm over the years flooded into my mind. Lottie as a baby, giggling in her stroller as the rabbits hopped around in the petting zoo. Lottie laughing with delight as a toddler as we bounced on the hayride. Our more recent fall visits to search for the best pumpkin in the pumpkin patch, shoot apples out of cannons, and get lost in the corn maze. And magical Decembers when the farm was transformed into a winter wonderland, decorated in Christmas lights and with rows of Christmas trees for sale. The thought of all of that disappearing, of no more happy memories being made, sent a pang of sadness right to my heart.

Matt shrugged. "Apparently, it's been running at a loss the past few years, so it's not exactly an appealing purchase. They've only had interest from Samadhi Resorts at this stage."

I frowned. Samadhi Resorts owned a number of exclusive health retreats across America. If they purchased the farm, it would be bulldozed and replaced with shiny state-of-the-art yoga studios, swimming pools, colonic therapy rooms and exclusive accommodations for the New York elite. I'd advised one of my clients against a potential investment in Samadhi a few years ago and knew their business model well. Charging thousands of dollars a night for services that had no basis in science—energy healing, sound baths, and contrast hydrotherapy. I pressed my lips together. It was a load of bullshit.

"Where are we going to get our pumpkins and Christmas trees from now on?" Lottie asked, the corners of her lips dropping down. "And what will happen to all the animals?"

"Lottie's been taking the news badly." Matt dropped his voice. "Her symptoms came on yesterday afternoon, just after we heard the news."

Lottie pushed in front of Matt, so her tragic face took up the entirety of my phone screen. "Can you do something, Aunty Roz? Dad said you fix sick companies."

My heart clenched. Lottie had been through a lot in the past twelve months. Mel leaving, appendicitis... Losing Red Tractor Farm was just another blow.

An idea popped into my head, sending a rush of adrenaline through my body. It was ridiculous. Absurd. I didn't know anything about farms. But Lottie was right. I did know a lot about saving businesses from bankruptcy. And wasn't a farm just another business?

CHAPTER FOUR

OLIVIA

I CLUTCHED my phone to my ear, waiting for a loud car to drive past before I continued speaking. "I'd happily share my knowledge on setting up a geothermal greenhouse and natural pest control methods with you if that would help?" *God, I sound desperate.*

"We have plenty of florists who are happy to buy flowers from us already, despite our use of pesticides," the farmer replied. "I'm sorry, but I can't help you."

"Thanks for your time."

He hung up. *Shit.* I kicked a small rock. It bounced down the pavement, hit one of the cast-iron lamps that lined Main Street, and fell into the gutter.

I was screwed.

I filled my lungs with air and took the final few steps to Builders Arms. While all I wanted to do was crawl onto my couch in a tiny ball, I'd committed to attending trivia night. Hopeful it would provide a welcome distraction, I pushed open the door to the pub and walked in, scanning the packed room for my friends.

"Olivia!" Jenny waved from a high wooden table near

the back of the pub, where Hannah and George were already sitting.

I waved back, making a detour to order a lemon-lime soda at the bar. Drink in hand, I weaved through the tables of trivia hopefuls and took a seat next to Hannah, managing a weak smile. "Hey."

"We've already chosen our trivia name: The Whisk Takers. No prizes for guessing who chose it." Hannah patted George's hand fondly.

God, they were cute together. All my plans to focus on dating had flown out the window with Jim's news about the farm.

George grasped her beer. "Well, no one else had any bright ideas. I also suggested Flour Power—spelled with an 'ou'—which I thought you might like, but The Whisk Takers was most popular."

"How are you holding up?" Hannah asked, turning to me with a sympathetic expression. I'd blown up the group chat last night, telling them about Jim's news and my concerns.

I groaned as I pushed an empty coaster around on the table. "I reached out to all the flower farms within a reasonable distance of Sapphire Springs today. A few grow flowers sustainably in spring and summer, but nothing during winter."

Hannah frowned. "So what do other flower shops do?"

"They import flowers, mainly from the Netherlands and South America, or buy from American farms who use energy-guzzling greenhouses." I sighed. "But I just can't stomach doing that. The carbon footprint is horrific. Not only is it completely against my principles, but I've built my whole brand around being sustainable and locally grown."

"That sucks," George said. "I'm sorry, Liv. What will you do?"

I swallowed, trying to dislodge the lump in my throat. I focused my gaze on the old grandfather clock in the corner of the pub. "I won't be able to keep Sapphire Blooms going without fresh flowers year round. I can't sell enough dried flowers and candles in winter to cover rent, and I can't think of anything else I could sell to bring in revenue." Tears welled in my eyes. "I'll have to close the shop and move back home with my parents until I can find another job." And this time, there'd be no job waiting for me at Red Tractor Farm to fall back on. I couldn't imagine finding another career I loved as much as working at Sapphire Blooms. And then there was that ticking clock. No one would want to date me if I was unemployed and living with my parents. I cradled my face in my hands. "God, I feel terrible about Maddie. I just hired her, and now I'll have to let her go."

I dug my fingernails into my hand in an attempt to ward off the tears and turned to Jenny. "I'll do whatever I can to honor all the weddings we've booked, but I won't be able to take on any new bookings until we know for sure what's happening with the farm. I'm sorry."

"Hey, let's not get ahead of ourselves. They might find another buyer for the farm—one who'll keep it going. And if not, you still have some time to investigate other options." Jenny leaned across the wooden table and patted my hand.

"I hope they find someone, because I'm all out of ideas," I said, my shoulders dropping. I'd even considered whether I could buy a block of land and establish a sustainable flower farm myself before quickly dismissing the idea. I knew a lot about flower farming, but I didn't have the money or the time to take on such a venture.

Dan, the pub's owner and trivia master, cleared his throat from the makeshift wooden podium he'd set up in the corner. "Okay, everybody, we'll be starting in fifteen minutes, so get your drinks and take your seats."

Jenny glanced at her phone. "Blake better be here soon, or we'll have no chance of beating The Gran Masters."

We all turned to face the table of older women near the podium. Helen, George's mom, and Barb, Hannah's beloved former nanny, smiled and waved when they saw us looking.

"They may look sweet, but looks are deceiving," Jenny muttered and then glared at Hannah. "I still can't believe you even considered joining their team."

Hannah laughed, lifting her hands. "Oh my god, will you ever let that go? I just suggested it once. Everyone in my book club, except me, is on the team and they were short a couple of people because it coincided with a burlesque show at the retirement home."

Jenny raised an eyebrow. "Uh-huh. It had nothing to do with them being the reigning champions and the free drinks they usually win?"

Hannah rolled her eyes.

"Can I just say that I hope the retirement home is still doing burlesque shows by the time I'm ready to move in," Blake said as she appeared holding a beer. "Sorry I'm late. Work emergency. And I bumped into Dana on my way and convinced her to join us." Blake stepped aside to make room for Dana, Jim's second-in-command at Red Tractor Farm. "We need all the help we can get if we're going to beat our arch-rivals." Blake narrowed her eyes at The Gran Masters and then pulled over another stool for the tall brunette farmer. We shuffled around to make room for her at the table.

"The more the merrier," Jenny said as Blake slid onto the seat next to her and kissed her cheek.

I looked at Dana. How was she holding up after Jim's news? I'd been so caught up trying to work out how I could save Sapphire Blooms that I hadn't thought to check in with her. While we weren't close friends, since she'd started working at Red Tractor Farm last year, we'd bonded over our love of flowers, and I always enjoyed catching up with her when I visited the farm. Though her grooming and outfit choices were standard—she had brown hair pulled back in her trademark ponytail and sported brown work shoes, faded blue jeans and a purple-and-red flannel shirt— her make-up-free face looked slightly paler than usual, and there were dark rings under her eyes. I wasn't surprised. Just like me, she was facing losing her job and being evicted from her home—a cottage tucked away near the back of Red Tractor Farm.

"Hopefully there are lots of horticulture and livestock questions, or I'll be no use to you, I'm afraid," Dana said as she took a seat, placing her drink in the middle of the table.

"Dan once asked how many compartments a cow's stomach has," George said.

"Four." Dana grinned.

"There we go." George chuckled. "If we'd had you here, we wouldn't have lost to the grannies."

A man walked into the bar, and his friends, sitting at a table near us, cheered loudly, waving him over. I waited for the noise to subside and then turned to Dana. "Jim told me the news about the farm. I'm so sorry. I don't suppose you have any updates?"

"Actually, I do." Dana smiled. "Jim might have found another buyer."

I straightened and leaned forward. "Oh wow! Who?"

"Someone named Roslyn Kennedy. Apparently her parents live around here."

I frowned, trying to remember the Kennedy family. Frank and Marie, who would have to be in their early seventies now, had bought flowers at Sapphire Blooms on a few occasions. If I recalled correctly, they'd lived in Manhattan and had both been high-powered lawyers or something similar, but they also had a large property partway between Sapphire Springs and Cloverdale which they'd kept as a vacation home. Had it been about five years since they moved here permanently? I thought their son lived in Cloverdale but didn't remember anything about a daughter.

"Frank and Marie," I said. "Does anyone know anything about Roslyn?" I looked around the table, letting my legs swing under my bar stool.

My friends shook their heads. Well, at least they didn't have anything bad to share.

I turned back to Dana. "Do you know what her plans are?" Would she save the farm?

"Not bulldozing it, thank god." Dana ran her hand over her smooth ponytail. "Jim said she wants to keep the farm going, but he hasn't told me any specifics yet—I'm not sure he knows himself."

I clasped my hand to my chest. "Oh, thank god! Do you know how serious she is?"

"She's coming to do a farm tour and meet with Jim, but it sounds like she's genuinely interested, and Jim is eager to sell to anyone who's got the cash and won't destroy it."

"Well, that all sounds very promising." I raised my glass, giddy with the good news. "To the Kennedys' daughter. May you purchase Red Tractor Farm and keep it and Sapphire Blooms going for generations to come!"

Everyone laughed and raised their glasses. "To the Kennedys' daughter."

I took a swig of soda. While I knew it was premature, gratitude for the woman I'd never met welled in me. If she did buy the farm and saved the flower fields, I'd have to restrain myself from throwing my arms around her when we finally came face to face. I refused to consider what would happen if she didn't. The Whisk Takers needed my undivided attention if we were going to beat The Gran Masters.

CHAPTER FIVE

ROZ

TWO BLACK BABY goats wobbled on their feet under the watchful eye of their mother.

Jim smiled, his eyes hazy. "They were only born a few hours ago."

New beginnings. For the goats and for me. I pursed my lips. *Good god, Roz. Don't get sappy.*

"So, what do you think?" Jim asked as we walked back from the petting zoo to the main farmhouse.

The scent of freshly cut grass wafted through the air. The large white two-story farmhouse, well over one hundred years old, was far too big for one person. Over three hundred acres of farmland, spanning Christmas trees, flower and strawberry fields, orchards, a corn maze, a petting zoo, and a café, was a lot for one person who knew nothing about farming. But I thrived on a challenge and I was a fast learner. I'd also learned from years at Saunders & Company that you were only as good as the people you surrounded yourself with. And Jim had some good people on his team. I was confident that, with their practical expertise and my business skills, we could make it work. I exhaled, my body buzzing. There was so much potential here. And unlike the matters I'd worked on at Saunders & Company, I wouldn't just be stepping in, fixing the business, and then walking away and washing my hands of it. I'd be here for the long haul.

I turned to Jim, who was patiently awaiting my response. "I'm in."

Jim's face broke into a broad grin. "That's great! And you'll keep it going as a farm and keep all the employees on?"

I nodded. "Yes. I'll have to make some changes to ensure it is financially viable, but I'll keep it running as an agritourism business, and I don't see any need for layoffs." I'd spent the last few days poring over all the farm's finances and had formed the view that, to make it profitable, some of its operations would need to be streamlined while other areas would need to be expanded. But keeping Jim's team of employees was critical to the farm's success. They had the farming knowledge and skills that I lacked. Especially Dana Hoffman, who Jim had brought on last year to manage most of the farm's day-to-day operations.

Tears welled in Jim's brown eyes. "Well, in that case, we'd love to sell to you." He held out his hand. "And the price I mentioned before still stands."

Jim's grip was so hard I thought I might lose circulation in my fingers.

"Penny and I have a cottage in Sapphire Springs we're planning to move into, so we can fit in with your timing. If you want to move in early, we can get out of your way. Rip the Band-Aid off, and all that." Jim looked wistfully at the fields stretching out in front of us. "And you're welcome to most of the furniture in the farmhouse as well. We won't be able to bring it with us."

"I'm excited to get going, so the earlier, the better, from my perspective." I gazed at the stunning farmhouse. I was more than ready to move out of my parents' place. After living apart from my parents for over twenty years, with only short visits back, spending the last two weeks in close quarters with them had been more than enough. "And I'll happily take any furniture you don't want." I had far more important things to focus on than interior decoration. Like getting the farm back in the black.

"Excellent. We'll move out this weekend then."

I blinked. This weekend. That was fast. "I'll ask my lawyers and my accountants to expedite the closing of the sale, but I'm not sure we'll be able to finalize the paperwork and get you the money by then."

Jim waved his hand through the air. "Once you sign the contract, it's a done deal from my perspective. I trust you."

I stared. I couldn't imagine trusting a stranger enough to hand over my farm to them before I got paid.

A cow mooed loudly nearby, and I flinched, jerking my head in the direction of the noise. Two sets of large brown eyes stared at me over a fence. One of the gigantic brown cows stomped, sending up a flurry of dust. The other gave a loud huff. I flinched.

"Don't mind Thelma and Louise," Jim said.

"I don't think they like me." I hadn't told Jim I'd keep all the animals. Perhaps these two could be rehomed—*to the abattoir.*

A twinge of uncertainty hit me as we went to sign the papers. Buying the farm was an enormous financial commitment. I was using all my savings, which were significant, to purchase it, and I'd need to get a bank loan or find an investor to make the changes I needed to ensure the farm's financial success. I'd turned around hundreds of businesses over the years, but it had always been someone else's money on the line. This time, if I failed, it would have significant repercussions for my future. At forty-two, losing all my savings would mean having to start again. I shook off my doubts. I would make this a success. For both my sake and Lottie's.

God, Lottie will be so thrilled when she hears I've bought the farm.

"Is everything okay?" Jim asked as he ushered me into his study and handed me a pen.

"Yes, yes," I said, signing my name on the contract that I'd had my lawyers review yesterday.

Fear was for the weak. And Roz Kennedy was not weak.

CHAPTER SIX

ROZ

I STOOD on the back deck of the farmhouse, following the path of a bald eagle as it soared through the blue sky. It swooped toward my neighbors' property, disappearing out of sight. I dropped my eyes, my gaze landing on the hay wagon parked next to my black Mercedes-Benz. *Shit.*

I glanced down at my watch. It was four p.m. The farm was closed to visitors and my family would be arriving in two hours, their first visit since I moved in over the week-end. I frowned. Did I have time to learn how to drive a tractor between now and then? The thought of Lottie's disappointed face spurred me on. How hard could it really be?

I scanned the property for any signs of Dana. A tractor was rolling along in the corn field, which was currently just an expanse of dirt. I took up a brisk pace in its direction.

The tractor slowed as I drew nearer. I waved my hand and Dana switched the engine off.

"Can you teach me to drive a tractor?" I asked, looking up at her.

Dana tilted her head. "Sure. Does tomorrow afternoon work?"

"No, I need to learn now. Before my niece comes at six."

Dana's brow furrowed. "Um, okay. Do you mind me asking why?"

"I promised I'd take her on a hayride."

"Ah." Dana glanced down at her watch. "Well, I've almost finished spreading manure here. Do you want to squeeze in with me, and I'll show you the basics?"

My lip curled at the mention of manure, but I steeled myself. *Think of Lottie.*

I clambered up and squeezed next to Dana. The hard seat was clearly only designed for one large farmer, rather than two medium-sized women. Frowning, I took in the various levers and pedals before me. Dana walked me through them all before starting the tractor and continuing to drive down the field, narrating what she was doing as she went. I wrinkled my nose. Now we were in the middle of the field, the smell of manure was overpowering.

"Do you want a turn?" Dana glanced at me.

"Sure," I replied. Yes, there were a lot of different things to remember, but I was used to mastering things quickly. Once I started driving, I was sure it would all come together.

Dana brought the tractor to a halt and shifted to the side so I could reach all the controls. I grasped hold of the large steering wheel and pushed my foot on the clutch before turning the rusty key and pushing down on the gas pedal. The engine revved loudly. I reduce the pressure, gritting my teeth. The gear lever was stiff and creaked as I moved it. I released the clutch, pushing the gas pedal down further. The tractor jumped forward, and I grabbed the wheel to avoid being thrown out.

"Good god, they should put seatbelts in these things," I yelled over the rumble of the tractor.

"They do nowadays, but this tractor is old. New tractors are usually also automatic, have better suspension, enclosed cabs, and even air conditioning," Dana responded.

I made a mental note to upgrade the tractors as soon as possible.

"A new one will set you back between fifty and a hundred and fifty thousand dollars," Dana said, as if she'd just read my mind.

I winced. A tractor upgrade would *not* be happening in the immediate future.

I pushed the hand throttle to get the tractor to pick up pace. *Why this damn thing needs a gas pedal and a hand throttle is beyond me.*

"You're veering left. You need to make sure you're driving in a straight line, or the manure won't be spread evenly."

I twisted the wheel, and the tractor slowly straightened. Good god, this was clunky. I yearned for my Mercedes-Benz, with its soft leather seats, twin turbo-charged engines, and power steering.

I drove up and down the field until we reached the corner closest to the main road.

"Okay, that's done now." Dana yanked a chain. "I've closed the spreader. I think you've got the hang of it. Why don't you drive back to the barn, and then we can drop off the spreader and hook up the wagon for your niece?"

I steered the tractor down the dirt road toward the barn, where Dana jumped off and disconnected the spreader.

"You know, if you're thinking about buying some new equipment, I'd love to upgrade the irrigation system for the flowers," Dana said as she swung herself back on the tractor.

"That won't be necessary," I replied, turning the tractor back on and driving toward the farmhouse where the wagon was parked.

While I kept my eyes focused on the road in front of me, I sensed Dana staring at me.

"What do you mean?" she asked.

"We're only turning a small profit with the flower fields. I ran the numbers, and we'd be better off leasing the land to another farmer for grazing than continuing to grow flowers." When my new neighbor had told me over the weekend that he'd be more than happy to lease any land that I didn't want for his cattle, I'd jumped at the suggestion. The passive income could be used to reinvest in the agritourism side of the business.

"You're getting rid of the flower farm?" Dana's eyes bore into me, a sharp bite to her tone. "I thought you were going to keep everything going."

"No." I frowned. The tractor drove over a bump, and I clutched the steering wheel tighter. "I told Jim I'd keep the farm going as an agritourism business. I never said I'd keep the flowers."

"But it's one of the best sustainable flower farms in the region—and the only one with a geothermal greenhouse. Jim worked so hard to establish it; you can't just get rid of it."

I pursed my lips together. I didn't appreciate Dana's tone. It was my money on the line. She should be thankful I'd bought the farm at all. "I can, and I will. I need to do what's best for the bottom line."

"But—"

"I've made up my mind, Dana. If I don't increase revenue, the whole farm will go under. And you'll be out of a job and a home. We need to streamline operations and focus on what the farm is best known for, and that's agri-tourism. Not growing flowers. I'm planning to build a taphouse and event venue space to capitalize on our strengths." Doing so would create synergies, as the café's large kitchen could be used for catering both venues, and the existing café staff could also work functions as required.

As I pulled the tractor up near the wagon, I spotted my parents, Matt and Lottie standing by the side of the house.

"I can reverse it so we can hook up the wagon," Dana said, her voice surly.

"No, I can do it," I insisted. "You can hop down. I've got this."

I hadn't practiced reversing, but how hard could it be? And with my family watching, I wanted to stay on the tractor.

"Fine," Dana said, sliding off the seat and jumping down.

"Auntie Roz!" Lottie yelled.

I waved at my family. "I'll be done in a second—just getting the hayride set up."

I put the tractor in reverse, twisting my head to look behind me as I inched the vehicle backward. I turned the wheel to align the rear of the tractor with the front of the wagon.

I frowned. From where I was, it was difficult to see clearly behind me. There was no rearview mirror and the large engine hood on the back of the tractor obscured my view. I could use the sophisticated 360-degree camera system in my Mercedes-Benz right now.

"You're turning too much!" Dana yelled from her vantage point on the ground near the house. "The steering wheel is more sensitive in reverse. Slow down!"

Sweat pricked my armpits as I pushed the throttle to slow the tractor.

The tractor jerked backward.

"Pull the throttle; don't push it!" Dana's shout was barely audible over the rumble of the tractor.

Shit.

Still twisting to try to see, I grabbed what I thought was the throttle and pulled it.

"That's the gear stick, not the throttle. Push down on the brake, or you're—"

Dana's words were drowned out by a loud crunching noise as the tractor hit something and started tipping forward.

Fuck. Fuck. Fuck. I gripped the steering wheel.

"Brake now!" Dana screamed.

I slammed my foot on the brake, and the tractor jerked to a stop, sending me toppling forward. My chest crashed into the steering wheel. The tractor was tilted on a thirty-degree angle, its back wheels presumably propped up on whatever I'd smashed into. Was it the wagon?

Dana sprinted over to the tractor. "Oh my god! Are you okay?"

Winded and with my heart still pounding, I wheezed out, "Yeah."

With trembling legs, I carefully climbed off the tractor and turned to survey the damage.

My heart plummeted.

My Mercedes-Benz.

One of the gigantic back wheels of the tractor was sitting on the crumpled front of my car. The hood, grille, and bumper were crushed under its weight.

"Fuck."

I had a terrible feeling my insurance wouldn't cover me

destroying my own car. I winced at the thought of the hundreds of thousands of dollars I'd just destroyed in less than two minutes.

I turned, glaring at the two cows in the paddock who were staring at me and chewing grass like they were enjoying popcorn at a movie.

"Show's over," I muttered.

"Are you okay?" Matt asked, appearing beside me, slightly out of breath from having jogged over from the house.

"Yes, I'm fine," I snapped, still shaken by the whole situation.

A loud creaking noise made me turn my head again. Dana was back on the tractor, slowly driving it off my car.

"The tractor seems to be fine," she called.

"Oh, thank god," I muttered, kicking the dirt. "The tractor that's probably as old as I am is okay."

I couldn't bear the thought of dealing with my car, so I strode toward my parents and Lottie, who were still standing next to the farmhouse.

"Sorry, Lottie, I won't be able to take you out on a hayride today," I said once I'd arrived. I'd need some time to recover and some more practice before I was willing to risk driving Lottie around on the wagon.

Lottie let out a sigh that sounded suspiciously like a sigh of relief. "That's okay."

Before anyone had a chance to comment further on what had just happened, I clapped my hands. "Let's go inside, and I can give you a tour."

I ushered them into the kitchen and then down the long hall and into the formal dining room, where Jim's huge walnut dining table took center stage. Back in the hall, I swung open the door to the small powder room before continuing to the sitting room, which held four cozy armchairs circled around a fireplace, empty bookshelves lining the walls. I led them back into the hall and then into the study and living room.

"This place is huge!" Lottie exclaimed as we walked up the staircase.

"How many rooms did you say are here?" Mom asked, peering into a spare bedroom.

I opened the door wider, so everyone else could see the empty room. "There are five bedrooms and three bathrooms."

"Well, that's too many for just one person," Mom said. "You'll have to find a nice woman to settle down with and have kids to fill up all these spare rooms. You know, I think that woman who drove your tractor off your car"—Mom grimaced—"might be gay. Diana?"

My jaw clenched. "Mom, seriously. I've got a lovely niece"—I rustled Lottie's hair—"and I've just bought a farm that will bring joy to thousands of children. That's enough for me." I began walking toward my bedroom.

Mom ran her hand along the balustrade. "But you always wanted kids—"

"Mom!" I swiveled on the oak floorboards. "I *used* to want kids. Not anymore. Can you just drop it?" Having children with someone was the ultimate show of trust. And my trust had been broken so strongly that I couldn't imagine putting myself in that position. "And even if *Dana* is interested in women, I'm not dating my employees. It would be highly inappropriate."

"Well, you should at least give dating a try again. It's been years since Sadie. When was the last time you went to that gay bar?" Mom raised her eyebrows, tilting her head forward.

I stiffened. I hadn't been back to Pryde for just over six months.

Not since Olivia.

"My dating life is none of your business," I snapped.

Mom looked away, but not before I saw the shimmer of tears in her eyes.

My chest tightened. Our relationship had always been rocky, even before I found out what she and Dad did to try to get me into college, but since we'd reconciled, I'd made an effort to keep things between us on good terms, especially for Lottie's sake. Right now, that felt like pulling teeth. Why did Mom always have to bring up my lack of a love life?

I opened the door to my bedroom. "And this is my bedroom."

Mom sniffed, walking inside and immediately began straightening the framed photo of my parents, Matt, Lottie and Mel that hung on the wall. Lottie's little eyes darted back and forth between us. Mom sniffed again.

"I did actually meet someone last time I went." Hopefully that would cheer her up a little. She didn't need to know how it had ended.

Mom's face lit up. "Oh, really? What's her name?"

I hesitated, but it was too late to go back. "Olivia."

"Well, you've kept that quiet! When can we meet her?"

I internally groaned. I should have kept my mouth shut. What a day. Totaling my car, and now this.

"So what are your plans for the farm?" Matt asked.

Tension in my chest released at the change of topic. *Thank god for Matt.*

I'd take talking about farm strategy over Olivia and my non-existent dating life any day of the week. Fingers crossed Mom would forget I'd said anything about her.

CHAPTER SEVEN

OLIVIA

HUMMING A TUNE, I pushed open the door to Novel Gossip and walked inside, pulling the cart of flowers and candles behind me. The mouthwatering scent of caffeine and baked goods hit me.

George rushed over from the counter to hold the door.

"Morning!" I said, grinning at her.

"Hey! I love the purple flowers!" George exclaimed as I parked the cart, and we began to unload the bouquets and place them on the café's tables.

"They're hyacinth. They're gorgeous, aren't they?"

A pang of sadness gripped me as I remembered Jim dropping off the hyacinth last week, his final delivery as owner of Red Tractor Farm. He'd been so proud of them. I sighed. Jim had been an amazing mentor and colleague. At least he'd moved into Sapphire Springs, so we'd be able to keep in touch. But I'd miss working with him.

"Do you have time for a coffee?" George asked.

I glanced at my watch. It was only 8:15 a.m., and I didn't usually open Sapphire Blooms until nine. "That would be great!"

We finished unloading the flowers and candles, and then I leaned against the spotless wooden counter as George made a latte for me and an Americano for her.

"It must be a huge relief about the sale," George said as she frothed a pitcher of milk.

"It all happened so quickly—Jim has already moved out and the new owner has moved in. I've been meaning to go over and introduce myself once she's settled. I know we're unlikely to have the close relationship Jim and I had, but hopefully we'll get along well enough. The fact she's keeping the farm running makes me like her already."

"Well, she seems to be the main topic for gossip here," George said. "I don't want to alarm you, but apparently Roslyn Kennedy is a little intimidating." George began pouring frothed milk into my cup.

"In what way?" Frowning, I straightened a pile of leaflets on the counter, advertising an upcoming paint and sip night George was hosting at the café.

"It sounds like she's a straight shooter and very much focused on the numbers. One of the teens who works at the petting zoo told me she cross-examined him about which animals were underperforming."

"Underperforming? What the hell does that even mean?" I wrinkled my brow.

"He thinks she wants to get rid of the less popular animals as a cost-cutting measure, so he gave a vague answer about how they were all loved." George handed me my latte. "She glared at him and stomped away. Oh, and she also asked him if the cows could be rehomed."

My eyes widened. "Not Thelma and Louise!"

George cupped her Americano in her hands and took a sip. "Don't worry, Liv. I'm sure she'll be fine. The kid probably misunderstood. She has an MBA from Harvard and was a partner in a top consulting firm, so I'm sure she just has a bit of a different style from Jim that'll take some getting used to."

My frown deepened. "So you're telling me she's totally unqualified to run a farm as well as an unpleasant person to deal with? Shit."

I'd been so focused on the fact she was going to keep the farm running that I hadn't thought to ask about her personality or farming credentials. I should give Dana a call and find out what was going on over there.

I took in a slow breath. I didn't need to be friends with this woman. I didn't even need to like her. As long as she kept supplying me with flowers, I'd be fine. Totally fine. And I hoped to god all the animals would be fine too.

I sipped my latte and closed my eyes. Thank goodness for George and her amazing coffee.

My phone pinged. I pulled it out of my pocket and frowned. It was a notification from the app I'd installed last night.

> Complete your profile to start dating!

"Is everything okay?" George asked.

"Yes, just a pushy app reminding me I haven't set it up properly," I replied, tucking my phone back into my pocket.

Perhaps it had been too premature to download the app, thinking Sapphire Blooms was out of danger and I had time to prioritize dating. I'd started to set up my profile last night but stumbled at the "sexual orientation" question. The app had listed over twenty options. Some I had heard of, others I'd had to Google. I loved how inclusive the app was, but all the choices were a little overwhelming. Was I bi, queer, pansexual, heteroflexible, homoflexible, a lesbian or something else entirely? I'd lived in Sapphire Springs long enough to know that someone in town would see me on the app, and word would spread about whatever orientation I selected. I needed to get it right. I was tired of choosing the wrong thing—whether it was a boyfriend or one of my failed business ideas—and suspected my family and friends were tired of hearing about it too. But this time, I wasn't going to rush into anything until I was sure. Perhaps tonight I'd look for some sexuality quizzes online that would give me clarity.

The bell on the front door jangled. George looked up, a smile spreading across her face, her right cheek dimpling. "Maybe Dana can offer you some comfort."

I turned around to see Dana walking up to the counter in brown boots and green overalls, her chestnut hair in a ponytail that fell down her back.

"I was just thinking about you," I said. "How are you doing?"

Dana shook her head, grimacing. "Ugh, don't ask."

"That doesn't sound good." George tapped the coffee machine. "You want your usual?"

"Make it a double shot," Dana said, flopping down onto the seat near the counter. "I'm going to need it."

My stomach churned. "What's going on?"

Dana snatched up a sugar packet and twisted it between her fingers. "The new owner is driving me up the wall. I love the farm, but I don't know if I can keep working with that woman."

Shit. So much for Dana bringing me comfort. She adored the farm and her little cottage next to the Christmas trees, so if she was considering leaving, things must be bad.

"What's wrong with her?" I pulled a chair up next to Dana and sat down, holding my coffee.

"Where to start?" Dana pursed her lips. "She doesn't

know the first thing about farming, she's obsessed with finances, and her people skills need a complete overhaul. Oh, and she's planning to get rid of the flowers."

"What?" I yelped.

Dana rubbed her forehead, wincing. "Yeah, I'm sorry, Liv. She told me she's planning to pull them all up and lease the fields to our neighbor for his cattle."

My hand clenched the handle of my cup. "Why would she do that? Jim told me the flowers were profitable, and he invested a lot of money building the greenhouse only a few years ago. It doesn't make sense to pull it all up if she's going to keep running it as a farm."

Dana held her hands up. "It doesn't make sense to me either. She said she wanted to focus her efforts on agri-tourism and that she can make more profit by leasing the fields than continuing with the flowers. She seems to have it in for them; I even caught her glaring at a bunch of tulips the other day. Maybe she's allergic or something?"

I huffed. "That's ridiculous! Does Jim know? Surely he wouldn't let her destroy his flowers."

Dana twisted the sugar packet so tight it broke, sending sugar spilling onto the table. "I spoke to Jim. He was upset, but he said he can't do anything about it. The farm is hers now. She can do what she wants with it." She swept up the sugar with her hands.

"Well, it's a stupid business decision. If she's so focused on money, she should know better." I gripped the handle of my coffee cup so tight my knuckles turned white.

"I tried to talk to her about it, and she totally shut me down." Dana grimaced.

"Well, I'm not going to just stand around and let her destroy the flowers." I slammed my coffee cup down loudly on the saucer. "Sorry, George. But I've got to go."

"Maybe you should sleep on it and speak to her tomorrow if you still think it's a good idea," George suggested, sliding Dana's double shot cappuccino over the counter.

I narrowed my eyes. George was always full of sensible advice, but I was too worked up not to take action right away.

"Okay, okay," George said, holding up her hands. "I'll pour your coffee into a to-go cup. I want you thoroughly caffeinated if you're going to face her. It sounds like you'll need it."

"Thank you." I shot George a grateful smile.

"Good luck." Dana stood up and grabbed her coffee off the counter. "And don't let her get anywhere near you with a tractor. You should see her car."

I stared at Dana, making a mental note to ask her about that curious comment later.

George handed me the to-go cup, and I stormed out of Novel Gossip, grabbing the cart on my way. I was going to give this Roslyn woman a piece of my mind.

Except... like Jim said, it was *her* farm. I didn't really have the right to tell her what to do.

But I could at least try to convince her not to get rid of the flowers. If she really was allergic to them, she could just take some damn antihistamines.

CHAPTER EIGHT

ROZ

I SAT at Jim's old oak desk, which was covered in scratches and faint ink stains, scrolling through the business plan I'd prepared on my laptop. An email notification from Mom popped up titled *Lesbian Speed Dating in Poughkeepsie!* I rolled my eyes, and focused back on the document in front of me.

This better go well. Thank god for Fred, the only person in my network who'd shown any interest after dozens of rejections from banks and private lenders. It wasn't ideal that he'd only consider coming on board as an investor—a bank loan would have been much more straightforward—but I needed the money one way or another. The farm needed far more money than my savings could provide. A lot of the farm machinery was old, to the point where it needed to be replaced rather than repaired, and other unexpected issues kept cropping up. *Like crashing an ancient tractor into my extremely expensive car.* I winced. The insurance company had refused to cover the damage. I wouldn't be able to afford to replace my car anytime soon, even if Fred agreed to go ahead with the investment. And if he didn't... I closed my eyes. I didn't know what I would do. But it would probably end in bankruptcy.

The doorbell sounded, and I jumped up, my eyes darting to the wooden clock on the wall. My pulse quickened. That must be Fred, although he was fifteen minutes early. I took a deep breath, pulled on my suit jacket, and walked down the hall. I opened the door, a large smile plastered on my face.

My smile vanished. It was Mom. She was holding a pie and a bag of groceries and beaming at me. My hand tightened around the door handle.

"Mom? What are you doing here?"

Mom lifted up the pie. "I thought I'd just pop by to check you're settling in okay and drop off some food to make sure you're eating."

"Thanks, Mom. You know, I do have the farm café literally fifty feet from my house and I can look after myself—I managed to eat for the last twenty years without you. But I appreciate the thought." I reached out for the pie and bag of groceries. "I've got a business meeting in ten minutes, so I'm afraid I don't have time to talk, but thanks for dropping by."

Mom pulled the grocery bag away from me. "If you're busy, I can put this all away for you. Don't worry, I won't interrupt your meeting."

"Okay, Mom, just make yourself at home," I muttered under my breath as she pushed past me into the hallway. Well, I did want to pitch the farm to Fred as a family farm. Having Mom around might help, as long as she didn't hijack the meeting or start asking Fred if he knew any single queer women of childbearing age I could date.

Mom entered the spacious kitchen with its expansive wooden countertops, blue cabinets and white farmhouse sink. She placed the bag of groceries on the island.

"Did you get my email about speed dating?" Mom pulled a can of tomatoes from the bag.

I did my best to hold back an exasperated sigh. "Yes, thanks."

"Apparently, tickets are selling fast. I know you're seeing someone, but perhaps you should buy a ticket just in case things don't work out with her." Her eyes lit up. "Oh, and I also have another possibility waiting in the wings." She looked at me expectantly, clearly waiting for me to ask for details.

"Uh-huh?"

"Margie's daughter." Mom grinned, a loaf of bread in hand.

"Holly? Is she queer?" I collected the yoghurt from the counter and popped it into the almost empty fridge.

"Well, I'm not *one hundred* percent sure. But she does have short hair and always wears pants. Oh, and your dad often runs into her at Home Depot."

I huffed, swinging the fridge door shut. Mom was really leaning into the lesbian stereotypes. I should probably have a talk to her about that, but now was not the time.

The doorbell rang. I glanced at my watch. Fred was right on time.

"Mom, that will be Fred. This meeting is really important, so I'll just introduce you, and then you need to leave." I took the pie from her and placed it in the pantry.

"Okay, sweetie," Mom said, folding the grocery bag and leaving it on the counter. She followed me to the front door, smoothing her dress as she went.

A loud knock made me pick up my pace. Perhaps Fred thought the doorbell wasn't working.

The knock sounded again, harder this time. I frowned. That wasn't like Fred.

As I reached the door, I wiped my damp hands on my pants, plastered another welcoming smile on my face, and swung the door wide.

And froze.

What the hell?

Standing in front of me, cheeks flushed and eyes flashing, wearing blue pants with yellow flowers on them and a pink t-shirt, was Olivia. From Pryde.

I blinked. *What is happening right now?*

"Olivia?"

She was even more beautiful than I'd remembered, her shiny brown hair framing her face in soft waves. For some reason, she appeared to be glaring at me.

Olivia's eyes widened. "Roz?"

We stared at each other in silence.

"Oh, Olivia!" Mom exclaimed, pushing past me and enveloping Olivia in a hug. "When Roz said she'd been seeing someone named Olivia, I didn't realize she meant you! How wonderful! It's so lovely to see you again. How's your flower shop going? Those dahlias we bought from you last year were gorgeous."

Olivia's expression changed from anger to confusion as she shot me a questioning look.

Oh god.

Mom knew Olivia? And Olivia lived somewhere nearby. *Shit.*

"Mom, Olivia and I are not—"

"Roz!" Behind Olivia, Fred stepped out of a black electric car in the parking lot. He flipped his sunglasses onto his balding head and waved before starting to walk toward us. Fred looked like he'd just come from the golf club in fitted navy pants and a white polo shirt.

Shit. Shit. Shit.

"Okay, sorry to cut things short, but I've got a meeting now with a potential investor for the farm. Can you both please leave?"

I couldn't let myself get distracted by Mom or Olivia. I could clear up the misunderstanding later. For now, I had to stay laser focused on securing the investment from Fred.

"Roz!" Mom crossed her arms. "That's no way to talk to your girlfriend."

"She's not my girlfriend," I said through a smile directed at Fred, who had almost reached us.

"Sorry, what's the word you use these days? Partner?" Mom tilted her head.

"Girlfriend, partner—I'm happy with anything," Olivia said, grinning.

"Mom, Olivia, can you *please* leave?" I muttered through gritted teeth moments before Fred reached us. "Hi, Fred!"

"Roz, it's great to see you again." Fred held out his hand.

"You too," I said, grasping his hand firmly in mine. "Thanks for coming all the way out here."

"And I'm Roz's mom, Marie, and this is her girlfriend—sorry, partner—Olivia," Mom chimed in.

Fuck.

Fred tipped his head. "Lovely to meet you both." He shot me a glance, an eyebrow slightly raised. No wonder he was surprised. In the ten years he'd known me, I'd never had a girlfriend.

I had to fix this situation now, before it got even more out of control. "Actually, there's been a misun—"

"Lovely to meet you, Fred." Olivia shook Fred's hand. "We're so happy you could visit. Aren't we, darling?" She shot a devilish sweet smile my way.

I stared into her brown eyes, lost for words.

She elbowed me. "Aren't we, *darling?*"

"Um, yes." My mind whirred. What the hell was she playing at?

Fred looked between us, his smile faltering. Shit, this was not a great start. And it would be even worse if I tried to explain that Olivia was not my girlfriend now that she'd started acting the part. It would probably result in Fred thinking we'd lost our minds and leaving. My best bet was to get rid of Mom and Olivia and go full steam ahead with the meeting. I could work out how to correct the record on our relationship status later.

"Please, come in," I said to Fred. "I can take you through the financials and my vision for the farm, and then I can give you a tour. Mom, Olivia, please excuse us."

"Actually, could we do the tour first? I've just spent the last hour and a half in the car. I'd love to stretch my legs and enjoy the fresh air." Fred inhaled a vigorous breath to make his point.

"Yes, of course." I turned to Mom and Olivia, who were both still hovering next to me. "Well, Fred and I will be off, then. I'll see you both soon." I stepped out of the door while trying my best to emulate Olivia's sweet smile.

"Oh, babe, I decided to open my shop later today so I can stay to show Fred around the farm as well." Olivia flashed a grin at Fred. "We have so many great plans for it that we can't wait to share with you."

I frowned. "That's really not necessary—"

"Excellent." Fred clasped his hands together. "The more the merrier. And I'd love to get to know the woman who has stolen Roz's heart."

I clenched my teeth together. *Stolen control of my meeting, more like it.*

In my long career, I'd experienced many meetings that

had gone off the rails, and I'd always been able to bring them back on course. But usually, I knew the motives of the person disrupting the meeting, and I was able to use that information to my advantage. However, while Olivia clearly had her own agenda, it wasn't clear what it was. I straightened my back. I couldn't let her throw me off my game.

"Before you three head off... how long are you in the area for, Fred?" Mom asked.

Fred swatted at a passing fly with his hand. "I thought I'd mix work with pleasure and stay for the weekend. I'd also love to explore the Hudson Valley some more. And considering it's not a small investment, I'll probably visit the farm a couple times before I make my final decision."

Damnit. I'd hoped Fred would decide quickly. How long could I put off fixing the backhoe?

Mom smiled. "Well then, we'd love to have you over for lunch if you're free tomorrow? You too, Olivia."

"Mom—" I cut in, eager to shut down any talk of the three of them regrouping. This conversation had already spiraled out of control after only a few minutes.

"That would be lovely, thank you," Fred said.

"Say about twelve?"

"Sounds great." Fred pulled down his sunglasses.

Goddamnit. The plan was set. How could I get out of it? I tried not to clench my jaw too hard. I did not need a fractured tooth on top of everything else.

"Well, should we get going?" I stepped forward. "I thought we could walk around the café, farm stand and petting zoo first, and then we can take my truck to see everything else. It would take too long to walk the entire farm." I nodded toward an old truck parked next to the house, an inheritance from the farm that I now relied on to get around after the tractor incident. The truck didn't have any back passenger seats, so hopefully, I could get rid of Olivia at that point.

"Sounds great." Olivia beamed at Fred as they turned toward the café, their backs to me. "I'm sure you'll love the animals and the flowers."

She glanced over her shoulder at me, shooting me another sugary sweet smile, and I glared at her. Not only was Olivia more attractive than I remembered, but she was also way more annoying. I needed to work out her ulterior motive stat, before this meeting completely crashed and burned.

CHAPTER NINE

ROZ

OLIVIA'S warm shoulder pressed against me as I drove down the dirt road. Much to my chagrin, Olivia had insisted on squishing into the front of the truck with me and Fred. The truck was so ancient it had a bench seat, which unfortunately was just wide enough to fit the three of us. Olivia's faint floral scent tickled my nose. The image of her body pressed to mine in a very different way that night at Pryde flashed into my mind. I tensed. *Do not go there, Roz.*

I accelerated as we passed my crushed car, hoping no one would notice. Out of the corner of my eye, I saw Olivia's eyes widen, but she didn't comment.

Olivia had been irritatingly charming during the tour of the café and farm stand, raving about the delicious apple fritters and cherry pies using homegrown fruit, and then introducing all the animals by name at the petting zoo. How did she know so much about my farm? Instead of being the liability I had expected, she was actually doing a good job selling it to Fred—maybe even better than me.

"What are these for?" Fred asked, pointing to the empty fields on either side of the path.

I pulled over. "We'll be planting corn and pumpkins there next week. By fall, they'll be transformed into a corn maze and pumpkin patch. They're a big draw with the families." I smiled at the memory of Lottie scrambling around pumpkins to find the biggest one last fall.

"I can imagine," Fred replied. "I wish my parents had left their Upper East Side bubble and taken me to somewhere like this as a kid. I didn't realize that milk came from cows' udders until embarrassingly late."

"Oh, that reminds me. Babe, we forgot to introduce Fred to Thelma and Louise!" Olivia slapped my thigh so hard I nearly jumped off the bench. The last time that hand had been on my body, it had been running up and down my bare back in the restroom at Pryde, driving me wild. A shiver shot down my spine. I clenched my jaw. Now Olivia was driving me wild in a much less enjoyable manner.

Olivia turned to Fred. "We'll have to show you on the way back. They're two of the sweetest cows."

"Mmm. Yes." I pursed my lips.

Of course Olivia would like the damn cows. Given everything else I'd had going on, I'd made no progress rehoming them, but I was still hoping to see the last of them. Their constant mooing near my study window was a distraction I didn't need, and whenever I ventured out the back of the house, they stared at me. If they were expecting more entertainment in the style of my car-crushing mishap, they would be sorely disappointed. Perhaps my neighbor who raised cattle would take them.

"Well, there's no mistaking what this section is." Fred chuckled, breaking me out of my thoughts. We'd reached the flower fields, where rows of yellow daffodils were blooming.

"Yes, isn't it gorgeous?" Olivia leaned forward, her shoulder brushing against mine.

"What are those ones?" Fred pointed at the rows of green shoots behind the daffodils.

Damn. It was the first question I couldn't answer. *It doesn't really matter since I'm proposing to get rid of them all anyway.* The business plan Fred had received hadn't included the proposal to lease the flower fields. I'd added that in after I'd realized how dire the farm's financial situation was. Now was an opportune time to tell him of the change of plans. "I'm actually planning to le—"

"They're tulips," Olivia interjected. "And farther on, we have ranunculus and anemones. Roz, honey, let's stop here so we can show Fred around."

I gritted my teeth. I had no intention of stopping. What was the point of giving Fred a tour of something that was going to be trampled by cows?

But Fred was already putting his hat on, clearly eager to explore.

Olivia shot me a sweet smile, but there was a steely glint in her eyes. Something clicked in my mind. Was she here because she didn't want me to get rid of the flowers? Mom had mentioned she'd bought dahlias off Olivia. Could she be one of the florists Red Tractor Farm supplied? I recalled the customer list Jim had given me included a flower shop in Sapphire Springs. Could that be Olivia's?

I reluctantly stopped the truck, and we hopped out.

Olivia led Fred down a small path between two rows of bright flowers, talking animatedly about heirloom varieties and sustainable farming practices. There was only room to walk single file, so I was stuck behind Fred, unable to get a word in. I stomped after him. Olivia singing the praises of the farm stand and café was fine, but I really didn't need her raving about how wonderful all these flowers were. And I was sure Fred couldn't care less about sustainability. I shot a withering glare at a particularly perky-looking daffodil, trying to distract myself from how perky Olivia's butt looked up ahead. While the floral pattern on her pants was horrendous, it clung to her curves in all the right places. I shook off the thought. We were almost at the end of the row now. Once we reached it, I could lead Fred and Olivia back to the truck and drive on to the Christmas trees.

"We also have some gorgeous tulips flowering in the greenhouse, which we'd love to show you," Olivia said as we walked out of the field. She kept talking quickly. It was almost like she could sense that if she paused, I'd try to move us on. "It's powered by geothermal energy, which means it can produce flowers all year round using a sustainable energy source. Did you know the flower industry is rife with questionable environmental practices? Huge quantities of flowers are flown into the US from overseas each year, fossil fuels are used to heat greenhouses, synthetic fertilizers and pesticides are widespread and packaging waste contributes to landfills." Olivia's eyes flashed again. "We're really passionate about sustainable farming, aren't we, babe?"

I clenched my jaw. "Let's not bore Fred with the details. I'm sure he's more interested in the bottom line than our carbon footprint."

"Actually, sustainability has become a passion of mine in recent years, ever since I visited Yosemite and saw the shrinking glaciers. I got solar panels installed on my house in the Hamptons and bought an electric car last year. Got to protect our planet for future generations," Fred said.

I blinked, my mind racing. Did Fred actually care about this stuff? I held back a sigh. Yet again, Olivia had put me in a position where if I disagreed with her or explained what my plans for the flower fields were, it would be extremely awkward.

I took a fortifying breath. When we got back to the farmhouse, I'd fill Fred in on my updated business plan, and hopefully he'd be so impressed with my financial projections he'd forget that the flowers he'd been admiring would be munched to oblivion by my neighbor's cattle.

"Well, why don't you show me this amazing greenhouse?" Fred asked.

Olivia nodded, grinning, and practically bounced across to the large greenhouse. I trudged after her.

The warm, sweetly scented, humid air hit us as Olivia pushed open the glass door, and we stepped inside. Bright sunlight filtered through the glass panes, illuminating the rows of flowers. I fought the urge to screw up my nose. *Ugh.*

"These two rows are ranunculus, then over there we have anemones and freesias—that's what the gorgeous smell is," Olivia said, pointing for our benefit.

Fred peered down at the ground. "You mentioned it was powered by geothermal energy? How does that work?"

Olivia's face brightened even further. "We have thousands of feet of piping under the ground to capture and store warm air, and fans that pull the air through the pipes into the greenhouse. Not only is it a sustainable energy source, but it also means that we're able to provide flower shops with locally grown flowers all year round, so they aren't forced to import them."

"That's fantastic," Fred said, scanning the greenhouse.

Olivia grinned. "Yes, it's just one of the ways we try to minimize our carbon footprint here at Red Tractor Farm. We also use other sustainable farming practices, such as reduced tillage and avoiding synthetic pesticides and herbicides."

"You seem to know a lot about the farm," Fred said, giving Olivia an assessing look.

"I used to work here—first at the café and then helping the previous owner, Jim, with the flowers—off and on during my twenties. I now run the flower shop in Sapphire Springs and the farm is my primary supplier. I love this place and I'm so happy Roz loves it too." Olivia patted me on the back, sending my skin tingling.

So I was right. Olivia was the owner of the flower shop in Sapphire Springs, which meant she had a vested interest in the future of the flower fields. The pieces were starting to fall into place.

"Oh, how wonderful." Fred turned to me. "Roz, you must be so pleased Olivia shares your passion for the farm."

I hummed noncommittally and glanced at my watch. "Let's head over to the Christmas trees, and then we can show you the orchards on the way back." Not only did I want Fred away from the flowers, but their cloying scent was starting to give me a headache.

To my relief, Fred nodded, and we headed back to the truck and drove toward the Christmas trees. The row of dark-green firs stretched for acres, at varying levels of maturity.

I slowed the truck. "These are Fraser firs. They take about seven years to reach maturity. This section will be ready this Christmas. We make about 30% margin on these trees, so it's one of the more profitable parts of the farm and an important attraction during the holiday season." I accelerated the truck. The sooner this was over, the sooner I could get rid of Olivia. Then Fred and I could get down to discussing business.

"Stop, Roz!" Olivia yelled.

I jumped in my seat, slamming on the brakes. Once the truck jolted to a halt, I peered through the windshield, my heart pounding. Had I hit something? *Not again.*

"Excuse me, babe. I'm just going to hop out for a second." Olivia looked expectantly at me. I frowned. I didn't like the idea of letting Olivia out without knowing her intentions first. At the rate we were going, I would be lucky if it was still light by the time I got Fred into my office. "You know what, never mind. I'll just climb over you."

Olivia clambered over my body, her soft hair brushing against my nose, her elbow bumping my breasts. I shut my eyes. Why did she have to smell so goddamn good? I opened them in time to see Olivia open the door and jump out. What the hell was she doing? A tic started under my eye.

She picked a sprig off the closest fir tree and handed it to Fred through his window.

"Doesn't it smell wonderful?" Olivia beamed.

I fought the urge to roll my eyes. Really?

Fred sniffed it. "It does. Reminds me of just how magical Christmas was when I was a kid." He inhaled again and closed his eyes.

Olivia clambered back over me and onto the bench. "Sorry, Roz, but I couldn't have Fred visit and not experience our amazing Fraser firs up close. We'll have to get you one for Christmas, Fred."

Fred beamed. "I haven't had a real Christmas tree for years. That would be lovely."

I made a mental note to send Fred a Fraser fir for Christmas if he agreed to invest in the farm.

"We'll head back past the orchards and strawberry fields now," I said, turning on the engine.

As we drove past budding cherry trees, Olivia turned to

look at them. "I've always thought not having a cherry blossom festival at the farm was a missed opportunity. Perhaps we could do it next year, hon?"

I glanced sideways to see Olivia smiling innocently at me, before focusing my attention back on the road.

A cherry blossom festival was a decent idea. It could be a good way to show the locals that Red Tractor Farm was still in safe hands, as well as bring in some more revenue. Even if the cherry blossom season was over, a spring festival might have a similar outcome. We could hold it sometime in late May or early June, which would give me at least five or six weeks to pull it together.

"Yes, that's definitely something to consider," I said.

"You'll also have to try the delicious cherry and strawberry jams that we sell in the café." Olivia wriggled in her seat. "We'll give you a jar of each to take home."

Fred rubbed his stomach. "You're making me hungry with all this talk of food. Perhaps we could drop by the café after this?"

Stopping at the café wasn't a terrible thought. There was a study that showed that judges were more likely to grant parole after a meal break... and I wanted Fred in the best possible mindset when deciding whether or not to invest in my vision.

I guided the truck over a rough section of road, chewing on my lip. Apart from putting me in a difficult position regarding my plans to lease the flower fields, Olivia had been surprisingly helpful. But I didn't want her around when I put forward my proposal to Fred. She'd been willing to pretend to be my girlfriend to protect the flowers, so who knows what else she might do if she saw the updated section about the future of the flower fields.

I pulled up at the parking lot and jumped out of the

truck before Olivia's impatience had her climbing over me again. "Here we are. I know you'll be needing to get back to work." I gave Olivia a look intended to convey that her presence at the café was not welcome.

Olivia held my gaze coolly for a moment then stared at the silver watch around her slender wrist. Her forehead creased, and I suspected she was having an internal struggle between wanting to stay here and needing to go and open her shop.

"Yes, you're right. I better be off." Olivia stretched out her arm. "Well, lovely to meet you, Fred, and please feel free to reach out to me if you have any questions about the greenhouse or the flowers. As you can see, we're very passionate about them, so we'd really appreciate your help to ensure they continue to flourish. And if you're interested, I'd love for you to visit Sapphire Blooms if you've got time."

My eyes narrowed. Olivia and Fred meeting without me present would be less than ideal.

"I might take you up on that offer," Fred said, shaking her hand. "It was great to meet you too, Olivia. I'll see you tomorrow for lunch."

Confusion flickered across Olivia's face for a split second. "Yes, of course." She turned to me, leaning in and brushing her cheek across mine, leaving my face tingling. "Bye, babe, see you later."

When she pulled back, her mouth curved up, her eyes sparkling, and my heart jumped. *She's putting it all on for show. Don't get sucked in by her beautiful smile.*

"Bye," I choked out.

Olivia beelined for an orange Volkswagen Beetle with large purple and pink flowers painted all over it. Humph. Of course she'd have a ridiculous hippy-looking car covered in flowers.

"She's such a delight," Fred said as Olivia opened the door to her car.

"She's certainly special," I replied, not willing to concede the point.

God, she was infuriating. Her parting words about the flowers would make it even more difficult to sell Fred on getting rid of them, especially since he seemed to be a huge fan of hers already.

"You two make a good team. You're the numbers woman, and Olivia is clearly focused on the heart."

My shoulders tensed. But I had to admit that, apart from Olivia's comments about the flowers, we had complemented each other well today.

A sinking sensation tugged at my stomach. Fred thought we were a team, but we barely knew each other. And because we'd just spent the last hour pretending to be a couple, I was now in a very difficult position.

Fred and I had known each other since business school, but we were acquaintances, not friends. We weren't close enough that I was confident we could just laugh this situation off and move on without jeopardizing Fred's potential investment.

My gut told me that the only reason Fred had been willing to consider investing in Red Tractor Farm was because he trusted me. If he found out we'd been lying to him, the entire deal might be off the table before I could even put it on there.

Without his money, I'd have to let go of a number of the staff and possibly take even more drastic steps in an attempt to keep the farm afloat. Surely not correcting the lie was the least worst of two bad options?

I clenched my jaw. Probably not. But it didn't feel like I had much choice now. I needed to focus my energy on convincing Fred to invest in the farm and work out how to get rid of the flowers after Olivia had extolled their virtues. And I also had to make sure Olivia planned on showing up tomorrow to avoid raising any suspicions with Fred. Hopefully, without her body pressed to mine in the confines of the old truck, I wouldn't have any more of those irritating flashbacks to Pryde.

CHAPTER TEN

OLIVIA

I WRAPPED THE RED, orange, and yellow ranunculus in brown paper, tied them together with string, and handed them to Mrs. Seabourne. "Have a lovely day." I waved as she exited the shop.

I'd been buzzing with adrenaline since I'd returned from Red Tractor Farm. I still couldn't believe what I'd done. I'd been about to tell Roz's mom, in no uncertain terms, that I was certainly not dating her flower-hating daughter who'd ghosted me and stolen my favorite t-shirt, when Fred had shown up and a half-baked plan to save the flower farm had materialized in my head. Before I knew it, I was playing Roz's girlfriend. And I had to admit I'd gotten a perverse pleasure from seeing Roz clenching her jaw as I sang the flowers' praises. Hopefully, I'd made it difficult for her to get rid of them now.

I turned back to the flower arrangement I was preparing for a wedding at Rivers Edge restaurant. As I added some greenery, a thought struck me. News traveled fast in Sapphire Springs. There was a real risk that Fred or Roz's family would mention our "relationship" to someone else, and within twenty-four hours, the entire town would know.

Shit. I was not ready to come out to my friends and family yet. Not like this. I needed more time to work things out. I took a deep breath. If word did spread, I could just explain to my family and friends that I'd pretended to be Roz's girlfriend to try to save Sapphire Blooms and conveniently not mention that night at Pryde with her. Unless I told them otherwise, they'd continue to assume I was straight.

The doorbell jangled. I didn't look up. I needed to secure the flowers first with twine, or the arrangement would collapse.

A shadow fell across the counter and someone cleared their throat. I jumped, letting go of the twine and the bouquet fell apart. *Shit.*

Roz stood in front of me, still in her ridiculous business clothes that were completely unsuitable for a farmer. Although, I had to admit she did look good in the dark suit that fit her long, lean body to perfection, a cream silk blouse underneath. I swallowed as I thought about what was beneath that blouse.

"Hello," she said, fixing me with a cool stare.

"Hi." I collected the fallen flowers. If she'd come here looking for an apology, she wouldn't get one.

She crossed her arms but said nothing. Silence fell.

"Can I help you with something?" I asked. "We have some beautiful tulips in stock. Although, they did come from your farm, so while I probably shouldn't tell you this, it would be cheaper for you if you just picked them yourself."

Roz pursed her lips. "I'm here about that stunt you pulled this morning—"

"Stunt? You were the one who told your mom we were

dating." I glared. Why *had* she told her mom that? Or perhaps she really was dating someone else named Olivia? At Pryde, she'd told me she didn't date, but maybe things had changed since then.

"It was a misunderstanding—one I was in the process of correcting when you jumped in. Anyway"—Roz's eyes darted around the shop—"I just wanted to confirm you're coming tomorrow."

I tilted my head. "Tomorrow?"

"To my parents' house. For lunch with Fred."

"Oh." While my "stunt" had hopefully achieved its intended result of forcing Roz to keep the flowers, I didn't want to spend any more time around the flower-hating, suit-wearing, rude woman than necessary. "No."

Roz stepped forward. "You have to."

My jaw tensed. "I'm sorry, but I don't *have* to do anything."

"You pretended to be my girlfriend, told my mother and Fred you'd be there, and for some reason, they are both looking forward to seeing you." Roz gritted her teeth.

I bit my lip. Roz's mom and Fred both seemed delightful. It was unfortunate that Roz was not. I would have to disappoint them. "I don't think that's my problem."

"Well, it'll be your problem when I lease the flowers for cattle fodder and you lose your supplier." Roz quirked a brow.

My chest tightened. She'd clearly put two and two together and worked out what I'd been up to. "But..."

"It's obvious what your agenda was this morning. And while it may have worked temporarily—I didn't put forward my proposal to Fred to lease the flower fields because you made it too difficult—if Fred's investment falls through, the flowers are gone."

I stared at Roz. "But Jim told me they were profitable!"

"They are, but I'll make more money leasing the fields to my neighbor. And if Fred doesn't invest, I'll need every cent I can get to keep the rest of the farm going."

My heart dropped. She was serious.

Roz's lips pressed into a thin line. "Investing the amount of money I've asked for requires a big leap of faith on Fred's part. He needs to be able to trust me, or the whole deal will fall through. While I don't like it either, you've backed us into a corner. You need to play my charming girlfriend, or we'll both lose. If you play along and he invests, then I'll keep the flowers." She wrinkled her nose. Why did she hate flowers so much?

I twirled the twine with my fingers. While it had been fun watching Roz squirm for an hour, keeping the act up was another story.

"I'll also need you to continue this dating charade while Fred is deciding whether to go ahead with the investment," Roz said. "Oh, and be available as necessary."

My eyes widened. "Available?"

"In case Fred asks for you. Or if we're doing something that a partner would usually attend, like dinner."

I picked up a pink petal on the counter and dropped it into the compost bin. "For how long?"

"Fred said he might come back again for some more visits before he makes up his mind, so it could be a couple of weeks."

My stomach twisted. "I don't want to lie to my friends or family about this." I also didn't want them learning I was interested in women just yet. I chewed on my lip. I was meant to be focusing on finding a partner to have kids with, not embarking on fake flings. I'd loudly announced on my thirtieth birthday that rocky relationships and failed businesses were a thing of the past. I didn't want my first "relationship" post that speech to be a short-lived fake relationship with Roz that everyone thought was real. But until Sapphire Blooms was safe, I'd have no bandwidth to focus on dating anyway.

Roz snorted. "Shame you only discovered your moral code after this morning's tour."

I held up a hand. "I know, I know. But it's one thing to get, um, a bit carried away and briefly pretend to be your girlfriend. It's another to continue the deception and expand it to include other people."

Roz shifted on her feet. "I don't like it either, but Fred is my only chance for funding, and without it, the farm's future is in peril—and this place as well." Roz looked around Sapphire Blooms, as if seeing it for the first time. The tiered round rustic wooden table in the middle, overflowing with colorful blooms. The wooden shelves featuring my homemade candles and greeting cards. The displays of hyacinths, crocuses and tulips in the front window. Her features hardened. "A fake relationship was not part of my business plan this morning, but you've given me no other choice."

I almost felt bad for Roz. *Almost.*

I sighed. It seemed like the best option was to fake date Roz but tell my friends and family the truth. At least that way, I could buy myself some more time to sort out my sexuality and avoid them thinking I'd entered yet another disastrous relationship with my eyes closed. Although they would almost certainly judge me for getting myself into this fake-dating pickle. I inhaled deeply through my nose. All things considered, it still seemed like the better option.

"I won't lie to my friends and family. They won't tell

anyone. I promise." I fixed her with a stare. "It's non-negotiable."

Roz held my gaze for a moment. God, she had incredible eyes. The blue reminded me of the Virginia bluebells that were currently in bloom across the Hudson Valley.

"Fine," she said.

"Okay," I said. "I'm in." Maddie usually worked Saturdays with me. I could still work in the morning, and she should be able to manage without me for the rest of the day.

"Okay, then." Roz pulled her phone out of her suit pants pocket. "We'd better get each other's numbers so we can communicate. Do you still have mine?"

"What?" Why did she think I had her number? "No, I don't have your number."

She stabbed the screen of her phone a few times with an elegant finger, then handed it to me.

I entered my number and then clicked on her camera icon, turned it on selfie mode, leaned across the counter and adjusted the camera settings so we were both captured in the frame. "Smile!"

Roz pulled back. "What are you doing?"

"If we're going to date, then we should have a picture of us together. Actually, let me come around so we're standing next to each other."

I walked around the counter and wrapped my arm around Roz's slim waist. When I'd touched it at Pryde, there'd been no shirt between us. Her skin had been so soft and smooth. Heat sparked low in my belly. I inhaled the faint scent of cedar I'd detected in the bar and again this morning when I'd been pressed up against her in the truck. *Focus, Olivia.*

I held my free arm out straight, pressing my cheek

against Roz's, smiling and trying to ignore the warmth emitting from her body.

"Okay, now smile!"

Roz's face pulled into an expression that was somewhere between a smile and a grimace. I pressed the button to capture the awkward moment and then quickly stepped back to put much needed space between us. I glanced down at the image. Roz's smile left something to be desired, but that would have to do. I handed the phone back to her, our fingers brushing. The heat in my belly flickered again.

Roz pursed her lips, and then her thumbs flew across the screen.

"I've sent you a text so you have my number. See you tomorrow." With that, Roz turned and strode out of my shop, the doorbell jangling behind her.

My phone lit up with a text, and I glanced down. Roz had sent me the photo along with a text message.

Don't fuck this up.

CHAPTER ELEVEN

ROZ

MY EYES DARTED to the grandfather clock in my parents' living room. Olivia was late.

I frowned. She better show. She was the whole reason I was in this mess to begin with. And if she didn't play the part she'd created for herself, we'd both be screwed.

"Auntie Roz, you're not paying attention!" Lottie yelped.

"Sorry, sweetheart." I focused back on the Monopoly board spread across the lush carpet in front of us.

"So why have you been keeping Olivia top secret?" Matt asked, sliding his thimble piece across the board. "Is she the real reason you moved back?"

I paused. I didn't like lying to Matt. But my parents were in the next room and could potentially overhear us. I couldn't risk that. Not only were they terrible actors, but they wouldn't approve of the fake-dating situation we'd found ourselves in. And they were both so thrilled to hear I was finally dating someone; I was eager to keep them in happy ignorance for a little longer. Mom's constant badgering about me needing to settle down was pressure I didn't need right now with everything else that was going on.

"No, it's complicated," I said. "I'll tell you later."

I stared at him meaningfully over Lottie's blond head. Matt raised an eyebrow but dropped the subject.

Lottie had just declared victory when the doorbell rang. My pulse quickened. Was it Fred or Olivia? I glanced around the living room. I was used to meeting business partners in sleek meeting rooms with associates I trusted. My family members were loose cannons. And having Olivia present was going to add another layer of unpredictability to the mix. For the tenth time today, I wished Mom hadn't insisted on Fred coming to lunch. I knew she was trying to be helpful by welcoming Fred into our family, but I preferred to keep business and family separate. My parents had a history of trying to be helpful in ways that were anything but. My chest tightened at the memory.

Lottie bounced up and raced to the door. I rose stiffly off the floor, following her.

By the time I'd reached the long hallway, Lottie had already opened the front door. Fred and Olivia stood on the doorstep, Fred dressed in tan pants and a navy polo shirt, and Olivia in a blue dress covered in purple flowers.

"Hello!" Lottie waved in their faces.

My mother's familiar footsteps echoed behind me. I quickened my pace.

"Hello, I see you've met my niece, Lottie. Come in." I smiled to mask my nerves as I shook Fred's hand and then turned to Olivia.

Shit. While it'd been a long time since I'd been in a relationship, I was fairly confident that in this situation, most people would kiss or hug or show some type of physical affection toward their girlfriend. I needed to do something.

As I stared at Olivia, frozen in place, she leaned forward and brushed her soft lips against my cheek.

"Hi, babe," she murmured, her breath tickling my earlobe.

A shiver rushed down my spine. Something like *that*.

I managed a strangled, "Hi," took a deep breath and then reintroduced Fred and Olivia to my mother, who was hovering behind us. Dad trotted out, wearing a navy apron over his jeans and checkered shirt, and extended a hand, and then Matt followed suit. Once the introductions were complete, Dad, Lottie, and Matt disappeared off.

Mom squeezed her hands together. "So lovely to see you again, Fred. And you too, Olivia."

"Thanks for having me," Olivia said as we walked back down the hall. "Is there anything I can do to help?"

"I'd love a hand with the salad," Mom said, whisking Olivia into the kitchen.

My stomach sank as they vanished out of sight. I didn't trust either of them right now. On the plus side, at least it gave me the opportunity to speak to Fred without Olivia present. I ushered him into the living room, taking a seat on my parents' cream couch, while Fred lowered himself into the matching armchair. The smell of roasted potatoes wafted in from the kitchen.

"Did you have a good morning in Sapphire Springs?" I asked, smiling.

Fred rested an elbow on the armrest. "It was lovely, thanks. I went for a stroll down to Dockside Park."

"Oh, wonderful." I leaned forward. "Have you had any more thoughts about our discussion yesterday?"

Fred nodded. "So far, I'm impressed. But I'd like to get some more information about supply and demand for your proposed event space and taproom. I want to understand what your competition is around here, whether they are booked out or have capacity, and how you'll differentiate your function space from other venues in the region."

My shoulders sank. I'd done enough research to know that the event space and taproom would be profitable, but I hadn't had time to do a deep-dive competition analysis. It had been a weak spot in my proposal, but I'd hoped Fred wouldn't notice. I should have known better. I was used to having minions to do this type of work for me.

"Of course. I can get all that information for you."

"Excellent. Thanks, Roz. I need to go back to the city tomorrow, but I'm planning to come back on Friday. Could you have it to me by then?"

"Yes, of course." I gave a swift smile. I could *really* do with a minion right now.

Dad popped his head into the living room. "Lunch is ready."

We made our way into my parents' expansive dining room, which looked out over the sprawling green front lawn. I took a seat at the large, oak table. Fred sat on my left, and a minute later, Olivia appeared, set down two bowls of salad, and slipped onto the seat on my right.

Mom and Dad brought out plates of salmon with dill sauce and roasted potatoes, placing them in front of us. Lottie and Matt arrived, flushed and slightly out of breath.

"We just had a very energetic game of catch," Matt said, gulping down some water.

As we ate, I couldn't stop myself from glancing at Olivia. It was strangely intimate, inviting someone I barely knew into my parents' home to have lunch with my family. The last date to meet my parents was Sadie. Not that this was a date. Olivia seemed to be enjoying herself, chatting to Dad about ways to deal with his rose slug problem.

"It's best to get onto them as quickly as possible, before they multiply," Olivia said.

"Speaking of multiples," Mom said, putting down her fork and focusing her attention on Olivia, "do you want children, Olivia?"

I spluttered, nearly choking on a mouthful of salmon.

"Mom!" I snapped, glaring at her. I'd hoped one of the benefits of this ridiculous charade was that it would keep my mother off my back about dating for a while. I hadn't anticipated she'd just change lanes to this other, equally annoying, line of questioning.

My eyes flickered to Olivia, who seemed unperturbed by my mother's inappropriate behavior. If anything, I thought there was a glint of amusement in her eyes.

"Okay, okay. I'm sorry," Mom said, holding up her hands. "I would love to hear how you met, though."

"We met at Pryde, the gay bar, remember?" I answered, trying to keep my tone civil. Fred was here, after all.

"I know that, but how did it actually happen?" Mom pressed.

"Marie." Dad placed his hand on her arm. "We don't need to pry."

Thank you, Dad.

"Hang on a second—is this the first time you've all met?" Fred asked, putting his water glass on the table and looking around with raised eyebrows. "I didn't realize I was crashing your 'meet the parents' lunch."

"Yes. Roz has been keeping Olivia from us for some reason," Mom said, fixing me with a pointed stare.

"Really? Well, don't let my presence hold you back, Roz. I'm quite intrigued to hear your love story." Fred leaned forward. "So how *did* you meet?"

Shit. We really should have prepped some answers beforehand. I gulped down a mouthful of water.

Olivia looked at me expectantly. From across the table, Matt raised an eyebrow. The silence, punctuated only by cutlery scraping across plates, stretched on far too long.

I had to say something—fast. Best to stick to the truth as close as possible.

"We sat near each other at the bar and started talking," I said, my tone crisper than I'd intended.

A frown flickered across Fred's face. Damn. This was clearly not the love story Fred had in mind.

A soft, warm hand grasped my arm. "It was a lot more romantic than that, babe," Olivia said, winking at Fred and then looking around the table. "I was being an absolute klutz and hit my head on the bar counter—before I'd even had a drink—and Roz struck up conversation with me on the pretense of making sure I was lucid. I then managed to spill my drink all over her, so we had to go to the restroom... And one thing led to another." Olivia's cheeks flushed pink. "And it's great having you here for the 'meet the parents' lunch, Fred. It takes the pressure off me."

"I'm happy to help." Fred grinned. "How long have you been dating for?"

My chest clenched. All this questioning was probably quite innocuous, but it felt like the Spanish Inquisition. Up until now, I hadn't directly lied to anyone—the situation we'd found ourselves in had been the result of misunderstandings we'd failed to correct. While my behavior was already morally questionable, I couldn't bring myself to lie outright to Fred. But I needed to say something. I couldn't leave him hanging.

"We met six months ago, but obviously Roz was living in New York then, so it's only recently we've been able to spend much time together," Olivia said, running her hand up and down my arm and smiling adoringly at me. Her hand left a trail of goosebumps on my skin, and it took all my effort not to scowl. Damn my body and its involuntary reactions. I stabbed a crispy piece of potato with my fork.

Fred leaned over and spooned some salad on to his plate. "Oh, that must be a relief to finally be in the same area. Long-distance relationships can be a challenge."

I popped the potato in my mouth and chewed. Fred was taking this well. Olivia seemed to be much better at fake dating than me. And she'd managed to give answers that were effectively true but also didn't blow our cover.

"Aunty Roz, are you good enough at driving the tractor yet to take me on a hayride?" Lottie piped up.

I swallowed too quickly, sending the potato traveling painfully down my throat. A change in topic was needed, but could it not be about my tractor-driving skills?

Mom handed Lottie the salad bowl. "I think she'll need a few more weeks of practice before it's safe to take you out, sweetheart." Mom turned to me. "Did you hear back from the insurance company about your car?"

I gave Mom a death stare, willing her to stop talking. "Let's not talk about insurance."

Fred raised his eyebrows. "Oh, what happened to your car?"

"It was nothing." I scrambled to think of another conversation topic. "So, is anyone watching any good TV shows at the moment?"

"She didn't tell you?" Mom looked at Fred then gave an awkward grimace. "Roz tried to connect the tractor to the hay wagon so she could take Lottie on a hayride. Thankfully, Roz survived unscathed. Her car was less fortunate. We all witnessed it. It wasn't pretty."

Fred's gaze shot to me. "Oh, yikes. That's rough."

The tic started up again under my eye. *What the hell is Mom thinking?*

Mom snapped her mouth shut, as if she'd realized that perhaps telling my potential investor that I'd negligently driven a tractor into my car was a bad idea. Which it most definitely was.

"Oh, it was just a little incident," she backtracked. "I'm sure her car will be repaired without any hassle."

Fred glanced at Olivia, who was staring at me wide-eyed.

Olivia blinked, her gaze shifting to Fred. "Um, yes. It wasn't a big deal." She wasn't very convincing, but at least she'd made an attempt to sound like she knew what Mom was talking about.

"It was like this!" Lottie jumped up on her seat, clenched her fists together, and smashed one down on the other. "Crunch, crunch, crunch!"

Matt tapped her back. "That's enough, Lottie."

Dad cleared his throat. "So, what do you think of the farm, Fred?"

Fred patted his mouth with his napkin. "I loved it. I was particularly impressed by the focus on sustainability. The geothermal greenhouse was fantastic."

Olivia put down her fork. "I'm so glad you liked that. I've got lots of other ideas for how we could make the farm even more environmentally friendly."

Not this again. I held back a sigh. This lunch couldn't end soon enough.

Fred turned to Olivia and tilted his head. "Oh, what were you thinking?"

Olivia leaned in, her eyes bright. "Solar panels on all the barns, a smart irrigation system to help with water conservation, and upgrading the tractors to more fuel-efficient models. Did you know you can get electric tractors too these days?"

I gripped my knife tightly. Yet again, Olivia was trying to hijack things with Fred to further her own agenda. Everything she had just rattled off would cost significant money. Money I didn't have. The last thing I needed was for Fred to decide to throw his money into sustainable farming instead of a new event space and tap house. While Olivia's suggestions would probably save some money in the long term, there was no way they'd bring in anywhere as much profit as my proposal would. I needed to shut this down—now.

Fred nodded. "That sounds terrific. Roz, you didn't mention any of this in your business plan."

"Yes, well the priority is getting the taphouse and event space built, and then we can explore some of the ideas Olivia mentioned."

Olivia straightened. "We can incorporate sustainability into the taphouse and event space too, making sure they're designed in an energy-efficient manner and installing solar panels and a rainwater harvesting system. We could even use reclaimed materials to build them." Her eyes flashed with excitement.

"Roz, could you update your business plan to include these ideas too?" Fred asked. "I'd love to hear more about them. Being able to market Red Tractor Farm as an eco-friendly sustainable business could be one way to differentiate it from the competition."

"Yes, of course." I plastered a smile on my face as I dug my nails into my hands. As soon as Fred left, I'd be having a word with Olivia.

CHAPTER TWELVE

OLIVIA

FRESH AIR HIT me as Roz and I walked out onto her parents' back deck, which overlooked a tennis court, swimming pool, and a large expanse of neatly cut grass, surrounded by rose bushes. The sprawling property and the gorgeous white two-story colonial revival mansion we'd just exited were a far cry from the cozy cottage I'd grown up in. Roz's family was clearly loaded.

Roz leaned against the railing of the deck. My eyes lingered on her firm-looking ass, which was encased by perfectly tailored black pants. While her back was to me, my gaze traveled up to take in the back of her purple silk shirt and her neatly cut short blond hair. Black oxfords completed the look. Her outfit was ridiculously formal for a Saturday lunch with family, but it did look good on her.

"I thought that went fairly well," I said as I rested my arms on the railing. Fred had left ten minutes ago.

Roz shoved off the railing and glared at me. "Are you serious? It was a disaster."

I opened my mouth to object, but Roz kept speaking.

"Did you miss my mother telling Fred I'd crashed a

tractor? Not exactly information that's going to instill Fred with confidence in my ability to run a farm. And then you hijacked the discussion with all your sustainability talk, which Fred now wants me to include in the business plan before Friday. Not to mention how I nearly blew our cover when I stumbled over Mom's and Fred's questioning."

I pressed my lips together. I supposed it wasn't great, but it could have been much worse. "But at least Fred liked my ideas, right?"

Roz huffed. "*Wrong*. You have to stop pushing your own agenda. You're making me look bad in front of Fred. It could make the whole deal fall through. Not only that, but I don't have time to become an expert in sustainable farming and buildings between now and Friday. So the two of us have a lot of work to do over the next few days."

I stared. "The two of us?"

"I'll send you the sections of the business plan I need you to update with your sustainability stuff."

I bristled at Roz's tone. "I signed up to fake date you, not work for you."

"You were the one who suggested it. You're clearly passionate about it and presumably know what you're talking about. So you should be the one to do it."

"And what if I'm too busy?" I could probably fit it in, but I didn't want Roz thinking I would just fall at her feet when she was so rude about it.

"If Fred doesn't agree to move forward, the flower fields are gone, remember? So you have a vested interest in making my business plan as good as possible."

A swallow dived and somersaulted over the lawn. Roz had a point.

I rubbed a hand along the smooth wooden railing.

"Okay, fine. Can we walk down to the roses? I told your dad I'd take a look at them."

"Sure." Roz turned and started striding toward the stairs. "And we have some other homework as well," she said over her shoulder.

I raised an eyebrow, hurrying after her. God, she was demanding. "What?"

"Our fake-dating arrangement." Roz took the steps two at a time. "We weren't very convincing today. We need to get our backstory straight, make sure we know the basic information two people dating would know about each other, or Fred might become suspicious."

We reached the perfectly manicured lawn, pausing for a moment.

"Okay." I folded my arms. "So what should I know about you?"

"Not right now." She gave a small shake of her head. "We should both write a list of key information—a family tree, where we went to school, that type of thing, and then exchange it. I'll prepare a questionnaire tonight and send it to you. I'll need both the questionnaire and the updated business plan done by close of business Wednesday so I'm prepared for when I see Fred on Friday."

We began walking toward the roses, my feet springing on the grass. Roz was right. If we were going to convince people we were dating, we should get to know each other. But I wasn't going to answer a questionnaire for her. I'd be spending enough time on my laptop as it was, working on her business plan.

"No thanks. If we're going to do this properly, we should do it in person. You don't learn about someone from reading a survey. And how are we going to get our beautiful love story straight that way? Why don't we have lunch tomorrow and talk about it?" I'd intended to hike up Break-back Ridge tomorrow, but saving Sapphire Blooms had to take priority.

Roz shook her head, slowing as we reached the roses. "I can't. I've got to do some more research for Fred on the local competition."

"Competition?" A flash of yellow caught my eye under a rose bush. Was that an American goldfinch? I bent down. No, it was just a tennis ball.

"Other taphouses and event spaces that Red Tractor Farm would be in competition with. He wants to get more information about them to make sure the business plan for investing in the farm is strong."

I frowned, leaning over and inspecting the rose bush. Roz's dad was right. Tiny green larvae dotted the underside of the rose leaves. Rose slugs. It was unusual for them to appear this early. I glanced up at Roz. "That's a strange way of thinking about it. Aren't they more your... colleagues than competition?"

"No." Roz shot me a withering look.

I raised my eyebrows but decided it wasn't worthwhile pressing the point. "Okay, so what does your research involve?" I straightened, and walked to the next rose bush, Roz strolling next to me.

Roz ran her hand through her hair. "I'm going to scope them out. The information I gave Fred already was based on desk research, but I'll need to do some field research to provide him with the level of detail he wants—covertly, of course."

An image of Roz wearing a fake mustache and cap, going undercover to get information about the other event venues in the area flashed into my head and I snorted.

"What?" Roz eyed me.

"Nothing. Sorry." I inspected a few rose leaves. No sign of larvae here. "Anyway, I can help you with your 'mission'. I know the event spaces around here pretty well from doing flower arrangements for weddings in them, and taprooms as well. Why don't I come along too, and we can get to know each other better?"

Hopefully it wouldn't be too painful. Sapphire Blooms was closed tomorrow, and we were supposed to have lovely weather. I'd also been having a craving for quark which they only sold at Lawson Grove Dairy's store. Fingers crossed that was on Roz's list. "Do you have a list of places you want to visit?"

Roz swatted away a fly with her hand. "In the plan I gave Fred, I included a high-level overview of all the venues in the region. But tomorrow I need to focus on the event spaces that would be most likely to compete with my proposal for Red Tractor Farm—so any function spaces that can accommodate around two hundred people."

I nodded, furrowing my brow. "Okay, let me think about it. My sister-in-law is an event planner, so I'll ask her for some advice and come up with an itinerary for tomorrow." Ideally one that involved visiting Lawson Grove Dairy.

Roz gave me a small nod. "Thank you. I'll pick you up tomorrow at eight a.m." We started to retrace our footsteps.

My eyebrows shot up. "Eight on a Sunday? No thanks. Let's say ten. That's a lot more respectable."

Roz pursed her lips. "Fine. Ten."

We walked across the lawn and back up the stairs, the trills of a warbler the only distraction from the awkward silence.

Roz paused at the top of the deck, rubbing the back of her neck. "So how did your friends and family take the news of our fake dating?"

"I haven't told them yet. I was planning to tell my friends today. We're meeting at Builders Arms for a drink this afternoon." I glanced down at my watch. "Shit, it's later than I thought. I'd better be heading off."

"Just to let you know, I'm planning to tell Matt as well," Roz said as we headed toward the back door. "I think he already suspects something is up."

I grimaced. "We weren't great, were we?"

"No."

Inside, we found Roz's parents cleaning up the kitchen.

"Thank you so much for having me," I said.

"It's our pleasure." Roz's mom dried her hands on a towel then reached out for a hug. "We're just so happy Roz has finally found someone as lovely and as youthful as you."

Roz's jaw tensed, but she said nothing. She walked me down the hallway.

At the front door, she faced me. "Can you text me your address?"

I bent down to pick up my handbag I'd left next to the door. "You have it already—I live above Sapphire Blooms."

"Ah, right. Well, I'll need your email address too, so I can send you the business plan sections for you to complete."

The last thing I felt like right now was working on a damn business plan. "I'll text it to you."

"Do it now so you don't forget." Roz held the front door open. "See you tomorrow."

I stepped outside and huffed. Thank god Roz had agreed to the ten a.m. start. There was no way I could deal with her any earlier than that. I needed at least an hour of lying in bed and two coffees to prepare me for more one-on-one time with her.

CHAPTER THIRTEEN

OLIVIA

"LIV!" George waved at me from a wooden table lit by dappled sunshine under a towering oak tree at the back of the Builders Arms' beer garden. Clutching a glass of rosé, I weaved through groups of day drinkers until I reached my friends.

"Sorry I'm late." I flopped down onto the seat next to Hannah.

Blake turned to me. "I was just saying that if we're going to beat The Gran Masters on Thursday night, we'll have to work on our economics and sports knowledge. We could each choose a sport to read up on—or economics if you'd prefer."

I stared at my sister. "I don't really have time at the moment, sorry." I already had enough homework from Roz. Blake's face dropped and I bit my lip. "Perhaps we could find someone who already knows about that stuff?"

Blake creased her forehead. "I can't think of anyone."

Hannah put her cider on the table. "I'm in procrastination mode at the moment with my book, so I can take a sport. Maybe hockey?"

"I can take baseball," George added, smiling at Hannah and squeezing her hand. God, they were cute.

Blake grinned. "That sounds great. I can pick up football and I'll text Dana and see if she's interested in researching golf or economics." Blake turned to me. "Is everything okay?"

"Yes. It's just the new owner of Red Tractor Farm is creating quite a bit of work for me." I closed my eyes for a moment and took a sip of wine.

George peered around Hannah, her face soft with sympathy. "From what I've heard at Novel Gossip, she's been rubbing everyone the wrong way. Dana is ready to quit, the kitchen staff at the farm café are furious that she wants to reduce the menu for cost-cutting purposes, and she apparently made one of the teens who works at the petting zoo cry."

"Oh my god, what happened?" I twisted to stare at George.

"He accidentally let the baby goats out of the yard—"

I clutched the stem of my wine glass. "Roz wasn't driving a tractor, was she?" After hearing about Roz's run in with her car, I had serious concerns about anyone or anything getting close to her in a tractor.

"What? No." George's brow furrowed. "They didn't get very far, but apparently she snapped at the kid who did it—something about him not being the GOAT of petting zoo employees and telling him if it happened again, he'd be fired."

I snorted, my shoulders relaxing. That sounded like Roz. She didn't strike me as the person who would suffer fools lightly. I imagined her pairing her cutting words with a withering glare. Poor kid.

The smell of fries wafted over from a neighboring table and my stomach rumbled.

"So how did it go confronting her yesterday?" George asked. "The way you stormed off, I expected we'd hear she'd been murdered or, at the very least, get some updates in our group chat, but this Roslyn woman is alive enough to make more enemies and you've been radio silent."

"Yes. Well, there have been some developments." I took a gulp of wine.

"Did you convince her not to destroy the flower farm?" Jenny asked.

"Well, sort of. We came to an understanding." I swirled my wine glass, creating a whirlpool which reflected the current state of my stomach. I was not looking forward to this conversation.

"What kind of understanding?" Blake glanced over to the other corner of the beer garden, where a group of men in their twenties were laughing raucously, before refocusing her gaze on me.

I shifted uncomfortably on the bench. "I'm helping her with some things, and in exchange she's going to keep the flower farm going."

"Olivia, you're being very vague right now. What's going on?" Blake's frown deepened.

"Yeah, you're sounding really shady," Jenny chimed in. "Have the two of you conspired to grow weed on her farm or something? Is this a *Breaking Bad* or *Weeds* type of situation? Please don't get arrested, Liv."

"No!" I exclaimed, nudging Jenny on her shoulder.

"What, then?" Blake leaned in.

"Well..." I swallowed. "I may have agreed to be her fake girlfriend in return for saving the flowers." I winced.

My friends stared at me, wide-eyed.

"What the hell, Olivia? What do you mean?" Blake ran her hand through her short hair. "Like an escort?"

I recoiled. "God, no! We're pretending to date to help get an investor for the farm. There's nothing physical involved." Except for when my lips brushed Roz's warm cheek earlier today. I pushed the memory away, trying not to blush.

"Hang on a second." George tilted her head, the dappled sun lighting her brown crew cut. "How did you go from wanting to strangle her yesterday to fake dating her?"

Hannah crossed her arms and leaned in. "Okay, you have to tell us all from the start."

Four pairs of eyes gazed at me expectantly.

I took a deep breath. "When I went to confront her, her mom was there. She assumed we were dating for some reason and then a potential investor showed up. I realized that if I went along with the dating story, I might be able to influence him to keep the flower farm. So I kind of pretended she was my girlfriend."

"Oh my god, Olivia!" Jenny screamed, attracting stares from the nearby patrons.

I groaned and covered my face with my hands. "I know, I know. I just really didn't want the flowers to be destroyed and Sapphire Blooms to go under."

"So then she just went along with it?" Hannah asked, looking at me with fascination. Was my ridiculous plight going to end up in her next book?

A tiny leaf in my wine glass caught my eye. I dipped my finger in and fished it out, flicking it onto the ground. "Yes. And now it's a little tricky to extricate myself without jeopardizing the investment, so I'll have to keep it up until the money comes through. It should only be a couple of weeks."

I didn't want to consider what would happen if Fred decided not to invest.

"Only? I hope you can last that long with Cruella de Farm." George grimaced.

"Yeah, she's not making it easy." Like ordering me to complete her business plan as if I was one of her employees. I kicked the brick paving under the bench.

"And you're okay pretending to be queer?" Blake asked.

My heart rate increased. *Shit*. I should have expected that fake dating a woman would raise questions about my sexuality.

George gave Blake a nudge.

"Sweet potato fries?" Dan asked from behind me.

Blake's gaze shifted to him, and I exhaled. *Thank god*.

"Yes, thanks," George said. "We're sharing them. Anywhere is good."

Once Dan left, I picked up a fry. "So about the whole fake-dating thing, can you guys please not tell anyone? We don't want it getting back to the investor that it's all a ruse. I'll tell Mom and Dad but will swear them to secrecy too."

"Yes, of course," Jenny said.

Hannah and George murmured in agreement. Blake was noticeably silent, staring at me instead. I ignored her and grabbed another fry. "Thanks. Oh, and Jenny, I need your help." I popped the fry, still piping hot, into my mouth, savoring the rich flavor.

"Help?" Jenny put down her drink. "With what?"

"Roz wants to build a function space and taphouse at Red Tractor Farm and the investor asked for more information about her 'competition.'" I rolled my eyes. "I said I'd come up with a list of venues of a similar size nearby she could visit."

Jenny's face brightened. "Oh, awesome! What capacity is she thinking?"

"Two hundred people." My hand bumped against George's as we both reached into the bowl of fries at the same time. "Sorry George."

"If she can make it even bigger, say two hundred fifty or three hundred, that would be best. We're really lacking spaces that can accommodate that many people around here, and there's definitely demand for it." Jenny's eyes sparkled.

"That's good to know," I replied, filing the information away to report back to Roz later.

Jenny tilted her head. "In terms of similar event spaces, I'd look at Lawson Grove Dairy and Rosedale Estate. And for the taphouse, Terry's Apple Orchards."

"Okay, great. Those are the ones I was thinking of too. Do you have any idea how many customers you're turning away because the event spaces are too small?" I suspected Roz would like firm numbers for her business plan.

My sister-in-law chewed on her lip for a moment. "Off the top of my head, no. But I can take a look tomorrow if that would be helpful? We do keep records of all the inquiries we get."

"That would be amazing." I leaned back, taking a sip of rosé. How would tomorrow go? I didn't fancy being driven around by Roz in that gas-guzzling old truck she'd used for the farm tour the other day, especially after learning about her questionable driving skills. A thought struck me. Gorgeous weather was forecast tomorrow, and the venues Jenny had suggested were all relatively close together.

I pulled out my phone and shot off a text to Roz.

Do you have a bike?

My phone buzzed before I'd pushed it all the way back into my pocket.

No. Why?

I turned to Blake. "Hey, could Roz borrow your bike tomorrow?"

She eyed me for a moment and then nodded. "Sure."

"Awesome. Thanks."

Let's meet at my sister's house instead. You can borrow her bike. 23 Apple Blossom Way. Everything is within cycling distance.

I'd prefer to drive.

I frowned. If things went badly, it would be best if I could just cycle away rather than being reliant on Roz for a lift home.

Cycling between the venues is very popular with tourists and locals. For research purposes, it's important you experience it.

Three dots pulsed on my phone screen. When the text finally came through, it was short.

Fine.

I grinned at Blake. "It's all sorted. We're meeting outside your house tomorrow at ten a.m."

"Hmm. I'm not sure how I feel about being an accessory to this," Blake said, rubbing her arm.

"What do you mean?" I asked.

Dan delivered a plate of nachos to the table next to me.

Damn, they smelled good. If we were going to stay much longer, I'd order some to share.

"Going on a bar crawl with the fake girlfriend you dislike doesn't sound like a terrible idea at all. What could possibly go wrong?" Blake arched an eyebrow.

"It's not a bar crawl. It's all for research. Don't worry, we're not going to drink irresponsibly and total your bike." At least, I didn't think so. Probably best not to mention Roz's recent run-in with the tractor in case Blake retracted her offer.

CHAPTER FOURTEEN

ROZ

I PULLED up in front of a white weatherboard cottage. Olivia leaned against the blue picket fence, looking effortlessly cool in a knee-length red floral dress and white sneakers, her wavy hair tied in a low ponytail. She raised a hand in greeting.

My stomach dropped. In retrospect, my standard gym gear—black tights and a racer back top—perhaps wasn't the best outfit for going undercover to explore the local venues on a gorgeous spring day. I had a sinking suspicion that the other patrons would be dressed more like Olivia and less like gym junkies.

I sighed and turned off the ignition. Olivia's eyes trailed up and down my body as I stepped out of the car holding my backpack, no doubt judging my clothing choices.

"Not a word," I said, lifting a finger. "You were the one who insisted on cycling."

"I didn't say anything," Olivia replied, her lips twitching.

Two bikes leaned against the fence next to her. One was black and sleek, and the other was burnt orange with a wicker basket decorated with fake flowers. No prizes for guessing which one was Olivia's.

I eyed the bikes with trepidation. "I hope the saying that you never forget how to ride a bike is true," I muttered under my breath. I hadn't ridden a real bike since I was a kid. But surely the hundreds of hours I'd spent in spin class had to count for something?

"Here's your bike," Olivia said, pulling the black bike off the fence and handing it to me. A helmet hung from one of the handles.

"Thanks." My hand brushed her fingers as I grabbed the bike, leaving a trail of warmth on my skin.

I shoved on the helmet, pulled my backpack over my shoulders and studied the bike. How was it possible that my entire five-foot-eight body was meant to balance on those two wheels? My stomach clenched. I should have insisted on driving. What was I thinking?

"Is everything okay?" Olivia clipped her pink helmet under her chin. "You do know how to ride a bike, don't you?"

"Of course I do." I threw my leg over the bike. *Ouch.* A pain shot from my groin down my thigh. I winced.

Olivia gracefully jumped onto her bike and started to pedal down the road. She made it look so easy, so effortless.

I placed my feet on the pedals and pushed. The bike wobbled. My stomach swooped as it fell sideways. I yelped, shooting my leg out to steady myself.

Olivia stopped and twisted around. "Are you okay?"

"I'm just a little out of practice," I snapped. *God, I hate being bad at things.*

Olivia raised her eyebrows but shrugged and set off again. I put my feet back on the pedals. I tried not to think about the fact that my entire body was defying gravity by balancing on two thin wheels. *Pretend I'm back at my spin class.* I hummed a techno track under my breath, pumping my legs in time, and was suddenly speeding ahead of Olivia.

"Hey," Olivia yelled, "this isn't the Tour de France! We're just out for a leisurely Sunday bike ride. I don't want to get all sweaty."

Olivia had a point. Not only that, but I had no idea where we were going. I slowed my pace, letting Olivia take the lead. I exhaled. I seemed to have found my balance and no longer had to go at spin-class speed to stay upright.

After a few minutes of cycling through the side streets of Sapphire Springs, Olivia disappeared off the road.

Grumbling under my breath, I twisted the bike handles to follow her. My heart lurched as the bike skidded onto a dirt path. I gripped the handles tightly, just managing to regain control.

After a few minutes adjusting to the bumpy surface, I peeled my eyes off the ground in front of me and looked around. Green pines and cedars lined the path. Chirping birds flitted between the trees. There was only a smattering of fluffy white clouds in the deep-blue sky. I inhaled a big lungful of fresh air and blew it out again. This was a lot more pleasant than a darkened spin studio.

Olivia slowed her pace so we were pedaling side-by-side. I shot a glance at her. Wisps of hair escaped out of her helmet, dark against her pink cheeks. My heart picked up pace. *It's just the cycling. Nothing to do with Olivia.*

"You know, you should really talk to somebody about having the path extended to Red Tractor Farm," Olivia said. "It'd only be another mile or two, and I think it would attract even more business, especially if you add a taproom. The path is very popular with the tourists in summer."

I frowned. It wasn't a bad idea. "Perhaps."

We continued cycling in silence until a driveway leading up to a white building came into view.

Olivia leaped off her bike and leaned it against a tree.

I pedaled backward to brake. My stomach flipped. The bike kept hurtling forward, toward a large white sign with a cow on it.

Oh god. Panic flooded my nervous system, sending my blood pumping.

The brakes weren't working. The sign loomed closer.

"You need to use the handbrake!" Olivia yelled.

I squeezed the levers on the handlebars just as the bike collided into the sign. My body jerked forward. For a second, I looked straight into the cow's beady eyes, and then I was falling through the air. I closed my eyes and braced myself for impact. But the painfully hard landing I'd expected was not forthcoming. Had I landed on a strategically placed futon or something? An unpleasantly sweet scent tickled my noise. My eyelids fluttered open. Purple flowers framed Olivia's concerned face, which was peering down at me.

"Are you okay? Thank goodness you landed on the violets and not a rock. Hopefully they cushioned your fall."

"I'm fine," I said abruptly, still reeling from the shock. "The foot brakes weren't working." I glared at the bike that was laying next to me.

Olivia frowned. "Adult bikes don't usually have foot brakes."

Heat rushed up my neck. *How embarrassing.* I grabbed her outstretched hand and stood up, brushing dirt off my black leggings.

"A dairy?" I asked, inspecting the large white sign for damage. Thankfully, it seemed to have survived the impact unscathed, as had the bike. The violets I'd landed on were, however, looking worse for wear. Not that I was bothered by the demise of the flowers. Their scent lingered on me. I narrowed my eyes at them.

"Don't worry, the violets should bounce back," Olivia said.

"I'm not worried." I wrinkled my nose, which seemed to have been irritated by something—most likely those damn violets.

"And yes, it's a dairy," Olivia continued. "I've had a craving for their quark."

I picked up my bike, balancing it against Olivia's. What the hell was quark? The purpose of this trip was to research my competitors, not eat bizarre-sounding dairy products.

Olivia swung her handbag over her shoulder. "But I didn't just bring you here to buy incredible cheese. As I'm sure you know, they also have a large wedding venue in the old creamery building."

"Yes, I remember," I said, even though my recollection was hazy.

I rubbed my nose, which was still decidedly itchy, and then followed Olivia as she bounced up a brick path toward a white-washed stone cottage. Her dress highlighted her curves, the fabric belt clinging to her waist before the skirt flared out at her hips, ending at her knees. My eyes dropped to her slender calves.

"I signed us up for a tour of the dairy so you can get a good feel for the place." Olivia turned to me.

Heat rushed up my face as I yanked my gaze from her legs. "Oh. Thank you." That was... nice of Olivia. *Don't take it personally. She's just looking out for Sapphire Blooms.*

We entered the cottage which had been converted into a small store and café. Olivia walked to the counter.

"Hi, Will."

A middle-aged man with short red hair and a large bushy red beard grinned at her. "Hi, Olivia! You here for more quark?"

"Well, yes. But we're also here for a farm tour. This is my... This is Roz."

Will, looking down at a piece of paper, didn't seem to notice Olivia's stumble. We hadn't discussed whether we'd pretend to be a couple while on our field trip. I frowned. Yet another thing I hadn't thought through fully. *You need to step up your game, Roz.*

"Oh, great. Yep, we've got you down. No one else has signed up today, so it's just the two of you." Will clapped his hands. "Should we get started?"

"Sounds fantastic." Olivia twisted on her feet to follow Will.

Will led us past tractors, the milking parlor and large concrete tower silos for storing feed as he explained the workings of a dairy farm. It was surprisingly interesting. That was probably a good thing. I was a farmer now, after all. When we reached the cows grazing in the pastures, I kept a safe distance from their powerful hooves.

On the way back, Will led us to a barn. "And now we've come to the most popular part of the tour."

An enormous black-and-white cow munched on hay in the middle of the barn. I looked around, my eyebrows pinched. The cow appeared to be roaming freely. Will strode up to her and stroked her back.

"This is Clara. She's a gorgeous girl. Roz, would you like to have the first go?"

"First go?" I asked, eyeing Clara's gigantic barrel-like torso and muscular legs.

Will gestured to a small wooden stool next to Clara's

swollen pink udders. I took a step back. *Oh god. He wants me to milk this bovine monstrosity?*

"Oh, no, I don't think that will be necessary," I said, clutching the straps of my backpack. "Unless Olivia wants to try it, I'm happy to skip this part of the tour."

Olivia turned to me. "Now that you're a farm owner, you really need to learn how to milk a cow. That's, like, farm ownership 101."

Will's eyebrows shot up and his face broke into a grin. "Oh, are you the Roslyn who bought Red Tractor Farm? It's great to meet you. I've been meaning to pop over and say hi."

I gritted my teeth for a moment before giving Will a polite smile. *So much for covert field research.*

"It's a pleasure to meet you too," I said, trying to focus on Will's face and not on Clara's giant nostrils.

"So, would you like to sit down?" Will asked.

My gaze shifted to Olivia. "Why don't you go first?"

"No, no," Olivia said, waving her hand. "I've done it before."

Goddamnit. Now Will knew who I was, for the sake of my pride I had to go through with it. I wanted him to take me seriously.

"Sure!" I said with forced enthusiasm, avoiding eye contact with Clara's sharp, unblinking dark-brown eyes that were fixed on me.

I took a step toward the tiny wooden stool. Clara stepped back.

"I don't think she likes me." I rubbed my nose.

"Clara likes everyone. The only thing that bothers her is loud noises, but that shouldn't be an issue." Will caressed Clara's back.

"Hmm, okay." I slowly moved closer to Clara. She

glared at me and let out a loud moo. I stopped still and looked at Will.

He frowned. "Huh. That's unusual. She can probably sense that you're nervous. You just need to relax."

Just relax. So helpful. My pulse increased.

I continued forward and then cautiously lowered myself onto the tiny wood stool. I eyed Clara's large black hooves, which were far too close for my liking.

Will handed me a warm, wet cloth. "Okay, so first you wipe down her teats."

I took the cloth and stared at the large, fleshy pink teats hanging off Clara's veiny, balloon-like udder.

Holding my breath, I carefully wiped them down. To my amazement, Clara didn't react.

"Good work. Now, put these gloves on"—Will handed me some disposable gloves—"hold the closest teat like this"—he held up his hand, demonstrating the correct grip—"and then squeeze and pull down at the same time, aiming for the bucket."

I pulled on the gloves.

"Sorry, Clara," I muttered as I grabbed a teat and followed Will's instructions. As much as I wasn't a fan of cows, I knew I personally wouldn't appreciate someone tugging my breasts in this undignified manner. Heat prickled my neck as I sensed Olivia watching me massaging Clara's nipple.

Milk shot out of the teat and into the bucket. It was surprisingly satisfying.

"Good work," Will said. "Keep going."

I fell into a rhythm, and before long, the stainless steel bucket was almost full.

"That should be enough now," Will said.

As I relaxed my grip on Clara's teat, my nose became

unbearably itchy. I wiggled it to no avail. Suddenly, the urge to sneeze overpowered me.

I tensed, trying to hold it in.

"Aaaaaachooo." My entire body jolted.

Clara bucked. Her hind legs kicked the pail of milk, sending its contents toward me. I shut my eyes just as the warm, sweet-smelling liquid made impact with my face and chest.

I sat in shock, my eyes firmly closed, as the milk dripped down my face and soaked into my clothes.

My jaw tightened. I knew this was a terrible idea.

"Shit!" Will exclaimed. "Olivia, can you grab that cloth over there?"

A furious stomping noise made me flinch.

Will's voice dropped to a more soothing tone. "Hey, Clara. It's okay, girl."

A cloth was shoved into my hands. Once I'd wiped my face as best I could, I opened my eyes, stood up and looked down. I was drenched. The rich, creamy, slightly sweet scent permeated the air around me.

At least Clara was now secured by a rope in the corner of the barn.

Will turned his attention to me. "I'll run and get you another towel."

"Well, that sneeze was quite something," Olivia said, one eyebrow raised. "I'm pretty sure it startled cows from New Jersey to Albany."

I glared at Olivia through milky eyelashes before wiping my face again. "I have a powerful sneeze." I winced at the defensive tone in my voice.

Olivia's lips twitched and suddenly a laugh threatened to erupt from my mouth. I pressed my lips firmly together and glared at her. God, she was infuriating.

"Here you are," Will said as he jogged back into the barn with two towels.

As I patted myself down, Olivia turned to Will. "Is it okay if we look inside the event space before we leave? Roz is thinking of building one herself and wanted to see what else is around."

I shot daggers at Olivia. What the hell was she thinking?

"Of course," Will said, smiling, apparently unperturbed by the prospect of more competition. "Are you okay now, Roz?"

"Yes. Thank you," I said, glancing down at the wet towels in my hand.

"Just leave the towels on the table. I'll get them later."

We followed Will out of the barn toward a much larger barn that was painted blue with white trimmings. My feet squelched in my shoes as I walked.

"This is an 1840 Dutch dairy barn that we repurposed as a wedding venue. It fits around two hundred people," Will said.

"It's gorgeous," I said as he swung open the large barn door, revealing rustic wooden beams and a soaring ceiling. "If you don't mind me asking, do you get many bookings?"

Will grinned. "Yep, we're booked out pretty much all year, except winter."

We wandered around the barn, the smell of sweet milk following me.

"If you don't have any more questions, we can head back to the store now and do a milk and cheese tasting," Will said.

I held back a shudder—the last thing I felt like was dairy when my clothes still clung to my skin with it—and plastered a smile on my face. After Will had been so friendly, I didn't want to come across as ungrateful. "That sounds great."

Five minutes later we were back at the store, sitting at one of the small wooden tables next to a window over-looking the front lawn. Our bikes were still where we'd left them, leaning against the tree near the path.

"First, we'll do a milk tasting." Will appeared holding two wooden paddles with three shot glasses of milk balanced on each one. "We have cow, goat and sheep's milk. Now, if you're at all competitive"—he eyed me—"and I'm sensing you are, can you guess which is which?"

I stared at the shot glasses, my stomach turning.

"Sounds fun!" Olivia snatched up the first shot glass. "Are you ready, Roz?"

"Sure." I swallowed.

I reached out for the glass and raised it to my mouth. A strong, tangy scent hit me. I winced but forced myself to take a tentative sip.

"It's all very fresh. Just out of the udder this morning," Will said.

I spluttered, nearly spitting out the milk, before forcing myself to gulp it down. I threw back the rest of the shot glass. If I did it fast enough, perhaps it would circumvent my tastebuds.

"Wow! You downed that like it was a tequila shot," Olivia said, grinning.

"So, what do you think that one was?" Will asked.

"It was more strongly flavored than normal milk. Goat?" I used all my willpower not to wrinkle my nose.

"Olivia?" Will asked.

Olivia pursed her lips for a moment. "I'm going with sheep."

Will nodded, tilting his head. "Interesting."

"So, who got it right?" Olivia asked.

"We'll wait until the end for the big reveal." Will grinned. "Now, if you ladies keep going with milk tasting, I'll get the cheese ready." He disappeared into a room behind the counter.

I stared at the two remaining shot glasses of milk, trying to hype myself up. Sweat pricked my armpits as my stomach roiled. *Oh god.*

"I don't think I can do it," I muttered under my breath.

"Do what?" Olivia asked, her brows furrowed.

"Drink any more milk. I'm going to be sick."

Olivia stared at me. "Well, don't then. Just tell Will."

"I don't want to offend him."

Olivia rolled her eyes. "He'll be fine. But if you're worried..." She grabbed the two remaining shot glasses off my paddle.

"What are you do—"

Olivia threw one in her mouth, swallowed, and then did the same with the other one. She placed them back on the paddle. I breathed out. *Oh, thank god.*

"There." She grinned. "Problem solved."

Before I'd had a chance to respond, Will reappeared holding a wooden platter with cheese. I didn't dare inspect it too closely in case it increased my nausea.

"Wow, Roz, you really polished that off! What do you think?"

"Um, the second one was sheep's milk and the third one cow's?" I guessed wildly.

"Very interesting." Will turned to Olivia.

Olivia downed her remaining shot glasses. "I think the second one was cow's milk and the other one was goat's."

Will grinned. "Good work, Roz. You got them all right!"

Pride welled up in me. *That was complete luck, you idiot.*

"There's no prize, I'm afraid, just the glory," Will continued, looking at me. "Although, you're welcome to another glass of milk if you'd like."

My stomach flipped. "Oh, no thanks. But what a kind offer."

"No problem. Here's your cheese tasting." Will placed the platter in front of us. "I'll leave you two to enjoy."

"I can't believe you won," Olivia muttered as Will walked away.

I smirked. It appeared Olivia had a competitive streak as well.

My eyes dropped to the platter and my smirk vanished. Will had provided us with generous servings of eight different cheeses, including some very pungent soft ones. Bile rose in my throat.

"Are you okay?" Olivia asked. "You're looking very pale. And a little clammy."

"I'm not sure if I can eat the cheese either. The smell, from the milk, it's all over me, and it's making me feel..." I gripped my stomach.

"Okay, okay," Olivia said, letting out a dramatic sigh. "I guess I'll just have to take one for the team and eat all of this delicious cheese myself."

Within minutes, Olivia had almost demolished the platter.

"Are you sure you don't want to try this one?" She pointed to a creamy, off-white cheese in a small bowl.

I shook my head. "Definitely not. What is it?"

"It's quark." Olivia spread the cheese on a piece of bread. Despite my newfound dislike of dairy, I couldn't help watching as she placed it into her mouth, leaving a smear on her upper lip. I wanted to reach out and gently wipe it off with my thumb. I resisted.

Olivia let out a guttural moan as she swallowed the bread and my stomach clenched. I frowned. *It must be because you've gone off cheese. There's no other plausible explanation.*

Olivia fixed me with her gaze, and I froze. *Shit. Did she catch me staring at her?*

"Can I ask you something?" She dabbed her lip with a napkin.

"You can ask. Whether I'll answer is another matter," I said, feeling slightly more inclined toward Olivia after she'd helped me out by eating all the dairy.

"Why did your mom think we were dating?"

Heat swept up my cheeks. "Oh." I took a sip of water. "She'd been pressuring me to date so to stop her, I said I'd met someone at Pryde. She asked me what their name was, and I... I said yours. I never thought our paths would cross again."

Olivia nodded slowly. "I see. That makes sense."

I cleared my throat. "Thank you for, uh, drinking all my milk. And eating my cheese." Two sentences I never thought I'd say.

Olivia laughed, a warm peal that did something strange to my insides. *It's just the milk.* Then why did it feel sort of... good?

"That's okay," she said. "How are we doing on time?" She pulled out her phone, her face brightening. "Oh great! My sister-in-law, who's an event planner, said there's a real lack of larger venues in the area—between two hundred fifty or three hundred—but there's definitely demand for it.

She's just emailed me exactly how many people her company has had to turn away because of space constraints. If you decide on having a bigger space to corner that end of the market, I thought the numbers might be helpful for your business plan to Fred. I'll forward it on to you."

"Thank you. That does sound helpful. And please thank Jenny as well." I cautiously took a sip of water. I'd have to look into the costs of building a larger venue. "So, does this mean you told your friends about our, er, arrangement?"

"Yeah." Olivia tucked a stray curl behind her ear.

I raised an eyebrow. "What did they say?"

"They think we're crazy."

"I don't blame them," I replied.

"I know." Olivia grimaced. "Are you ready to head off now? If you want to stay and sample some more of Will's dairy delicacies, I completely understand." Her eyes twinkled and again my stomach whirled. It didn't feel like nausea, despite the churning dairy.

"Ha ha. No, I'm all good." I stood, ready to escape into the fresh air, and grabbed my backpack from the floor.

We thanked Will again and walked back to the bikes. Olivia placed the large container of quark she'd purchased into a cooler bag in her basket.

"So, what's next on the itinerary?" I asked as I threw my leg over my bike. "Please tell me it doesn't involve any dairy."

Olivia laughed as she started to pedal. "Nope! Next stop, Terry's Apple Orchards and then Rosedale Estate Winery."

I exhaled. Apples and wine—that I could handle.

"Are you coming or not?" Olivia called, cycling surprisingly fast for someone who had just eaten their body weight in dairy.

I sighed and began pedaling after her, trying to escape the sickly sweet scent of dairy lingering in the air.

CHAPTER FIFTEEN

OLIVIA

THE DELICATE CITRUS flavors of Rosedale Estate's prized Riesling swept over my taste buds as I gazed at the rolling hills covered in rows of vines. Prue had given us a tour of the event space and the vineyard and then secured us a prime table on the patio of her restaurant. My eyes flickered across the white tablecloth, dominated by two large pizzas and a bowl of arugula salad, to Roz. She leaned back, her arms resting on the sides of her chair, looking out over the vista. Her blond hair was slightly tousled from the bike helmet, but it suited her. It gave her a rakish look. My eyes dropped to the curves of Roz's Lycra-clad upper body. The milk appeared to have dried now, leaving off-white stains and a faintly sweet scent.

Roz shifted her gaze to me. "Well, should we get down to business?"

I blinked. "Business?"

"The whole point of this little adventure was to get to know each other. I've prepared a list of questions for us to run through." Roz pulled a leather Moleskine notebook and pen out of her backpack.

I crossed my arms. "Can't we just have a casual chat and learn about each other organically? I mean, I feel like I've already learned a lot about you this weekend."

Roz narrowed her eyes. "Such as?"

"Your sneeze would cause an avalanche. You are highly competitive, stubborn as hell and assume the worst of people." I ticked them off on my fingers as I spoke. *You have Catwoman's body but not her grace or agility.* "But you also adore your niece, are intent on making Red Tractor Farm a success, and while you're rude to them, you also care enough about your employees that you don't want to fire them."

Roz leaned over and helped herself to a slice of pizza. "While all of those things you listed off *may* be aspects of my personality, you need to learn some other basic things about me that a girlfriend would know. Which is why I have prepared this list." Roz snapped open her notebook.

"Fine," I said. "Hand it over."

Roz placed the leather notebook in front of me.

I wiped my hands on my napkin and scanned the list. *Ugh.* This reminded me of a more boring version of the dating profile I still hadn't completed. Roz was intriguing, there was no doubt about it, and I had a number of questions I wanted to ask her, but they were not on this list.

It also reminded me of something else. I chuckled. "Did you hear about that study that theorized that if two people asked each other a list of questions and then stared into each other's eyes, they'd fall in love?"

Roz shook her head. "That's ridiculous."

A warm breeze sent a few strands of hair dancing across my face. I brushed them aside. "Someone wrote a *New York Times* 'Modern Love' article about it. It sounded legit." I grinned. "Are you sure you want to keep going with the list?"

"Yes." Roz reached out her hand. "Give me back my notebook."

"I can read," I replied, waving her away. "But if you're madly in love with me at the end of this session, don't say I didn't warn you."

Roz settled into her chair. I was confident the list of questions in the study had been a lot more interesting than *Age?, Family?* and *Education?*, but I enjoyed teasing Roz too much to let that stop me. I took a bite of the capricciosa pizza, my eyes closing as my teeth sunk into the delicious combination of wood-fired sourdough pizza base, tomato, ham, mushrooms, and a generous topping of mozzarella cheese. *Damn.*

Roz's gaze darted to my lips and then away again. I swallowed. Did I have cheese hanging out of my mouth or something? I dabbed my mouth with my napkin.

"Hurry up. We don't have all day." Roz picked up her wine glass and took a long sip.

I swiped my tongue along my front teeth to ensure they weren't covered in food before I spoke. "Okay. Question one. How old are you?

"Forty-two. You?"

"Thirty-one." I raised my eyebrows. "So we have quite an age gap then. Does that bother you?"

Roz narrowed her eyes. "Am I bothered by the age gap in our *fake* relationship?"

Someone cleared their throat. I looked up to see Prue beaming at us. *Oh god. I hope she didn't overhear us.* "Hi ladies! I thought I'd bring over two complimentary wine flights as a *Welcome to Sapphire Springs* gift for Roz."

My eyes dropped to the tray she was holding and

widened. Was that all for us? Prue placed six glasses in front of each of us. "And here are the tasting notes." She handed us a piece of paper. Damn, I loved Prue. Being a Black woman in an overwhelmingly white, male industry couldn't have been easy, but she seemed to take it in stride. Not only were her wines incredible, but her restaurant made some of the best food in the area and she played a key role in the local farming community.

"Thank you. That's very generous," Roz said, gazing at the row of glasses in front of her.

"And very generous pours too," I said, picking up a glass of sparkling and sniffing it. I wasn't a wine connoisseur, but it smelled amazing—kind of yeasty, but in a good way.

"I told the bartender not to be too stingy. You look like you've really settled in over here, so I wanted to make sure you were well hydrated." Prue dropped the tray to her side.

I was confident wine was not good for hydration, but I appreciated Prue's intentions. Perhaps the wine would alleviate the dullness of Roz's questions.

As Prue left, I took a sip of the sparkling. It tasted even better than it smelled.

"Now, where were we?" I stared at the notebook. Did I need to know where Roz was born? Probably not. "Why do you hate flowers and sustainability so much?"

"That's not on the list." Roz stabbed some arugula with her fork. "Next question."

I leaned in. "No, but seriously, I'd like to know."

Roz watched Prue's Labrador walk across the lawn and slump down under a tree, and then she sighed. "I don't hate sustainability. In fact, in my last job I was going to implement a number of changes focused on building up our environmental, social, and governance practices and ensuring our company followed our own advice..." Her hand gripped her fork tightly. "Anyway, I'm not against making sustain-ability improvements at the farm, but my priority is getting the farm into the black. Which reminds me, did you receive my email last night with the business plan sections I need you to complete?" She shoved the arugula into her mouth.

"Yep," I replied, still processing Roz's admission that she'd been a sustainability champion in her past role. She hadn't explained her hatred for flowers, though. "I'll work on it tonight."

"Thank you. Next question." Roz's lips closed around the rim of her wine glass. They were soft and full, a red that reminded me of the dogwood blossoms that were just begin-ning to bloom. *Don't ogle her lips.* My eyes dropped to her long, slender fingers, elegantly cradling the glass. *Or her fingers.*

I dragged my gaze back to the list in front of me. "Fami-ly." Now that could hold some more secrets to Roz's intriguing personality. "I've obviously met yours, but tell me about them. Your mom was a lawyer?"

Roz nodded. "Mom and Dad were partners at a big law firm in Manhattan. They retired a few years ago and moved out here."

"And Matt?" I asked.

"He's in construction."

I sighed. Roz was not exactly forthcoming with informa-tion. "Are you guys close?"

"Yes." Roz picked up a slice of margherita pizza and took a bite.

Good lord. This was like pulling teeth. "If you don't mind me asking, is Lottie's mom in the picture?"

Roz nodded. "Yes. Mel is in the army. She's a helicopter pilot. She's been deployed for twelve months in the Middle East. When she's not deployed, she works at West Point."

"Oh, wow, that must be tough for Lottie and Matt," I said.

"Yes." Roz paused, her face softening slightly. "It was a factor in me deciding to move here—so I can support them both while Mel is away. Lottie also adores Red Tractor Farm, so she was thrilled when I bought it."

Well, that was kind of sweet.

"That's enough about my family." Roz lifted her wine glass. "Tell me about yours."

"Well, you're riding Blake's bike. She's the local doctor and married Jenny last year. My brother Dave lives in New Jersey. He's an accountant and has six-year-old twins who are also big fans of Red Tractor Farm." I nibbled on a pizza crust.

Roz's face broke into a broad smile. For once, it wasn't tinged with sarcasm. "I'm glad to hear it. And what about your parents?"

"We're pretty close—I usually see them at least once or twice a week." I leaned over and piled more salad on my plate. "Mom is a retired schoolteacher. Dad used to work at the local bank and now works at Blake's medical practice as her receptionist."

Roz's eyebrows shot up. "I can't imagine working with my parents. They'd drive me up the wall. How does she find that?"

I chuckled. Was Roz warming up a little? "Well, he certainly drives Blake up the wall on occasion, but on the whole, they love it. Having said that, I'm glad he didn't try to get a job at Sapphire Blooms."

"What's next?" Roz asked, peering over the table at the notebook and attempting to read upside down.

We raced through schooling, before moving onto hobbies and interests. I filled Roz in on my pastimes, from hiking and kayaking to boardgames and candle making. "What about you?"

"The gym. Weights and spin class. Although I haven't been since I moved here." Roz stretched out her arms. They still looked pretty toned to me, long and lean but with clear muscle definition.

I dragged my eyes away from her arms. "Ah, spin class. That explains why you couldn't stop your bike, but you could pedal at a hundred miles an hour. What else?"

Roz frowned at a glass full of a deep burgundy wine in front of her. "I do like a good Broadway musical."

I chewed on some salad. Was that it? I'd been hoping for something a little more revealing—like a Dungeons and Dragons obsession or a secret passion for Disneyland. An image of Roz wearing Mickey Mouse ears flashed into my mind and I sniggered.

Roz fixed me with a stare. "That's all. I haven't had time for anything else. Too busy working."

I downed the rest of the sparkling and took a sip of the second wine in the flight. I wrinkled my nose. "Hmm, I'm not so sure about this one. It kind of tastes like tires."

"Tires?" Roz took a sip. "Huh. I see what you mean. I quite like it." She took another sip.

Of course Roz would like wine that tasted like tires. I looked down at the notebook and paused. Something was missing. "What about relationship history? Any past serious relationships your girlfriend should know about? Ever been married or engaged, left at the altar, that sort of thing?"

Roz clenched her napkin. "That wasn't on the list. Next question." She stared out to the middle of the vineyard, where a worker was bent over a vine.

I frowned. Had I hit a nerve?

"You don't need to share any details with me, of course,"

I said. "But if there's anything a girlfriend would know, it might be a good idea to tell me just in case it comes up while Fred's around."

"Nothing recent," Roz replied. "What about you?"

"Nothing serious." I took a deep breath. "But you should probably know..." I swallowed, pressing my palms into my lap. "I've never dated a woman before."

Roz's jaw dropped. "You haven't?"

My face flamed with heat. "No. It's taken me a while to work things out, which is ridiculous because my sister is a lesbian and pretty much all my friends are queer." I gulped down a mouthful of the tire wine and studied a spot of pizza grease on the tablecloth.

"That's not ridiculous," Roz said.

My head jerked up, and I met Roz's gaze. Instead of the judgment I'd expected, her eyes were soft. My heart kicked.

"So if you don't mind me asking, what have you worked out?" Roz asked.

"Um. Well, I know I'm attracted to women." I'd die before I confessed to Roz that it had been our kiss at Pryde that had confirmed my attraction. My eyes dropped to her lips. *Eyes up.* "But that's about as far as I've gotten. I haven't told my friends or family yet."

Roz's eyebrows rose. "So they think you're fake-dating and fake-gaying?"

"Um, yes." I scratched the back of my neck.

Roz tilted her head, her blue eyes framed by surprisingly dark lashes. "Why haven't you told them?"

"I wanted to wait until I'd worked out what my sexuality was—whether I'm bi, pan, a lesbian... or something else."

"You know, you don't need to put a label on it if you don't want to," Roz said. I stared at her. I'd never heard her voice so gentle before. "Or you could just use a general term, like queer. Not that I'm telling you to come out or how to do it. But I thought I'd say it in case that's what's holding you back."

I blinked and exhaled, lightness spreading through my chest. "Thank you. I think all my friends have just been so confident with their sexuality from an early age that I've been putting some pressure on myself to choose a label." No thanks to that dating app, which I'd had to put on hold until our fake dating was over. "But you're right. Perhaps I don't need to." I pushed the tire wine aside and took a sip from the next glass of wine, a chardonnay, savoring the oaky flavor. "Okay, I like this one a lot better."

Roz lifted the wine glass to her lips and tilted it back, exposing her long neck. "Oh, this one is nice. I might need to buy a bottle."

Swallowing, I leaned forward. "Did you work out your sexuality early?"

Roz swished the straw-colored wine around in her glass. "Yes. I was twelve when I realized I was a lesbian. Thankfully it wasn't something I struggled with, and my parents and friends were accepting, so it never felt like a big deal."

"That's good." It would be nice if it was that easy for me.

"But it sounds like it is a big deal for you. If you need someone to talk to about it, as an elder millennial lesbian, I'm happy to be a sounding board." Her lips curled into a soft smile.

I chuckled. "Thank you. I may take you up on that offer."

My eyes dropped to Roz's list of questions. Career history. *Ugh.* I did not feel like reliving that right now. I skipped to the next question.

"Food dislikes and allergies. Any deadly allergies to nuts, crustaceans or anything else I should know about?" I asked.

"I have a mild pollen allergy. When it gets annoying, I take antihistamines."

I slammed down my wine glass. "Aha!" I exclaimed. "Is that why you hate flowers?"

"No." Roz pressed her lips together.

"Oh." My shoulders slumped. For whatever reason, Roz clearly did not want to discuss it and I didn't want to push her when it finally felt as though we'd been getting along. "And any foods you hate?"

Roz's face relaxed. "I may have very recently developed a dislike of dairy, but I hope it's temporary. It would be very tragic if I was put off triple cream brie and Ben & Jerry's butter pecan for life."

I laughed. I liked this lighter, joking version of Roz. "I still think you should try my quark. It really is very good."

Roz wrinkled her nose. "Are you sure it's going to be okay by the time we get home? It's very warm today."

I glanced over the rows of vines, lit by the strong after-noon sun. "Yeah, I'm sure it'll be fine," I said. "I've got a few cooler bars in there."

Roz took another sip of wine and leaned back in her chair. "What about you? Any dietary restrictions or foods you can't stand?"

I filled Roz in on my allergy to pineapple and then snapped the notebook shut. "Well, I think we're done."

Frowning, Roz reached over and grabbed the notebook. She scanned the page. "You didn't ask about job history. I know you worked off and on at Red Tractor Farm in your twenties. But when you were 'off,' what were you doing?"

I sighed. I didn't feel like listing all my failures off to a highly successful businesswoman. "I was pursuing various, um... ventures."

"What kind of ventures?" Roz asked, her eyes fixed on me.

Heat rose in my cheeks. "Fine." I took a fortifying gulp of the pinot noir I'd moved on to. "I'll answer, but if you've finished can we walk? I feel like I need to start moving after all that food—unless you want to drink any more of the wine?"

"I'm all good, thanks," Roz said, surveying the row of half-full glasses. "I want to make sure I get your sister's bike home in one piece." She placed her napkin on the table and pushed back her chair.

We walked over to the counter and paid, thanking Prue again for the lovely meal and wine, and then stepped out onto the grassy lawn between the restaurant and the events space.

I filled my lungs with air, exhaling slowly. "You wanted to know about my job history. Some of my greatest hits include worm farms, making biodegradable cardboard coffins, recycling cooking oil, and dog walking." I dropped my gaze to the ground and braced myself for the laughter and snide remarks.

"Biodegradable coffins?" Roz asked.

I looked over to Roz and blinked. Her head was tilted and she gazed at me with interest rather than mockery.

"They're very environmentally friendly," I explained, as we walked toward the vines. "But it turns out there isn't a huge market for them around here and the local funeral homes were reluctant to sell them." I kept my voice light, not wanting to let on to Roz just how devastating it had been when it had failed. The cooking oil recycling business had been even worse. An image of me meeting with bank representatives in the city, pleading to give me more time to repay the loan before they repossessed my assets flashed into my head. My chest constricted. Hopefully Roz and I could pull off this fake-dating charade. I couldn't bear to have another failed venture on my hands.

Roz nodded. "I'm surprised dog walking didn't take off."

We reached the vines. I stopped, admiring their gnarled trunks and woody arms twisted around the trellis wire. "It turns out most people in these parts actually like getting outside with their dogs, so demand was low." I managed a weak smile. At least dog walking required few upfront costs, so when it failed, I didn't need to deal with the debt collectors.

Roz trailed her hand along the trellis wire. "Makes sense. So after all these, um... career mishaps, you eventually decided on floristry?"

I breathed out, my smile widening. Thank god for floristry. "Yes. It's perfect for me. I get to be creative, be around gorgeous flowers all day, interact with customers and, while I'm by no means saving the world, I am bringing a bit of color to people's lives in an environmentally sustainable way. It's just a shame it took me so long to work it out." My smile faltered. I started walking again, down the row of vines. The buds studding the branches were swelling and starting to break open, new growth unfurling from them. I raised my hand to shield my eyes from the sun, which was surprisingly warm.

"Well, the fact you kept going, until you found something that worked, is... commendable," Roz said, stepping in time with me. "There's a reason why there are so many sayings about failure being the steppingstone to success. Most people give up too soon. I worked with a lot of successful businesspeople when I was a management consultant, and that's one thing they all shared. They didn't give up."

I shot Roz a glance to check if she was teasing or not. She looked genuine, her face as soft as someone with incredible cheek bones and startling blue eyes could be. My heart squeezed. I swallowed. *Maybe all that dairy has clogged my arteries and is giving me palpitations.* "Thank you. That's nice of you to say. I think most people just think I'm a bit scatterbrained, jumping from one thing to the next, unable to settle down."

We came to the end of the vines and stopped at a strip of wildflowers Prue had planted to attract bees. I bent down, gently lifting up a Virginia bluebell and inspecting it. They really were a striking color.

I stood, brushing my hands down my dress. "What about you? Did you always want to be a... was it a management consultant? And agritainment farm owner?"

Roz snorted. "Management consultant, yes. Farmer, no."

I tilted my head. "Why did you want to be a management consultant?"

"I was good at problem solving, had strong analytical skills and enjoyed learning new things. My parents wanted me to be a lawyer, but I wanted to do something different from them, prove I could make it without their help." Roz pursed her lips. "Well, I think that's the last of the questions."

"Just one more." I grinned at her. "Are you in love with me yet?" I cringed after the words left my mouth. It was a joke, but it had come out a lot more flirtatious than intended.

"No, but perhaps we haven't stared into each other's

eyes for long enough," Roz deadpanned. "Do you want to give it a go?"

Her gaze held mine and my stomach flip-flopped. Was there tension in the air between us, or was it all in my head?

An engine revved in the distance. I steadied myself and forced a casual grin onto my face. "I think I'll pass." I turned on my feet. "We should probably get moving."

When we reached the bikes, I sniffed the air. What was that smell? Could it be Roz? The smell got stronger as I approached my bike.

"Oh no!" I exclaimed as I peered into my cooler bag in the front basket and wrinkled my nose. "I don't think my quark is okay. The cooler packs have melted and it smells kind of rancid." We'd talked a lot longer than I'd expected.

The blood drained from Roz's face and she clutched her stomach. "Oh god, please don't talk to me about rancid cheese. I don't think I can handle it."

I sighed and resealed the cooler bag. No quark on my granola tomorrow morning. "I'll deal with it later. We better get a move on. I'm supposed to go over to my parents' house for dinner."

As we cycled back to Sapphire Springs, I replayed the events of the day in my mind. It had been a surprisingly enjoyable excursion. I was shocked just how much I'd liked the glimpses of Roz I'd seen under her terse exterior. When she let down her walls, she was funny and easy to talk to, and far less critical than I expected.

My eyes lingered on her Lycra-clad body ten feet ahead of mine. I frowned. I shouldn't be checking her out. Our fake-dating arrangement was complicated enough. *She doesn't date. She doesn't even like me.* And once this is over, I needed to focus on finding someone to settle down with. *Don't forget that ticking clock.*

As I stared at Roz, my bike bounced over a rock I hadn't seen and skidded. I clutched the handlebars, managing to wrest back control of the bike before it fell. *Pay attention, Olivia.* The last thing I needed was to crash my bike and break an arm or a hand. I couldn't afford any injuries or other distractions impeding my ability to do my job, especially not with the busy spring and summer wedding season approaching and the high-profile wedding I had coming up in the next few weeks. I needed to knuckle down and focus. I pedaled harder to overtake Roz so I didn't have to look at her perfect butt anymore, breathing out as I shot past her. *There. Out of sight, out of mind.* But was it really that simple? My feelings toward Roz felt... complicated. And she was most definitely a distraction. It was probably best if I avoided her as much as our fake dating arrangement would allow. No more long lunches and bike rides.

As we pushed the bikes into Blake's yard, her door opened and Blake appeared on her doorstep.

"Hi, I'm Blake, Olivia's sister," she said, a hint of wariness in her tone.

Roz carefully leaned Blake's bike against the fence, wiped her hands on her top and then held one out to shake. "I'm Roz. Thanks for lending me your bike. Apologies if I smell. I managed to spill milk all over myself earlier today."

Blake raised an eyebrow.

"Don't ask," I said, grinning. "The smell could also be my quark, which I left in the sun."

Blake grimaced. "Okay, please don't eat that, Liv."

"I'm not going to!" I replied indignantly. I might have been Blake's "little" sister, but I was also a fully grown woman who knew eating rancid cheese was a terrible idea.

"Good." Blake turned to Roz, a calculating look in her

eyes. "So I heard that you were a management consultant in New York before you moved out here?"

I frowned. Where was Blake going with this?

"Yes. That's right," Roz said.

"Do you know much about economics?"

Oh no. I thought I knew where this was going. I glared at Blake.

"Yes," Roz said. "I majored in economics and have an MBA."

Blake's face lit up. "What are you doing Thursday night?"

I sighed. So much for avoiding Roz as much as possible.

CHAPTER SIXTEEN

ROZ

"THANKS FOR DOING THIS." I held the back door of the farmhouse still while Matt positioned the drill. The door had fallen off its hinges this morning with a spectacular clang that had sent Thelma and Louise mooing loudly.

The nail glided smoothly into the doorframe. I tentatively let go.

"No problem," he said, opening and shutting the door to make sure it worked.

The last of the farm's visitors were trickling out of the petting zoo and back to the parking lot. The laughter of pre-teens and the wail of an overtired toddler carried on the cooling breeze.

"Can I still hang out with the animals?" Lottie yelled from the entrance to the petting zoo.

"That's fine," I called back. "You can give Ronnie a hand feeding the chickens. Just don't get too close to the cows!" I glared at Thelma and Louise. As usual, they were placidly eating grass. I would speak to my neighbor tomorrow about rehoming them.

Lottie let out an excited yelp and disappeared.

I turned to Matt. "Do you want a beer?"

We retrieved two beers from the fridge and parked ourselves on the wicker chairs on the back deck.

"How's the tractor driving going?" Matt asked, sipping his beer as he stared at the grassy patch where my crushed car had sat. I'd finally gotten it towed this morning. The local mechanic had confirmed it was a write-off.

I managed a weak smile. "I'm improving. I drove it up and down the hayride route a few times this morning before the farm opened. No fatalities to report. I should be ready to take Lottie out soon—if she's not traumatized by witnessing the crash." I winced.

Matt grinned. "She's still excited to go."

"Good." Lottie ran out of the petting zoo holding two carrots, her blond hair bouncing and her cheeks flushed. My chest filled with warmth. *This is why I've turned my life upside down.* Ronnie, one of the farmhands, jogged behind her.

"Is it okay if I feed Thelma and Louise?" Lottie asked, poking her head through the deck rails. "Ronnie said they like carrots."

I furrowed my brow. I'd seen countless children feed the cows under Ronnie's supervision since I'd taken over the farm. Lottie would remain safely on this side of the fence, away from their powerful legs. But still...

"Pleeeease, Auntie Roz."

How could I say no? "Fine. Just no loud noises near them, okay?"

Lottie squealed and scampered away. My lips curved up.

Matt chuckled and then took a sip of beer.

"Any news from Mel?" I asked, keeping a close eye on

Lottie as Ronnie demonstrated how to present her flattened palm to the bovines.

Matt smiled. "She's good. We spoke to her yesterday. Loving the challenge, but missing Lottie terribly. She was supposed to be finishing up in August, but she's asked if she can finish earlier to be home in time for Lottie's birthday, so we're just waiting to hear if that will be approved. We're not mentioning it to Lottie yet—don't want to get her hopes up in case her application is rejected."

"Well, I hope she gets the green light." I jolted as Lottie offered one of the cows a carrot, exhaling as its long tongue scooped it into its mouth without taking any of Lottie's little fingers with it.

"Me too." Matt took another sip. "If you hadn't invited me over, I was going to call you."

"Oh?" I dragged my eyes away from Lottie and back to Matt.

"To find out what's going on with you and Olivia. You'd never mentioned her before, but suddenly you've been dating for six months?" Matt raised an eyebrow.

I sighed. "Do you remember in October, when I went to Pryde and met that woman?"

Matt frowned. "The one you kissed and then ran out on?"

"You know that's not exactly what happened." The memory of Olivia breathing heavily, her body pressed to mine in the restroom, slammed into me. I shook it off. "Well, anyway, that was Olivia."

Matt's eyes widened. "But I thought you left your number and she never called?"

"That's right." I tipped back my beer, letting my body sink into the chair.

"Then how have you two been dating for six months?"

I filled him in on my fake-dating fiasco.

"I thought you were the smart one of the two of us," Matt said once I'd finished. "Surely there was another way to handle it. Faking a relationship seems a little drastic."

I sighed. "Do you really think Fred would have agreed to invest if I confessed I'd just pretended to be Olivia's girlfriend for the farm tour?"

Matt shrugged. "Maybe if you'd told him the whole story he might have."

Frowning, I took another sip of beer. "Well, we're in too deep to turn back now."

Matt shook his head. "Why didn't you just ask Mom and Dad for the money? That would have been a lot more straightforward. They would have lent it to you, even after you came clean to them about Olivia. Unconditional love and all that." He waved his hand.

My stomach roiled and I glared at him. "Absolutely not. You know how I feel about asking Mom and Dad for favors. I'd rather sell it all and go back to working at Saunders & Co."

"But is it really a worse option than continuing this fake relationship nonsense?"

"Yes." I fixed my eyes on a black bird that was pecking the dirt near the petting zoo. "It's only for a few weeks. Borrowing money from Mom and Dad would undermine everything I've done over the past twenty years to prove I can succeed without them."

Matt sighed. "Look, I know what they did was shit, but it was a long time ago. They've changed, Roz."

"But have they? I heard them going on at you the other night about Lottie's school again." The public-versus-private-school showdown had struck once again.

Matt rolled his eyes. "It drives me up the wall that they

won't drop that, but their heart is in the right place. They just don't always go about it in the right way."

"And sometimes they go about it in illegal ways," I muttered.

"Okay, okay." Matt raised his palm placatingly. "And your insistence on fake dating definitely has nothing to do with the fact your fake girlfriend is gorgeous and lovely to boot?" He grinned behind his beer.

The image of Olivia teasing me about my newfound dislike of dairy yesterday, her eyes bright and her broad smile flashed into my mind, and my heart stuttered. *Stop that.* "Don't be ridiculous. She never called me, remember? And anyway, I'm not looking for a real relationship. This fake one is as close as I'm willing to get."

Matt rested his beer on the round wicker table in front of us. "Are you sure that's what you really want?"

"What?" My eyes flickered to Lottie, who had thankfully moved away from the cows and was now climbing a bale of hay.

"To be single forever?" He leaned forward. "If it really is, that's fine. But I just want to make sure your reluctance isn't because of that psychopath or Mom and Dad. Or both."

Heaviness tugged at my chest. Matt was really making me relive all my trauma tonight. "Yes. It's what I want." I never wanted to be hurt like that again. "Anyway, please don't tell anyone. Olivia has told her close friends and family, but they're all sworn to secrecy. We don't want this getting out. If it does, I'm screwed."

The rumble of a truck attracted my attention. Dana pulled up near the petting zoo, jumped out and walked over to us.

"Sorry to interrupt," she said, not sounding particularly

apologetic. "Roz, the chainsaw we use for cutting the trees has broken. Are you okay if I order a new one?"

I frowned. "How much will that be?"

"Around a grand."

My heart sank. "Fine. But if you can do it on the cheap, such as buying one second-hand, do it that way."

"Okay." Dana's surly face relaxed slightly. "Oh, and I heard Blake roped you in to coming to trivia too. She's got me studying up on golf." Dana grimaced. "Has she assigned you a topic too? She took our loss last week quite badly."

Huh. I didn't realize Dana was part of Olivia's friendship group. I shook my head. "No. Was that all, Dana?"

Dana yanked the truck keys from her pocket. "Yes. I'll put in the order. Bye."

When Dana was out of earshot, Matt turned to me. "Roz, this isn't the cutthroat world of consultancy. People around here are used to a warmer and, well, a more personable approach. I know you're a straight shooter, but I think you may need to add a few more pleasantries and open up a bit more if you don't want to get your employees against you."

I crossed my arms. "Dana wasn't exactly being the epitome of warmth."

Matt's gaze bore into me. "I did sense some tension between you two. But I thought she was trying to extend an olive branch with her question about trivia, and you shut it down."

I pressed my lips together.

"I know you find it hard to open up to people, but I think you'll get a lot further in Sapphire Springs if you can be a bit... nicer," Matt said.

My mind flickered to Olivia, who was so friendly with

everyone, and her comments about how the local farmers all worked together. "I'll think about it."

A patter of footsteps made my head snap up. Lottie ran toward us, grinning. "Did you see the cows eat the carrots right out of my hands? It was so cool. Can I come feed them every night?"

I laughed. "Not every night. That would be a lot of driving for your dad. But you're welcome to feed them whenever you visit."

"Yay!" Lottie jumped up and down.

Of course, of all the animals Lottie would fall in love with, it would be the damn cows. I sighed. I couldn't get rid of them now.

CHAPTER SEVENTEEN

ROZ

CLUTCHING THE COOLER BAG, I approached the pub. Faint music and chatter drifted out from the open windows on the warm spring breeze. The sun was sinking behind the mountains, a soft pink-and-blue haze filling the sky.

As I pushed the door open, the music and voices grew louder. The cozy pub was packed full of people. If Red Tractor Farm's taproom was half as popular as this place, we'd stay in the black.

I looked around until my gaze landed on Olivia sitting at a circular table near the back of the pub. She laughed, her head thrown back and her eyes flashing. She was wearing a t-shirt tonight, a gray V-neck with a flower and something written on it. Blake was beside her, one arm around a blond woman who was gesticulating wildly. That must be Jenny. On Jenny's other side was a brunette with shoulder-length wavy hair and glasses, sitting close to another woman with light-brown hair cut even shorter than mine. And then there was Dana.

I beelined toward the bar where I ordered a non-alcoholic beer from a friendly bartender. I wanted tonight to go well. I wasn't sure why I cared so much, but I wanted Olivia's friends to like me. Holding my own at trivia would be a plus. It was clearly why I'd been invited in the first place. Matt's words from earlier in the week echoed in my head. *People around here are used to a more personable approach.*

The bartender slid the beer across to me and I tapped the card reader with my phone. Clutching my drink, I plastered a smile on my face and walked over to the table. No one noticed me, so I pulled out the spare stool next to Olivia. It scraped loudly on the old oak floor. Five pairs of eyes turned to me.

I cleared my throat. "Hello. I'm Roz."

They went around the table, introducing themselves. Did I sense a slight hesitation in their body language? Perhaps I was just overthinking things after Matt's feedback.

"That table over there are the ones to beat," Blake murmured, nodding her head toward a table in the corner. "The Gran Masters."

I followed her gaze and blinked. Four sweet-looking elderly ladies were our main competition? Well, this should be easy.

"This is for you." I shoved the bag into Olivia's hands.

Her eyes widened.

"It's a thank-you for showing me around on Sunday." Why did my voice sound so gruff?

Olivia opened the bag and peered in, her brow furrowing.

"I learned from your mistake and covered it in cooler blocks. But it's quark. Extremely well refrigerated quark." As the words left my mouth, I second-guessed them. Was it weird to bring someone a tub full of quark to a pub trivia night?

An expression I couldn't place flickered across her face before she broke into a smile. "Oh, that's too kind of you. So, you've recovered from your temporary dairy intolerance?" Olivia's tone was teasing, but I could have sworn there was a hint of wariness in her eyes.

"It seems that way." I wasn't about to tell Olivia that I hadn't been able to consume any dairy since our excursion and had nearly thrown up going back to the dairy to buy the quark today. My gaze dropped to Olivia's t-shirt. At the bottom of the V-neck, a hint of the delicate skin between the curves of her breasts caught my eyes. I forced my gaze farther down to the writing scrawled on her shirt in cursive: *That's ranunculus!* A red flower, presumably a ranunculus, bloomed next to the words, over the arc of her left breast. I held back a chuckle, yanking my eyes away before anyone thought I was ogling her chest. *I should really give her the t-shirt back.* It was sitting neatly folded in my drawer next to my bed.

"So, Roz, how are you finding life as a farmer?" George asked, placing her beer on the table. "It must be a big change from being a consultant in the city."

My thigh pressed against Olivia's as I turned to George. She jerked her leg away.

"It's been..." My impulse was to say it was going great, but Matt's voice in my head made me reconsider. "It's been a steep learning curve."

George tilted her head. *Come on, Roz. Elaborate.* While I was looking at George, I was deeply aware of Olivia's presence next to me, of her chest gently rising and falling as she breathed, of her slightly sweet floral scent. I wiped my slightly clammy palms on my pants. *Focus.*

"I'm good at the business side, at the numbers, at strategy, at looking for efficiencies"—in my periphery, Olivia shot Dana a look and rolled her eyes—"but I'm not familiar with the day-to-day running of a farm, so I'm having to rely heavily on my staff. Thankfully, they're all very good at what they do." I looked at Dana and gave her a little nod before turning to Jenny. "Thanks again for sending Olivia that email about the event spaces, by the way. It was incredibly helpful." There. I leaned back in my chair. Matt would be proud at how personable I was being. I'd admitted a weakness, showered my employees with praise and thanked Jenny. You couldn't get more personable than that.

"No problem." Jenny smiled. "Let me know if you have any other questions. I'm excited that we might get another venue."

I glanced at Olivia, who was sipping from her wine glass. Was I imagining it, or had she shifted her chair slightly away from mine? "I also need to thank you for sending through the sustainability sections of the business plan." *So personable.*

"Was it okay?" Olivia asked.

"It was really good." Surprisingly good.

Olivia's face brightened. "I'm glad. All the practice I got doing business plans in my twenties finally paid off."

Blake gazed around our table. "It looks like Dan's getting ready to start. Does anyone need to do some last-minute brushing up on their topics before we put our phones away?"

George groaned. "I can't read another word about baseball. Dan better ask a question about it."

Hannah laughed, wrapping her arm around George and squeezing. "And I'm now an expert on the NHL. I should probably take up writing hockey romances."

George elbowed her gently. "You have to finish your current series first. I need to know what happens!"

I surprised myself with a chuckle. Why wasn't I finding their PDA off-putting? It was almost... cute. I glanced over at Olivia, who was studying her wine glass with great interest.

"Okay everyone! We're starting now," a man announced. "Please take your seats."

Blake grabbed a pen and paper from the middle of the table.

"For those who don't know me, I'm Dan, and I'll be your host tonight. Now remember, no phones are allowed while we're playing. Is everyone ready?" He looked around the packed pub and a cheer broke out. "Excellent. The first question is: what happened in 1929 on the day that became known as Black Tuesday?"

My heart jumped. I leaned in. "That's easy. The stock market crashed."

As Blake scribbled down the answer, Olivia brushed her fingertips over the black coaster in front of her, following its contours. Her nails were neatly cut and there was a long thin red scratch across the back of her hand. Had she hurt herself at work? Scratches were probably an occupational hazard for florists, given all those unpleasant thorns and twigs they had to handle.

"Question two. What is the hair-like material on an ear of corn called?"

"Silk!" Dana and Olivia hissed in unison. They high-fived each other, laughing. Olivia's eyes crinkled, her white teeth gleaming between her pink lips. Her face, framed with glossy brown hair, was so expressive. My breath caught, and I realized I was grinning as well. I'd also completely zoned out of the trivia questions.

"Question five. What is the Gini coefficient most often used to measure?" Dan scanned the groups of people huddled over their tables.

"Oh god," George said. "I don't have a clue."

"Income inequality," I muttered, earning myself a smile from Blake.

By the time the third round was over and Blake handed our answer sheet in, I was buzzing.

"I have a good feeling about this," Jenny announced, rubbing her hands.

Blake elbowed her. "Hey! Don't jinx us!" She turned to look at The Gran Masters, who were now digging into a bowl of fries. "The grannies are looking confident as well."

George had just finished telling us about a Major League Baseball manager who was ejected from a game and tried to sneak back in wearing a fake mustache and borrowed clothes when the music was turned down and Dan cleared his throat. "We have a tie for first place tonight." I bit my lip. Could we be one of the winning teams? I was surprised how invested I was in our success. "There's only one prize, so we'll go to a tie-breaker round between The Whisk Takers and The Gran Masters." Our table cheered. Dan continued. "So we're not here all night, whichever team gets the first question wrong or fails to write an answer within one minute of the question being asked will lose. I'll be checking The Whisk Takers answers in real time and my trusty bartender Zach will be monitoring The Gran Masters." Zach put down a pint glass he was drying with a dish towel and stepped out from behind the bar.

Blake gripped the pen, looking around the table. "Okay. We can do this, folks."

"I wish I'd convinced Mom to stay a few more days in

Florida," George groaned, gazing at a smartly dressed woman with a gray bob at The Gran Masters table. "She definitely got that one we missed about Bhutan."

I peered at George. "That's your mom?"

George nodded. "She's been making use of the discount I give her at Novel Gossip and reading a lot of non-fiction books lately. All of a sudden, she's become a wealth of knowledge on a whole lot of useless facts that are only good for trivia."

Olivia laughed. "You need to stop giving her that discount!"

George's mom looked harmless enough. She caught me looking at her and shot me a death stare. I quickly averted my eyes. *Or not.*

"Are you all ready?" Dan roared, positioning himself behind Blake so he could see our answers.

We nodded.

"Who or what is rumored to have started the Great Chicago Fire?"

"I'm pretty sure it was a cow," Hannah whispered, leaning in with her elbows on the table.

Humph. Sounded like exactly the sort of thing a cow would do.

Blake wrote it down and Dan nodded in confirmation. *So far, so good.*

Sensing Olivia staring at me, I shifted my gaze. It landed on her just in time to see her eyes dart to Blake. My gaze lingered on her face in profile, traveling over the brown arch of her eyebrow closest to me and down the smooth bridge of her nose to her pink lips. I blinked. *Don't let yourself get distracted again.*

"Next question!" Dan boomed. "Which later-assassinated president was a sitting member of the House of

Representatives immediately prior to being elected president?"

Our table was silent. Sweat pricked my armpits as my mind raced. *I think I know the answer to this...*

"I think it was Garfield," Dana said, gripping her pint glass.

I frowned. "I don't think it was Garfield. Lincoln, JFK and McKinley were assassinated as well. I'm pretty sure it was McKinley."

Blake's gaze darted around the table. "Anyone else? I don't have a clue."

Everyone shook their head.

"Shit." Blake's pen hovered above the paper.

"You've got twenty seconds left," Dan said.

I closed my eyes, trying to remember the book I'd read on American presidents a few years ago. My confidence grew. "I'm almost certain it was McKinley."

A vein pulsed on Blake's forehead. "Okay." She shot an apologetic look at Dana and wrote down McKinley. On The Gran Masters' table, George's mom also scribbled down an answer.

Dan peered over Blake's shoulder and then glanced at Zach, who nodded. "We have a winner!" he yelled. My heart jumped with excitement. Had we— "The Gran Masters win again, for the fifteenth week in a row!"

Shit.

As a cheer rose from The Gran Masters' table, Blake's face dropped, and Dana pressed her lips together.

I slumped back in my chair, my chest deflating. "Damn. I'm sorry."

"Don't worry. It's just a game." Olivia squeezed my thigh, leaving it tingling and then snatched her hand away as if it had burned her. I stared down at her hand. What was going on with her tonight?

"There's always next week," Hannah added. "We wouldn't have even gotten to the tie breaker if it wasn't for you."

"You're both required attendees from now on," Blake announced, looking between Dana and me. "Who wants another drink? Now that we don't need to keep our minds sharp, I'm going to grab another beer."

I shook my head, absentmindedly running my fingers over a seam in the table. I needed to keep my mind clear for my presentation to Fred tomorrow morning, which reminded me... I glanced at Olivia. She was staring at my fingers, an odd look on her face.

"Hey, is there any chance you'd be able to come to the meeting with Fred tomorrow morning? Just in case he asks anything about the sustainability sections?" Fred would hopefully make his decision shortly after—or even during—the meeting, so I needed it to go perfectly, especially in light of all the bills that had been piling up recently.

Olivia's head jerked up. Her cheeks were pink, accentuating the long, dark lashes that framed her warm brown eyes. My chest twinged.

"Sure, I can do that." She glanced over at the old grandfather clock in the corner of the bar. "I should probably head home. Need to get some sleep to make sure I'm on the ball for tomorrow." She grabbed her bag and stood up. "Good night, guys! Great work tonight. I'll see you tomorrow, Roz."

She all but sprinted out the door.

My gut pinched. Why was she behaving so strangely? I hadn't realized how much I enjoyed Olivia's open, warm personality until it disappeared.

Perhaps tomorrow I'd find out.

CHAPTER EIGHTEEN

OLIVIA

I GAZED open-mouthed at Roz from my vantage point on the couch. She stood in front of Fred and me, her eyes sparkling under the gold dome pendant light that hung from the study ceiling, her voice confident and passionate. I'd heard the phrase "competence is sexy" before, but I'd never understood it... until now. *Damn.* Surely Fred would be throwing his money at Roz after this performance. With Roz's attention focused on Fred, I let my gaze drop down her body. She was wearing another ridiculous suit, a sleek black one with a starched gray shirt underneath that made her blue eyes pop even more than usual. I bit my lip. *Ridiculous. Or ridiculously hot,* suggested a small voice in the back of my head. I clenched my jaw. *Not helpful.*

I looked up to find Roz and Fred staring at me expectantly. Heat spread across my cheeks. "Sorry, what was that?"

"I just asked whether the solar panels on the roof would generate extra electricity that could be used elsewhere in the farm, not just for the event space?" Fred said.

"Oh, sorry." I cleared my throat. "Yes, we'll definitely be

able to use the electricity for other purposes as well, like powering the irrigation systems and lighting the barns."

"Excellent." Fred slapped his hands on his thighs. "Well, I don't have any further questions. That was very impressive. Thank you both." He smiled and rose to his feet. "Before I head off, would you mind showing me where you're planning to put the new buildings? They're going to be a lot larger than I thought, so I'd like to visualize how it might change the farm's aesthetics."

"Of course. We can go now," Roz said, taking off her jacket and then ushering Fred out of the study. I followed them out of the house and over to the field where Thelma and Louise usually roamed. I twisted my head, looking for their familiar brown bodies. My chest constricted. *She hasn't gotten rid of them, has she?* I exhaled as I spotted them in the far corner of the field. I squinted. Someone— possibly Dana—was bending over the fence. Thelma and Louise appeared to be keeping them company.

Roz gestured at the ground. "It's a little muddy here, so watch your step." Her shiny black leather shoes were already splattered with dirt. Did the woman not own any sensible footwear? Even Fred had dressed down for today's meeting, wearing hiking boots, jeans and a checkered shirt.

"If you need to run to change, Roz, that's fine," Fred said, his eyes dropping to her feet. "Or you can just show us from here."

"No. No. I'm fi—*argh!*" Roz's feet slipped, shooting off the ground.

Heart pounding, I yanked my hands out to steady her as she tipped back. I wasn't fast enough.

My heart ricocheted into my throat as she tumbled, landing flat on her back with a thud.

"Shit! Are you okay?" I crouched down next to Roz.

She struggled into a sitting position, wiping hair off her brow and streaking mud across her forehead in the process. "I'm fine." She clambered to her feet.

Brown mud plastered the back of her shirt. I dropped my eyes farther and—*oh god!* Her black pants had split down the seam, revealing a glimpse of shapely ass and black underwear, both a little smeared with mud. I bit my lip and then blinked. *Now is not the time to leer at Roz's butt.*

Springing into action, I wrapped my arm around Roz and repositioned her so she was facing Fred, her exposed ass out of Fred's sight.

"Why don't we just show Fred from here, babe?" I said, trying to keep my voice light.

Her eyebrows furrowed. "Let's go a little farther into the field so Fred can really envision it."

"No!" I yelped.

Fred tilted his head and looked at me.

Shit. If Roz turned and kept walking in front of Fred, her butt would be on complete display. And as annoying as Roz could be on occasion, she didn't deserve to be humiliated in front of her hopefully future business partner.

Fred was too close for me to whisper a warning to her. There was only one way I could think of to let her know...

Holding my breath, my hand slipped down Roz's back and over the curve of her butt until it reached the split seam. *Damn. She has a nice, firm body.* I tapped her bare bottom with a finger.

Roz's eyes widened. Mission accomplished, I yanked my hand away before I was tempted to let it linger.

"Actually, here is fine," she said, before launching into a description of how the new building would be positioned.

I watched her, fascinated. How did she manage to

remain so cool while covered in mud and with her butt exposed to the breeze? Perhaps twenty years in the cutthroat world of management consulting prepared you for every eventuality, including unfortunate wardrobe malfunctions. I tugged at the collar of my dress. Whatever the reason, Roz's butt was not helping me shake off the annoying attraction I'd developed toward her one iota.

"That was great," Fred said as we walked back to his car, Roz keeping a step behind him.

Roz smiled. "I'm so glad to hear that."

A group of teens passed us, heading toward the petting zoo. Roz twisted her back slightly away from them and wrapped her arm around my waist, pressing her body close to mine. Roz's cedar scent, the earthy tones stronger than usual, danced in my nostrils. My pulse increased. *She's just doing it to protect her modesty, remember?*

I watched Fred as he pulled his keys from his pocket and pressed a button. Surely he now had enough information to give an enthusiastic yes.

"Do you have any other questions?" Roz asked.

"Not at the moment." Fred reached for his car door. "But this is such a great area, I've decided to look for a vacation home around here." He grinned. "I'll be staying here for the next week and working remotely. So if I think of anything else I'll be in easy reach. I'll probably pop in once or twice to have lunch at the café—those fritters I had last time were delicious."

"Oh, excellent." A muscle twitched under Roz's eye. "Talk soon."

"How do you think it went?" I asked as Fred reversed his car out of the parking spot.

Still smiling, Roz muttered through her teeth, "Terrific.

My butt's hanging out of my pants and I'm covered in mud."

I laughed. "Thankfully, Fred didn't seem to notice the butt situation."

"Yes, well let's head back inside before anyone else does." Roz scanned the parking lot. "Thank god the farm is quiet this morning."

We walked across the lot. As we stepped onto the path to the house, my eyes dipped to Roz's butt. Heat shot up my cheeks as I yanked my gaze away and focused on Roz's face instead. "So butts aside, do you think he's interested?"

"He loved your sustainability sections and he seemed impressed with all the information we included about supply and demand." Roz pressed her lips together. "But I think he's worried I don't have enough practical farming experience."

"Really? He seems so enthusiastic. Well, he clearly hasn't seen you milk a cow," I said, grinning. "If he did, he'd realize exactly how good at farming you are."

Roz narrowed her eyes. "Ha ha."

"And the fact he's considering buying a house around here has to be a good sign, right?"

Roz shrugged. "I hope so."

"I did have one big takeaway from today's meeting," I said, picking up my speed to keep up with Roz's fast stride so I wasn't tempted to peek at her butt again.

"Hmm, what's that?" Roz gave a muddy patch of dirt a wide berth.

"You need some new clothes." I watched Roz closely. Would she be offended by my suggestion?

Roz's forehead wrinkled. "These pants are a write-off, but I've got plenty more at home."

"I don't mean more of those pants. I mean a whole new

wardrobe. While your clothes are very, um... business-like, they're not exactly designed for farm life. They seem better suited for impressing rich CEOs of Fortune 500 companies than convincing people you're a farmer."

Roz paused for a moment and then gave an abrupt nod. "You're probably right. I have been thinking that I need some new clothes." She sighed. "I've been putting it off because I can't stand shopping."

"Well, if you want, I could take you." My mouth slammed shut. What the hell was I doing? I was trying to avoid spending unnecessary time with Roz, and here I was, volunteering to be her personal shopper? But I'd seen the way Fred had stared at her shoes. Making Roz look more like a farmer might help convince him that she knew what she was doing. And I had no confidence that Roz would select the appropriate clothes if she was left to her own devices.

Roz shot me a sharp look. "Are you sure?"

I stopped at the front steps of the farmhouse. "Why don't we go now? Maddie is covering for me at Sapphire Blooms. And I need to buy a new hat anyway."

"Okay." Roz sprang up the steps and pushed open the front door. "I'll just run upstairs and get changed. Feel free to make yourself at home. Oh, and before we head off, we should have lunch. Shopping is bad enough at the best of times. Shopping on an empty stomach is even worse."

An image of Roz, always so proper, having a toddler-like hangry meltdown on the floor of Tractor Supply Co. flashed into my mind. I chuckled. "Sounds great."

"My treat." Roz paused in the doorway. "As a thank-you for attending the meeting today."

While waiting for Roz, I examined the books lining the walls of her study. *Team of Rivals: The Political Genius of*

Abraham Lincoln; Playing to Win: How Strategy Really Works; Real-Time Leadership: Finding Your Winning Moves When the Stakes Are High. Yikes, they sounded dry. Roz's steps echoed down the hall and she appeared in the door frame, dressed in yet another pair of black tailored pants and a crisp white shirt. My heart skipped a beat. As impractical as her clothes were, Roz could really rock a suit.

We headed over to the farmhouse café. Roz nodded at the young man behind the counter, who rushed out with menus and a jug of water, beads of sweat on his forehead as he handed his boss a menu with shaking hands. Poor guy.

"Ohhh," I said, perusing the menu. "I see there have been some changes since I came here last. After Fred's rave review, I think I'll get the fritters."

Roz's brow furrowed. "Let me check something. Tom, can you come over here, please?" She waved at the poor server, who hurried back over to our table. "Do the fritters have pineapple in the salsa?"

"No, no, they don't. It's mango, ma'am, not pineapple."

"You don't need to call me ma'am, Tom."

"Sorry, m—I mean Roz." His Adam's apple bobbed. "Um, are you ready to order?"

We gave Tom our orders, and he scurried away again.

I took a sip of water. "Thanks for checking about the pineapple."

"Well, I don't want you to collapse in my café. Not only is it a liability issue, but I need you to help me buy these clothes." Roz straightened her knife and fork.

I chuckled. "Of course. I'll wait till I'm out of your café and you've gotten a new wardrobe before I mess up your day."

"You know that's not what I meant." Roz's eyes locked

on mine for a moment, and a zing of electricity jolted down my spine.

I stiffened. *Not again.* This was a convenient business arrangement—nothing more. If she wanted something more, she wouldn't have just disappeared without a trace that night at Pryde. The memory of sitting at the bar, nursing my drink and waiting for her to reappear shot through my mind. Why had she disappeared that night?

I was tempted to ask her. But was it worth risking the tenuous equilibrium we appeared to have reached to uncover the answer, especially when I was almost certainly not going to like the answer? She'd likely decided she just wasn't that into me, or she was swept off her feet by another, more experienced woman while I was sitting on the toilet hyping myself up. No, I'd leave asking her about that—and demanding my t-shirt back—until it would be easier to avoid her. We were, after all, going to be stuck fake dating each other for at least another week.

My pineapple-free fritters and Roz's burger arrived.

I cut off a piece of fritter and popped it in my mouth, savoring the fresh herbs and juicy corn kernels. "Oh, this is delicious."

"Good, I'll let the chef know that you approve." Roz bit into her burger, chewed and swallowed. "So, where should we go shopping?"

"There's a Farmer's Own twenty minutes away. It should have some decent farming clothes."

"The name sounds appropriate. I'm in." Roz sunk her white teeth slowly into her burger again and I averted my eyes. How did she even make eating a burger attractive? This shopping trip was definitely a bad idea.

I spent the entire drive staring at the road, relieved I had something to focus on that wasn't Roz and her distracting face. I pulled into a parking spot and turned off the ignition.

"We're not going in there, are we?" Roz asked, her eyes wide.

I checked the large sign on the storefront to make sure I'd driven us to the correct place. Yep, it was Farmer's Own. "Yes. Do you have a problem with that?"

"It says '*Guns, Ammo.*'" Roz pointed to the writing under the sign.

"Oh." I grimaced. I'd forgotten it sold firearms. It did look a little intimidating. I waved my hand through the air. "It'll be fine."

"Perhaps we could go to an Anthropologie instead?" Roz sunk farther down into her seat.

"Roz, real farmers don't shop at Anthropologie. If you want to convince Fred you're up for the job, you need to get some heavy-duty farming clothes." I leaned over and released her seatbelt.

Roz slipped out of the car, moving at a snail's pace. "I knew we should have taken my truck. There's no way these gun dealers are going to take us seriously with this ridiculous car." She glared at the spray-painted flowers.

"Stop being so dramatic," I said, hooking my arms through hers and pulling her along. "You're making it sound like we're going to do an illegal arms deal or something. We're just getting some clothes. We'll stay well away from the guns."

Inside, we scanned the large store for the clothing section. There were only a few customers, and they all seemed to be middle-aged white men. We certainly did stand out—I doubted they got many androgynous women in immaculately tailored business suits or women in floral dresses.

I spotted a sign saying *Women's Clothes* in the far corner of the store, thankfully well away from the firearms. "Ah, here we go." I strode over to the clothes. "Now, these would be perfect." I held up some navy-blue bib overalls, fairly confident I'd guessed Roz's size correctly. "They'll stand up nicely to mud and manure management."

"Manure management?" Roz wrinkled her nose. She held up a hand before I could elaborate. "Actually, don't tell me. I don't want to know." She eyed the overalls, her lips pursed. "I haven't worn overalls since I was a kid. I'm not going to start now."

"They're very practical. They'll keep you manure-free." I grinned.

"Okay, fine," Roz said, snatching the clothing out of my hands. She peered at the label. "They should fit."

"These work pants would be a good idea too." I pulled them off the rack and handed them to Roz. "Oooh, and flannel. You definitely need some flannel." I grabbed some red and blue flannel shirts and piled them into Roz's arms.

"You're enjoying this far too much," Roz murmured as we made our way to the changing room.

I laughed as Roz swished the changing room curtain closed. I hovered outside the changing room like a shop assistant working on commission. I couldn't wait to see what Roz looked like in my hand-picked outfits.

"Is everything all right in there?" I asked after a minute or two of hearing Roz mutter under her breath.

"Yes, fine."

A few moments later, the curtain flew open, and Roz emerged, dragging her feet. The navy overalls and a red flannel shirt perfectly fit her slim frame. The colors suited her too, complementing her blue eyes and blond hair in a way her usual monochrome wardrobe did not.

I blinked. "Wow."

"What?" Roz snapped.

I swallowed. "You look... good."

Roz stared at me, unconvinced.

"No, seriously. If I was meeting you for the first time, I would hardly believe that you hadn't spent your whole life on a farm."

The overalls really brought out the blue in her eyes, sharp glare aside. I jerked my gaze away, rubbing my neck.

I needed a distraction. "We should get you some proper boots as well. I'll grab some while you try on the rest. What size are you?"

"Nine," Roz replied, arms crossed. Good lord, it was as if she was handing over a state secret under duress.

"I'll be right back." I selected a few pairs of sturdy boots in the footwear section. On my way back, I passed a row of fleece jackets and grabbed one for her too, along with a selection of hats.

I pushed the jackets and shoes under the changing room curtain.

A few minutes later, Roz reappeared, this time wearing a blue flannel shirt, tan work pants and a pair of dark-brown work boots. *Damn.* I'd never thought of farming clothes as particularly sexy before, but this fashion parade was showing them in a whole new light. I pictured Roz in a barn, tossing hay onto a wagon. Her eyes locked with mine and she dropped the pitchfork on the ground and pushed me onto a hay bale, ripping off my dress. *Oh god.*

"Nice." I cleared my throat. "You look like you're ready to get your hands dirty."

Roz raised an eyebrow.

"In a good way, of course." I tugged at the collar of my dress.

Roz wriggled around. "They are surprisingly comfortable. I can see why farmers wear them. And they aren't as ridiculous as overalls."

I stared at her like we were on an episode of *Queer Eye* and I was Tan France. "Hmm, something's missing." I grabbed a brown wide-brimmed leather hat from the pile of headwear I'd collected and carefully placed it on her head. Her soft breath tickled my face. I dropped my gaze to her shirt. One side of her collar was tucked in. I flipped it out, my fingers tingling at the contact with the soft skin of her collar bone. My breath hitched.

I pulled back, my heart racing, and clapped my hands. "There! I'd trust you with my cows any day of the week, Farmer Roz. And if I was Fred, I'd trust you with my money."

Roz chuckled. "Let's hope Fred feels the same way." She slipped back into the changing room. When she came out again, her face was barely visible over a pile of clothing.

"Do you want me to return anything while you pay?" I asked.

"No, I think I'll grab it all. And I'll pick up a few more pairs of pants and flannel on the way to the counter."

My eyes widened. "Even the overalls?"

"Yes, even the overalls. Just in case, god forbid, I need to help with manure management." Roz's mouth twisted to one side. "Hang on." She stopped. "Didn't you say you needed a hat as well?"

I nodded. I'd been so engrossed in Roz's wardrobe makeover, I'd forgotten.

"What about this one? I think this would suit you."

Roz placed a wide-brimmed straw hat on my head and gently tugged it down, tucking a strand of hair behind my ear. A shiver ran down my spine.

She stepped back and stared at me. "Perfect," she whispered.

My stomach flipped. What was wrong with me? *She gives me one compliment and I turn to jelly?*

I looked in the mirror, focusing on my reflection. "That's actually quite nice. Maybe I should take you shopping more often."

"Hard pass. Now I know my sizes, all future clothes will be ordered online." She paused, holding my gaze. "But thank you for accompanying me. I wouldn't have stepped foot in here by myself."

We stared at each other for a moment, the air suddenly heavy between us. *It's all in my head. It's all in my head.*

I cleared my throat. "No problem. Anyway, I guess we'd better pay and head back."

CHAPTER NINETEEN

ROZ

I STOOD on the back deck, thermos of coffee in hand, surveying the farm. It was hard to believe all of this—hundreds of acres of fruit and Christmas trees, strawberry fields and green pastures—was mine. A hint of pine wafted on the southerly breeze. Now all I needed was for Fred to greenlight the investment and I could really relax.

A loud thump, followed by muttering, broke my reverie. I followed the noise to the side of the house. Dana was inspecting the locking mechanism on the door of the van we used to transport produce.

"Is everything okay?" I asked.

Dana turned, her cheeks pink and jaw clenched. "The door won't shut properly."

I gripped my thermos tighter. Everything around here kept breaking down. As I approached the van, I spotted a colorful assortment of flowers through the window.

"Are you heading over to Sapphire Blooms?"

Dana nodded. "Yeah, I've got to drop these off to Liv."

My pulse leaped. "I'll figure out the door and drive it

over. I know you've got a lot on your plate with fixing the irrigation to the strawberry fields."

Dana frowned. "Are you sure?"

"Yes, it's fine. I know I'm not much practical help around the farm, but this is something I can do. Besides, I owe you for the other night and the whole McKinley debacle." Insisting my answer was right *had* led to our defeat, after all.

But more than that, I wanted to see Olivia.

I stiffened at the thought. *It's just because I need to ask her something, that's all.*

"You don't want to give Ronnie a hand with Thelma and Louise?" Dana raised an eyebrow. "He's just heading over there now."

"News travels fast around here, I see." I pressed my lips together.

"Welcome to small-town life." Dana smirked. "Will may have mentioned your milk bath at the pub the other night."

I ran my hand over the side of the van door. "Yes, well, I think I'll let Ronnie stick to his area of expertise, and I'll focus on things I can actually help with."

"Just don't crash the van." Dana threw me the keys and winked. "We only have one of them. By the way, I like the new wardrobe."

"Thanks." I wasn't going to admit it to Olivia, but I'd been loving my new clothes. They were so much more practical than my usual attire. I'd even worn the ridiculous overalls yesterday when cleaning out one of the old barns.

I strode back into the house, grabbed a can of WD-40 and sprayed it at every conceivable section of the door that could be jamming. I yanked the handle, and after a moment of resistance, the door slid shut.

THE BELL to Sapphire Blooms announced my arrival with a loud jingle. Olivia stood behind the counter, wearing a green apron over a pink floral jumpsuit, her hair tied in a messy bun. Mason jars full of flowers sat in front of her. Brow furrowed, she added frilly red flowers to the jars.

I cleared my throat, and her head jerked up.

A slight frown flittered across her face before she broke into a smile. "Well, hello, Farmer Roz." Her eyes scanned me up and down. "How are you liking your new clothes? Any more mooning incidents?"

I snorted, heat burning my cheeks at the memory of Olivia's soft finger tapping my bare-naked butt.

"I'm pleased to report I have not exposed myself to anyone. And the clothes, they're... comfortable. And not dry-clean only, which is nice." Especially since I no longer had an assistant to take care of things like that. "How's your hat?"

"Very sun protective, thank you." Olivia plucked up another red flower and placed it in a jar. "Have you heard from Fred?"

I shook my head. "Unfortunately not."

Olivia's face fell, and my shoulders dropped. Olivia clearly wanted this whole arrangement to be over. Why did that bother me so much? I shook myself. *It's not personal. She just wants reassurance her business is safe, just like I do.*

"So what do I owe this visit to?" Olivia asked, straightening a purple flower that had flopped over.

"I've got the van outside with your delivery." I nodded my head toward Main Street. "Dana is very busy, so I thought I'd bring them over."

Olivia's eyes widened. "Oh, thanks. I'll come out and help you bring them in."

Once we finished moving the flowers into Olivia's climate-controlled storage room, I nodded at the mason jars. "Are these for a wedding?"

"No. I'm about to drop them over to Novel Gossip. They're for the café tables. George has been doing a great job at selling my candles, so I'm taking an extra box of those as well."

Olivia eyed a small metal trolley on the side of the counter. A large cardboard box sat on it.

"I'm probably being a bit ambitious trying to walk it all over at once. I might need to do two loads." She glanced at the clock on the wall. "Scrap that, I didn't realize how late it was. I'll just run the flowers over now and drop off the candles after I close. Sorry, I'd better hurry."

I took a step closer to the counter. "I can help. I can carry the box and you can use the trolley for the flowers. I've been meaning to check out the café anyway."

Olivia's face brightened. "Are you sure? That would be amazing. Although the box is fairly heavy. Lift it first and see what you think."

I bent down and picked up the box. It was heavier than it looked and my arms were sore from cleaning out the barn yesterday, but Novel Gossip wasn't far away. "This is fine."

"Excellent!" Olivia grabbed another red flower. "Let me just finish adding the ranunculus into the jars and then we can head off."

My arms burned as we walked down Main Street. I glanced over at Olivia, who was staring straight ahead, and cleared my throat. "I asked my architect to draw up revised plans of the events space, with your sustainability suggestions included. They're going to send them through this afternoon. I was wondering if you'd be willing to take a look? It would be good to get another pair of eyes on them and given many of the changes arose from your suggestions, I'd love to get your input. If we're both happy with them, I might forward them onto Fred as an excuse to prod him."

Olivia's eyebrows dipped for a moment. There was that hesitation again. Was she trying to think of an excuse not to help?

Olivia guided the trolley around a bump in the footpath. "I'm coming over to the farm on Wednesday to talk to Dana about planning for some upcoming weddings. Would that be too late?"

"No. That's perfect," I said, trying to ignore the pain in my arms.

By the time we reached George's café, my arms were shaking.

I pushed open the door with my back, letting Olivia pull the trolley through. As soon as she was inside, I tried to place the box gently on the nearest free table. It landed with a thud.

As I stretched out my arms, I took the opportunity to look around. It was nicely set up. Customers sat at circular wooden tables chatting or reading. Exposed red brick walls with floating bookshelves gave the café-bookstore a warm, comforting vibe. Aisles of books stretched back on the left side of the store. On the counter, there was a display of delicious-looking baked goods. My stomach rumbled. Even though it was still early, a line of customers was queued in front of the register.

George stood behind a large shiny red coffee machine on the counter, a tall man taking orders beside her.

"It looks like George and Ben are swamped," Olivia said. "Do you mind helping me swap out the flowers on the tables with the new ones, and we can leave that box with the candles in the corner for George to unpack later?"

I set to work taking the jars of slightly wilted blooms off the table and replacing them with new jars full of fresh flowers. My nose tickled. I really needed to remember to take my antihistamines.

"Olivia!" A woman with short gray hair approached us, peering over her glasses. "Is this your new employee?"

Olivia laughed. "No, Mrs. Harding. She's—"

"I am for the morning." I grinned. "Hi. I'm Roz Kennedy. When I'm not Olivia's assistant, I'm the new owner of Red Tractor Farm." I placed the jar I was holding on the table and extended my hand.

Olivia stared at me and blinked. "Mrs. Harding was my English teacher. She's also Blake and Jenny's neighbor."

"Nice to meet you," Mrs. Harding said, grasping my hand. "Olivia was one of my star students. I always thought she'd become a journalist or find some other way to use those skills." She peered over her glasses at Olivia. "Although, you've had quite a few careers already, haven't you, dear? Perhaps there's still time."

Olivia gave a small but firm smile. "I think I've found my calling with floristry."

"Back in my day, we usually just had one career, often with the same employer. But you millennials seem to love constant change." Mrs. Harding shook her head. "Although, Blake has been very consistent."

Olivia's hands tightened around the mason jar she was holding.

I jumped in. "Work is such an important part of our lives—it makes sense to take some time to find a career that you love rather than just sticking out the first one you choose for the sake of it. It's often hard to know what a job entails until you're in the trenches."

"Perhaps." Mrs. Harding's eyes lit up and she gave someone a wave. "My coffee date is here. Nice to meet you, Roz. I'll see you around, Olivia." She bustled off.

"Is everything okay?" I asked Olivia once Mrs. Harding was out of earshot. "She reminded me of a nosy math teacher I had in seventh grade."

Olivia nodded. "It's fine. I just didn't need the reminder about my chaotic career history before I've had my morning coffee."

"Well—" I started to say.

"Roz! Olivia!"

My heart jumped. I recognized that voice. *Fred.*

Olivia's gaze shifted behind me, her face breaking into a smile.

I swung around to find Fred holding a takeout cup and a paper bag, beaming. "Hi Fred! How's your house hunting coming along?"

I flung my arm out to wrap it around Olivia's waist. *Ouch.* Pain shot up my already sore arm. *What the...?* I glanced down. Our arms had smashed into each other halfway between us. Olivia must have had the exact same idea as me.

I chuckled awkwardly. "Sorry, babe." I slid my arm carefully behind Olivia's waist and squeezed.

"I haven't found anywhere yet," Fred said, eyeing us. "But there's a few promising open houses this weekend."

"Oh great! Well, at least you've found the best coffee shop in the area." Olivia smiled. "Always a top priority."

Fred laughed, his gaze dropping to the cart. "Are these your creations, Olivia?"

She nodded. "Yes. All locally grown at Red Tractor Farm."

"They look terrific, don't they?" I added, smiling at Olivia.

She faced Fred, her smooth cheek so close to mine I could see the fine hairs on her face and a smattering of light freckles. Maybe... Perhaps I should kiss it? As a little show of affection, for Fred's benefit. Yes. A quick peck on the cheek might make up for our clumsy embrace earlier. I leaned in, pouting my lips.

Olivia's head moved suddenly, a blur of pink, white and brown. My lips made impact with something soft, warm and pillowy. My stomach flipped, my eyes widening as I gazed directly into Olivia's deep-brown eyes. I wasn't kissing her cheek. I was kissing her lips. *Oh god.* Her lips parted slightly. My arm gripped her waist even tighter. Something clenched in my core. She smelled incred—

Bang!

Water sloshed over my leg. I pulled back, looking down. Shit. A mason jar, surrounded by water and flowers, lay shattered on the floor. Did I knock that over?

Olivia and I crouched down, and our heads collided. Pain reverberated through my skull. *Seriously?*

Fred grabbed the largest piece of the jar. "Here, let me help."

"Thanks, Fred. Between the two of us, we'll have this cleaned up in no time," I said as I collected the flowers between my fingers carefully.

"Don't mind us." Olivia picked up another piece of large glass, her cheeks flushed red. "We're always a hot mess until we have our coffee."

I nodded, placing the flowers carefully on the table. I'd already drunk my thermos of coffee this morning, so caffeine withdrawal couldn't explain my sudden bout of clumsiness. Or why my lips had lingered on Olivia's mouth. Or why I wasn't finding it difficult to compliment Olivia anymore. My head pounded.

"I'll go see if they have something to sweep it up," Fred said, hurrying off.

"I've got this," Olivia murmured, picking up another large shard of glass and delicately placing it in a small pile of glass she'd collected. "Why don't you check in with Fred when he comes back?"

"Here you are." Fred reappeared with a dustpan and broom.

"Thanks, Fred." Olivia grabbed it and began to sweep up the glass.

I clambered to my feet, wiping my damp hands on my flannel shirt and turned to Fred. "Do you have any more questions about the farm?"

"No, not yet. I've been too busy with work and house hunting." Fred picked his takeout cup off the table and took a sip. "But if I think of anything, I'll let you know."

Goddamnit. My cheek muscles worked hard to keep my smile in place. "No problem. You know where to find us."

"I should let the two of you get coffee before you sustain any further injuries." Fred chuckled.

"Lovely to run into you!" Olivia said as she stood up, the glass now swept into the dustpan.

"See you soon." *Hopefully, with good news about the investment.*

Fred walked out the door.

"That was a bit of a disaster," I murmured. "Sorry about the kiss. I was aiming for your cheek."

Olivia's face tinged with pink. "It's okay. I was just turning to look at you and was a little taken by surprise. But yes, we didn't do the best job. Hopefully Fred bought my story about caffeine withdrawal. Ouch!" Olivia sat down heavily on a chair and lifted her left foot.

"Are you okay?"

Olivia undid her sandal and inspected her foot. "I think I cut my toe on some glass."

"Is there any glass still in it?" I crouched down next to her, my eyes lingering on Olivia's slender ankle and then lower, to her elegant toes tipped with neatly manicured nails. I'd never been much of a foot person, but I suddenly understood their appeal.

Olivia peered closer. "I don't think so."

I leaned in, lifting her foot gently with my hand and staring at the drop of blood on the tip of her big toe. "I can't see anything either."

"That feels nice," Olivia said. I blinked, realizing I'd been rubbing the arch of her foot with my hand. I stopped, my head jerking up. She stared, a strange expression on her face. She pulled out her phone and frowned. "Shit. I really need to get back to the shop to open up. It's already past nine."

"Are you okay to walk?"

"Yeah. I'll be fine." Olivia stretched her feet.

I picked up her sandal and gently slid her foot inside. *Imagine what this must look like as an onlooker.* Heat shot up my cheeks. *Were we serving Cinderella and Prince Charming vibes?*

"Thanks." Olivia stood, then stepped in the puddle of water that had been left by the mason jar topple. "Shit. We'd better clean that up too."

I clambered to my feet. "Why don't you head back to the shop and I'll sort this out?"

Olivia tilted her head. "Are you sure?"

"Yes. I knocked it over. Go on, you head off. We don't want to keep your customers waiting." I shooed her with my hand.

"Okay. Thank you! I'll see you Wednesday." Olivia grabbed the cart and started walking toward the door. I ran to hold it open for her, watching her closely for any sign of a limp.

Satisfied she was walking normally, I closed the door and walked over to the counter where George was standing, frothing milk.

"George, do you have something I can use to mop up the water I spilled?"

George handed me a green-and-white striped dish towel over the gleaming red expresso machine. "Let me know if that's not enough and I can grab the mop. Is Liv okay? It looked like she cut herself."

I met George's worried expression and gave a nod. "She seems fine. She had to rush back to open up."

"Okay, good." George grinned. "While you're here, would you like a coffee?"

"Could I grab a long black to-go?"

George nodded. "Sure."

Olivia's forlorn face as she realized she'd run out of time to get a coffee flashed through my mind.

"And, um, do you know Olivia's coffee order? I might run one back to her."

George shot me a knowing look. "A triple shot latte."

My cheeks burned with heat. "I'll get one of those as well."

CHAPTER TWENTY

OLIVIA

BUTTERFLIES FLUTTERED in my stomach as I drove up the dirt road to Red Tractor Farm.

Why had I agreed to do this? I should have told Roz to email me the architect's plans. The memory of her soft lips touching mine at Novel Gossip on Monday, her elegant hands massaging my foot and then her reappearance at Sapphire Blooms twenty minutes later with a triple shot latte sent the butterflies fluttering at double time.

I sighed. There was no point denying it to myself. I'd developed a crush on Roz, which was exactly what I'd been trying to avoid. Unrequited crushes were annoying at the best of times, and this was definitely not the best of times. After our clumsy performance at Novel Gossip in front of Fred, I needed to keep my mind on the game. Not only that, but I had a massive wedding next week between a local politician and the owner of a chain of bridal boutiques. If it went well, it could be huge for Sapphire Blooms. *As long as we still have a supplier to fulfill all the potential new orders.* I clenched my jaw. That was exactly why I couldn't afford to get distracted by Roz.

I slowed as I neared the farmhouse and blinked. Someone was bent over the roses lining the front of the parking lot.

Was that...? Surely not.

It *was*. I'd know that outfit anywhere—I'd handpicked it myself.

Roz, dressed in overalls and a red flannel shirt, was pruning the roses. I pulled up next to her and rolled down my window.

"Ouch." Roz pulled her hand back from the bush and shook it. "Damn thorns."

I cleared my throat, and she turned, a scowl on her face.

"Nice morning for a prune," I said, leaning out the window, unable to keep the grin off my face.

Roz pursed her lips. "I asked Dana if I could do anything to help and she suggested *this*. Why anyone plants roses is beyond me. Very unpleasant."

"The gorgeous flowers make up for the thorns." A little like Roz—prickly but surprisingly sweet. *No. No. No.* My eyes dropped to her long, slender fingers. *Also a mistake.* I dragged my gaze away. "Didn't Dana give you gloves?"

Roz shook her head. "Just these." She held up the pruning shears.

"Well, I recommend getting a pair, stat."

Dana must still not be a fan of Roz, sending her out here without gloves.

Roz pressed her lips together. "I think there's some in the laundry. Dana is over at the flower fields. Do you want to talk to her first and then come back to look at the plans?"

"Sure." Happy to delay our meeting for as long as possible, I started the engine and continued on. The grass lining the road was surprisingly overgrown. Jim would never have let it get that long.

Next to the road, part way down the flower field, Dana was crouched over inspecting a red tulip.

She looked up as my shadow crossed her vision. "We've got aphids."

My stomach dropped. "Shit. How bad is it?" A severe infestation could destroy an entire crop of flowers.

"There aren't too many—yet. But I'll need to get on it before they multiply." Dana wiped her forehead with the back of her hand. "And did you hear that the heat pump in the greenhouse broke too, as well as the ride-on lawnmower?"

"Oh no! That explains why the grass was looking so overgrown." I wrinkled my brow. "And heat pumps are expensive." Another financial hit was the last thing the farm needed.

"Yeah. Thank god it'll be fairly warm for the next few weeks, so the flowers in there should be okay for now." Dana brushed dirt off her pants. "It feels like the farm is just falling apart since Jim left."

I crouched next to her and examined a yellow tulip. Dozens of tiny green aphids were crawling on its stem. "I can't help with the heat pump, but I'm going to Lowe's this afternoon to get more supplies for the store and can pick up some neem oil if you'd like."

Dana smiled. "That would be awesome, thanks. I'm run off my feet at the moment. Jim used to do so much around here whereas Roz is... Well, she's no Jim."

"I saw you had her pruning roses without gloves," I said, raising my eyebrows.

Dana smirked. "Yes, well." She stood up and straightened her shirt. "Look, Roz isn't my favorite person, but at least she's willing to get her hands dirty and learn more about farming. And she finally bought some sensible clothes, thank god. It was excruciating watching her walk around here in her fancy business suits." She led me down the field, beside a row of purple tulips. "I need her to succeed, otherwise I'm screwed. I did notice she seems to be taking interest in you." Dana glanced sideways at me.

"Me?" My stomach twisted. Shit. I had no idea if Dana thought we were dating or not. Probably not, or she wouldn't have been so open with me about Roz's failings. I should say something. Although, perhaps I should speak to Roz first, in case she wanted to control the message. Dana was her employee, after all. But was it weird not to mention it?

Dana shrugged, oblivious to my internal panic. "She wanted to do the flower delivery the other day. And whenever your name arises, I've noticed her ears prick up."

"Huh," I said noncommittally. That was interesting. "Oh wow, these hyacinths are incredible. They're going to look fantastic in the table centerpieces for the wedding next week."

"They're stunning, aren't they?" Dana tilted her head toward the old glass greenhouse, which was now used primarily as a workspace. "Should we head over and go through the orders?"

I RETURNED to a pile of thorny branches in front of the farmhouse, with Roz nowhere to be seen. I peered at the rose bushes. The cuts were neat, and she'd done a nice job thinning the bushes out. *Not bad.*

I walked up the stairs to the porch. The front door was open, so I tentatively poked my head inside. "Roz?"

"I'm in the study," Roz called. "Come in."

I entered the large room. Light streamed through the open window, which looked out over the grassy lawn and parking lot. Roz sat behind the imposing oak desk, plans spread out in front of her. She looked so... confident and in control.

"Take a seat," she said, flipping the drawings around so I could see them and gesturing at the wooden chair opposite her.

I sat down and poured over the artist renderings of a large, red brick building with floor-to-ceiling, black steel-framed windows. "Wow, these are great!" The architect had included the solar panels and rainwater collection system I'd suggested and it looked like most of the building would be constructed from sustainable materials.

Roz stood and walked around the desk so she was directly behind me. She leaned over and pointed to the large building. "So, this will now fit up to three hundred people and function as both an event space and a taproom." She moved her finger over to a smaller building, which looked like a barn. "And this is for the catering kitchen and storage." She pulled over another drawing of the event space's interior.

Roz's arm brushed against my shoulder. Damn, she smelled nice. I took a deep breath through my nose. Sandalwood and cedar with earthy undertones. *That would make an amazing candle. Eau de Roz.*

I shook myself, refocusing on the designs in front of me. My eyes widened as I studied the artist's rendering of the interior. Wooden floors, incredible views over the farm from the large windows and a soaring ceiling.

"This is amazing! I can't wait to see my flower arrangements here."

"Oh, good. I'm glad you think so. Do you have any other

thoughts?" Roz was so close to me that her warm breath tickled my cheek. *Don't turn around. Focus on the plans.*

I shuffled on the chair to create some space between us, bumping the paper in the process. We reached out to straighten the plans at the same time, our hands touching. I yanked mine away.

Roz looked at me. "Is everything okay?"

"Yes, sorry." I swallowed and returned my gaze to the plans. "Have they mentioned insulation?"

Roz nodded. "Yes. All the glass will be double glazed and the walls insulated."

"Great." I bit my lip. "From a design perspective, perhaps you could put a ledge across the back wall, to hold more flowers?" I pointed to the wall. "I saw something similar at a wedding I went to in a Brooklyn warehouse a few years ago. It would break up the brick wall."

I looked up at Roz, who was staring at my finger. We were only inches apart. She nodded and turned her gaze to me. Our eyes locked, and a shiver shot down my spine. Instinctively, I wet my lips. Roz was so close. And her soft, generous lips were so inviting. What would happen if I just leaned—

"Shit!" A loud yell cut through the silence. We flinched.

"What the hell?" Roz turned and sprinted out of the room. I jumped out of my seat and followed closely behind, my heart pounding in my ears.

Oh god. I hoped there hadn't been a terrible farming accident. Growing up in a small town and having a sister as a doctor, I'd heard enough stories about them.

We raced down the hallway, through Roz's kitchen and out onto the back deck.

Ronnie and Dana stood near the petting zoo, Ronnie

gesticulating wildly. I scanned them both, looking for any sign of injury. I couldn't see anything obvious from this distance.

"Is everything okay?" Roz yelled as we ran over to them.

"Thelma and Louise have escaped," Dana said. "Again."

I scanned their field. No sign of the cows. While the farm was fairly quiet today, having two cows on the loose, even if they were good-natured cows, was less than ideal. Despite that, I couldn't help taking a little jab at Roz. "You didn't sneeze again, did you?"

Roz narrowed her eyes at me. "Well, they must be around here somewhere. How long ago did they escape?"

"I'm not sure. I just noticed they were missing a minute ago," Ronnie said, his brow still furrowed in concern. "I don't know how the gate was open. I know I locked it this morning."

Roz froze, the blood draining from her face. "Shit. It might have been me. I went into the field earlier with the plans for the new buildings."

Dana's jaw clenched. "Well, we'd better find them ASAP before they cause any damage."

She'd just been telling me how busy she was. A cow search party was probably the last thing she needed.

Roz nodded, her face still pale. "Let's split up and search for them. Olivia and I will head over to the flowers and Christmas trees, and you two take the front of the farm and the orchards." Without waiting for a response, Roz strode toward a pick-up truck parked behind the house and jumped in.

"Sorry, I shouldn't have assumed you'd help," she said as

I eased onto the bench seat next to her. "If you want to leave, that's fine."

"That's okay. Maddie is working today and I've got a vested interest in ensuring Thelma and Louise are found without damaging the farm... or anyone on it."

As the truck bumped down the road, I scanned the farm. "They better not have stampeded any flowers."

"Surely they wouldn't have gotten that far," Roz said, gripping the wheel. We bounced over a pothole as we drew closer to the flower fields.

"Cows can run faster than you'd expect." I glanced at Roz. "So, Dana told me about the heat pump breaking."

Roz's brow wrinkled. "Yes. Very unfortunate. I'm going to hold off on fixing it until I hear from Fred about the investment."

"And she said the lawn mower isn't working either. I'm sure Prue would be happy to lend you hers while you're getting yours fixed. The grass is looking pretty overgrown."

Roz's frown deepened. "That's okay."

"Jim and Prue used to help each other out all the time. She won't mind at all. You could just borrow it for half a day."

"I don't like asking people for favors." Roz's fists tightened around the steering wheel.

I raised my eyebrows and was about to insist that it really wasn't a big deal when something brown in the distance caught my eye. My heart shot into my throat.

"Shit! They *are* in the flowers!" I pointed to where Thelma and Louise were standing, in the middle of the field. "Shit, shit, shit!"

Roz slammed on the brakes. I jumped out and sprinted toward the cows, running beside a row of vibrant-orange ranunculus. I slowed as I got closer to Thelma and Louise, not wanting to startle them and cause even more destruction.

Their heads were low to the ground, their eyes half closed and their jaws moving in a circular motion.

My stomach dropped. They were eating the glorious white and yellow daisies that we were going to harvest for the wedding next week. *Fuck.*

I approached Louise cautiously. She was the ringleader of the two. If I walked her out of the field, there was a decent chance Thelma would follow.

Roz came panting up from behind me. "Be careful."

"They're fine. Thelma and Louise wouldn't hurt a fly. I'm just worried about them stepping on the daisies. So, whatever you do, *do not sneeze.*"

"Why would you say that to me?" Roz asked, wrinkling her face. "You put the thought in my mind. Now my nose is itchy."

Louise looked at me with her big, brown innocent eyes and let out a friendly moo in greeting.

Roz flinched and jumped back. "Why don't I just call Dana and Ronnie so they can get them?"

I nodded. "Call them. We'll need reinforcements to get them back to their paddock. But I want to get them out of the field before they destroy all the daisies." I eyed the two bovines. "Thank god they have their halters on."

Roz stepped a few feet back and pulled out her phone.

"Hey, Louise," I said softly, reaching out for her halter and grabbing it. "Good girl."

I eased Louise between the rows of flowers toward Roz's truck. Thelma followed behind.

We'd just reached a patch of violets when Louise suddenly stopped, bent her head, and opened her jaw, snapping the heads off at least four of them.

"Not the violets, Louise," I yelped.

I tugged her halter, but she was intent on making fast work of the gorgeous purple flowers. Thelma stomped over a bed of tulips to join her. I winced.

"Dana and Ronnie are on their way," Roz said from behind me.

"I'm worried that, by the time they get here, Thelma and Louise will have eaten all the violets. Do you have any food in the truck we might be able to use as bribes? Bananas, apples, that sort of thing?"

"I don't think so, sorry," Roz replied. "Oh god."

I turned to find Roz standing still, her eyes closed and her face scrunched up.

"What's wrong?" I asked, my pulse quickening.

"I think I'm... going to... sn— AHH CHOOOO!"

I jumped as Roz's explosive sneeze reverberated through my ear drums. Louise's halter yanked out of my hand and she took off down the field, Thelma stampeding close behind.

"Keep off the flowers!" I yelled. Yes, it was completely futile and possibly counterproductive, but I couldn't help myself.

"It looks like they're mainly sticking to the furrows between the flowers," Roz said, a hand on her forehead shielding her eyes from the sun as her gaze followed their path.

"No thanks to you," I said as I broke into a jog.

"I wouldn't have sneezed if you hadn't brought it up." Roz picked up her pace to keep up.

"Calm down, I was just teasing." I squinted in the direction of Thelma and Louise. "On the plus side, it looks like they are almost out of the flower beds now." The roar of a truck sounded. I turned to see Dana and Ronnie driving up the road toward us. "And Dana and Ronnie are nearly here."

We jogged down between the flower beds until we were close to the cows, who were currently stomping on Dana's prized lilacs. I winced. Dana and Ronnie approached from the other side. Ronnie greeted Louise and pulled out some carrots from the bucket he was carrying. Louise looked up, gave another moo, and moved toward the carrots. Dana grabbed Louise's halter and together Dana and Ronnie led Louise out of the flower beds. Thelma followed closely behind. I exhaled. *Thank god.*

"Thank you," Roz said once we were all standing on the dirt road again.

"This isn't our first rodeo with these two escape artists," Dana said, stroking Thelma's neck as Ronnie attached a lead to each of the cow's harnesses. "We can walk them back if you two don't mind driving both of the trucks?"

Dana threw me the keys to their truck.

"I'll just stay here for a few minutes to assess the damage to the flowers," I said. "I have a bad feeling it's going to affect the wedding that's next week."

Roz stopped in her tracks. "I'll stay too. There was something else I wanted to discuss before you head off."

I tilted my head. We'd discussed the architect's plans. What else did Roz want to talk about? After my vivid thoughts about kissing Roz in the study, I was eager to put some distance between us.

Dana's gaze flitted between us. "Okay then. I'll see you later."

I began to retrace Thelma and Louise's path of destruction through the flower fields, Roz trailing behind.

Once Dana, Ronnie and the cows were out of earshot, Roz cleared her throat. "After our run-in with Fred at Novel

Gossip, I think we need to work on being a more believable couple. We're at a critical point right now. We can't afford to be head butting and generally being awkward around each other, especially when Fred could pop up unannounced at any moment."

I stopped and turned to her. "What exactly are you proposing?"

Roz pressed her lips together. "I'm not sure. Perhaps we could agree on some couple-ly things to do in front of Fred if he reappears?"

"Well, in the fake-dating movies they often..." I slammed my mouth shut. *What the hell was I thinking?* Telling Roz about the practice make-out scenes in fake-dating movies was a terrible idea. My gaze dropped to her lips. I swallowed. An absolutely terrible idea. I dragged my eyes away, refocusing my attention on the yellow tulips at our feet. They hadn't been trampled, thank god. And no signs of any aphids either.

Roz blinked. "Hang on a second. Fake-dating movies?"

My head jerked up. "Yeah, you know, like *The Proposal* or *10 Things I Hate About You.*"

Roz shook her head. "Never heard of them."

My eyes widened. Good lord. What planet did Roz come from? "What? Come on, you must have seen at least one fake-dating movie. You've seen *Pretty Woman*, right?"

"I don't have time to go to the movies. And when I do watch something at home, it's usually a documentary." Roz swatted at a fly. "So, you're telling me there are a whole lot of movies made about fake dating that might have helped us with this situation and you're just mentioning it now?"

I held up my hands. "I thought everyone knew. And I'm not sure how much help they'll be anyway. Most of them are rom-coms, so it's typically them just making a whole lot of silly mistakes and nearly getting their cover blown."

"Sounds familiar." Roz pursed her lips together, one corner twitching up.

A thought entered my mind and left my mouth before I'd had time to consider whether it was a good idea. "Well, what are you doing tonight? I could give you a crash course on fake-dating movies. Even if they're not useful, at least you'll be filling a gaping hole in your movie knowledge."

Roz's left eyebrow arched. After a moment of silence, she said, "You know, that's not a bad idea. It'll also give us something truthful to say if Fred pops around this week and asks what we've been doing. A movie night sounds like something people who are dating would do."

And something to avoid doing when trying to squelch feelings for your fake girlfriend. My stomach dropped. But now that I'd suggested it, I couldn't exactly take it back.

"Okay," I said, shielding my eyes from the sun behind Roz. "Should we meet at your place, around seven? We should be able to stream them on most of the apps." My apartment was a mess. Judging by the state of Roz's study, she was much neater than me.

"Sure," Roz said.

"I'll bring pizza. Was that all you wanted to talk about?"

Roz nodded. "Yes."

"Okay, great. Well, don't feel like you have to hang around with me. I'm sure you've got better things to do than fuel your allergies by surrounding yourself with flowers." Hopefully that didn't sound too harsh, but I really needed some time to myself. Away from Roz.

Roz stared at me for a moment. "I'll head back then. See you tonight." She turned and made her way back down the field toward her truck.

I exhaled and refocused on the flowers. My chest tightened as I reached the daisies. Petals were strewn on the ground, the heads of many of the yellow flowers missing, others crushed. Damn. I'd definitely need to rethink the flower arrangements for next week's wedding.

I trudged back to the truck. Could I use ranunculus instead? I'd need to talk to the couple to check if they were onboard. What a pain.

I glanced at my watch. I needed to get a move on if I was going to stop in at Lowe's, do an inventory check of the storage room and also get pizza for tonight.

The memory of Roz in the study earlier, bending close to me, smelling so damn good, came flooding back. What would have happened if Thelma and Louise hadn't escaped?

An image appeared, uninvited, in my head: me sitting on Roz's desk, naked with my legs splayed, as Roz, standing between my thighs, trailed kisses down my neck. A lick of heat unfurled from my core.

No, no, no. I shook my head. *Do not go there, Olivia.*

I'd order extra garlic on the pizza so I didn't get any ideas.

CHAPTER TWENTY-ONE

ROZ

I STARED AT MY WARDROBE, naked and still slightly damp from my shower. Shit. What was appropriate movie-night attire?

While my clothing selection had expanded considerably thanks to my shopping trip with Olivia, there was still a gaping hole when it came to clothing to socialize in. My options were a suit, my gym clothes or farm clothes. The memory of Olivia staring at me as I stepped out of my truck wearing Lycra on the day of the bike ride was still fresh in my mind. Gym clothes were definitely off the table. I pulled out a pair of charcoal gray suit pants and a white shirt and held them against my body in front of the mirror.

I sighed. No, that looked way too formal to eat pizza in.

Tan work pants and a red flannel shirt it would have to be.

Olivia's movie night suggestion had surprised me, especially given her strange behavior lately, but I was looking forward to having a distraction from worrying about the farm, especially after the discussion with the accountant I'd had earlier in the week. We didn't just need the funding to keep the flower farm going. We needed it to keep the entire business above water. A heavy sensation pulled at my chest. *There's no point dwelling on it now.*

My doorbell chimed. I flung on my shirt and pulled on the pants, then glanced at my reflection in the mirror. It would have to do.

Running my hand through my hair, I jogged down the stairs, slowing my pace as I approached the front door. I didn't want to be out of breath to greet Olivia.

I opened the door and blinked.

Mom and Dad stood in front of me, beaming. They looked like they'd come directly from playing tennis, both wearing white shoes and white polo shirts, Mom in blue capris and Dad in white shorts.

I folded my arms. "What are you doing here?"

"Nice to see you too, sweetheart," Mom said, pulling her sunglasses on top of her head.

Dad's gaze shifted to the perimeter of the parking lot. "Your roses are looking good, Roz."

Despite myself, my chest welled with pride. "I just pruned them." I refocused my attention on my parents. "So, what do I owe the pleasure of this impromptu visit to?"

"Ah, yes. Surprise!" Dad threw something at me.

Ouch. A small hard object hit my chest. I grabbed it just as it slid down my shirt.

Dad grimaced. "Sorry. I forgot about your poor reflexes."

I stared at the object in my hand and frowned. Were they playing some weird joke on me? It looked like the car key for my old car, just without any scratches on it.

"It's parked over there." Mom pointed in the direction of the parking lot.

My gaze fell on a shiny black Mercedes-Benz. My eyes narrowed. *They didn't.* "What's that?"

"It's your new car." Mom grinned. "Since your insurance company wouldn't cover it, we thought we would."

They did. My blood pounded through my veins with ferocious intensity.

I sucked in a deep breath, held it and then released it. *Stay calm.* "That is very generous, but you know how I feel about accepting gifts." Especially gifts worth hundreds of thousands of dollars from my parents, of all people. "And I'm quite happy driving the farm trucks around. It's a lot more practical than a Mercedes. Can you please return it?"

"Come on, Roz," Dad said, glancing at Mom whose smile was faltering. "Just take it. We want you to have it."

Mom nodded. "We have more than enough money."

"No. I—" A door slammed. I shifted my gaze toward the parking lot. Olivia jumped out of her car, wearing jeans and a light red sweater. She leaned back in and pulled out four pizza boxes. My eyebrows shot up. "Olivia has just arrived for dinner. I'm not arguing about this. I know you mean well, but I don't want the car."

"Hello." Olivia smiled as she approached the steps.

"Olivia!" Mom embraced her, nearly knocking the pizza boxes Olivia was holding to the ground. "Can you please talk some sense into your girlfriend? She—"

"Mom! That's enough! Don't rope Olivia into this."

"We just want you to be happy," Mom pleaded.

"Well, the car won't make me happy." I reached out and slipped the keys into the pocket of Dad's shorts. "Our dinner is getting cold. Would you mind leaving? We can talk about this some other time."

I put a hand on each of my parents' backs and led them toward the parking lot.

"Just think about it, darling. Surely you want a nice car when you're driving outside the farm?"

"Actually, no. I want people to take me seriously around here. Driving an overpriced luxury car is not going to aid that cause." I was surprised how little I'd missed my old car, and how little interest I had in getting a new one.

I opened the door to the Mercedes and ushered Dad in. "I'll see you at dinner on Sunday."

To my relief, Dad didn't put up a fight. Mom grumbled as I accompanied her to her car and she slipped into the driver's seat.

"We will talk about this more on Sunday." Mom gazed up at me and then yanked down her sunglasses.

"Bye, Mom." I closed her door and stood with my arms crossed until they both drove off, clouds of dust swirling up from the dirt road.

I hiked back to the house and up the front steps where Olivia leaned against the wall next to the front door.

"What was that all about?" she asked.

I grabbed the pizza boxes from the wooden floor of the porch next to Olivia's feet. "Just my parents trying to help me by giving me a new car I don't want."

Olivia turned her head to see Dad driving off in the car. Her eyes widened. "They bought you a new Mercedes-Benz?"

I shifted the pizza boxes in my arms, a comforting heat radiating through the cardboard. "Yes. I think their love language is gift giving. Unfortunately, gift receiving isn't mine. And their gifts are usually over the top and unnecessary. Like a new car that's completely impractical on a farm. I think it might be tied up in residual guilt for working so hard when we were kids and never being around."

"Yikes." Olivia grimaced, opening the front door wide.

"Yeah. They don't seem to have gotten the message yet that I don't need their money, despite me rebuffing their offers of help for the past twenty years." I watched Mom turn out of the long driveway, already feeling a little lighter. "I also don't need the judgement that would come along with accepting help from them. If I accepted the car, they'd be sure to comment if they felt I wasn't taking good care of it or if it got scratched." Or run over by another tractor, god forbid. "Anyway, sorry to keep you waiting. Let's go in." I strode through the front door. "This is a lot of pizza, by the way. Did you invite the whole trivia team over as well?"

Olivia chuckled as she followed me into the house. "No, I just wasn't sure what you liked so I got a selection. I don't know about you, but I like eating cold pizza the next day. So, I'm more than happy to live off the leftovers for the next two days. I assure you, none of this will go to waste."

"Hey, I'm not complaining." I grinned. Olivia's confident stride reminded me of the first time she'd come storming to my house, demanding to speak to me. It was hard to believe that was only two weeks ago. If someone had told me back then that we'd be having a movie night together, I would have laughed in their face.

"How's your foot?" I asked as I led Olivia through to the living room.

"It's fine, thank you," she said. "Although, if you were planning to offer me another foot massage, then, uh, yeah, it's excruciatingly painful." Olivia's cheeks flushed.

I laughed. "Well—"

"Oh, my God!" Olivia exclaimed, stopping in her tracks. "What is that?"

"What?" I asked, eyes darting around. Had a gigantic spider made a nest here or had Louise broken in and taken a giant dump on the couch?

Olivia pointed at the television, her eyes wide. "That TV. It's tiny. You didn't tell me I needed to bring binoculars. Is it from the eighties or something?"

Hmm. It was rather small. "Jim left it when they moved out, because they were getting a new one."

"I'm not surprised they upgraded." Olivia stepped forward and inspected it more closely. "Can you even get any of the streaming services on it?"

Oh, shit. I hadn't thought to check. I grabbed the ancient-looking remote and examined it. It didn't look promising. I pressed the power button, and the TV came to life. A news show blared. I winced. The sound quality was terrible and a black line flitted a quarter of the way down the screen. *Damn.*

"Uh, no, I don't think it does. I've never actually turned it on before. Sorry."

"So where do you watch your documentaries, then?" Olivia tugged at her handbag, looking around.

Heat pricked my neck. "My bedroom. I know it's not good sleep hygiene but there's nothing better than watching a good documentary about the Great Recession and then turning over and going straight to sleep."

Olivia snorted. "Jeez, that sounds *so* relaxing. I guess that would put me to sleep right away too." She took the pizza boxes out of my hands. "Well, I guess we're watching a movie in your bedroom then."

I followed her into the hall. I didn't love the idea of pizza crumbs in my bed, but it wasn't like there was another option. "Do you even know where my bedroom is?"

"No," she admitted, walking past the study and peering into the formal dining room.

"It's upstairs," I said, gesturing to the staircase at the end of the hallway.

Olivia strode ahead of me, bouncing up the stairs. On the second floor, I squeezed past and opened the door into the bedroom. *Thank god I made the bed this morning.*

"Wow, this room is huge," Olivia said, taking in the spacious room with its massive oak wardrobe, king-sized bed with a matching oak headboard, large TV on the wall and dark-green upholstered armchair by the window. I'd inherited all of the furniture except the TV from Jim, and while they showed signs of age—a few dents and scratches on the wood and faded upholstery—they made the room feel cozy and lived in. Olivia walked over to the window. "Oh, the view is incredible."

The window looked out over the farm, from the petting zoo all the way past the corn maze, orchards and flower fields to the Christmas trees. Orange and purple hues were spreading across the sky as the sun dipped behind the mountains, bathing the farm in the last of the evening light.

I smiled. "Yeah, I love it up here."

Olivia turned and looked at the bed, the smile fading from her face. "I'll sit in the armchair."

"You're welcome to sit on the bed. The TV is firmly stuck on the wall, so it would be an awkward angle to watch from the chair."

"I'll be fine." She placed the pizza boxes on the side table.

"I'll go grab some plates and drinks. What would you like? I've got wine, cider from Terry's Apple Orchards, beer, Coke, water..."

Olivia slid off her shoes and tucked them neatly under the bed. "A cider sounds great, thanks. I'll cue up the first movie. I narrowed my list of favorite fake-dating movies down to two and also selected one I haven't seen yet, so we'll need to make a start ASAP if we're going to finish at a decent hour."

"Sounds like a plan." I handed her the remote from the bedside table and ducked out of the room.

I returned a few minutes later to find Olivia sitting on my bed, leaning against its headboard. She was perched perilously close to the edge of the bed. I surreptitiously sniffed myself. Did I smell bad or something? All I could smell was pizza.

"I couldn't get the chair into a good position, so this will have to do," Olivia said.

I handed her a plate and a bottle of cider and then jumped onto the other side of the bed. "Okay, so what's first on the list?"

"*Pretty Woman*, followed by *The Proposal* and then *Love to Hate You*. The first two are old classics. *Love to Hate You* just came out, but I've heard it's great."

Olivia pressed play, and I bit into a slice of pizza—very garlicky, but delicious. If I didn't smell before this pizza, I would now. Julia Roberts appeared and I lost myself in the fun but incredibly improbable plot.

"Shit!" Olivia screeched.

I twisted my head just in time to see Olivia disappear off the side of the bed, followed by a loud thud.

I scrambled across the duvet and peered over the side of the mattress. Olivia lay groaning on the floor. "Are you okay?"

"I think so. I was reaching for my cider on the side table and suddenly toppled off the bed."

I slipped off the bed, leaned over Olivia and offered her my hand. "Let me help you up."

She gripped it and I pulled her up, studying her for any signs of injury. "Do you need an icepack?"

"No thanks. I think I just need my balance checked." She sat back on the bed.

"Well, perhaps if you sat a little closer to the center of the bed, you wouldn't fall out. I don't bite, you know. I just consumed an extremely garlicky pizza, so I'm definitely not a vampire."

Olivia laughed and scooted slightly closer to me on the bed. "Now, what did we miss?" She rewound the movie until we recognized the scene.

I was chuckling away at Julia Roberts enjoying the luxury hotel room when I sensed Olivia's eyes on me.

"What?" I turned to her.

Olivia paused the movie and grinned. "I don't know. I guess I just didn't expect you to be into it." She must have shifted toward me while I was watching, as she was even closer to me than she had been when I looked last. If I reached out, I could rub her thigh with my hand. I frowned. Why would I even think that?

I shrugged. "It's not terrible."

Olivia rolled her eyes. "By the way, what is your love language?"

I did a double-take, my head jerking back. "I'm sorry?"

Did Olivia's cheeks just flush, or was it the glow from the TV screen?

"Your love language... You said it wasn't receiving gifts. I was just wondering what it was—in case it comes up with Fred." Her eyes skittered away.

I tilted my head. I couldn't imagine Fred bringing it up, but Olivia seemed genuinely interested. We'd been getting along surprisingly well, so I didn't want to dismiss her question out of hand, especially with Matt's words still echoing in my head about being more personable. "I'm not sure." Definitely not gift receiving or words of affirmation. Sadie and my parents had seen to that. The pizza sat heavy in my stomach. "Perhaps acts of service and quality time? What about you?"

"I think I'm the same. And physical touch." Olivia was definitely blushing. She turned back to the screen and pressed play, breaking into a laugh as Julia Roberts teased Richard Gere. I couldn't help smiling. God, Olivia was pretty, all glossy hair, bright eyes and pink cheeks. And she had such an infectious laugh. I forced my gaze back to the screen.

Pretty Woman led to the next movie, and the one after that. I turned off the TV as the credits rolled on *Love to Hate You*.

"Well, they were all entertaining, even if they weren't full of helpful advice." I turned to Olivia, who was uncharacteristically silent. "Olivia?"

Her body was slumped against the headboard only inches from me, her eyes closed. Her chest rose and fell. Warmth welled inside me. I leaned over and removed her empty plate, then glanced at my watch. It was past midnight. Too late for her to drive home. Besides, if I woke her now, she'd feel really groggy. Better to let her be.

Not wanting to disturb her, I pulled a spare duvet out of my closet. I placed it over her, tucking the edges around her body. I yawned and lay beside her, my gaze running over her long, dark lashes and pink lips. I'd just rest here for a few minutes and then go sleep in the spare room.

CHAPTER TWENTY-TWO

OLIVIA

MMM. I snuggled into something warm. I sniffed. And it smelled so good. Like I was in a gorgeous forest, full of cedarwood. It reminded me of something. Was it one of my candles? No. Not a candle. Something else...

My eyes flashed open. *Oh shit.* The warm, nice-smelling thing I'd been snuggling into, that I had my arm flung around, was Roz. I froze for a moment before carefully removing my arm from her stomach and inching away from her. Thank god she was still asleep, dressed in the flannel shirt and pants she'd been wearing last night. My eyes lingered on her peaceful face, her blond hair flopped over her forehead. It felt so intimate, seeing her lying there, oblivious to my gaze. I dragged my eyes away.

What had happened last night? We'd been lying in the bed, watching *Love to Hate You*, and then... I must have fallen asleep. I winced. Hopefully I hadn't snored loudly or gotten too handsy while I was dead to the world. Why on earth had I suggested going to her bedroom? It wasn't until I was staring at her bed, my heart palpitating, that I realized what a terrible idea it was. Why did I keep putting myself in these situations?

I rolled silently to the side of the bed and grabbed my phone from the nightstand—7 a.m. I slipped off the bed and tiptoed to the window. Below, Thelma and Louise munched on grass in their field. Nearby, Ronnie was feeding the chickens. In the distance, a pick-up truck drove toward the fir trees. Only a few fluffy white clouds dotted the bright-blue sky. I liked my cozy apartment above Sapphire Blooms, but its view over Main Street had nothing on this.

A rustling behind me caught my attention. Roz was pushing herself into a seated position. My heart skipped two full beats. Her blond hair was mussed, her eyes bleary, but she still looked good. *Too good.*

"Sorry," she said, her voice thick with sleep. "You dozed off and I was going to sleep in the guest room, but I must have fallen asleep too."

"I should be the one apologizing for passing out on your bed," I replied. "Well, I'd better get going." I started toward the door.

"Unless you have to rush off, you're welcome to stay for coffee and breakfast," Roz said, then cleared her throat. "I don't want you driving home on an uncaffeinated empty stomach."

I stopped. Coffee would be nice. But I could do with getting some distance from Roz after our unplanned sleep-over. My head began throbbing. Perhaps some caffeine would help. I'd have a quick coffee and a bite to eat and then make my escape.

"That sounds amazing, thank you. I might just freshen up in the bathroom if that's okay."

"I'll grab you a towel." Roz opened her wardrobe and peered in. "Unfortunately, I think most of my clothes will be too big for you, but you're welcome to borrow a shirt if you'd like." She pulled out a blue flannel shirt I'd selected last week.

I looked down at my red sweater and sniffed. A distinct scent of garlic and pizza clung to it. "That would be great, thanks."

I'd only intended to splash water over my face, but after being provided with a thick, soft towel and a fresh shirt, the shower beckoned.

Once I smelled less like a walking vampire repellent, the scent of coffee drew me down the stairs and into the kitchen, where Roz stood over the stovetop, prodding something in a frying pan with a spatula.

She turned and grinned. My heart did that beat-skipping thing again.

"Does scrambled eggs with bacon, avocado and toast sound okay? I've also got granola, cereal, jam or peanut butter, if you'd prefer. Or last night's pizza." She winked at me. "Oh, and here's your coffee." She handed me a mug, her fingers brushing against mine.

I shivered. "Thank you." With my hands wrapped around the warm ceramic, I took a sip, the strong latte sliding down my throat. "This is just what I needed. And eggs and bacon sounds incredible." When was the last time someone cooked me breakfast?

I leaned against the kitchen island, watching Roz. The sleeves of her flannel shirt were rolled up, and the muscles of her forearm flexed as she flipped the bacon. I licked my lips. "Is there anything I can do to help?"

"Nope, I've got it all under control." Roz scooped up a large spoonful of scrambled eggs and placed them on a plate already waiting with toast and avocado. She added two pieces of streaky bacon and handed me the dish.

"Here you are. I thought we could sit out on the back deck."

Cool air hit us as Roz swung open the back door of the farmhouse. I took a seat on one of the wicker chairs overlooking the farm. Ronnie had disappeared and Thelma and Louise had drifted closer to the fence, perhaps to keep an eye on us. The soft cluck of chickens and the bleating of the baby goats provided a relaxing soundtrack to the morning.

I shoveled a forkful of creamy scrambled eggs into my mouth and groaned. Roz's eyes jerked in my direction.

Heat flooded my cheeks. "Sorry. This is really delicious." So much for a quick bite. I'd definitely be staying until I'd finished the entire plate of food. Between the coffee and the food, my headache was already subsiding.

Roz grinned. "The eggs were freshly laid—I ran out and got them while you were in the shower."

"Thank you, chickens!" I yelled in the direction of the petting zoo.

A rooster crowed back.

Roz chuckled. "Typical man, taking all the credit."

I snorted and pierced a strip of bacon with my fork. "So, what did you think of the movies last night?"

"Surprisingly enjoyable," Roz said after she'd swallowed her bite of toast.

"Oh good! I found it very difficult to narrow it down to three, so if you want to watch any more, I've got plenty of suggestions." My cheeks warmed for the second time in minutes. Had I just suggested another movie night? I didn't want to make a thing of this, especially not movie nights in Roz's bed. That felt... dangerous.

"That would be nice." Roz shifted in her seat. Her shirt rose up, revealing a strip of smooth skin above her pants. I yanked my eyes up. *Very dangerous.*

"I could invite some of the others. And we could all hang out... as friends." I cringed. It suddenly felt very important to clarify that. I took a bite of toasted sourdough, slathered with butter, and resisted the urge to moan again.

"I'd like that. To be friends." Roz's tone was stilted, but she looked genuine enough. "But I'll need to replace the TV in the living room before I can host. I don't think we could fit the whole trivia team in my bed—if that's who you were thinking of inviting."

I laughed. "Yes, it might be a little cozy. We don't want any more falls." I looked down at my plate and scooped up a chunk of avocado.

Roz placed her mug on the table. "You know I really related to Richard Gere in *Pretty Woman.*"

I looked up and snorted. "Why? Because you're so rich and handsome?" My neck prickled. Handsome? Why the hell did I say that?

Roz's lips twitched. "No. But thank you. Because he was a corporate player, focused on money and short-term gain, but then moved to a more rewarding, ethical business model."

I tilted my head. "So, were you a ruthless corporate raider before you moved out here?"

"Not quite." Roz stared out over the petting zoo. "But I helped my clients be ruthless corporate raiders. This farm feels like an opportunity to start things over and do things a bit differently."

I nodded slowly. "That makes sense. It must feel pretty incredible, knowing that this farm is making invaluable memories for thousands of children. Oh, and did I ever mention that both Blake and Jenny and Hannah and George had big moments in their early relationships here?"

"No. But I'd believe it. 'Red Tractor Farm, bringing

queer women together since 1886.'" Roz quirked an eyebrow.

I laughed again. "Hang on a second. If you're Richard Gere, does that make me Julia Roberts? If so, I'll take it." I tossed my hair behind my head.

Roz smiled, a warm, wide, breathtaking smile. Not the tight smile I'd captured in our selfie or the smirk I'd become so well accustomed to. My stomach fluttered. *Friends like making friends laugh.* Yes. But did they like it this much?

To distract myself from the fluttering, I jumped on the first conversation topic I thought of. "So, did you learn any fake-dating tips from our evening of research that you think we should implement?" I slammed my mouth shut. There was one, very obvious, answer—the one I'd thought of yesterday—that had featured in *Love to Hate You*. But surely Roz wouldn't suggest that...

"You were right that the movies were generally a crash course in what not to do when fake dating. But one thing did stand out to me." Roz's gaze was fixed on me.

I swallowed. "Oh?" I shoveled a forkful of egg in my mouth, hoping it might squash the flutters that seemed to be increasing by the second.

"We haven't really practiced being affectionate with one another. If we had some agreed moves that we'd prac-ticed, it might help avoid a repeat of the fiasco at George's. A bit like what I was suggesting yesterday."

My breath caught. I'd clearly underestimated Roz's dedication to saving the farm. But what types of moves was she proposing?

A slide deck of potential moves flashed through my mind. Roz pushing me up against the wall of a barn, her tongue exploring my mouth. Roz taking me bent over her study desk. Me straddling Roz in her bed.

Get a grip. She's talking about moves we could do in front of Fred. Not moves for a lesbian porn movie.

I swallowed and a chunk of egg got stuck in my throat. I tried swallowing again, but it felt as though my throat had constricted. My chest squeezed, my eyes watering.

"Are you okay?" Roz asked.

I raised my hands to my throat, panic flooding my body. *I can't breathe.*

"Shit!" Roz sprang up, lurching for me. "Are you choking? Try coughing."

I couldn't. *Shit. Shit. Shit.* This was how it was going to end: dying on a mouthful of farm-fresh eggs. I scrambled to my feet, dizziness washing over me.

Roz jumped behind me, her warm arms enveloping me. She thrusted into my upper abdomen with force.

Egg sprayed out of my mouth, covering the deck. I gasped for air.

Roz guided me back to the chair. She crouched down, studying my face. "Can you breathe okay now?"

I nodded, my cheeks burning. "Sorry. I think the egg just went down the wrong way."

"Here, have some water." Roz handed me my glass.

I gulped it down. "Thank you for that," I said once my heart rate and breathing began to slow back to their normal rhythm. "For both the water and saving my life."

"Anytime." Roz's lips quirked up. "That's what friends do for each other."

My shoulders relaxed as I took a sip of my coffee, watching a swallow swoop down onto the fence of Thelma and Louise's paddock. It appeared my near-death experience had distracted Roz from her previous topic of conversation. *Thank god.*

"Now that you're breathing again, I was saying that if

you're okay with it, I think we should practice a few moves we could do in front of Fred, just in case he appears again."

Shit.

"M-moves?" I swallowed again, thankful I only had saliva and no egg to contend with. "So exactly what are you proposing?" I tried to keep my voice casual.

Roz pushed her now-empty plate away. "Some moves we can do sitting or standing, depending on the circum-stances."

An image of me sitting on Roz's face sprang into my mind. A jolt of heat rushed over my body. *Not that kind of sitting. Good god.*

"Okay. Like what?" I looked at Roz for guidance. I didn't trust myself to suggest anything right now.

Roz's brow furrowed. "If Fred came up while we were sitting somewhere—like right now, for example—perhaps I could rub your leg affectionately? That's a thing people do, right?"

"I think so." I gulped down another mouthful of coffee.

"Do you mind if we practice doing it now?" Roz asked, leaning forward.

"Yeah, sure." Hands shaky, I placed the mug on the table. *It's just a friendly leg rub. For practice. For keeping up appearances.*

Roz's palm skimmed my thigh, soft at first, then firmer. I breathed out. That was nice. Warm and comforting. Why had I been so worried?

Roz tilted her head, as if she was trying to think of what else we could do.

An idea struck me. That seemed harmless enough. "Per-haps if you said something funny—"

"If?" Roz interjected, an expression of fake hurt in her face. "Don't you mean when?"

"Haha," I replied, rolling my eyes.

Roz wagged her finger. "Definitely don't roll your eyes at me. That doesn't scream 'I love my girlfriend.'"

"Well, I don't know, some couples like teasing each other. Maybe that's us." I arched an eyebrow. "Anyway, what I was saying is that if you said something funny, I could put my hand on your shoulder, look adoringly at you and laugh, like this."

I reached out and patted Roz's shoulder, letting out a forced laugh. Roz grimaced.

"Sorry. That wasn't great, was it?" I pressed my lips together.

Roz snorted. "It reminded me of my grandpa slapping me on the back when I was a kid."

"Grandpa is definitely not what I was going for." I brushed a piece of egg off my jeans.

"Okay, let's try that again," I said. "But it would help if you said something funny for real."

"Hmmm, the stakes are high. You want me to say something a-moo-sing?" Roz said, her lips twitching.

"Oh my god," I groaned. "As your friend, I need to tell you... That was terrible." I laughed again, and this time I rubbed my hand more gently on Roz's back. It felt warm and strong and suddenly, I had the urge to run my hand lower, to wrap my arm around her waist.

Roz held my gaze. "That's good, except for the fake laugh. But I'm sure whatever I say will be so hilarious you won't need to fake it."

I laughed for real this time.

"There you go." Roz leaned back, arms folded in triumph.

The space around me grew cold. "What else?"

She bit her lip, eyes skating over me. "Sometimes your

hair sort of falls down beside your face. Would it be too much if I leaned over and tucked it behind your ear?"

A warm glow lit in my belly. "That would be sweet."

She leaned over and brushed a strand of hair out of my face. It was such a small gesture, but her fingers skimmed my cheek and then my ear, sending a shiver down my spine. Our eyes locked. *Shit.* What would it feel like if she bit down on my lobe? *Olivia, get a hold of yourself.* Friends didn't have these thoughts. It had only been fifteen minutes since we'd agreed to be friends, and I was already failing miserably at it.

Roz pulled back as if I'd given her an electric shock. "Of course, given the circumstances, with Fred being a potential business partner, he wouldn't expect us to be all over each other in front of him."

"That's true." I couldn't blink, my eyes still locked on hers.

"If we were standing..." Roz continued, rising to her feet.

My breath hitched. *Standing like we had against the restroom wall at Pryde, her body pressing against mine.* My eyes flickered to her lips. *Stop it, Olivia. Don't look there.* But...

Roz held a hand out to me. "Would you be okay with a kiss on the cheek or if I wrapped my arm around you?"

"Yes." My throat thickened as she pulled me to my feet, my legs wobbly. "Do you... Do you want to practice that?"

"It's probably a good idea." Roz's blue eyes shone, her breath quickening.

My pulse raced as we each took a step forward, drawing close. *It's all the caffeine I just swallowed.*

A cough pierced the silence. "Good morning."

Roz and I jerked apart.

Dana stood at the bottom of the deck, eyeing my blue flannel shirt with one eyebrow arched. God, could we look any more like a stereotypical lesbian couple, standing here in matching flannel shirts? If she didn't think we were dating before, she would now.

"Sorry to interrupt. Roz, I just want to check if I can order a new fork for the forklift? It would be great to have it to help with moving the fence posts to fix the fence in the apple orchard."

Roz hesitated, just enough for me to notice. "Yes, that's fine, Dana. Go ahead."

"Great, thanks. Enjoy your breakfast, ladies." Dana's lips curved up into a knowing smile as she twisted around and strode away.

Once she was out of earshot, I turned to Roz. "By the way, did you tell her that we're dating—or fake-dating?"

Roz grimaced, her gaze following Dana. "You know, I don't think I did. Thank god it didn't come up when Fred was at the farm. But I think she has her suspicions now." Roz looked at me. "Where were we?"

"Um. We were going to practice wrapping your arm around me and a kiss... on the cheek." I flushed.

Roz nodded. "That's right. Stand over there." She pointed at the railing. "Face out."

Swallowing, I took the three steps over and rested my stomach against the top rail.

"I could wrap my hand around your waist, like this." Roz's arm encircled my waist.

I slipped my arms over hers, my throat dry. "Good. Much better than our attempt at Novel Gossip." I exhaled and relaxed into the embrace.

She was so warm and smelled so damn good. When this was all over I'd definitely need to create a candle to capture her scent. It would sell like hotcakes. I tentatively leaned my head back against Roz's shoulder. Unlike our bumbling efforts at Novel Gossip, this felt so natural. Like we were standing on the deck, as we did every morning after breakfast, admiring our gorgeous farm. We gazed over the fields, the corn maze, studded with tiny green seedlings, the dirt road and the petting zoo. A tractor putted in the distance. The fresh smell of grass wafted on the light breeze.

Roz moved, and suddenly soft lips were grazing my cheek. My eyes fluttered closed. That was nice. Very nice.

Knock. Knock.

I flinched. Was that someone at Roz's door? I pulled back and twisted my head to look at Roz.

"Are you expecting visitors?" I asked.

Roz shook her head. "It's probably my parents trying to offload the car on me again. Let's just ignore them."

"Hello?" a man's voice called.

I stared at Roz, my eyes wide.

It was Fred.

CHAPTER TWENTY-THREE

OLIVIA

"GOOD MORNING!" Fred stood on the front step of Roz's house, beaming at us. "I hope this isn't too early. I figured farmers are usually up at dawn, and the farm will be opening any minute now anyway."

"No, no, not at all. We've been up for a while now, haven't we, babe?" Roz gazed at me, wrapping an arm around my waist just as we'd practiced.

I leaned in slightly, smiling up at Roz before returning my focus back to Fred. "We have! Come in." I stepped to the side, ushering him in as if I lived here.

I suppressed a wide grin. We were acing playing a loved-up couple. It couldn't have been better timing, Fred appearing at Roz's place while I was here, the practice session fresh in our minds. If Fred had any doubts after our run-in at Novel Gossip, surely this would put them to rest.

"We were just sitting on the back deck, enjoying the view. Would you like to join us?" Roz asked.

Fred smiled. "That sounds delightful, thank you."

I followed Fred and Roz down the hallway. Was Fred

here to tell us his decision about the investment? My heart beat picked up pace.

We reached the deck and Roz pulled out a chair for Fred. "Please, take a seat."

I grabbed our empty plates from the table. "Would you like a coffee or tea?"

"A coffee would be lovely, thank you," Fred said.

"No problem." I ducked back into the kitchen, put our plates in the dishwasher and began opening cupboards, looking for a mug. Plates. Glasses. *Aha, mugs.* I grabbed a large one.

Now, where would Roz keep her coffee... I scanned the kitchen, my gaze falling on a large, shiny black espresso machine with an Italian-sounding name. *Hmmm.* I hadn't noticed it in Roz's kitchen earlier this morning. I'd clearly been too distracted by... the eggs and bacon. I stepped forward, examining it more closely. It had a lot of knobs and buttons, none of which were clearly marked. I frowned. Surely Roz had a French press or drip around? Even some instant coffee would do. I opened more cupboards, locating a stash of dark chocolate and a container of ground coffee, as well as a number of standard kitchen utensils, but nothing that would enable me to make coffee without using Roz's machine. I walked back to it, pulled out my phone and Googled the name of the machine. Surely, there would be an instruction manual online?

Aha! I clicked on a link that looked promising and zoomed in on the PDF document that opened. My stomach sank. It was in Italian.

I pressed my lips together. Why had I volunteered to make Fred coffee? I couldn't very well go back out to the deck and announce I didn't know how to use Roz's espresso maker. That wouldn't be in keeping with our claimed relationship history.

I went back to the search results, my eyes widening as I saw its price. Three thousand euros. Good lord. I kept scrolling down, only finding instruction manuals in Italian. Had Roz imported the damn thing from Italy? No wonder her coffee tasted so amazing.

I sighed and turned my attention back to the coffee machine. *You can do this.* I pressed the power button on and the machine lit up. Good. I placed the coffee cup under the machine and pressed a random button. The machine whirred to life. Okay, that sounded promising. Water started dripping out of the machine and into the cup. I peered into it, my brow furrowing. It was very watery. Once the liquid reached two-thirds of the way up the mug, I turned off the machine and studied the mug's contents. *Hmmm.* Perhaps if I added some milk it would look more like an actual coffee. I opened Roz's fridge, grabbed a gallon of milk and poured some in. It still didn't look great. I grabbed a soup spoon from a drawer, dipped it in the mug, sipped from the spoon and winced. *Ugh.* It was like warm, slightly milky water with dirt in it. I couldn't serve this to Fred. I poured it down the sink and rinsed the mug.

Sweat pricked my armpits. I didn't have all day to press every button on the damn machine. I needed Roz. I leaned against the counter, my mind ticking over, then walked back out to the deck.

"Sorry to interrupt, but I'm having a few issues with the coffee machine. Roz, would you mind giving me a hand?" Okay, that sounded casual and believable. Good work.

Roz jumped up. "Of course."

"I don't have a clue what to do," I muttered as soon as we were in the kitchen and out of earshot.

"Ah, yes. Do you want one too?" Roz reached for the mug.

I shook my head. "I'm all good, thanks."

Roz pulled a handle thing out of the machine and emptied it, opened the cupboard, pulled out the container of ground coffee, refilled the handle, pressed a few buttons and before long, the machine was humming and a steady golden stream of coffee poured into the mug.

"There you go. I'll let you hand it to Fred."

Our fingers touched as Roz handed me the mug, sending warmth shooting down my arm.

"Do you think he's made his decision?" I murmured.

"Yes. He just told me that's why he's here."

Our eyes locked and the enormity of the situation sank in. The moment we'd been working toward for the last two weeks was finally happening. The future of Sapphire Blooms and Red Tractor Farm would be revealed any minute. My stomach fluttered with nerves.

We walked back outside together and sat back down on the wicker chairs. I handed Fred his mug.

Two small children ran past, screaming with excitement, a man jogging after them. Despite my nerves, I managed a smile. The farm was open for business.

Fred took a sip of his coffee and leaned forward. "So, as I was saying to Roz, I've reached a decision about the investment."

I clutched my mug, my heart pounding, and took a steadying breath. *Oh god.*

"And I've decided that I'd love to come on board as an investor." Fred beamed at us.

My heart leaped. "That's fantastic news!"

Blinking away happy tears, I placed my mug on the table before I splashed it all over me in excitement.

"I'm so happy to hear that, Fred." Roz was smiling ear-to-ear. "I won't let you down."

I fought the urge to jump up and fling my arms around her. We'd done it. Sapphire Blooms was saved. The farm was saved. *Thank god.*

A ring tone sounded. Fred pulled his phone out of his pocket and frowned at the screen.

"Apologies, I'd better take this one." Fred jumped out of the chair, and walked down the back steps of the deck, holding his phone to his ear and his coffee in his other hand. He strolled down the side of the house and disappeared out of view.

I stood up, my body still buzzing with adrenaline at the news.

Roz rose to her feet and stepped over to me. She wrapped her arms around my waist, pulled me to her and then swung me around, laughing. I was giddy. Giddy with the news the flower fields were safe. Giddy from being swung around. Giddy at Roz's uncharacteristic show of excitement. I joined in, laughing, and circled my arms around Roz, squeezing tight.

"I can't believe it!" I pulled back to look at Roz's beaming face.

Our gazes locked. Her face was only inches from mine. Her mouth, red and soft, was only inches from mine. My pulse quickened, my tongue darting out to wet my lips. Were we...? Adrenaline shot through my body. Goddamn, I wanted to. I really wanted to.

Her eyes drifted to my mouth, and I leaned in.

Our lips locked.

Tingles zapped through all the way down to my core. Our bodies pressed together. I closed my eyes, a soft whimper escaping my throat as Roz's tongue teased my lips apart. My mouth parted, my body turning into a puddle of molten lava as our kiss deepened. *Oh god.*

Roz's hand cupped my cheek. She let out a small moan, sending my stomach swooping. I fisted the back of her flannel shirt with my hand.

Kissing Roz was just as amazing as I'd remembered. My mind felt like mush. Why hadn't we been doing this all along?

My mind cleared enough for the reasons to bubble up. *We are friends and, until very recently, enemies. Roz doesn't want a relationship. I do.*

My eyes snapped open. My cheeks flaming, I disentangled myself from Roz's arms, and focused on tugging down my shirt, which had ridden up slightly during the kiss. What the hell were we doing?

We'd just gotten carried away in the moment. It didn't mean anything.

I studied Roz's face for clues as to how she was taking this development. Her cheeks were flushed, her breathing labored. She reached out her hand and my breath hitched. *What is she doing?* She gently swiped her thumb across my cheek, her gaze soft.

"You had a little egg on your face," she murmured.

I swallowed. "Oh. Thank you."

Movement behind Roz caught my eye. Fred was heading back toward us. I stepped away from Roz and straightened my shirt.

"Sorry about that, ladies," Fred said as he sprang back up the stairs. "A work emergency. Unfortunately, I have to head back to my bed and breakfast to sort it out, but I'd love to celebrate tomorrow night if you're both free? I've heard good things about Rivers Edge."

"That sounds lovely." Roz glanced at me. "Are you free then, babe?"

"Yes. I'd love to come," I said, smiling. My only plans this weekend were working and catching up with my brother and his family who were in town.

We shook hands with Fred and walked him back to his car.

I exhaled loudly as we watched Fred drive off down the dirt road. "What a relief."

Roz nodded. "I just wish he hadn't suggested dinner."

I glanced at her. "Why?"

Roz scratched her hand. "Until the investment documents are signed, Fred can pull out. I'm worried about just the three of us spending so much time together tomorrow night. There's a lot of opportunity for us to slip up."

"We've come this far. Surely we'll be fine," I said as we began walking back toward the farmhouse. "I thought things went pretty well this morning, all things considered."

"But that's exactly it." Roz frowned. "We're so close now. What if we fuck it up and lose everything?"

CHAPTER TWENTY-FOUR

ROZ

I HIT the turn signal and pulled up in front of Sapphire Blooms. As the truck slowed, the door to the store flung open and—*oh boy*.

Olivia stepped on the sidewalk in a black dress that hugged her curves, giving a hint of cleavage and a lot of leg. Her hair was piled on her head in an elegant updo. She smiled at me, raising her hand in greeting, and my stomach fluttered. *It's just nerves about the dinner with Fred.* But why did I feel like a high school senior taking the hottest girl in my class to prom?

Perhaps it has something to do with the kiss yesterday? I clenched my jaw. That had been... that had been a mistake. A mistake I couldn't stop thinking about.

Olivia's gaze shifted to the front of the truck, her eyes widening. Shit. I slammed on the brakes only seconds before I would have rear-ended Olivia's car. The truck jerked, throwing me forward, and came to an abrupt stop.

"Hi! That was close." Olivia jumped into the passenger seat. For the first time in weeks, I wished I had my old car. This battered pickup truck didn't do Olivia's outfit justice.

"Hello. You look—" I swallowed. Stunning? Hot? Sexy? No. They were all too much. "Good."

Her gaze dropped down my suit and back again. "You scrub up pretty well yourself."

"Thanks." I started the engine and began the drive down Main Street toward Rivers Edge. The sun had almost disappeared behind the mountains. Pink, purple and gold-tinged clouds stretched across the sky.

"How are you feeling about tonight?" Olivia asked as we passed the pub, two men doubled over laughing on the front steps.

"I'll be glad when it's over. But I think we've done all we can—hopefully our practice session yesterday will pay off."

We reached the end of Main Street, and I did a quick right and then left turn, pulling into the Rivers Edge parking lot.

Once the engine came to a halt, I turned to look at Olivia. This was it. Our last hurrah as a fake-dating couple. The last hurdle before Fred signed on the dotted line.

Olivia broke into a small smile. "We'll be okay." She reached out and squeezed my hand.

I ignored the tingle on my skin from her touch. "I hope so. I guess we'd better not keep Fred waiting."

Inside, Fred sat at a table next to the floor-to-ceiling windows that provided a stunning view of the sunset that had deepened to dark purple and red. Its reflection rippled on the water.

"Sorry we're a few minutes late," I said as we reached him. I rested my hand on the small of Olivia's back, trying not to let the warmth of her body distract me from Fred.

"No problem." Fred beamed. "I've just been enjoying the view and a glass of champagne." His smile widened. "It turns out we have two things to celebrate tonight. Our new business arrangement and my new house! I bought one in Sapphire Springs today." He reached for the bottle of champagne that was sitting in the ice bucket on the table. "Would you each like a glass?"

"Congratulations!" Olivia said as we sat down. "I'd love one, thank you."

"Roz?" Fred angled the bottle over a glass.

"That would be great, thanks. And congratulations on the house. That's fantastic news." As Fred handed me a glass of champagne, my stomach swirled. I knew he was looking but hadn't realized he would move so quickly. *It's just a vacation home. He'll probably hardly ever be there.*

I sipped my drink and glanced at Olivia. She was asking Fred something, leaning forward, her eyes bright with interest. She laughed at his response, her eyes crinkling. My insides fizzed. *It's just the champagne.*

I took another sip. Perhaps I should rub her thigh, just like we'd practiced. Yes. That was a good idea.

I reached out and placed my hand on her thigh, just below the hem of her dress. Her skin was smooth and deliciously warm. I moved my hand toward her knee and back again. Maybe I'd just leave it there, for a little while. I shifted my chair closer to Olivia so I could rest my hand there comfortably.

"So, when will you get the keys to your new house?" I asked Fred.

"Not for another three months. The sellers wanted a long settlement period."

"Well, when it's time, you're very welcome to borrow one of our trucks or our van to move if that helps." Three months. Assuming tonight went well, by then I'd well and truly have Fred's investment and Olivia and I would have officially broken up long ago. I shot a glance at Olivia and my chest tightened. We'd agreed we were friends, so I'd still see her around. Not only that, but I was her key supplier. There just wouldn't be any reason to massage her thigh like I was doing right now.

"Are you ready to order?" a young woman dressed in black asked.

I looked down at the menu in front of me. "Sorry, we haven't—"

"I was thinking we could do the chef's tasting menu," Fred chimed in. "If that's okay with the two of you?"

I scanned the menu and my stomach dropped. An eight-course tasting menu? We'd be here for hours. And the longer we were here, the more opportunity we had to screw things up. I forced my face into a smile. "That sounds great. It takes the pressure off having to decide."

"Any dietary restrictions?" the woman asked.

"Olivia is allergic to pineapple," I said, pleased to show off my knowledge. I patted Olivia's thigh.

"Thanks, babe." Olivia smiled at me, placing her hand on my hand. She squeezed, sending a rush of warmth up my arm and into my chest.

My eyes dropped to her cheek. Now was as good a time as ever. I leaned in, pressing my lips to her smooth cheek. Mmm. I wanted to do that again. And again. But that would be too much, wouldn't it?

"Olivia?" a woman's voice broke the moment.

Olivia's eyes widened. Oh god. What now? I twisted my head. A man and a woman weaved between the tables in our direction.

"Dave! Rach!" Olivia stood, her face flushed, and gave them both a hug.

Olivia turned back to the table. "This is my brother, Dave, and my sister-in-law, Rachel. They're visiting from

New Jersey this weekend. And this is Fred and Roz, of course." Olivia's cheeks turned an even darker shade of pink.

Dave's brow furrowed, his eyes darting between me and Olivia. *Oh shit. They don't know.* Had they seen me kiss Olivia on the cheek? Would Fred think it was odd if Olivia's own brother didn't know who I was? Should I pretend I already knew them? *Fuck.* My heart thumped loudly.

Fred and I rose to our feet. Fred reached out and shook their hands. In usual circumstances, I would shake someone's hand when greeting them for the first time. But nothing about this was usual. I took a deep breath and went in for a hug instead, fighting the urge to say it was nice to meet them in case it set off alarm bells for Fred. "Hello." That was safe, right?

"I thought you were having dinner with Mom and Dad tonight?" Olivia shifted uncomfortably on her feet.

"They offered to look after the twins so we could have a date night. We got here at 5:30 and we're just leaving to save them from the nightmare that is bedtime." Dave grimaced and turned to Fred and me. "We have six-year-old twins."

Olivia laughed, but it sounded a little strained. "Well, good luck with that."

Rachel's gaze dropped to my arm and her eyes widened. Shit. My hand had made its way back to the small of Olivia's back without me even noticing it.

Dave straightened the cuff of his sleeve. "We'll let you enjoy your dinner. Assuming we survive tonight, we'll see you Sunday, Liv."

"Nice to meet you both," Rachel said, smiling at me and Fred.

My eyes shot to Fred. If he'd registered Rachel's

comment suggesting we'd never met before, he showed no sign of it. *Thank god.*

We waved goodbye to Rachel and Dave and were taking our seats when a man cleared his throat. "Your first course, a black garlic and caviar macaron."

The server placed a large plate with a tiny black macaron on it in front of me. Okay, if all the courses were this minuscule, perhaps we wouldn't be here all night long.

I popped the macaron in my mouth, eyes widening as a kaleidoscope of flavors and textures exploded in my mouth. "Wow. That's incredible."

Fred leaned over and grabbed the bottle of champagne from the center of the table. "I thought it would be nice to do a toast to celebrate our new partnership."

He refilled our half-empty glasses and then lifted his own glass high and cleared his throat.

"Over the past two weeks, Roz—and you too, Olivia—has made a very convincing business plan for my investment in Red Tractor Farm."

Olivia placed her hand on my thigh and smiled at me.

"And while the facts and figures you presented have certainly been compelling and I've also been impressed by Red Tractor Farm's commitment to sustainability, the deciding factor for me was always going to be you." Fred fixed me with his gaze. "With this investment, we're entering a long-term business relationship. Before I made my decision, I wanted to make sure all the key building blocks of a good relationship were there. Trust, communication, respect and shared values. From our friendship over the years, I thought they would be, and all our interactions over the past few weeks have confirmed that for me. I'm confident that, together, we will make Red Tractor Farm a success. So, I wanted to raise a glass and say

cheers. To Red Tractor Farm and long-lasting relationships!"

"Cheers," Olivia and I echoed, clinking our glasses

Guilt twinged in my chest as I sipped my glass of champagne. Trust, communication, respect and shared values. If
Fred ever found out about Olivia and I... I squeezed Olivia's
hand. *He won't. We just need to get through another seven
courses and then we'll be safe.*

We moved on to discussing Fred's vacation plans as one
mouthwatering course after another was delivered to our
table. The tension in my shoulders dissipated.

As the server cleared the plates for the eighth and final
course—a pistachio soufflé—Fred yawned and glanced at his
watch. "I'm clearly getting old. It's not even ten o'clock and
I'm ready to hit the hay. But don't feel you need to leave too.
The night is still young."

Olivia glanced at me, a questioning look in her eyes.

I nodded. "We might stay here and grab another drink.
Thanks so much, Fred. I'll definitely do everything I can to
make your investment a success."

"I don't doubt it," Fred said, his voice warm. "I'll have
my lawyers send over the documents. Knowing them, it'll be
at least a week or two. They're very fastidious but not the
fastest group around."

My chest tightened. A week or two? Until the investment documents were signed, Fred could still back out. But
surely nothing could go wrong now. Fred had made his
decision. We survived our celebratory dinner. He was
heading back to the city tomorrow. Now all that was left
were the formalities.

We stood to say goodbye to Fred. Once he left, we
slumped back in our seats and looked at each other.

"Thank god that's over," Olivia said, lifting her water

glass and taking a sip. "I nearly had a heart attack when Dave and Rachel appeared."

I groaned. "I take it you haven't told them about the fake-dating situation?"

Olivia shook her head. "But I'm sure Mom and Dad will fill them in when they get home."

"Apart from their unexpected arrival, I thought it went pretty well. All our practicing paid off." My hand was back on Olivia's thigh again, our legs pressing together. I swallowed. We didn't need to pretend anymore. "Should we just go order at the bar?"

Olivia nodded and stood.

At the bar, we waved down the bartender. "I'll have a smoked Manhattan and..." I looked at Olivia who was studying the cocktail menu.

"A paloma for me, thanks Sam," Olivia said.

We leaned against the bar, waiting for Sam the bartender to work her magic.

A curl of hair had fallen from Olivia's updo, resting against her cheek. I reached out, gently brushing it behind her ear. Goosebumps pricked my neck.

Olivia smiled. "Very nice. Just how we practiced it."

"You know, I think we did all the moves we practiced yesterday, except one." I grinned.

"Oh?" Olivia raised her eyebrow. "We definitely did a few leg rubs." There had been a *lot* of leg rubbing. "And I did put my hand on your shoulder and laugh at your joke about horses, which was terrible, by the way."

I crossed my arms. "Fred thought it was hilarious."

Olivia pressed her lips together. "So which one didn't we do?"

I disentangled my arms, wrapping my left one around her waist and pulling her to me.

"Ah yes." Olivia laughed, wrapping her right arm around my waist.

My pulse quickened. I'd demonstrated the move. Now was the time to let go. But it just felt so right. *And Olivia is not letting go either...*

After tonight, there'd be no more reason to touch Olivia. My chest hollowed. *There's no reason to touch her now. Fred is gone.*

Perhaps this was just a friendly embrace. We were friends now, after all. *Friends who kissed yesterday.*

Olivia smiled, looking at me with her gorgeous brown eyes framed with dark lashes.

Did someone just turn up the heat in here? I tugged at the collar of my shirt, my eyes dropping to her soft, red lips.

A rush of desire flooded over me. I wanted to kiss her.

I wanted to do more than kiss her... things that friends definitely didn't do to each other.

Oh shit.

I slowly lifted my eyes to meet her intense gaze. Her arm was still around me, her breathing heavier than usual. Was she feeling it too, or was I misreading the signs?

I clearly misread the signs at Pryde. Maybe it's happening again.

I blinked as the memory jolted through me. Why had she never called me? The question that had been percolating in the back of my mind—and sometimes in the front of my mind—for over six months suddenly felt urgent. *Don't do it. You won't like the answer.*

"Olivia." My voice was low.

Her neck bobbed gently with a swallow. "Yes."

"Why didn't you reach out to me after that night at Pryde?"

She pulled back, frowning at me. "What? Why would I

have called you? You left without a word. Even if I'd wanted to, I had no way of contacting you."

My brow furrowed. "You didn't get my note?"

"Note? What note?"

I stared. "The note I left with Brenda, apologizing for running out, asking if we could raincheck?"

Olivia's eyes widened. "You left a note with Brenda?"

"You didn't get it?"

Olivia shook her head, the curl springing free from behind her ear again. "When I got out of the restroom, both you and Brenda were gone."

"Oh shit." It had never even crossed my mind that Brenda might not have delivered my message.

"What did your note say?"

"Something along the lines of: *My niece has been rushed to hospital. I'm sorry to run off, but can we take a raincheck?* It was the night Lottie got appendicitis. Mel had just left and Matt called from the ambulance, freaking out."

We stared at each other, realization slowly sinking in.

Olivia stepped forward, filling the void between us. She was so close now, her gaze electric. My entire body vibrated with anticipation.

"So, you weren't so repulsed by me that you ran away?" Olivia studied my face.

I lifted my hand and stroked her cheek with my thumb, tucking the curl back again. "God no. I haven't been able to stop thinking about that night, about you, since it happened."

Damn. She was so beautiful. I wanted to kiss her again so badly.

I leaned in, my heart pounding.

Olivia leaned closer too.

Oh. My eyes fluttered shut as I lost myself to the softness of Olivia's delicate skin. Our lips parted at the same time, hot tongues slipping into each other's mouths. I grasped her hips, pulling her closer to me. She felt so damn good. Her breasts pressed against mine and I fought the urge to let my hands to wander down to the curve of her bottom.

Through the waves of desire, alarm bells rang through my hazy brain. This was real. Not faked for Fred or the result of us getting carried away with excitement. Was it really a good idea?

Olivia moaned softly, sending a bolt of heat to my core. *Fuck.* Perhaps we just needed to finish what had been started that night at Pryde and then move on with our lives. My core throbbed with need. *Yes. Just one night.*

I swallowed. "So, how about that raincheck?"

CHAPTER TWENTY-FIVE

OLIVIA

MY HANDS TREMBLED as I fumbled with my key in the door.

Goddamnit. My body had become so attuned to Roz's presence I could sense her standing behind me, watching me.

After what felt like an eternity, the door to Sapphire Blooms swung open.

We stumbled inside, Roz slamming the door shut. I reached out and turned the lights to the back of the store on. A warm glow lit Roz's face, the hunger in her eyes on full display. The same hunger was gnawing at me, a desperate ache making me too impatient to suggest we retreat to my bedroom upstairs.

She grabbed me by the hips and pulled me to her. The warmth of her body, the curves of her breasts against mine sent my arousal, already high, skyrocketing. I tugged at her white shirt, slipping my hands underneath and pulling her even closer.

"I've been waiting for this moment for over six months," she murmured in my ear. The hairs on my neck prickled.

What the hell am I doing? Roz kissed my neck, sending a shudder down my spine. *I don't know. But it feels so right.* She kissed me again. Maybe the problem was that I had never gotten the one-night stand I was promised. I closed my eyes and let out a shaky breath. Yes. That was most likely the problem. We'd have one night together, and then I'd focus on finding someone who actually wanted a relationship.

Roz's lips trailed down to my collar bone and I gulped. What if I didn't know what to do? What if I was terrible? At Pryde, Roz seemed like the perfect candidate for my first time: an experienced older woman who lived in a completely different city. But if I embarrassed myself now, there'd be no avoiding her. Run-ins at Novel Gossip, visits to the farm, walking down Main Street. And I knew her now. I cared. The pressure weighed down on me.

"Is everything okay?" Roz murmured into my neck. "Do you want to go upstairs?"

"No, it's not that..." I cleared my throat. "Um, in case it's not clear from what I said earlier, this is my first time with a woman."

"Well, I better make it fucking incredible then." Roz walked me backward until I was pressed against the front door. She took my hands in hers and pinned them over my head.

A groan of pleasure escaped me.

"You like that? Me taking control?" Roz asked.

"Yes," I whimpered.

"Excellent," Roz rasped. "But tell me to stop any time you want, okay?"

I nodded, my entire body quivering with anticipation for what would come next.

Roz released my hands and took three steps back, a rush of cool air filling her place.

I furrowed my brow, stepping forward. "What are you doing?"

Roz smirked. "Take your dress off."

The hunger flared in Roz's eyes again, and a shiver shot down my spine. The idea of stripping down under Roz's unwavering gaze was a surprising turn-on.

Keeping my eyes fixed on Roz, I slowly reached for the zipper at the back of my dress and tugged it lower, letting the top of my dress fall, exposing the black bra I wore underneath. My breasts tingled with anticipation.

Her eyes dipped to my chest. "Keep going." Her voice was hoarse.

I tugged the zipper down farther until it slipped off my hips and onto the floor.

"Mmmm," Roz murmured with approval as her eyes lingered on my body. "Now... take off everything else."

My breath caught as I unclipped my bra, dropping it on the ground. I slipped off my panties, and then stood there while Roz drank me in. The ache between my legs was almost unbearable now, and all Roz was doing was looking me up and down, gazing at me as if she wanted to devour me.

I hoped the light was dim enough that she couldn't see the desperation in my eyes.

Roz took off her jacket and threw it on the counter.

"Good girl," she said. "Now, come here."

I took two steps, my legs weak. She lifted her hands and trailed those long, delicate fingers over my breasts, twirling my nipples with her thumbs until they hardened.

"Your breasts are incredible," she said, her voice low,

looking at them with wonder as she continued to caress them, every so often gently pinching the pink pebbles.

I moaned, my mind hazy. I'd never been so turned on.

"Can I..." I tugged at her shirt.

She nodded. "Only my shirt to start with."

With trembling hands, I unbuttoned her shirt, my breath catching at the sight of the small curves of her breasts encased in a plain white bra. I bit my lip, tracing a finger around the upper seam of the bra.

Still teasing one of my breasts with her hand, Roz slid her other hand down my stomach and trailed her fingers in patterns around my inner thigh. Her hand was so close to the ache that was now becoming all-consuming.

"Eyes up," she directed.

As I looked up, her face was suddenly illuminated by the lights of a car driving down Main Street, shining through the store windows, and I froze.

I'd gotten so carried away I hadn't thought about the fact that Roz might not be the only person to see me standing naked in Sapphire Blooms. It was late, and this section of Main Street was usually quiet at night, but it was a Friday, and the pub and the local bar would still be open. Some car and foot traffic would not be unusual.

I stared at Roz, who calmly walked me back to the door, so I was pressed up against it again.

"There," she whispered. "You're safe here."

I glanced to the side. Roz was right. No one would be able to see me here. Even still, an unexpected thrill shot down my spine. "This is... The threat of being discovered is actually quite hot. I think I may have discovered a new kink tonight."

"Let me know if you discover any others," Roz said, then her tongue slipped into my mouth.

I closed my eyes, giving myself over to the heat of her mouth. She grabbed my right breast firmly, pinching my nipple between her fingers, and I moaned again.

Just then, the sound of people laughing and talking outside reached my ears. My eyes widened. Roz placed a finger to my lips.

"You will just need to be very still and very quiet," she murmured.

Before I realized what was happening, she sank to the ground, all the while continuing to tease my breast with one hand and maintain eye contact with me.

I sucked in a breath. Roz Kennedy—proud, confident, sometimes infuriating, smoking hot Roz Kennedy—was on her knees in front of me. Her hair was slightly disheveled and her white shirt was splayed open, offering a tantalizing peek of her cleavage between the cups of her bra.

"Spread your legs," Roz ordered as the noises outside grew louder. She trailed her fingers down the crease of my inner thigh.

I obeyed, and Roz turned her attention to the brown curls between my legs, her fingers running gently over my clit before slipping farther in. She coated the fingers of her right hand in my hot wetness, and then circled my clit, setting all my nerve endings on fire. She pinched my nipple with her left hand, and I gasped, closing my eyes as the sensations rolled over me. This was unlike anything I'd ever experienced in my life. Roz continued working my clit and my nipple at the same time, until I could hardly bear it anymore.

Her left hand abandoned my breast and firmly slid down my body. I opened my eyes to find Roz staring up at me, her gaze intense. She moved her fingers to my opening.

"Can I fuck you with my fingers?" she rasped, her voice thick.

Another wave of desire shot through me, almost knocking me off balance. "Yes," I said breathlessly, bracing myself against the door.

Roz stared up at me as she pushed her fingers in, circling my clit with the thumb of her other hand as she did so.

My legs trembled. "Oh fuck." I groaned, parting my legs farther to give her better access.

Roz held my gaze as she slowly moved her fingers in and out, her thumb gradually increasing the pressure and speed against my clit. I whimpered, pressing the palms of my hands against the wall.

Roz began to drive her fingers harder, each thrust sending waves of pleasure washing over me. I let out another moan, my head dropping back against the door.

Through the haze of pleasure, I heard voices approaching again.

I looked down at Roz. "I'm so close."

"They can't see you." Roz thrusted her fingers even faster, her thumb increasing the intensity on my clit at the same time. "If you don't make a sound, they'll never know."

The voices were so close now, and so was I.

The people talking outside were about to walk past, completely oblivious to the fact I was having the best sex of my life only feet away from them, on the other side of the door. A shot of adrenaline rushed through me.

Roz gazed at me with pure, unadulterated lust burning in her eyes. She slipped in another finger, and I was gone, tipping over into ecstasy. It took all my willpower not to cry out as the orgasm wracked my body. I pushed my head against the door, closing my eyes and riding the waves of pleasure as Roz continued her thrusts, trying to stabilize my quaking thighs by pressing my weight against the wood.

The voices receded as my orgasm tapered off, leaving me gasping for air and feeling like my body might melt into a puddle on the floor.

Roz clambered to her feet and leaned in, placing one hand on the door next to my head.

"You are so fucking hot," she said, her voice husky.

The sight of Roz, hair mussed and eyes ablaze, those gorgeous red lips only inches from mine, sent another rush of desire over me.

"That was incredible." I cupped her chin with my hand and ran my thumb along her cheek before leaning in to kiss her.

Our tongues slipped into each other's mouths, my hands running down Roz's chest and over her breasts, down to the small of her back where I pulled her even closer to me.

"Can I..." I murmured, in between kisses. Nerves whirled in my stomach. What if I couldn't make Roz come? But the thought of not trying, of not exploring her body and at least attempting to bring her pleasure, was even worse.

"Yes. But not here."

I pulled back and looked around Sapphire Blooms, my eye catching on the rococo-style chaise lounge covered in cream fabric with gold wooden trimming in the back corner of the shop. Designed for customers to rest their weary feet, it wasn't long enough for Roz to lie flat on, but she could lean against the raised end with her knees bent while I had my way with her. Perfect.

"The chaise lounge?"

Roz stepped back, eyed the chaise lounge, and then

nodded. She pulled her jacket off the counter and handed it to me. "You can put this on, just in case anyone walks past."

"Thank you." I slipped my arms into the soft material, the faint scent of cedar tickling my nose.

Roz's gaze travelled over my body, now partially cloaked by her black jacket, which fell to my upper thigh, barely covering my ass.

"It suits you," she said, approval clear in her voice.

I grabbed her hand and led her to the chaise lounge.

"You won't be needing this," I said, my voice teasing as I tugged at her shirt, letting it fall to the ground. I slid my hands around her back and undid her bra. "Or this."

Her bra slipped off, revealing small, firm breasts. I stared at them in awe, tracing my fingers around their curves and then up to her mauve nipples, which hardened at my touch. To my delight, Roz let out a small moan, so I continued my exploration.

Roz's moans amplified. I dropped my gaze to her pants, my heart thumping. I slowly trailed my fingers down her smooth stomach to the button on the waistband of her navy trousers. Hands trembling again, I undid the button and pulled down the zipper.

Her trousers dropped to her knees, revealing plain black boy shorts underneath.

"Sit," I said, trying to channel confidence.

Roz obeyed, and I crouched down at her feet, untying the laces of her tan oxford shoes and easing them off before slipping her trousers the rest of the way off.

I looked up at Roz while I knelt in front of her. A thrill, equal parts nerves and excitement, shot through me. For one night only, this cool, sexy woman, who looked like an androgynous queen, her long limbs on glorious display, was mine.

"How do you want me?" she asked.

I licked my lips, barely able to contain my desire. It was clear from Roz's question that I was in control now. As terrifying as it was, it was also titillating.

"Lie back there," I said, nodding to the sloping arm of the lounge.

Roz followed my direction. She looked even more regal, lying back on the cream upholstery, watching me with an expectant and slightly amused glint in her eye. Perhaps she liked being ordered around a little too.

I straddled her waist, relieved to find there was just enough room on the chaise lounge for my legs on either side of hers, and bent over her, some wisps of hair falling out of my updo and hanging between us.

I pressed my lips to hers and ran a hand through her hair while propping myself on the opposite elbow to steady my body. Roz's mouth parted, and the kiss turned hungry, our tongues dipping in and out of each other's mouths. I dropped my hand to her chest, cupping one of her breasts while I rolled my thumb over her nipple until she moaned into my mouth.

I slipped my hand lower still, running it over her boy shorts and between her legs, groaning at the wetness soaking through the material.

"As you may have noticed, I don't need a lot of foreplay," Roz said, a smile twitching against my mouth.

I ran my fingers lightly over the wetness, circling the space a few times.

"Actually, scrap that." Roz breathed heavily. "I don't need any foreplay."

I swallowed. "Can I go down on you, then?"

Roz nodded, and I slowly made my way down her body, trailing kisses along her neck and collarbone, then her breasts and stomach, until I reached the seam of her shorts.

Heart pounding, I tugged at the fabric. Roz lifted her ass so I could slip them off.

I looked up, relishing the vision of Roz completely naked before me, taking in her firm breasts studded with small, hard nipples and the golden-brown curls of hair between her legs. Dropping my head, I returned to kissing the soft, warm skin of her lower abdomen.

Anxiety spiked in my chest as I slipped my fingers through her soft curls. What if I couldn't make her come? But as my fingers reached a little nub that was most definitely her clit and then dipped into wet heat, and the scent of Roz's arousal hit me, something instinctive kicked in. I lowered my head, swiping my tongue from her opening to her clit in one long, slow lick. Damn. Her taste sent another wave of desire crashing over me.

Roz let out a soft moan. Emboldened, I repeated the move a few times, and then focused on her clit, swirling my tongue over it, listening as Roz's breathing grew more labored. I experimented with different pressures and movements, paying close attention to how she reacted to my touch. In an attempt to replicate the effect of my favorite vibrator, I placed my mouth over her clit, lips parted, and sucked gently while circling my tongue around the small hard nub in the middle.

"Oh, that's good," Roz moaned.

I flicked my eyes up just in time to see her hand grip the side of the chaise lounge. Goddamn, that was hot.

"Fingers," Roz gasped out. "In me. Now."

I slid two fingers inside her, groaning into her clit at the sensation of my fingers fully encased by her. My mouth and tongue continued to work her clit, falling into rhythm with the movement of my fingers. Shit. This was so hot.

Roz tilted her hips up, letting out small moans, and I glanced up at her again. She was biting her lip, her eyes dark pools, one hand holding onto the chaise lounge for dear life. In the dim light, I could see a faint flush on her cheeks and chest.

"Faster," she groaned.

I picked up the pace, pushing my hand in and out with speed, curling my fingers slightly, just as Roz had done to me, all the while circling my tongue in time.

"Fuck!" Roz exclaimed, her body quaking as her muscles squeezed against my fingers in quick contractions.

I kept going as Roz writhed under me. It was hot, messy and sticky and so incredibly sexy. Roz Kennedy was falling apart at the mercy of my fingers.

"Enough!" Roz cried out, and I stopped, pulling my head up to look at her.

Her gaze was heavy, her red lips slightly parted, her chest rising and falling. I had never seen anything more attractive in my life.

A wave of performance anxiety rippled through me. It seemed like Roz had enjoyed herself... but could she have been faking it for my benefit?

As if she sensed my concerns, Roz grinned. "Come here."

I clambered up, straddling her hips, and leaned down so my face was only inches from hers. Roz lifted her head and gave me a deep, lingering kiss, slow and passionate.

"Was that okay?" I asked after we'd come up for air.

"That was far more than okay," Roz said. "I don't know where you learned how to do that thing with your mouth but it was... it was something else. Mind blowing."

Warmth swept over me at Roz's words.

"Do you want to come upstairs?" I asked. "While I don't think I'll ever look at the chaise lounge in the same way again, it's not so comfortable for snuggling."

I snapped my mouth close. Snuggling? While I had the urge to wrap my arms around Roz's warm body and nuzzle my head into her neck, Roz did not strike me as a snuggling person.

Not only that, but Roz had made it clear that first night at Pryde that she didn't date. This was just a raincheck on the one-night stand we'd missed that night. And snuggling wasn't part of a one-night stand, was it?

But Roz was already nodding. "That would be nice."

We collected our clothes from the floor of the shop. Roz tugged on her shirt, not bothering to rebutton it, and I led her up the stairs at the back of the shop and into my apartment, my body trembling.

Roz's eyes widened as I turned on the light switch, illuminating the open-plan living-dining room we'd just stepped into.

"Wow. This is very... floral." Floral wallpaper lined the walls and framed prints of some of my favorite flowers—dahlias and ranunculus, in different shades of red, orange and yellow—hung from them. Flower cushions dotted the orange couch and green armchair.

"I should have warned you. I know how much you dislike flowers," I said, taking Roz's hand and leading her down the hall. "I'll let you know now—the bedroom continues the theme. If you want to make a run for it, now's the time."

Roz chuckled. "Nope, you promised me snuggles. I'm not running away now."

I laughed and then pushed open the door to my bedroom and flicked the light switch.

"You weren't kidding." Roz's wide eyes surveyed the yellow and white daisy duvet cover and pillowcases and the muted-yellow-and-pink floral wallpaper.

"I can turn off the light."

Roz stepped toward me, her eyes glinting. "But then I wouldn't be able to see you."

I laughed. "Okay, but no complaints, then."

Roz stood in front of me, gazing into my eyes. "Absolutely no complaints." She lifted her hand and brushed her thumb over my lips. "You know, I think flowers are growing on me." We fell into the bed, snuggling together under the daisy duvet, Roz gazing at the yellow daisies and pink dahlias that decorated my walls. "Maybe being around you has acted like some form of exposure therapy."

"Happy to be of service," I said, grinning up at her before closing my eyes to enjoy the warmth of Roz's smooth, lean naked body against mine.

So, this was what sex with a woman was like. It blew all my previous experiences with men completely out the window. Maybe I was a lesbian? All I knew was that the attraction I felt toward Roz was stronger than anything I'd felt before. And I didn't want this one-night stand to end.

CHAPTER TWENTY-SIX

ROZ

I WOKE to the sound of pattering rain interspersed with the occasional gentle snore.

Smiling, I opened my eyes to look at the source of the snores. Olivia lay next to me in pink daisy pajama shorts and matching t-shirt, the duvet thrown half off her body, her relaxed face framed by silky brown hair falling across the pillow. My heart skipped a beat. Damn, she was gorgeous. My gaze dropped to her chest, the soft curves of her breasts just visible, and my core began to thrum.

I closed my eyes. *What the hell am I doing?*

Last night certainly hadn't gotten my attraction to Olivia out of my system. Quite the opposite, as the throbbing sensation between my thighs reminded me. The image of Olivia, leaning against the front door of Sapphire Blooms, trembling legs parted as she came over my fingers, did not help matters. *Shit.*

I stared at Olivia's ridiculous floral wallpaper, hoping it would act like a cold shower on my libido, but it did nothing. I should leave before this got even more out of hand. I sat up, looking around for my phone. Before I located it, my gaze fell back to Olivia's face. She was distractingly beautiful. My gaze lingered on her soft, pink lips and long lashes. Her eyes suddenly snapped open wide. I flinched.

"Good morning," Olivia said, giving me a sleepy smile.

My heart ballooned with warmth. *Goddamn my body and its involuntary reactions.* I couldn't help smiling back at her. Olivia wriggled closer to me, and I sank back down into the bed. Suddenly, we were kissing again, hands roaming over each other's bodies, and Olivia was tugging off the t-shirt she'd lent me to sleep in. *Maybe just one more time...*

When we finally came up for air, we lay facing each other, our heads on the same pillow. Olivia gazed at me, her eyes soft, her lips curved slightly upward. She reached out and gently traced her fingers across my jawbone.

She was looking at me with such tenderness, my bones felt loose, like I might melt into the bedspread.

I used to look at Sadie like that. My heart squeezed. *I should go.*

"How do you feel about coffee? And possibly pancakes?" Olivia ran her hand down my stomach.

No. No. You need to leave. But you also need to eat... I glanced out the window. It was pouring rain outside. *Fuck it.* I'll head home once I'd eaten. I smiled at Olivia. "I feel very good about both those things."

"Excellent." She swung her legs out of the bed.

As Olivia mixed the pancake batter with a large wooden spoon, I sat on the counter stool, sipping my coffee in my boy shorts and borrowed t-shirt that said, "Flower Dealer".

"Do you have any plans today?" Olivia asked.

I should go to the farm, throw myself into work now that Fred had given the investment a greenlight and pretend last night—and this morning—never happened. But that seemed very unappealing. I shook my head. "No."

"Me either. Maddie is working today, and since it's raining, the shop will be quiet." Olivia poured the batter into a hot frying pan. It let out a satisfying sizzle. "If you feel like it, we could continue your movie education. Since we don't need to worry about fake dating anymore, we could move onto some other tropes that tickle your fancy. Enemies-to-lovers, grumpy/sunshine, forbidden love?" She wiggled her eyebrows, her eyes twinkling.

I glanced out the window. The rain was even heavier than before. I took a deep breath, savoring the scent of the pancakes. I'd just eat a couple pancakes, watch one movie, and then excuse myself.

"I THINK enemies-to-lovers is my favorite trope," Olivia announced as the credits rolled on yet another rom-com.

I smiled down at her, snuggled in my arms. "I'm still partial to fake-dating."

I glanced up at the yellow-and-white flower clock on Olivia's living room wall and my chest constricted so hard it squeezed the air out of my lungs. How the hell was it Sunday afternoon?

Despite my best intentions, we'd ended up having a movie marathon yesterday, followed by what could only be described as a sex marathon, and then today we'd managed to fill the morning with lazing in bed before finally getting up and watching another movie. Every time I vowed I was about to leave, I'd end up staying, tumbling back into bed with Olivia or lazing on her couch, chatting or watching movies.

Magnetic attraction. That was what it felt like. An irresistible pull toward Olivia that I couldn't shake. She was so warm, funny and gorgeous. And I couldn't get enough of her body. Alarm bells rang in my ears. I'd only felt like this once before in my life, and it had ended with me devastated and alone.

"One more?" Olivia asked, grabbing the remote. "I know it's not the right time of year, but have you seen *Happiest Season*?" She looked at my blank face and rolled her eyes. "Of course you haven't. What was I thinking? Well, it's a lesbian holiday rom-com. Kristen Stewart is in it. Her character actually reminds me of a younger, shorter version of you. Blond, a penchant for suits, a dry sense of humor." Her eyes twinkled.

"She sounds like the perfect woman." While my lips twitched, a string tugged at my chest. This felt so domestic, so intimate and cozy. I didn't know what Olivia was looking for, but I was starting to suspect it was more than just a one-off weekend of sex and movie watching. And anything more than that was more than I could give her. I swallowed. "But I should head off."

"You're welcome to stay for dinner, if you want," Olivia said, pulling her head off my shoulder and looking up at me. "No pressure, though."

I steeled myself. I couldn't let myself get carried away again. An image of Sadie flashed into my mind: her sitting on the other end of our couch in Manhattan, refusing to engage with me after some minor failing on my part.

I had to leave now, before I got even more entangled. It wasn't just my heart and my mental health on the line this time. The farm was at a critical point. I needed to have all my time and energy focused on ensuring its success, not getting swept up in another intense relationship that would crash and burn.

I leaped to my feet. This time, I was really leaving. "Thank you. It's very tempting, but I'd better go."

"Okay." Olivia stood, running a slender hand through her hair.

Not trusting myself to stick to my resolve if I lingered for too long, I strode into Olivia's room and changed back into the clothes I'd been wearing Friday night, shoving my phone in my pants pocket and returning to the hallway.

Olivia walked me to the door. My gaze dropped to her lips. Warning sirens blared in my ear. *Get out now.* I grabbed the door handle.

I smiled, my face tight, barely able to meet her gaze in case I got pulled back in. "Thank you for the wonderful weekend."

And with that, I bolted.

CHAPTER TWENTY-SEVEN

OLIVIA

ROZ JOGGED DOWN THE STAIRS. I pressed the door shut, leaning against it for a moment, unease swirling in my stomach. What had just happened?

I trudged to the kitchen and switched the kettle on. I must have misread the signs. It had been stupid of me, thinking that the last forty-eight hours might have been more than a one-off weekend of mind-blowing sex. I grabbed my sunflower mug from the cupboard and leaned against the counter, staring blankly at the kettle as it began to tremble. Roz made it very clear the first night we met that she didn't date. I chewed on my lip. She'd been so warm and affectionate this weekend, such an entertaining rom-com watching companion, that I'd foolishly let myself imagine what it would be like if we were actually together. Cozying up on the couch for pizza and movie nights, enjoying coffee together on the back deck every morning, raising kids on the farm... A pang vibrated through my chest. I'd gotten way ahead of myself there. *Roz doesn't want that.*

I dropped a tea bag in my mug and poured the water on

top. I finally understood the U-Haul jokes about lesbians. I hadn't wanted Roz to leave. God, I was pathetic.

I grabbed my phone from the charging station on the kitchen counter and returned to the couch, sitting down and drawing the throw blanket over me. It was no substitute for Roz's warm body. I pulled it up to my neck. The house felt very quiet. The falling rain, which had been delightfully cozy when I was snuggling with Roz on the couch, suddenly seemed gloomy. I pulled out my phone, ready to do some mindless scrolling.

The photo of Roz on my phone wallpaper stared back at me. Another pang hit me, harder this time. Even with her mouth pulled into a half grimace, half smile, she looked stunning. It was hard to believe it had only been just over two weeks ago that I'd snapped it in Sapphire Blooms.

My stomach dropped as I paid attention to the notifications on the screen. Shit. I'd been so consumed with Roz I hadn't looked at it since breakfast.

A message from Jenny.

> Hey! Just checking in that everything's okay for the wedding on Friday? I know you mentioned there were a few issues with the flowers.

My chest constricted. I'd planned to finalize the new plan for the politician's wedding, taking into account the flowers damaged by the aphids and cows, yesterday. Needless to say, I'd made absolutely no progress on that front.

There was also a text from Mom.

> Are you coming to lunch? Dave, Rach and the kids are here.

My stomach twisted. I was dropping balls left and right.

I glanced at my watch. 2:30 p.m. I was supposed to be at my parents' house for lunch at noon. My brother and his family would be heading back to New Jersey any minute, if they hadn't already left. *Shit.* I shot off a text apologizing for missing the lunch to Mom and Dave.

I pressed my lips together and stood. As appealing as moping on the couch was, I couldn't let Roz distract me anymore. I'd already missed out on some quality family time, but at least I could get back on top of work. I made my way downstairs to Sapphire Blooms. As I walked to my workbench, my gaze fell on the front door. The memory of Roz's body pressed up against mine, of her fingers inside me, slammed into me, sending my core tingling. I dragged my eyes away. *Goddamnit.* I'd never be able to look at the door or the chaise lounge in the same way again. Even so, I had no regrets about Friday night. But letting it continue over the weekend, letting myself hope it might be something more... That had been a mistake.

Just then, a family walked past the shop window. I froze, watching them. A small child, perhaps three years old, squealed with delight as his parents, holding a hand each, swung him up and down. His mom was laughing, while his dad was smiling at his older sister, who was pushing a scooter down the street, rainbow ribbons streaming from the handlebars. Invisible strings tugged at my heart. That was what I wanted. And Roz couldn't offer me that.

Letting out a loud sigh, I made my way to the workbench, where I grabbed my laptop, pulled up a seat, and threw myself into work.

"MORNING! YOU'RE EARLY TODAY," George called, rushing to get the door as I pulled the cart of fresh flowers into Novel Gossip. I'd vowed to be completely on the ball this week and had set my alarm for the crack of dawn to ensure Monday got off to a good start. As a result, I'd arrived before George opened the café to the public. "How was your weekend? You must be relieved about Fred greenlighting the investment." I'd told everyone the good news after Fred had left on Thursday.

"I am." I smiled. I'd gotten so caught up thinking about Roz, the fact that the farm and Sapphire Blooms had been saved had been pushed to the back of my mind. "My weekend was good. How was yours?" I wasn't about to tell George that Roz and I had spent the weekend having sex before she ran out on me.

"Pretty busy! We took Mom and Barb to visit Saugerties and it was a mission to stop them from buying the entire antiques shop." George grimaced.

I chuckled at the thought of George's mom and Hannah's former nanny grumbling, their arms piled high with knickknacks, as Hannah and George tried to round them up and push them out of a dusty antiques store.

We unloaded the flowers, a spring mix of pink and purple anemones, and swapped out the older flowers on the tables.

George surveyed the café once we'd finished and gave an approving dip of her head. "They look great. Thanks, Liv. Do you have time for a coffee?"

I glanced at my watch and nodded. There was plenty of time before I had to open Sapphire Blooms and I was in desperate need of more caffeine. I hadn't slept well last night, tossing and turning, painfully aware of Roz's absence.

"So, how are things going with Roz?" George asked as she frothed the milk, peering at me over the shiny red coffee machine.

Heat rushed to my cheeks. Did George suspect something?

"Fine," I said, my mouth dry. "Now that Fred has agreed to the investment, I don't think I'll be seeing much of her."

George fixed me with a steady gaze. "Look, Liv, you obviously don't have to tell me what's going on, but if you want to talk, I'm here."

Tears welled in my eyes. The subtext to her comment was clear. George knew. Why was I feeling so emotional all of a sudden? I blinked the tears away.

"Oh, shit." George turned off the steam. "Are you okay?"

A lump formed in my throat. Was I ready to talk to people about this? I'd kept it so close to my chest for so long now that it felt like a bigger deal than it probably was. *She already knows. And talking to someone might help.*

"Yes. I—" I swallowed. "Roz and I, um... actually slept together."

I watched George closely for her reaction. To my relief, it was almost immediate. George's face broke into an enormous, genuine beam, her dimple on display. "That's awesome, Liv!"

The corners of my mouth wavered. "It was amazing. We spent almost the whole weekend together. But then she ran out acting weird yesterday afternoon."

George's dimple vanished, replaced with a frown. "Shit. I'm sorry. Do you know what happened?"

I shook my head. "Nope. And I haven't heard from her since."

George dropped her head to focus on pouring the frothed milk into two mugs and then slid one across the counter to me. I took a large sip of the warm, golden liquid.

George cradled her mug in her hands, her elbows resting on the counter, and stared at me. "Can you go and talk to her about it? I know it can be awkward, but Roz seems like a complicated woman. Who knows what's going through that sleek blond head of hers?"

I laughed weakly. "Definitely not me." I took another gulp of coffee. "But she made it clear when we first met that she wasn't interested in dating. So, it was presumably just a one-off thing for her. That's what I thought it was at the start of the weekend too. But by yesterday things felt different, like maybe there was more to it."

"Is that what you want?" George's eyes were soft.

I shrugged, swallowing down the lump again. "It doesn't really matter what I want if Roz doesn't want the same thing."

I should throw myself back into dating again, find someone who actually wanted to have a relationship and kids, before it got too late. Once the politician's wedding was over, I'd finish setting up that dating profile. Although, I probably shouldn't make it public until Fred's investment paperwork was all signed, just in case Fred somehow got wind of it—assuming Roz let me know when the documents were signed. My chest tightened again.

George brushed a few coffee grains off the counter. "Ugh, I'm sorry, Liv. That sucks. Are you going to mention this to the others—about Roz and being interested in women?"

"I don't think so. Things between us clearly aren't going anywhere. I'm not even sure if I'm bi, pan, a lesbian or something else." I peered at George over my coffee cup, the corner of my mouth twitching up. "Honestly, after this weekend I'm veering toward lesbian."

George chuckled. "It was that good, huh?"

I laughed. "It was incredible." I looked down at the golden-brown coffee in my mug, my laughter subsiding.

"But in all seriousness, you don't have to label your sexuality if you don't want to. You don't owe anyone a label." George's voice was so warm and kind my eyes filled with tears again. Roz had said something very similar while we were at Prue's winery. God, that felt like eons ago.

"That's true... But I'm sure people will want to know."

George pressed her lips together. "Maybe. But that's really none of their business."

"Given my history of choosing the wrong thing, whether it's jobs or boyfriends, I think I'll keep it quiet for now." I snorted. "Knowing me, I'll announce I'm a lesbian and the next day fall madly in love with a man. Everyone is sick of watching me flip-flopping around, making terrible decisions. I'll save them the pain of having to hear about the time I had a weekend of amazing sex with my enemy-turned-fake-girlfriend."

The memory of me standing in the beer garden of Builders Arms on my thirtieth birthday, holding a glass of champagne, and loudly declaring that failed businesses and relationships were a thing of the past, flashed through my mind. I winced. Well, that hadn't lasted long. Why had I thought another turn around the sun would magically improve my judgment?

George set down her mug and stared at me. "Liv. No one thinks you've been flip-flopping around, making terrible decisions. You've just been working out who you are, what you want to spend your life doing and who you want to spend it with. That takes time. It took me ages to work out I wanted to be a café owner and find Hannah." George smiled. "There's no pressure to come out or talk about Roz if you don't want to. You should do it on your own time—or not at all. But I just want to make sure you know that everyone will be here for you if you do."

I smiled at her, my chest filling with warmth. "Thanks." George was seriously the best.

The door jingled and Ben walked into the store. "Morning! Should I flip the sign to *open*?" Ben asked. "A line of cranky uncaffeinated customers has begun to form outside." His hand hovered over the sign hanging on the window of the door.

George glanced at her watch and straightened. "Shit, how did it get that late already? Yes, thanks, Ben."

"Well, I think that's my sign I should be getting back to the store," I said. "Thanks for the coffee and the pep talk." I downed the last of my drink and headed toward the door, standing aside to let the rush of customers enter. Being trampled by caffeine addicts desperate for their hit was not on my bingo card for this year.

My step was lighter as I walked back to Sapphire Blooms. It felt good to finally talk to someone about Roz. Now I'd gotten that off my chest, maybe I'd be able to move on from this weekend and focus on what really mattered—Friday's wedding and finding someone who actually wanted to spend time with me.

CHAPTER TWENTY-EIGHT

ROZ

I STEPPED out onto the back deck of my house, coffee in hand. The rain had finally stopped on Sunday night, and Monday and Tuesday had been gloriously warm. I scanned the scene in front of me. Ronnie was in the petting zoo, preparing for the farm to open. Thelma and Louise had their heads low to the ground, munching on grass in their pasture. There was no sign of anyone else.

My eyes dropped to the railing where Olivia and I had stood, gazing over fields, an arm around each other only days ago, moments before Fred appeared. My heart twinged. I clenched my jaw, forcing my eyes back up.

I should be in a better mood. Fred had agreed to invest in the farm. According to Dana, the rain followed by the warmer weather would be fantastic for all our crops. And the stress of fake-dating was now behind us. *Us.* My chest tightened. I took a sip of my coffee. It tasted bitter in comparison to the coffee Olivia had made on Sunday. I sighed. Why did all my thoughts keep circling back to Olivia? It wasn't healthy.

I gulped down another mouthful of the disappointing

brew and walked down the steps. Some fresh air and a brisk walk would do me good. As I passed their field, Thelma and Louise ambled over.

One of them—I was pretty sure it was Thelma—let out a mellow moo. I tilted my head and stared at her. She looked back at me, her brown eyes soft. Surprised, I stepped closer to her.

"Moo to you too." I tentatively reached out like I'd seen Ronnie do a thousand times and gave her long, slow strokes down her neck and shoulders. She leaned toward me, her tail swaying. "You like that, do you?"

Thelma—I was confident it was her now; she was giving me distinct Thelma vibes—gave me a lick, her sandpaper-like tongue swiping my hand.

I chuckled. "I'll take that as a yes."

I wish Olivia was here to witness this. My smile faded.

Louise nudged at Thelma, trying to get her head in between my hand and Thelma's body. "Okay, okay." I lifted my other hand and began stroking them simultaneously. The rhythmic movement of my hands was surprisingly soothing.

"I don't know what to do about Olivia," I murmured.

Their large soulful eyes calmed me a little, but no answers were forthcoming.

With a sigh, I gave them a parting pat and continued on past the petting zoo. When I reached the corn fields, I blinked in amazement. The green corn shoots sprouting out of the earth seemed to have doubled in size since I'd seen them on Friday. Dana had been right about the weather causing a growth spurt.

I kept going, arriving at the flower fields, but all I could see was the image of Olivia's gorgeous naked body splayed out on her yellow-and-white-daisy duvet, surrounded by even more flowers on the walls. I ran a hand through my hair. This walk was not helping matters at all. My nose itched. I'd also forgotten to take my antihistamines for the past few days.

I needed to talk things through with someone. Someone who was not a cow. And I needed to get away from the flowers.

I pulled out my phone. It was 8:30 a.m. With any luck, Matt would have just dropped Lottie off at school and be driving to work now. I dialed his number and began striding toward the apple orchard.

"Hi," he answered, the noise of road traffic faint in the background.

I smiled. "Hi, how are you? Do you have time to talk?"

Matt cleared his throat. "Yep, I'm just on my way to work." His voice sounded slightly rough.

I frowned. "Is everything okay?"

He sighed. "Yeah, I just had a stressful morning. Don't know if you saw the news, but an army helicopter crashed near where Mel is stationed. Four casualties."

My stomach turned heavy. "Shit, is she okay?" I'd been so caught up with my own worries that I hadn't checked the news this morning.

"Yes, thank god. I just heard from her a few minutes ago, and she's fine. But I spent the last two hours having breakfast with Lottie, getting her ready for school, and driving her there, trying to behave completely normally, all the while freaking out that it might have been Mel."

My heart squeezed. "Oh my God, that must have been awful. I'm sorry, Matt."

The rhythmic click of his turn signal sounded. "It was. I can't wait until she's home."

I reached the apple orchards. Rows of apple trees, some

already in bloom, stretched out before me. I inhaled the light sweet scent of the blossoms. The memory of Olivia's floral scent hit me, its phantom molecules invading my nasal passages. *Goddamnit.* Guilt tugged at my chest as I realized I'd zoned out on the conversation with Matt. *Focus.*

"Any news on her application to come home early?"

"No. It's not looking promising." He cleared his throat again. "Anyway, how are you doing? You must be thrilled about Fred's investment coming through."

I smiled, walking between two rows of leafy green trees. "It's a huge relief."

"I was looking forward to celebrating with you at Mom and Dad's on Sunday night, but Mom said you were feeling tired."

"Yes. I was exhausted." I took a deep breath and braced myself. Matt was the only person I spoke to about my personal life, but even with him it could be a struggle. "Olivia and I... well, we slept together on Friday night and spent the weekend together."

Matt did a slow whistle. "Wow! So... are you together now?"

"No." I stopped, inspecting a cluster of soft pink apple blossoms up close. "It was supposed to be a raincheck on the one-night stand we missed out on that night at Pryde—it turns out she never got my message—but then it just... kept going. I started to worry she wanted something more serious and I may have freaked out a little and rushed away." I stabbed the toe of my shoe into the dirt.

There was a pause. "Are you sure it wasn't because *you* wanted something more serious?"

My brow furrowed. "No. Of course not."

"It's just..." The turn signal sounded again. "Since you two started your fake-dating shenanigans, you've been the happiest I remember seeing you in a long time, even with all the stress of the farm. Your face lights up when you talk about her—and you talk about her a lot, by the way."

A bee landed on an apple blossom, drinking its fill of nectar.

I swallowed. "We're friends. That's all."

"Uh-huh. Friends who have been basically dating for weeks—bike rides, trivia nights, clothes shopping—and spent the whole weekend in bed?" Matt's voice softened. "Look, Roz, I understand why you're wary about getting serious with her, after what happened with Sadie, but I can confidently say that Olivia isn't Sadie, and you're also not the person you were fifteen years ago."

I pressed my lips together and kicked a rock down the row of apple trees. It hit a root and bounced behind a trunk, disappearing out of sight. It was true that I couldn't imagine Olivia manipulating and gaslighting me and, in the unlikely event she did, I'd be much better equipped to identify it and extricate myself quickly. But that wasn't all I was worried about.

"Even if there's no love-bombing involved, what if it's all just infatuation, and Olivia wakes up one morning and realizes she's not into me after all? Or I wake up and realize the same?" Pain stabbed my chest as it tightened. I couldn't go through that all again.

"It could be infatuation, or it could be genuine, very strong attraction. If you pursue the relationship, you'll work it out one way or another soon enough. Either the attraction will grow, or the infatuation will fade away. Does it really make sense to stop a relationship because you're worried you might be into her too much?"

I frowned. "The farm is at a critical point right now. I can't let myself get distracted by a real relationship. A fake relationship was hard enough. Not to mention there's an eleven-year age gap. We're at different stages of life. She still hasn't even told her family or friends that she's queer."

"Okay, now it feels like you're just grasping at straws. If you're worried about the farm, then just take things slow with her. But from what you've said, she's actually been a huge help with the farm so far. And on the age gap, if she was twenty, I'd be more worried. But she's in her thirties and has her shit together. Don't kid yourself that you're much more mature than her." There was a pause and then Matt yelled, "You idiot!"

I did a double-take, my brow furrowing. "That's a bit harsh."

Matt laughed. "Sorry, that wasn't directed at you. Someone just cut me off. Look, I'm nearly at work, but please don't dismiss the idea of dating out of hand. I really think it could be good for you."

My neck prickled. "I don't even know what she wants. She might think the whole thing was a huge mistake."

"Well, you'll only find out if you talk to her." The turn signal clicked again. "Sorry, Roz, I've just arrived. I'd better go. I'm already a few minutes late. But I can talk later tonight if you want."

"Thanks. I'm so glad Mel is okay. Tell her I said hi and to stay safe."

I hung up with Matt and turned toward the farmhouse, making my way back through the orchard.

I passed a low branch full of blossoms. The image of me trailing my mouth slowly down Olivia's delicate neck to her collarbone, drinking in her faintly floral scent, slammed into me, leaving me slightly winded and full of desire. Goddamn, I wanted her. And I missed her.

I groaned. As I'd said to Matt, I didn't know what Olivia wanted.

I stepped out of the orchard and back onto the dirt road. The domestic bliss of the weekend—cooking and eating together, watching movies together—had fueled my assumption Olivia wanted a serious relationship. But we were also friends. And those activities were also things that friends did. I bit my lip. Was there a chance we'd unwittingly fallen into a friends-with-benefits situation?

My step lightened. That could be the answer. We could still hang out together, still sleep together, just without the risk of our hearts being broken. If we went into it knowing it wasn't going to last, that it wasn't anything serious, surely we'd be more prepared when it ended, right? It wouldn't need to be for long, just until the infatuation we were feeling wore off. And then we could drop the benefits bit and return to just being friends.

CHAPTER TWENTY-NINE

OLIVIA

"COME ON," I muttered under my breath as I crouched down on the grassy lawn at Prue's vineyard, holding a tent peg steady with one hand while the other hand lifted the hammer. I needed the arch to be nice and secure. The last thing I needed was for a gust of wind to knock it over, taking out the high-profile bride and groom in the process. I could just see the news headlines now: *Breaking news: Floral arch kills happy couple moments before exchanging vows.* I gritted my teeth. The hammer made contact with the peg, but instead of driving into the ground, the peg fell down for the fifth time in a row. *Goddamnit.*

I glanced around. Lines of empty white chairs covered the lawn, ready for the wedding later this afternoon. A few feet behind the arch, rows of grapevines stretched out, their bright-green leaves unfurling after a winter of dormancy. *At least no one's around to witness my ineptitude.*

Usually, I enjoyed wedding setup, but today, everything seemed to be going wrong. I'd forgotten the chicken wire and had to rush back to the shop to get it. An hour ago, I realized I'd underestimated how many lilacs would fit in the large vases inside the venue and had called Dana in a panic asking if she had any more I could use. As a result, I was running short on time.

I wiped the back of my hand against my forehead. Even after not having seen or heard from her for five days, Roz was still throwing me off my game. All week, I'd been having flashbacks to our weekend together, triggered by the smallest of things. Sitting on the couch, an image of me writhing on it under Roz's naked body would strike me out of the blue, sending tingles shooting to my core. Opening the front door to Sapphire Blooms, the sensation of being held against it by Roz's firm hands would hit me. A woman's voice faintly resembling Roz's would bring back memories of Roz murmuring "good girl" in my ear. And then I'd remember Roz's abrupt disappearance. If I hadn't been struck by a particularly vivid, high-resolution image of Roz reclining on the chaise lounge while I was packing, I was sure I wouldn't have forgotten the chicken wire.

I took a deep breath, lifted the hammer and swung it down again.

"Fuck!" Pain shot through my finger as the hammer smashed into it, sending tears welling in my eyes.

Blinking furiously, I examined my finger. A shadow fell over me.

"Are you okay?"

My heart leaped so ferociously I wobbled and nearly fell.

I knew that voice.

Brown work boots appeared, a foot away from where I crouched.

I knew those boots.

I looked up to see Roz peering down at me, her brow furrowed. Forget butterflies, my stomach felt as though it was bursting with winged unicorns, flapping wildly and poking me with their horns. I'd been thinking about this moment since Sunday, but I still wasn't prepared for it.

I swallowed. "I think so." I bent my finger. "It still seems to be working. What are you doing here?"

"Good. You need working fingers... to do your flower arrangements." Roz crouched down next to me.

I resisted the urge to inch closer to her, to breathe in her scent I'd dreamed about every night, to run my thumb down her jawline, put my hand on the nape of her neck and pull her lips to mine. I sunk my teeth into my lower lip instead, avoiding direct contact with Roz's eyes.

"I've got the lilacs in the van," Roz said. "And Dana said you were sounding a little stressed, so I'm also here to help— if you need me."

"Oh. Thank you." I could certainly use another set of hands, especially for the fiddly arch, but were Roz's elegant ones a good idea? I needed to stay focused.

A gust of wind hit and the arch gave an ominous wobble. *Shit.* I shot out my hand to steady it. This was definitely a two-person job.

I swallowed my pride and nodded. "Okay." I handed Roz the hammer. My hand grazed hers, leaving warm tingles on my skin. "If I hold the peg here, would you mind trying to hammer it in?" I grasped the peg with both hands.

Roz stared at the ground, brushing the dirt next to the peg with her long fingers. A small shiver shot down my spine. *Those fingers were trailing all over my body last weekend.*

"I think there's a rock just here, which may be why you're not having any luck," Roz said. "Can we shift it a few inches?"

Heat rushed up my face. Of course the rock-hard patch

of dirt I was trying to drive the tent pegs into was actually a rock. "That's fine. Thanks."

Together we shifted the arch back and then tried again. This time the tent pegs slid smoothly into the soil.

"Thank you," I said, standing and wiping my hands on my orange overalls.

"No problem." Roz cleared her throat. "I'm sorry I left so suddenly on Sunday." Roz's gaze slid to the arch. "What do we need to do now?"

I blinked. *Oh. She's asking what the next step for the floral arch is, not our relationship.* I pressed my lips together. As apologies went, that was a disappointing one. Where was the explanation, the details as to why she ran out the door? Was she going to say anything more?

I yanked the chicken wire out of the box. "Now it's secure, we need to wrap the wire around the arch so we can attach the flowers."

We began twisting the wire around the metal arch in silence, punctuated only by the faint sounds of the caterers setting up inside the venue and birds flitting between the vines. Roz started at one end of the arch and I took the other. I focused on the task in front of me, trying not to look at how gracefully Roz's fingers were working. As we made our way up each pillar of the arch, we drew closer together. In my periphery, Roz opened and then closed her mouth a few times. I swallowed. Was she working up to say something else?

We were so close now, our bodies almost touching, as we reached up above our heads to wrap the wire around the top of the arch.

"I like you. A lot." Roz's voice was low and soft.

My heart jumped, my eyes darting to her face. Was she—

"But I need to be upfront with you. I'm not looking for a serious relationship."

Heaviness washed over my body, a lump forming in my throat. I swallowed. "That's fine. You made that clear when we first met."

I twisted the last piece of wire on the arch and stepped back. "Now, we need to feed the greenery through the chicken wire, like this." I picked up a leafy frond from the box next to me and weaved it through the wire.

Roz watched closely and then copied my actions. She bit her lip, her brow slightly furrowed, her blond hair flopping on her forehead. A pang hit my chest. *Stop ogling her. She doesn't like you like that.*

"That's great." I dragged my eyes away from her face and pulled out another frond to thread through. Thank god I had something to keep me busy. This conversation would have been excruciating if we'd just been sitting out on Roz's back deck together with nothing to do but sit in the long silence. Should I say something else? My mind was blank.

When the box was almost empty, Roz cleared her throat again. "I was wondering if you would be interested in something less serious?"

I froze, my eyes jerking up to her face. Her cheeks were tinged with pink. "Less serious?"

"Yes. More of a... casual arrangement."

I chewed on my lip, my heart sinking. "I don't think so. I really want to find someone to settle down with, have kids together. I can't afford to be distracted by a relationship that's not going anywhere."

Roz's face fell. "I understand."

Everything I'd said was true, and yet my chest ached at the thought of never kissing Roz again, never running my hands over her breasts and watching her as I made her come. The lump in my throat expanded.

I bent down, picking up the two last fronds and pushing them into the wire.

"The flowers are next. But I can finish that part myself." While Roz had done a surprisingly good job, I just wanted to be alone.

Roz shook her head. "I'm happy to stay."

I glanced at my watch. The timing was still tight. *Suck up your pride and accept her help.* "Okay. We have to insert the roses carefully into the chicken wire, like this, making sure they're secure." I pulled a white rose out of the bucket next to me and pushed it into the top of the arch. "We'll do the bigger roses first and then add the smaller spray roses."

Roz bent down and inspected the roses suspiciously.

"Don't worry, I de-thorned them already."

"Thank god." Roz let out a sound somewhere between a huff and a chuckle and then bent down, picked a large pink rose out of the bucket and tenderly threaded it into the wire. She tugged at it gently. "It seems stable enough. Is that okay?"

"Perfect." The lump was still there, bobbing as I spoke.

I selected another dusty-pink rose and inserted it into the arch. The silence felt heavy. Perhaps talking about something that wasn't related to our non-existent relationship would help.

I asked the first thing that jumped into my mind, something I'd been wondering for weeks. "Why do you hate flowers so much?"

Roz went very still. Had I hit a nerve? After a moment, she peered around the arch to look at me, her lips pressed together, as if she was trying to decide whether or not to let me in on her flower-hating secret. "Have you ever gotten sick after eating something and never wanted to eat that thing again?"

I tilted my head and stared at her. "Is this about quark again? If you really don't want to try it, I won't force you to."

Roz let out a small chuckle. "No, it's not about the quark. But something similar happened to me with flowers."

I frowned. "You ate flowers and got sick? Um, you do know most flowers aren't edible." I thought Roz was smarter than that. "I mean, you can eat pansies, violas, lavender and even roses, but I personally think flowers are better admired for their looks rather than consumed."

Roz snorted. "No, I didn't eat flowers."

I stared, waiting. "Okay..."

Roz turned her attention back to the red rose she was holding, pushing it slowly into the greenery. "I dated women when I was at college, but after that, work really became my life. When you're working fifteen-hour days, it's hard enough to fit in exercise and sleep, let alone see people."

My stomach sank. The whole point of this conversation was to steer clear of discussing our relationship. Why was Roz talking about dating?

"I can imagine," I said, plucking a gorgeous deep-purple rose from the bucket. "I found dating tricky enough in between hanging out with friends, doing all the things I love —like kayaking, hiking and reading—and work, and I don't even work long hours." Although, I had managed to fit fake dating Roz into my life quite easily... so perhaps the issue wasn't that I hadn't had time before, but that I just wasn't that interested in it.

Roz paused, staring into the distance. "When I was twenty-seven, I met a woman, Sadie, at my parents' holiday party. She was a couple of years older than me and worked at my dad's law firm. Things got intense quickly... She wanted to see me all the time, showered me with compliments, bought me expensive watches and told me she loved me after only a few weeks. We moved into her apartment after six weeks."

My heart clenched. I really didn't want to hear about Roz's amazing love story right now. Could I change the subject, or would that be rude? It felt rude. And I was still curious about the genesis story for Roz's disdain of flowers, even if she seemed to have gone off on a tangent.

I held back a sigh. "Oh wow. That does sound intense."

"Yeah. I think deep down I knew something was off—"

Off? Okay. Maybe this wasn't the amazing love story I'd first assumed.

"But Sadie was so into me and she seemed like the perfect partner on paper—attractive, successful, smart, outgoing and wanted a family like me."

I nearly dropped the rose I was holding. Roz wanted a family?

"And"—Roz cleared her throat—"I think I was flattered by her attention. She proposed to me after three months, and I said yes."

My eyebrows shot up. Roz getting engaged after three months did not compute. She was so measured and sensible.

Roz sighed. "After that, things went rapidly downhill. Instead of giving me over-the-top compliments all the time, she started constantly criticizing my appearance, making comments about how socially awkward I was, that sort of thing. I rarely socialized, but the few times I did go out, she'd get furious if I didn't respond to her messages or calls immediately. She even accused me of cheating on her with a straight friend once. I was devastated. I couldn't work out what I'd done."

Heat shot through my veins. What an awful way to treat someone. "It doesn't sound like you'd done anything wrong at all. So, what did you do?"

"I felt trapped. We'd announced the engagement. I'd given up my apartment lease. My parents were thrilled their daughter was dating an eligible woman who was on the partnership track. We'd moved so quickly; we had our future all planned out—buying a house, having kids, getting a dog. Leaving her seemed like such a huge step. And my job was so busy—you have to work to the bone in management consulting firms, especially if you're trying to make partner—so I barely had time to myself to figure out what to do. Every time I started seriously considering leaving her, she'd get better again, for a period, and I'd think maybe things weren't so bad after all."

I grimaced. "It sounds like she was a master manipulator."

"Yeah. That's what Matt said when he finally pulled me aside at a family lunch, told me I looked like shit and asked what was going on. I'd never heard the term 'love-bombing' before, but when Matt sent me an article about it afterward, it all started to fit into place. Matt also raised the possibility that she might be pursuing me partly to advance her own career, given she worked at the same law firm as my dad and he was a senior partner with a lot of influence. He was convinced—and still is—that she was a psychopath." Roz pressed another flower into the arch.

"Jeez!" I'd stopped trying to work now and was just standing still, listening intently.

"After that conversation with Matt, it was like a switch had been flipped. I suddenly saw how toxic our relationship was and that I needed to get out. Two days later, I moved in with Matt and Mel while I looked for a new place to live."

"That sounds really awful," I said. "I'm glad you left."

"Me too." Roz pressed her lips together.

As interesting as her story had been, I was still none the wiser on the reason for Roz's flower phobia. "So, um, how did your dislike of flowers come about?"

Roz chuckled softly as she pushed some more roses into the chicken wire. "Ah, yes. Sorry, I got so carried away I forgot why I was telling you in the first place. Sadie sent me flowers. Almost every single day we were together. I could tell how she was feeling about me based on the arrangement. If she was angry or annoyed with me, she'd get me a small bouquet of carnations or daisies—or not send me anything at all. If she was in her 'showering me with affection' mood, I'd get these over-the-top designer flower arrangements that were almost too big to lift. My office at work was filled with flowers; you could have mistaken it for a small flower shop. My colleagues thought it was hilarious. By the end of our relationship, I couldn't stand the sight or smell of the things."

My stomach sank. "Oh shit. And here you are, surrounded by them."

Roz smiled across at me. "Perhaps they're not so bad after all."

My heart ballooned. I furrowed my brow. She'd just said she wasn't interested in anything serious. But she also used to want kids, and she clearly changed her mind about that. Perhaps she might change her mind again? I clenched my jaw. Pursuing something casual with Roz on the faint hope that she might change her mind was a terrible idea.

Roz knelt down on the grass and carefully selected another rose, which she pressed into the bottom of the arch.

I couldn't help picturing Roz, kneeling before me, my back pressed to the front door of Sapphire Blooms as she pushed her fingers inside me. My eyes dropped to her mouth. *Big mistake.* The sensation of her soft lips making their way down my stomach last Friday night flooded my memory and sent my core thrumming. I swallowed. *Don't look at her mouth.* My gaze lowered to her hands delicately maneuvering the rose into position. *Or her hands!* I jerked my head away, focusing on the arch. That was safer.

But even with my eyes averted, my body still pulsed with desire. My mind whirred as I stared blankly at a particularly spectacular red rose. I wasn't planning to start dating again until after the paperwork for Fred's investment was signed anyway. Would it be such a terrible idea to extend our fling another week or two, until it was all finalized? Surely in that time I wouldn't get more attached than I already was... I swallowed. It quite possibly was a terrible idea, but never getting to kiss Roz again felt even worse. *Fuck it.*

I looked down at Roz through the foliage. "Okay."

She looked up at me, tilting her head. "Sorry?"

I cleared my throat. "Let's try casual. But only until Fred's paperwork is signed."

Roz's eyes widened, her face breaking into a wild smile. "Really?"

I nodded. "Yes."

"Are you sure?"

Doubt washed over me. I could just imagine the look of horror on George's face when I told her. And Blake would be even worse. Casually dating my enemy-turned-fake girlfriend when I wanted more than she could offer? Heat pricked my neck.

"Yes. But do you mind if we keep this between us? It's

just that I announced to the world last year I was turning my life around. Instead of jumping from one job and one relationship to another, I was going to make my thirties all about settling down."

Roz chuckled. "Sure. We'd just mastered the art of fake dating; now we can hone our skills in the art of fake not casually dating. We don't want to get too comfortable."

Roz's eyes twinkled and I laughed, feeling lighter. Maybe it all would be okay. If it was anything like our fake-dating experience, at least we'd have some fun along the way.

Roz stood on the other side of the arch to me, roses framing her head, her gaze soft. "Can I kiss you?"

My eyes darted around, checking no one was about. Making out under the floral arch hours before my clients would be married under it did not feel entirely professional. But the only sign of life was a bird flying overhead.

"Yes." I laughed, leaning in to kiss Roz. Our lips met and I closed my eyes, letting out a low moan as Roz's hot tongue slipped into my mouth. Tingles raced down my spine. *Oh god.* I fisted the collar of her flannel shirt. Roz's hand slid to my ass, giving it a squeeze, and I grabbed onto the arch to stabilize myself. The arch wobbled, bringing me back to reality.

I was under a time crunch to finish setting up for the wedding. I couldn't let myself get carried away or bring it all toppling over in a fit of passion. I disentangled myself from Roz.

"I would love to continue this later, but I really need to finish getting the rest of the flower arrangements done before Jenny and the wedding guests arrive."

Roz stepped back, grinning. "Another raincheck? I'm

okay with that, as long as it doesn't take as long as last time to call it in."

I laughed. "There is absolutely no risk of that."

"What are you doing tonight?"

My grin widened. "You?"

Roz chuckled. "Sounds like a plan."

I watched her go, the winged unicorns back again and flapping harder than ever in my stomach.

CHAPTER THIRTY

ROZ

"I NEVER THOUGHT I'd say this, but I think your expensive Italian coffee machine might be worth every penny." Olivia let out a satisfied sigh as she placed her mug of coffee on the wicker table and turned back to the farm stretched out in front of us.

The coffee did taste particularly delicious this morning—rich and nutty. *Everything's better with Olivia.* I frowned. *Don't be ridiculous.*

Dana's truck rumbled down the road toward the farm exit. I raised a hand in greeting and she waved back. As Olivia requested, we hadn't told anyone we were seeing each other casually, but Dana must have suspected something given how often Olivia's car was parked at the farm. Dana wasn't one to gossip, but I should talk to her, let her know we were keeping it quiet.

That reminded me... "Dana thinks I'm finally ready to drive the hayride." I grinned. It had only taken six weeks of practice and one very expensive crash.

"That's awesome! Lottie will be thrilled." Olivia broke into a wide smile, her eyes crinkling. My heart bounced.

"Would you be interested in joining her on my inaugural hayride around the farm? I thought I'd ease into it with a friends-and-family-only ride before I expand to strangers. Perhaps tomorrow afternoon after the farm has closed?"

Olivia laughed. "I'd be honored."

The familiar warm glow I felt each time Olivia and I planned another meet up filled my chest. For two people who were casually dating, we had spent a lot of time together in the past two weeks—rom-com movie nights, lazy mornings in bed, a dinner at Prue's vineyard. *Fred will be sending through the paperwork any day now. Might as well enjoy it while we can.*

Heaviness washed over me. I hadn't checked my emails today.

I unlocked my phone and clicked on the mail icon, my pulse increasing as I scrolled through the emails, scanning for Fred's name. I should have been experiencing unbridled excitement at the prospect of finally receiving the investment contract—it would be the culmination of everything we'd worked so hard for over the past few weeks. But to say my feelings were mixed was an understatement. Because once the papers were signed, Olivia and I would go back to just being friends. My shoulders relaxed as I reached the end of the new emails. Nothing from Fred. There was a short email from Prue, which I skimmed over.

I put down my phone and turned to Olivia, grinning. "Prue's in for the spring festival."

"Oh great! We'll—I mean you'll—have heaps of stalls, then."

My body buzzed. There'd be local produce, live music and spring activities. While I'd made a number of behind-the-scenes changes at the farm already, the festival would be my first very public initiative. It better be a success.

I spooned nutty granola into my mouth, watching the wispy clouds slowly moving across the blue sky.

"Moooo!" Louise stuck her head through the fence, her soft brown eyes focused on us.

"Your BFF has come to say hello," Olivia teased.

"Don't worry. I'll be over soon!" I yelled toward the cows, then chuckled. Over the last few weeks, Louise and I had formed a bond—a special bond based on a steady supply of carrots and apples.

"I was thinking of heading over to the flowers after we finish eating to see how the irises are coming along," Olivia said, leaning back on the chair. "I'm hoping to use them for a wedding next weekend. Do you want to come?"

"Sure, but I'm more interested in seeing how the lupines are doing."

Olivia let out a peal of laughter. "Look at you, taking an interest in the flowers."

I shrugged, the corners of my mouth lifting. "I mean, they're not terrible looking. They are nice and... purple."

Olivia snorted. "That's strong praise, coming from Roz 'I hate flowers' Kennedy."

I rolled my eyes. "And as long as we can swing past Thelma and Louise on the way to say hi and deliver a couple of carrots."

"It's a deal," Olivia said, picking up her empty bowl and stacking it on mine. "And do you feel like heading to Novel Gossip later for lunch? George was telling me about the special this week—crème brûlée French toast with berries— and I really want to try it."

"Yes please. My mouth is already watering."

This was shaping up to be yet another weekend spent

completely with Olivia. Was this really wise, spending so much time together? I pushed the thought out of my mind. This could be our last weekend together; it would be nice to end it on a high.

OLIVIA PUSHED OPEN the door to Novel Gossip and moaned. "Oh god, I think I can smell the French toast. I hope it hasn't sold out."

I stepped in after her. A distinctly sweet smell hit my nose, sending my stomach rumbling. The café was buzzing today. Most of the tables were occupied and there was a line of people waiting to order. My gaze flitted over them, looking for any faces I recognized.

Dana stood in the middle of the line, talking to a man who had his back to us. A man who, even from that angle, looked very familiar.

My heart stopped.

Fred.

My heart started beating at twice its usual speed.

"Shit, Fred's here," I muttered to Olivia.

Olivia followed my gaze, her eyes widening. "Oh." She grabbed my hand, the heat of her soft skin sending a comforting rush of warmth up my arm. "It'll be okay. We're pros at faking it now."

My stomach swirled. Why was I so uneasy about Fred's unexpected appearance?

Olivia squeezed my hand. "I guess we'd better go say hi."

My body did not agree. As we walked over to them, sweat pricked my neck and my legs itched. I wanted to run —fast—in the opposite direction.

Despite Fred facing away from us, his voice travelled clearly. "Once the contract is signed, it'll be full steam ahead with the event space. I know they've only been dating for six months or so, but I'm kind of hoping Olivia and Roz will be the first people to get married in it. Assuming all the approvals go smoothly, it should be done by April next year —just in time for a spring wedding." He chuckled.

"Six months?" Dana frowned. "More like one month—if that."

I froze, my stomach plummeting to the floor. *Shit. Shit. Shit.*

"Sorry?" Fred asked.

"Olivia and Roz. I don't know exactly when they got together, but it definitely wasn't last year. Olivia didn't even know who Roz was six weeks ago. When Roz took over the farm, Olivia asked me what she was like."

Olivia and I stared at each other, our eyes wide. *Shit.*

"That doesn't sound right," Fred said.

My heart pounded in my ears. *We should get out of here —quickly. Buy ourselves some time to work out what to do.* I started to turn, tugging gently at Olivia's hand.

Dana's eyes landed on us and Fred turned, following her gaze.

"Roz! Olivia!" Fred waved.

Blood drained from my face. I plastered on a smile and we walked toward them.

"Excellent timing. I was planning to come around later today with a little delivery." Fred patted the black leather satchel slung around his shoulder. *The investment contract.* "We were just talking about you. The two of you started dating around October last year, right?"

I swallowed. *Oh god.* Put on the spot, I couldn't bring myself to lie directly to Fred.

"We met in October last year." Guilt stabbed me in the chest. I sounded like an evasive politician.

Fred frowned. "But Dana said Olivia didn't know who you were when you took over the farm?"

I shot a glance at Olivia. Her face was pale.

"She didn't realize I was the same person she had met in October." I cringed at how confusing that sounded.

Fred's eyes narrowed. "You two were dating, but she didn't know you'd bought the farm?"

Fuck.

"Not exactly."

Fred's eyes darted between me and Olivia. "I don't actually care when the two of you started dating, but it's beginning to feel like there's something else going on and you haven't been totally honest with me."

Olivia and I looked at each other. *We have to tell him the truth.* She gave me a tiny nod.

"We did meet back in October, but we didn't keep in touch. It was only when I moved back here that we reconnected and in the last few weeks we started dating—casually," I said, my heart beating fast.

"You're telling me you were lying about being together?" Fred stared at me.

"I'm sorry, Fred," Olivia said. "It's all my fault. You see, when I—"

Fred's nostrils flared. "I trusted you. Both of you. I don't know what you were playing at, but finding out you were lying about your relationship is just..." Fred ran his hand through his hair. "Honestly, it's baffling."

"I'm sorry, we—"

Fred pressed his lips together, shaking his head. "I'm out. I can't go into business with someone I don't trust. If you're comfortable lying about this, what else will you lie about?" He stared at me, a mixture of anger and hurt swirling in his eyes. "I really thought you were better than this, Roz."

"Look, I know it sounds weird, but I didn't intentionally set out to deceive you. We—"

Fred shook his head again. "I don't want to hear any more excuses. The deal is off."

CHAPTER THIRTY-ONE

OLIVIA

"SHIT!" Roz slammed her hand on her study desk. She'd spent the afternoon in her study, poring over the farm's finances, her lips pressed into a tight line.

"Should we try calling Fred again? If he'd just let us explain..."

Roz shook her head. "We've left two voicemails. We can't keep harassing him. At this rate, he'll block my number."

I slumped back on the couch. What else could we do? I didn't blame Fred for his reaction. He was right—trust was critical for successful business relationships and we'd completely blown up his faith in us.

"We're fucked," Roz announced, snapping her laptop shut. "I've already spent more money than I have on the basis Fred's funding was coming through. I'll have to dig into my 401(k) to pay my employees' wages at this point."

My stomach dropped. *Damn.* Things really were bad.

Roz lowered her eyes to her desk. "I'll have to take immediate action to have any chance of keeping the farm afloat."

My shoulders tensed. The combination of Roz avoiding eye contact and the words *immediate action* sent a chill down my spine. "Like what?"

She raised her eyes. *Oh no.*

"I'm sorry, Liv, but I'm going to have to shut down the flower farm operations." My lungs squeezed. *No. No. No.* "I'll do my best to honor all the weddings you've committed to and we'll keep the flowers going until the spring festival, but once that's done we'll need to stop ASAP. They are just too labor intensive and fixing the greenhouse in time for the cooler weather will cost too much. If I can lease the fields out, then at least I'll have some money coming in and that will free up Dana and our seasonal workers to focus on preparing for fall."

I swallowed, trying to dislodge the enormous lump in my throat and failing miserably. "There has to be another way. Couldn't you lease out the land the corn maze and pumpkin patch is on instead, or the Christmas trees or something?" My voice was an octave higher than usual.

"The fall festivities are one of the farm's highest-grossing activities. They bring crowds of people to the farm. I can't afford to lose them. I'm sorry. I don't want to do this, Liv, but it's my only chance of keeping the farm afloat. And even then, I don't think we'll make it past winter."

My mind whirred. There had to be another way. "What about finding another investor or lender? Surely there's someone else out there."

Roz shook her head. "The banks wouldn't lend to me and I've exhausted all the connections I have."

I exhaled, wracking my brain. Did I know any rich people?

The memory of Marie and Frank's gigantic house on their sprawling property came into focus. *Roz's parents.*

Why hadn't I thought of them before? "What about your parents? I mean, they were lawyers for years. Surely they have a shitload of money?"

"No." Roz ran a hand through her hair.

I leaned forward on the couch. "They seemed to love the farm. Wouldn't they be willing to help out?"

"Possibly. But I'm not taking any money from them." Roz pushed her laptop away.

I stared at her, wide-eyed. "Hang on a second. So you're willing to throw it all away, to destroy the flowers and destroy my business, because you are too proud or stubborn or whatever is going on to ask your parents for help?"

Tears welled in my eyes. I was back at square one again. By winter, I'd have no job and all I'd have to show for the past six weeks would be another ex to run into at the general store. So much for turning over a new leaf in my thirties.

Roz clenched her jaw. "I've spent my whole life proving that I can do things without my parents. I can't just turn around and ask them for help now, when times are tough. That would invalidate all the years I spent trying to get out of their shadows."

"It could just be a loan. You could pay it all back," I pleaded.

"No!" Roz snapped.

I gritted my teeth. "I know you don't like to ask people for help, but choosing to ruin the farm and my business, because you're not willing to accept a loan from your parents is... is incomprehensible." I narrowed my eyes. "Is it really because you hate flowers? You're still hung up on Sadie and this is your excuse to get rid of them once and for all?"

"No." Roz furrowed her brow. "That's ridiculous. You don't understand."

"You're damn right. I don't." A wave of hot anger crashed over me. "Well, I guess this is it, then. You're getting rid of the flowers. The investment has fallen through. Sapphire Blooms is screwed. And yet again, I've wasted my time on a relationship that wasn't going anywhere and have a failed business on my hands. I'll see you around, Roz."

And with that, I stormed out of Roz's study and headed toward my car, dodging a busload of happy families who had just arrived at the farm.

CHAPTER THIRTY-TWO

ROZ

I STARED BLANKLY at the numbers in front of me, Olivia's words from yesterday ringing in my ears. Was my pride, and perhaps some lingering subconscious dislike of flowers, clouding my judgment?

But the numbers didn't lie. Closing down the flower operations was the only hope I had of keeping the farm going through to Christmas. And after that... My chest tightened. Unless there was a miracle, I'd have to put the farm on the market.

Unless I ask my parents for a loan...

I shut my eyes, rubbing my forehead. No, that was off the table. I felt terrible for what it meant for Olivia's shop, but surely she could find another supplier? While there wasn't another local farm that grew flowers sustainably, couldn't she make some compromises, just like I was having to do, to stay afloat? Was importing some flowers from overseas really that bad?

The memory of Olivia's eyes, wide with disbelief, as I refused to ask my parents for the money, sent a sharp pain shooting into my heart.

Fuck. I needed to talk to someone who'd understand. I picked up my phone.

"SO SHE THINKS I'm being completely unreasonable not asking Mom and Dad for money," I concluded. "What do you think?"

I leaned against the fence to the petting zoo. The delighted squeals of two toddlers, taking turns to pet a fluffy white rabbit with long floppy ears under one of the farm-hand's watchful eyes, were so loud Matt opened and then closed his mouth.

Once their joy subsided to a slightly lower decibel level, Matt fixed me with a steady gaze. "I get why you're reluctant, but you've spent the last twenty years proving you can achieve amazing things without them. Is it really such a big deal to ask for help this once?"

I clenched my jaw. "But that's just the thing. I've spent twenty years proving I can do it alone. Accepting a loan from them will undo it all."

The baby goats bounced around their enclosure. Lottie crouched down next to the fence, watching them. They began head-butting each other playfully and Lottie's face broke into a broad smile. A small glow lit in my chest. This would all be gone if I didn't get the money from somewhere. The glow vanished.

Matt shook his head. "Asking them for a loan is very different than what happened when we were kids. They were effectively bribing people to let us get ahead. There's nothing underhanded or illegal about having your parents give you money. And it's just a loan, for god's sake. You'll pay them back."

I gripped the railing so tightly my knuckles turned white. I didn't want to ride on the coattails of my parents at all, even if I would eventually repay them. I took a deep breath, inhaling the scent of fresh hay mixed with animal manure.

"It's not just that. You know what they're like. If they loan me money, they'll want to be involved in running the farm. There'll be those raised eyebrows, the 'helpful suggestions' and a constant stream of questions about how it's going. I'll have them looking over my shoulder twenty-four seven. It will drive me up the wall."

Matt frowned. "You could try talking to them about that, see if you can come to an agreement on what involvement, if any, they would have."

I stared at Matt. "Do you really think they'd stick to it?"

He shrugged, his eyes following Lottie as she sprang up and ran over to Ronnie, who was supervising the pony rides. Ronnie looked over to us, his eyebrows raised in question. Matt nodded. Ronnie smiled and handed Lottie a helmet.

"I'm sure there will still be some raised eyebrows and pointed comments, but if they agree upfront they won't be involved, then at least you'll be able to shut them down by reminding them about the agreement," Matt said.

Lottie was on a brown pony now, being walked around by Ronnie. She waved to us, grinning from ear to ear, and we waved back. I couldn't believe she'd be turning eight tomorrow. My heart constricted. Mel hadn't gotten approval to come back early in time for Lottie's birthday, so it would just be my parents, Matt and me at her birthday dinner tomorrow night.

"I haven't seen you this happy for years. Maybe ever. Don't throw the farm and Olivia away because of your pride, Roz." Matt's voice was almost pleading. "I thought you were having a mid-life crisis when you decided to buy the farm, but now it makes total sense to me. You clearly love this place. I've never seen you so excited about work before. And the same goes for Olivia as well."

A heaviness tugged at my chest. "There's nothing to throw away where Olivia is concerned. We'd agreed it would all end when the investment paperwork came through, which would have been yesterday if Fred hadn't found out about us." I shook my head. "It's over. The whole thing was a mistake. I should never have let myself get so carried away. I can't even make business decisions clearly because this infatuation with Olivia is clouding my judgment."

Matt turned to me. "Or the two of you are just madly in love and you care about her so much that you don't want to do something that will hurt her."

Love. For some stupid reason, the word sent tears welling in my eyes. I blinked them away, pressing my lips together. Matt was being ridiculous.

But the tears kept coming. A lump formed in my throat. Was it... Could it be possible?

If I did sell the farm, I'd have to move back to New York, find another job as a management consultant and start rebuilding my savings and my 401(k). I might never see Olivia again. Pain stabbed my chest at the thought.

I'd only really known her for six weeks—if you didn't include that night at Pryde—but in that time, she'd helped me find my footing at the farm, learn to ride a bike again, get a whole new wardrobe, make new friends and business connections, develop a love of rom-coms and plan a spring festival. And not only that, but all of it had been fun. Fun in a way I'd never experienced before. I loved her kindness, her desire to make the world a better place, her sense of humor, not to mention our off-the-charts chemistry. What I felt for her was deeper, more grounded, than anything I'd felt for Sadie.

Fuck.

I loved her.

I looked around. At small children petting the animals, their faces bright, as their parents watched with indulgent grins. Dana driving a hayride full of families down the dirt road toward the orchards. Two teenagers holding hands, shooting each other shy smiles as they walked toward the petting zoo, home-made strawberry ice creams in their hands. Lottie, still high on her pony, chatting to Ronnie as she clutched the reins.

And I loved this farm.

It had only been six weeks, but I couldn't imagine my life without Olivia or the farm. I couldn't let them go without doing everything in my power to keep them—even if it meant me putting my pride aside and begging my parents for a loan.

CHAPTER THIRTY-THREE

OLIVIA

"EARTH TO OLIVIA!" Blake waved her hand in front of my face.

I jerked, sending the water in the cup I was holding splashing onto my jumpsuit. "Sorry."

"What is going on with you today?" Blake stared at me.

I blinked. Jenny, George and Hannah, sprawled out on the tartan picnic blanket under a large oak tree in Dockside Park, were all staring at me as well.

My body ached from our kayaking session. When Jenny had messaged this morning, asking if anyone was interested in a paddle followed by a picnic lunch, I'd hoped the exercise and fresh air might clear my head. It hadn't.

"Nothing." If I told everyone, I'd start crying again. And it wasn't just that. To give them the full story, I'd have to tell them about what was going on with me and Roz. Sure, I could leave that part out, try to skirt around it, but I was sick and tired of obfuscating, of only telling half-truths. It hadn't exactly ended well with Fred.

I smoothed out the patch of picnic blanket next to me, brushing away imaginary crumbs. At least Dana hadn't shown up. She was the only one who now knew the whole story, and I'd been so distracted yesterday I hadn't thought to ask her not to mention what had happened to anyone else for now.

"Liv." Blake's voice softened. "You just spent the last hour paddling like you were being chased by a school of ravenous sharks, leaving us all in your wake, and ever since we sat down, you've been staring glumly at my shoes." Blake wiggled her black sneakers. "I mean, they're nice shoes. But not that nice. Something is clearly wrong."

George tilted her head, looking at me with her brow furrowed. She'd been standing too far away at Novel Gossip to hear the discussion between Fred, Dana, Roz and myself yesterday, but she'd seen enough to text me later to ask if everything was okay. I'd brushed her off as well.

"I don't feel like talking about it right now. Maybe later." I looked over the blue expanse of river to the green, tree-covered hills opposite us. Perhaps getting out in nature, just by myself, would help. Roz and I had talked about doing the Breakback Ridge hike together next weekend. A lump formed in my throat. That wouldn't happen now.

"Okay," Blake said, grabbing a smoked salmon bagel from the picnic basket. "Well, can everyone make trivia night this week? With Roz, George and Hannah away last week and Dana missing the week before, we haven't stood a chance against The Gran Masters. I've been reading up on politics, so I think we have a chance if we get the entire brain trust together."

"We'll be there." Hannah squeezed George's hand.

I nodded. I could always pull out at the last minute if I wasn't feeling it.

"Do you know if Roz can make it?" Blake asked.

A pain stabbed my chest. "Um—"

"Hi. Sorry I'm so late." Dana appeared, lowering herself to the ground. She looked like she hadn't slept either—dark circles under her eyes and her face a few shades paler than usual. Her gray pants and white t-shirt were faintly crumpled. "I brought some dips." She opened a small cooler and pulled out some containers, peeling back their lids and placing them in the middle of the blanket next to the rest of the food. "Hummus, baba ganoush and tzatziki. And carrot sticks and pita chips."

I swallowed. Hopefully the topic of Roz and the farm wouldn't arise.

"Yum!" Hannah leaned in, grabbing a pita chip and swiping it through the hummus.

"Is everything okay, Dana?" Jenny asked.

Dana's brows shot up as her eyes flicked to me. "You didn't tell them?"

I shook my head.

Dana slammed her mouth shut. "I've said enough already this weekend."

A gray bird swooped overheard, dipping down into the river with a splash and reappearing with a fish in its beak.

Jenny's gaze darted between us. "What's going on? Did something happen with the flowers? I thought you got the aphids under control?" Her eyes widened. "You didn't have another cow-trampling incident, did you?"

"No." Tears welled in my eyes. I blinked them away, but they began dripping down my cheeks. I swiped them away. "Shit."

Jenny jumped up and bounded over, wrapping her arms around me. I leaned into her warmth, letting out a shuddering breath.

"Oh, Liv. What happened?" Jenny asked.

Five pairs of eyes stared at me sympathetically. My

world was imploding. I was losing Sapphire Blooms, the farm and Roz in one fell swoop. If ever there was a time I needed to talk to my friends, it was now. I couldn't do this alone.

I cleared my throat. "Fred backed out of the investment and now Roz is going to shut down the flower operations—and she thinks the farm may not make it past winter."

There was a collective intake of breath.

"Shit! Why did he back out?" Blake asked.

"He found out we were fake dating." I struggled to hold back a sob.

Jenny tilted her head, wide-eyed. "How did he find out?"

My eyes flicked to Dana, who cradled her face in her hands.

"He ran into Dana at Novel Gossip yesterday and made a comment about how we'd been dating for six months. Dana corrected him, saying it was only one month at the most. Roz and I showed up just as all this was happening and Fred asked us on the spot. We had to tell him the truth."

"Oh no!" Hannah groaned.

"Yeah, it was really bad." Dana grimaced.

"Like we said yesterday, it wasn't your fault." I reached out and rubbed Dana's back. "It's all on me and Roz—well, mainly me. I was the one who got us into the stupid fake-dating situation to begin with, and we never explained to you what was going on."

"I'm so sorry, Liv. If it's any consolation, I thought you two were quite convincing. If I hadn't known better, I would have thought there was something going on between you." Blake picked up a carrot stick and dipped it in the baba ganoush.

Dana shot a glance at me.

My stomach clenched. This was the perfect opening to tell everyone what had really been going on. But nausea rocked my stomach at the thought of them hearing how stupid I'd been, letting myself get pulled into a fling that had no future, after swearing off dead-end relationships. Not only that, but I'd have to talk about my sexuality. And I still didn't know how to answer those damn dating profile questions. I'd hoped to have a clearer idea before I had this conversation. Olivia in her thirties was meant to be all about knowing what she wanted and grabbing it by both hands. So far, that wasn't going so well.

Roz's advice floated through my mind. *You don't need to put a label on it if you don't want to. Or you could just use a general term—like queer.* Tears pricked my eyes again.

"Yeah, um, well, actually..." I sniffed, glancing over at George, who gave me a small, encouraging smile. "There was."

Blake's jaw dropped. "What?"

My heart thudded in my ears. Who'd have thought coming out to three queer women, all of whom were close friends and one of whom was my sister, would be so nerve-racking?

"We started dating—casually—a few weeks ago." I ran my hand over the wicker picnic basket next to me. "But it's over now. We had a big argument yesterday. Anyway, it was only supposed to be until Fred's investment paperwork came through."

Blake's stare continued to bore into me.

"Oh wow!" Jenny said. "I'm really sorry that you guys had an argument, but hooray for more gays?"

I managed a weak laugh. "Thanks, Jenny."

My gaze shifted back to my usually composed sister. Her cheeks were flushed, her mouth still open wide.

"Shit, Liv. I always just assumed..."

"That's okay," I said. "I also assumed I was straight for a long time."

Blake's gaze flickered. "But why... why didn't you tell us?"

"It's something I wanted to work out for myself first. I know you all figured out your sexuality pretty early on, but it's taken me a long time. And I'm still working it out. I'm not sure if I'm bi, pan or a lesbian or something else."

Hannah put her arm around my waist and gave it a squeeze. "Hey, that's okay. You don't have to decide one way or another. You do you."

"Thanks, Hannah. That's what Roz said too." My voice wavered.

The others offered me similar words of solidarity. George passed around some salted caramel and pecan cookies and I bit into one, savoring the salty-sweet crunch.

"Surely there's something Roz can do that doesn't involve destroying the flowers and losing the farm," Jenny said, wiping cookie crumbs from her face.

I pressed my lips together. "That's what we were arguing about. Her parents are loaded, but she's refusing to ask them for help."

"What?" Jenny dropped the pita chip she was holding. "Why not?"

I frowned. Despite suggesting it was connected to Sadie and Roz's dislike of flowers when I'd stormed out yesterday, I didn't really believe that. That wouldn't explain why Roz would rather lose the entire farm, not just the flower fields, than ask her parents for help. From what she'd said yesterday, it was clear she had a long-standing aversion to asking her parents for help. She'd indicated as much when her parents had tried to give her the new Mercedes-Benz. But I didn't know the details.

"I'm not completely sure," I admitted. "But she's generally very reluctant to accept any help from her parents." Or anyone else, for that matter.

"Maybe she's worried about mixing business with pleasure and it affecting her relationship with her parents?" Hannah suggested.

"Maybe..." I replied. It was a valid concern. While Blake and Dad worked well together, as much as I loved my parents I couldn't imagine involving them in my business. And my relationship with my parents was a lot stronger than Roz's. When Roz had refused the new Mercedes-Benz, she'd mentioned if she accepted their help, it would come with judgement.

Perhaps Roz did have valid reasons for refusing the loan. But whatever they were, she was prioritizing them over me and the farm. And that still hurt.

"Is there anything we can do? Maybe I could organize a fundraiser or something?" Jenny asked, her face brightening.

"We could all help," George said, leaning in. "I could do the catering."

Blake, Hannah and Dana nodded.

Despite how miserable I was feeling, warmth washed over me. God, I loved my friends.

"Thank you, but we couldn't raise the amount of money she needs. I've seen the financials. We're talking millions of dollars."

"Oh shit." Jenny's face fell.

"Yeah."

A dog bounded into view, running across the expanse of

grass in front of us, and jumped into the river, its tail wagging. *What I'd give to be that carefree right now.*

"What are you going to do?" Hannah asked.

"I don't know." I sighed. It seemed like Sapphire Blooms would just be another addition to my long list of business failures. I stared glumly back at Blake's shoe.

Failure is the steppingstone to success. The conversation I'd had with Roz weeks ago at Prue's vineyard echoed in my head. *Most people give up too soon.*

I took a deep breath. I was not going to give up on Sapphire Blooms, Red Tractor Farm or Roz. Not yet. Not until I'd exhausted every possible avenue.

CHAPTER THIRTY-FOUR

OLIVIA

I WISH ROZ WAS HERE. *She'd be at home in this world.*

I stared up at the soaring skyscraper and swallowed. My eyes dropped to the foyer of Fred's building. People in dark suits swarmed through the formidable revolving doors, ready to throw themselves into another week of making rich people even richer.

A chill shot down my spine. Drew, the cheating banker I'd dated, had worked in a building just like this. *Maybe this was a bad idea.*

A man pushed past me, briefcase in hand, jerking me forward.

"Ouch!" A pain shot through my shoulder. I glared at him. He looked like my loan officer—the one who'd refused to give me more time to pay back my loan for the recycled cooking oil business. I only needed a few more months to start turning a profit, but he wasn't willing to wait any longer. My stomach roiled with nausea.

In fact, the last time I'd been inside a building like this, it was to speak to an attorney about the best course of action after I'd received intimidating legal notices from the bank. She'd charged me thousands of dollars to tell me that I should give up, liquidate my assets and find another job to pay back my debt.

And this was why I hated suits.

I clenched my jaw. Well, I wasn't going to give up so easily this time. All I had to do was try to convince a man I'd just spent the last six weeks lying to that he should invest millions of dollars in Red Tractor Farm. How hard could it be?

I strode up to the revolving doors, jumping in quickly as they swung past. My heart pounded in my ears, but I managed to get in without losing any limbs.

The foyer of the building was covered, floor-to-ceiling, in expensive-looking marble. Footsteps and voices echoed around me. I strode up to the reception desk.

"Hi, I'm here to see Fred Stockdon, of Stockdon & Associates."

A bald white man looked up at me. His eyes dropped to my clothes, and heat shot up my cheeks.

When I'd dressed this morning, I'd thought my pink-and-blue flower-print pants and purple silk blouse looked smart. But I was in Roz and Fred's world now. I should have gone with something more subdued. However, unless I was willing to race to Macy's and purchase some suit pants I'd never wear again, I was stuck with this outfit. I certainly wasn't about to make the hour and a half trip home to Sapphire Springs to change.

"ID please." The man held out his hand.

Fumbling, I pulled my wallet from my handbag, took out my driver's license and handed it to him.

"One minute." He raised a phone to his ear. "Olivia Mitchell to see Fred Stockdon."

After a moment, the man frowned and looked at me. "You don't have an appointment?"

I shook my head. "Can you tell him it's important?"

He turned back to the phone. "She says it's important."

My heart pounded in my chest. Were they going to send me away? When I hopped on the train this morning, I knew it was a real possibility. My stomach sank at the thought of coming this far and not even getting to make my case to Fred.

The man put down the phone. "His assistant is checking with him. Can you step to one side please?"

I hovered near the desk while the man gave a temporary visitor's pass to an employee who'd left theirs at home and then took another phone call.

Once he put down the phone, he waved me over. "Okay. They say you can go up. Here's a temporary pass. Thirty-first floor." He handed me a small white card with a barcode on it. I exhaled.

I scanned the card at the security gate, passing through into the elevator banks. I looked around, confused. Where the hell was the up button? It took me a few moments to register that, instead of pressing a button to call an elevator, I had to enter the floor number into a touch screen, which then told me which elevator to take.

The elevator shot up to the thirty-first level. I stared at the floor, trying to avoid the mirrors that reflected my bright floral outfit to infinity from all angles, making it seem even more garish. It was almost a relief when the doors opened and I walked out into a stark white foyer with yet another reception desk.

A woman sat behind the desk in a black pantsuit with a sleek headset on her black hair that was tied in a ponytail.

"Hi. Um, I'm Olivia Mitchell. Here to see Fred. I mean,

Mr. Stockdon." Sweat prickled my armpits. Was it suddenly very hot in here?

The woman's eyes flicked down to the screen in front of her. "Mr. Stockdon is in a meeting right now, but he said he'd see you once it has ended, which should be around eleven a.m. Please take a seat." She gestured to three black leather couches near the enormous floor-to-ceiling windows.

I walked over and sat next to the window. I peered out, hoping the view would calm my nerves. *God, we were up high.* Tiny people scurried down on the pavement, while cars, taxis, buses and motorcycles moved slowly down the street. If I leaned in, I could just spot a green glimpse of Central Park. I smoothed my hands over my thighs and then stood up and peered out the window from a different angle, before sitting again, this time with my legs jiggling. The receptionist shot me a look. *I need to calm down.*

I took a deep breath, trying to visualize myself in the middle of the flower fields, dahlias stretching out around me, inhaling their earthy, slightly sweet scent. *My happy place.* My shoulders relaxed. Suddenly, a herd of cows appeared in the fields, trampling my precious flowers and snapping them off at the stems with their teeth. My chest constricted. So much for a relaxing meditation.

"Olivia."

I started at Fred's voice.

Heart racing, I jumped up and walked toward him. He wore a charcoal-gray suit, polished black shoes, and a white shirt. His face matched his voice—calm and serious.

"Come through." Fred swiped his pass next to a door, opened it and ushered me through. I followed him down a hallway of glass offices until we reached a large corner one. Expensive-looking landscape paintings adorned the walls. The windows offered a view of Rockefeller Center.

When he'd shut the door behind us, he gestured for me to take a seat in front of his large redwood desk. He walked around and sat facing me.

I gulped. "Thanks for agreeing to see me."

Fred shuffled some papers on his desk. "I thought about turning you away, but since you came this far, I'll give you a few minutes."

"Thank you." I cleared my throat. "I'm so sorry for lying to you, Fred. I completely understand we betrayed your trust. I was hoping you'd be willing to let me explain what happened, in case it changes your mind."

Fred put down the papers and fixed me with a stare. "Okay. Go ahead. I've got five minutes."

Despite the time constraints, I started from the beginning—the very beginning. I spoke fast, the words jumbling out as I told Fred about Roz and I meeting at Pryde, the phone number mishap and then Roz blurting out my name as a way to get her mom off her back. And then me showing up at Red Tractor Farm, guns blazing.

"Roz wasn't trying to trick you into lending us the money on false pretenses. I just jumped at the opportunity to take advantage of Roz's mom introducing me as her girlfriend to try to influence you and Roz to save the flower farm and, by extension, Sapphire Blooms. It was a spur-of-the-moment decision and Roz was so taken aback, she played along, only afterwards realizing what a hole we'd dug for ourselves."

Fred frowned. "You could have come clean to me then."

I dropped my head and gazed at my hands in my lap. "What we'd done just sounded so ridiculous, we thought you wouldn't want to lend money to idiots who'd gotten themselves into that position." I peered up at Fred.

Fred snorted. "Well, perhaps."

"Not only that, but Roz worried that you'd already feel it was a betrayal of trust. At the time, it felt like an innocuous enough lie. Why did it matter who Roz dated? And then, what began as a rather acrimonious partnership developed into something else." I swallowed.

Fred raised his eyebrows. "I see."

"I'm so sorry, Fred. I put Roz in an impossible position, one she felt terrible about. It was my fault."

Fred nodded, his face still serious. "I can think of a number of ways the two of you—not just you—could have handled the situation differently, but I appreciate the context and the apology."

I took a deep breath. "Even though I've only properly known Roz for six weeks, I can assure you that she's a very trustworthy and sensible person, and that this whole situation was very out of character for her. Both of us will do everything we can to regain your trust."

I looked at Fred, trying to gauge his reaction, but his face was neutral. *Shit. Give me something, Fred.*

"Not only that, but the investment is an excellent business decision. Roz has the vision and the drive to make Red Tractor Farm an incredible success, and if you—and Roz—still want me to be involved, I'll happily continue to make myself available. Or I—I can stay away, if that would make you more comfortable." I winced at the increasingly desperate tone to my voice.

Panic bubbled in my chest. Fred's gaze held mine, his face expressionless. He did not appear to have been swayed by my speech.

"I came here to try to save both Red Tractor Farm and Sapphire Blooms. If Roz shuts down the flower operations, Sapphire Blooms will need to close. But I completely understand if the flowers and Sapphire Blooms aren't your priority, especially not after the role I played in this whole situation. But please... please at least invest enough money to keep the farm going and to build the event space. You know Roz would make it a success. You've seen how passionate she is. She's smart and determined and loves the farm fiercely."

I shuffled in my seat. As painful as it was, I could live with the fact that my actions had caused Sapphire Blooms' demise. I had no one to blame but myself and I'd do everything in my power to ensure Maddie found a new job. But the farm... that was more than I could bear.

"It seems she's not the only one." Fred smiled weakly.

I sat up straighter. Could he...? "You've seen how incredible the farm is, providing entertainment to thousands of families year round. It would be a huge loss to the Sapphire Springs community and the greater region if it was bulldozed to the ground." I blinked away the tears that had started to brew in my eyes. "Not only that, but Dana, Ronnie and all the other employees you've met would lose their jobs."

Fred's face softened. "Discovering the two of you had been lying felt like a huge breach of trust. And based on what you've said, Roz wasn't completely blameless in this." He sighed. "But while it seems like a completely bizarre set of events, I appreciate that you didn't set out to trick me into investing in the farm. And while there are clearly much better ways you could have handled this situation, it does make some strange kind of sense to me—not that I would have ever gotten myself into this position."

A lightness rose in my chest. Was he going to agree to the funding after all?

Fred opened his mouth again. "I can't promise you anything, but I'll think about it."

At least it wasn't a no. Not yet.

"Thanks, Fred. I really appreciate you hearing me out, and I'm so sorry that things happened the way they did. Even if you don't decide to invest, I hope you'll pop into Sapphire Blooms to say hi." If it hadn't closed already. I dug my fingernails into my hand. *Do not cry.*

"Thanks for coming in, Olivia." Fred reached out his hand and I shook it. "I'll walk you out."

We walked in silence back to the reception area, my chest heavy. In my more hopeful moments, I'd imagined Fred agreeing to invest after all and me racing to the farm to tell Roz the good news and apologize for storming out on her.

As the elevator doors closed behind me and I began my descent to the ground, I exhaled. Whatever happened next was out of my control, but at least I'd tried my best. I would go back to Sapphire Springs knowing that I'd done everything I could to try to save Red Tractor Farm.

CHAPTER THIRTY-FIVE

ROZ

"HAPPY BIRTHDAY TO YOOUUUU!" We were out of tune and out of time, but Lottie didn't seem to care.

She knelt on a chair at my dining room table and blew out the candles on the chocolate cake with a giant puff. I cheered along with my parents and Matt. This was Lottie's first birthday without her mom, so I was trying my best to push my worries aside and focus on ensuring she had a good time. It had been easier to be present earlier in the afternoon when, as a special treat, I'd taken her on a pony ride outside the usual petting zoo route, weaving through the apple orchards and out to the Christmas trees and back again, the fresh air tinged with blossoms and pine and Lottie's squeals of delight keeping me in the moment.

I cut the cake and served everyone a slice. Hopefully, it tasted good. I'd never baked a cake from scratch before.

Lottie gobbled hers down, then looked up with chocolate smeared across her little face. "Can I open my presents now?"

"Okay, fine." Matt grinned.

Lottie shrieked and began ripping the wrapping paper off an enormous box. Would Matt be able to transport its contents home in their small Toyota Corolla?

"Oh, wow!" Lottie exclaimed, as her efforts revealed a drum set, complete with cymbals. "Thanks, Nana and Pop. This is amazing!"

Matt shot me a horrified look, his eyes wide and his mouth puckered. I choked back a laugh.

Lottie smashed a drumstick on the cymbals, sending an ear-shattering clang reverberating around the room. I flinched. If Matt couldn't fit it in his car, I'd insist on dropping it off to him at the first available opportunity.

"Perhaps we could keep it at Nana and Pop's house." The corner of Matt's mouth pulled up. "We could turn their library into your drum studio, honey. I'm sure they wouldn't mind."

Mom frowned at Matt, and I chuckled under my breath.

I walked over and knelt next to Lottie, putting an arm around her shoulders and pulling her into me. "Happy birthday, gorgeous." I handed her my present.

Lottie unwrapped the box. Her face lit up as she pulled out the headlamp, kids Swiss army knife and sleeping bag.

"You said before that you'd like to go camping, so I thought the two of us could camp out at the farm—and that these would come in handy."

Little arms enveloped me. "Thanks, Auntie Roz! Can we do it tonight?"

"Not on a school night, sweetie, but perhaps next weekend?" I glanced over to Matt, who gave me a thumbs up and a grin. He didn't get many nights to himself these days.

"Speaking of school, Margie was telling me that

Radford has just finished building a state-of-the-art science lab and that her grandchildren are doing robotics and virtual-reality field trips to explore the solar system." Mom put down her fork and peered over at Matt.

A muscle twitched in Matt's jaw, but he kept his voice calm. "That's nice, Mom."

"Our offer still stands. I know you took Lottie off the waitlist, but we can pull some strings."

"We're very happy with Cloverdale Elementary, Mom." His tone had shifted, taking on a distinctly steely edge.

"But is she still struggling with math? Radford would be able to give her support in a way a public school just wouldn't have the resources to provide."

"Mom! Not on Lottie's birthday. We can speak about this later." Matt shoved a forkful of cake into his mouth.

A cold shiver shot down my spine. Mom and Dad just wanted the best for Lottie, but the best wasn't always the most expensive or the most exclusive option. Throwing money at things or pulling strings to get your loved ones ahead wasn't always the best option either, as I knew all too well. My stomach roiled with nausea. I was dreading the discussion I planned to have with them later tonight.

After we were full of cake and Lottie had opened the rest of her presents, Matt stood and placed his hand on Lottie's shoulder. "Well, I'd better be taking the birthday girl home. It's getting late and it's a school night."

Lottie's face crumpled, but she stood and started packing away her presents.

"Roz, do you mind if we leave the drum kit here for now?" Matt asked.

I narrowed my eyes. "Fine. But I'll be dropping it off to one of your houses if it's not gone by the weekend."

We walked them to the door, waving goodnight as they stepped out into the dark. Thirty seconds later, a little light appeared. I grinned. Lottie must have turned on her headlamp.

Mom and Dad headed back inside and began collecting their belongings.

"It's a shame Olivia couldn't make it," Mom said as she put her phone into her purse. "We'd love to see her again soon."

I took a deep breath and turned to them. "Mom, Dad, there's something I was hoping to talk to you about before you leave."

Mom put her purse back on the dining table and took a seat. "What is it, sweetie? Is everything okay with Olivia?"

As I sat, pain shot through my chest. I really did not want to do this. I hated it. I'd worked hard my entire life to ensure I was completely self-sufficient. But as Olivia said, I had to suck it up. I had to put my pride and my principles aside. At the end of the day, saving Red Tractor Farm, my employees' jobs and Olivia's business was more important. While I was stubborn enough that I'd rather ruin myself financially than ask my parents for help, this was far bigger than just me. I clenched my hands tightly and took a deep breath.

"It's the farm." I swallowed. "Fred decided not to invest." My chest felt so tight I could hardly breathe. "I'm out of options with finding financiers." I looked at my parents, who were staring at me, brows furrowed in sympathy. Here goes. I resisted the urge to close my eyes. "I was wondering if you would be willing to lend me the money? I'd pay it back, of course, with interest. I can give you all the documents I prepared for Fred, setting out my business plan and projected revenue. I need a lot. Two or three million. I completely understand if you're not comfortable doing it." I didn't know my parents' exact financial situation, but I did know they had both been earning salaries of over a million dollars a year for at least twenty years. While the amount I was asking was enormous, I thought—I hoped—they would have it.

Dad glanced at Mom, an eyebrow raised. She nodded.

"Of course," Dad said. "We'll talk to our accountant. It might take us a few weeks to get it to you, but that will be fine, Roz. We're happy to help."

"But I think we would want to have an agreement drawn up, setting out our roles and responsibilities," Mom chimed in. "Not just so we're on the same page, but also so it's all documented in case we need it for tax purposes."

My stomach dropped at the mention of roles and responsibilities. What kind of involvement were they expecting? "Of course. I was thinking the same thing. Apart from giving me the loan and me paying it back over time, was there anything else you were thinking of?"

Dad tilted his head. "It would be good to be consulted on any major changes that might affect the farm's profitability."

Mom leaned forward. "I'd also like to take a look at the plans for the new venue too, just in case I can value-add."

Nothing they were asking for was really that unreasonable, but my throat constricted at the thought of them poring over my plans, making suggestions that I almost certainly wouldn't agree with, and then me having to tightrope walk between trying to keep them happy while also staying true to my vision. If it hadn't been for our history, perhaps I wouldn't be so sensitive to the whole thing. But the thought of them meddling in my business again made me sick to my stomach.

But at least the farm, and Sapphire Blooms, would be saved.

I took another deep breath. "Thank you."

Now all I had to do was talk to Olivia.

CHAPTER THIRTY-SIX

ROZ

I STOOD LOOKING out the window in my study. The last family made their way to the car, an exhausted toddler asleep in a stroller, their older sister skipping along, talking to her parents at a million miles per hour. They laughed at something she said, shooting each other a smile over her head. An invisible string tugged at my heart. Could that be me one day? I hadn't considered the possibility in years, but now... I glanced down at my watch. Olivia should be here any minute.

Movement caught my eye. An orange Volkswagen Beetle covered in large purple and pink flowers was driving into the parking lot.

Butterflies fluttering in my stomach, I slowly made my way to the front door, arriving just as Olivia hit the bell. I swung the door open and my heart skipped a beat.

God, she's gorgeous. Olivia stood before me, wearing a green checkered dress studded with prints of colorful blossoms, her dark silky hair in waves framing her face, a dash of red lipstick accentuating her lips.

Shit. I didn't know what to do with my body, especially

my face and my hands. I wanted to smile at her, to throw my arms around her and apologize but that probably wasn't appropriate.

I cleared my throat. "Hi. Please come in." I winced at how formal I sounded.

I led Olivia into the living room and turned to her, biting my lip. I took a deep breath. "Thanks for agreeing to meet me here. I'm so sorry for Saturday. You were right, I was putting my pride before everything else by not asking my parents for a loan. But I asked them last night, and they said yes. So everything will be okay—the flower fields, the farm, Sapphire Blooms."

Olivia's eyes widened. "Oh, wow!" She frowned, studying me closely. "Are you... Are you sure that's okay?"

I shrugged, ignoring the heaviness that settled in my stomach each time I thought about the loan. "It's not ideal. But it's better than the alternative."

Olivia stepped forward, flinging her arms around me. I pulled her in, enveloping her, closing my eyes as I inhaled her sweet scent, reveling in the warmth of her body.

"Thank you. I'm sorry too," she murmured into the crook of my neck. "I shouldn't have said what I did and stormed out. I was just so upset about losing the flowers, about losing Sapphire Blooms."

"I know. It's okay." I rubbed her back.

I stayed there, gathering strength for what I wanted to say next. Eventually, I pulled my head back so I could see her beautiful face.

"There's one other thing," I said, brushing her hair back from her cheeks with my fingers. "I've done a lot of thinking over the past few days, about us and what I want..." I gazed deep into Olivia's eyes, my heart pounding in my ears. I had to get the words out, otherwise I'd live in regret. "And I've come to the conclusion that I want to wake up next to you every morning, have coffee and breakfast on the deck every day and grow you the best damn flowers for your shop. And assuming things go the way I think they'll go—with us only growing closer and closer—one day I'd like to have kids with you and let them run rampant on the farm." I swallowed. "I would love to date you in a very real, not at all casual or fake, way. That is, if you're still interested?"

I held my breath, waiting for her response. Had I come on too strong? Perhaps she'd reached the opposite realization over the past few days, deciding she was better off without me in her life. My stomach flipped at the thought.

Olivia reached out her hand, running her thumb down my jawbone. My heart fluttered.

"I would love that," she said, staring up at me. Her face broke into a smile. "Although, can we leave the flower growing to Dana for now? While I appreciate the sentiment and trust you in every other way, I don't trust you with my dahlias."

I chuckled. "Come here, you." I pulled Olivia in and kissed her gently on the lips. A warm glow lit in my belly. My lips parted and I deepened the kiss, running my hands over Olivia's back.

"I've missed this," I murmured as we came up for breath. "Before we get too carried away, would you like to stay for dinner?" I glanced at the clock on the wall. "I have something in the oven that will be ready very soon."

Olivia smiled. "That would be amazing. I was wondering what that delicious smell was."

I took her warm, soft hand in mine and led her down the hallway and through the kitchen. She froze as we stepped onto the deck, her eyes wide.

"What the...?" Olivia's mouth dropped open.

I grinned as she looked around, taking in the vision before her.

In the middle of the deck stood a square table covered in a white tablecloth, with two place settings and chairs. A small bouquet of dahlias sat in the middle of the table—I hadn't wanted anything too ostentatious that would obstruct my view of Olivia over dinner. However, I'd taken a no-holds-barred approach for the rest of the deck. The wooden railing was covered in glowing candles and vases of coral, pink and purple dahlias. A wine bucket sat in a stand next to the table, overflowing with red, orange and yellow blooms.

"Don't worry, I checked with Dana on whether you needed them for your shop and weddings, and ended up buying some from Charlie's Flower Farm in Shenorock to make sure I didn't use too many. I've also taken my antihistamines, so I won't be sneezing all over you."

Olivia turned to me, the side of her face lit with the soft glow of the candles. "This is gorgeous, Roz."

"The flower arrangements are probably not up to your standards, but I tried my best."

"I love them."

A loud moo sounded.

Olivia laughed. "And so do Thelma and Louise, by the sound of it."

I shook my head, chuckling. "Thelma and Louise watched me set up all afternoon, adding commentary like that on a fairly regular basis. Thelma kept licking her lips like she thought I was preparing a chef's tasting menu of dahlias just for her."

I pulled out a chair for Olivia and gestured for her to sit.

"Oooh." Olivia's eyes lit up as her eyes focused on the table. "Is this what I think it is?"

I chuckled. "Yep, it's quark and chive spread. And it's actually not bad. I may have gotten a little carried away with the quark dishes tonight." I could have spent the day trying to work out how I could put some reasonable boundaries around my parents' involvement in the farm, but instead I'd spent it creating flower arrangements and cooking Olivia a three-course meal centered around quark. I didn't regret it, though. I could deal with my parents later. Right now, I just wanted to focus on Olivia.

We were just polishing off the quark soufflé when both our phones pinged.

Olivia raised her eyebrows. "It's probably Blake, checking if we're all still in for trivia on Thursday. She's convinced if we all show up we'll win this time." She pulled her phone out of her bag on the floor and her eyes widened. "Oh shit, it's Fred."

I frowned. "Fred?"

I grabbed my phone from my pocket.

> Roz, Olivia. Are you free to talk?

I looked at Olivia. "Are you okay if we call him now? I'm sorry, I know this is supposed to be a romantic evening but—"

Olivia smiled. "Roz, it's fine."

My hands flew over my phone screen as I typed out a response.

> We're free now. Would you like us to call you?

Three dots pulsed on my screen.

> Where are you?

I frowned. "That's weird."

We're at the farm.

Is it okay if I come over?

"You think he means now?" I stared at Olivia, who'd been following the conversation on her phone.

She furrowed her brow. "It looks like it. Let's say yes and see how he responds."

Yes, you're always welcome here.

Okay great, I'll be there in a minute.

I blinked. A minute?

"Okay, wow." Olivia put down her phone, pushed her chair back and stood up. "I guess he must have been messaging us from the parking lot."

I rose to my feet. "I'm so sorry this is derailing our evening."

Olivia walked over and placed her hand on the small of my back, smiling up at me. "Don't worry about it. I'm as intrigued as you are to hear what he has to say."

We walked inside, through the kitchen and down the hall. Heart racing, I clasped Olivia's hand in mine. The comforting warmth of her hand spread up to my chest, soothing my pulse back to a more normal beat. As we reached the front door, a knock sounded. We exchanged glances and then I opened the door.

"Hi, Fred." I struggled to keep my voice calm and professional.

Fred ran his hand through his hair. "Sorry. I drove all the way from the city after work tonight and then realized that I really shouldn't just turn up on your doorstep unannounced."

"No. Of course. Please, come in."

I ushered him to the living room. Olivia and I sat on the cream couch, Fred lowering himself onto the matching armchair next to it.

I folded my hands together. "I'm glad to see you. I just want to apologize again for—"

Fred held up a hand. "I know you're sorry, Roz. Olivia told me everything."

My head jerked toward Olivia, my eyebrows raised. "She did?"

I'd texted, called and emailed Fred without any luck. How the hell did Olivia manage to get through to him and what had she said?

She ducked her head. "Yes. Sorry, I was going to tell you... I was just waiting for the right time."

Tell me what, exactly?

Fred chuckled. "She turned up at my office yesterday morning, saying it was her fault and begging me to still invest in the farm."

I blinked. Olivia had gone all the way into the city to find Fred?

"And while I don't think Olivia is entirely to blame for the situation by any means, I understand how the misunderstanding with your mom snowballed and got out of control. I don't agree with what you did, but I can see how it could have happened. Aside from that, you've been frank and open with me about the farm's issues and your proposal really was very convincing. And so, I've reconsidered my position."

Adrenaline pumped through my body. I gripped

Olivia's hand to steady myself. "You've reconsidered your position. So does that mean you'll invest?"

Fred nodded. "Yes." He smiled at Olivia. "Olivia reminded me of all the reasons why I was interested in the opportunity to begin with: your business savvy, the farm's potential, investing in a community—a community I'll now soon be part of. I will be writing a clause into the investment agreement that will allow me to withdraw money if you do anything that significantly undermines my trust in you. But I have a feeling I won't need to rely on that."

"You have my word," I said, holding in a slightly hysterical laugh that was threatening to erupt.

I wouldn't be beholden to my parents after all. *Thank god.*

Fred slapped his thighs and stood up. "Well, I'd better be going. I'd planned to come up on Friday to start furniture shopping for my new place, so I thought I'd come up a bit earlier to let you know my decision in person. I'll be working remotely for the rest of the week, probably a lot of it from Novel Gossip, so I might see you two there. My lawyers will be in touch with the paperwork."

I couldn't keep the grin off my face. "Thanks, Fred. I really appreciate it."

We walked Fred to the front steps, shook hands and waved him off.

As I shut the door, a mixture of relief and wonder washed over me. My body felt like it might float away if it wasn't tethered by Olivia's hand. What had just happened?

I wrapped my arms around her waist and pulled her to me.

"Wow. Thank you for speaking to Fred."

Olivia smiled at me. "Well, someone very wise once told

me that successful businesspeople don't give up. So I didn't."

I chuckled. "What an intelligent person."

Olivia laughed and then let out a long exhale. "Thank god our fake-dating days are now behind us. I'm never faking anything again."

I raised an eyebrow. "I should hope not." I grinned. "At least, not while you're dating me." Our eyes locked, and an ache started low in my core. "I may have decorated my bedroom too. Would you like to see it?"

CHAPTER THIRTY-SEVEN

OLIVIA

ROZ DIDN'T NEED to ask twice. Blood pulsing through my veins, I grabbed her hand and bounced up the stairs to her bedroom door.

"Just give me a minute." Roz opened the door just enough so she could slip inside.

I bit my lip. What was she up to?

Roz reappeared, peering through a small crack in the door. "Okay." She swiped her hand through her hair, her cheeks flushed and then swung the door all the way open.

My jaw dropped as I stepped into the room. Over the head of the bed was a huge arch, covered in gorgeous pink, purple and white dahlias and lush greenery. Two large candles flickered on the side tables at each end of the arch. Her normal gray duvet had been replaced with a purple one that perfectly complemented the flowers.

I pressed a hand over my thudding heart. "Oh my god, Roz. How long did this take you?"

"A while." She grinned. "Good thing a very talented florist gave me a masterclass on floral arches a few weeks ago."

I laughed, closing the gap between us and wrapping my arms around her. "It's incredible. Thank you."

Gazing up at her blue eyes, I leaned in and pressed my lips to hers.

A smile spread across my face and I gently pulled away. "You know, these candles remind me of a prototype I was working on yesterday."

"Oh?" She looked down at me, her eyes soft. One of her hands began a gentle, rhythmic stroking over my hair.

I loved that I didn't feel at all nervous about talking to Roz about sex, about proposing we try something I'd never done before. "Jenny is organizing a few bachelorette parties over the summer and asked if I could create some, um, X-rated candles. I showed her the prototypes I came up with this afternoon at Novel Gossip."

Roz's eyebrows shot up. "Oh really?"

My smile widened. "Yep! Lots of penises and vulvas, made out of soy wax. They can be used as candles or... for other erotic purposes. I have a prototype vulva in my bag, if you're interested." I raised an eyebrow.

The corner of Roz's mouth curved. "You want to play with fire?"

I chuckled. "I mean, I think I should test that they work okay in an intimate setting before they're handed out at bachelorette parties... But I can do it by myself if you'd prefer. I did drip some on my hand yesterday. I quite liked it. A little sting of heat and then a warm sensation. It doesn't burn your skin because it has such a low melting point."

"No, no. I'm happy to offer myself up as a human test subject. Or be the tester. Or both." Roz grinned. "You know what else could be fun... I'll be back in a second."

I sat on Roz's bed, gazing at the arch. She'd done an incredible job, weaving dozens of dahlias and ferns through the wire. This was, by far, the most romantic thing anyone had ever done for me.

Roz returned a minute later, slightly out of breath, holding my bag and the ice bucket that had previously been full of dahlias. It was now full of ice, an elegant curved purple glass dildo sitting in the middle of it.

"Fire and ice." She shot me a wicked grin from the doorway. "What do you think?"

I laughed. "I love it." It was perfect. We'd played with fire and skated on ice over the past six weeks as Roz's icy exterior slowly melted away. Now we were bringing some of that energy to the bedroom.

Roz placed the ice bucket on the side table and then sat next to me on the bed, handing me the bag.

I rummaged through it, pulling out the white vulva candle and placing the bag on the ground next to the bed. "Here we go. Let's try a drop on your hand first, to make sure you're comfortable with it."

I reached out, dipping the wick in the flame of the large candle next to the ice bucket until it lit. Roz held out her hand. My eyes lingered on her delicate fingers. A delicious shiver spread over me.

A drop of wax melted near the flame.

"Are you ready?" I murmured.

"Yes."

I tilted my hand, holding my breath. The bead of wax dripped off the candle and onto the back of Roz's hand, forming a round opaque dot that quickly set back to white. I blew out the flame. I didn't want it to melt away before we'd had a chance to properly use it and, unlike the other candles Roz had lit, it wasn't safely ensconced in glass. The last thing we needed was for the farm to burn down just after it had been saved.

"Was that okay?" I ran my fingers over her skin where the wax had fallen.

Roz nodded. "Yes. You were right—a second of pain that transforms into heat." She raised her hand to her nose and sniffed. "Mmm. This smells nice."

I laughed, my face warm. "It's eau de Roz."

Roz blinked. "What?"

I shifted on the bed. "I may have also spent yesterday trying to recreate your scent because I missed you so much. Cedar and sandalwood, with some earthy notes." For the bachelorette parties, I'd make them rose-scented or something a bit more traditional—not everyone might be into cedar-scented vulvas as much as I was.

Roz's eyes twinkled. "Eau de Roz. I love it." She peeled off the dot of wax on her hand and put it on the table.

"The wax might be more intense on more sensitive parts of your body. If it's too much, we should have a safe word." I pressed my lips together for a moment, then the perfect safe word hit me. "I know, how about *moo*"?

Roz's eyebrows shot up. "Moo?"

"Well, it's not exactly a word that would come up by accident. If you don't like it, we could use *quark* instead, but *moo* is easier to say."

"Okay, fine. Let's stick with moo." Roz shook her head, chuckling. "Now, where were we?" Her voice dropped low. Roz scooted closer to me, cupping my jaw in her hand and running her thumb across my lips. My stomach fluttered.

Roz dropped her gaze to the top of my dress and began to slowly undo the buttons.

She bit her lip, her blond hair flopping over her forehead as she stared at my chest with intense concentration. "Goddamn buttons. I want to rip this damn thing off you, but I also don't want to ruin it. You look gorgeous in it."

I smiled. "I can just pull it over my head if you want. That might be easier—unless you really want to work for it."

Roz chuckled. "Please, go ahead. At the rate I'm going, all the ice will have melted by the time it's off."

I tugged the dress up and over my head, Roz pulling off her pants at the same time and then peeling off her black t-shirt.

"Much better," Roz murmured as she reached around and unclipped my bra. She then pulled her own over her head. "Since I made the arch for you, I think it's only fair you get to enjoy it first."

She gently pushed me down onto the soft bed and then clambered on top of me, straddling my hips and leaning down.

My breath caught as I drank in the vision above me. It was too much. Roz, eyes smoldering, dahlias and ferns providing a stunning backdrop, her small breasts tantaliz-ingly close to me. I licked my lower lip and reached out a hand to cup her breast.

"Now, do you want fire, ice—with or without the toy—or just me?" she murmured, her breath soft against my face.

I bit my lip. "Ice and the toy, I think—and you, of course."

Roz leaned to the side, plucked an ice cube from the bucket, and slowly licked it while holding my gaze. A thrill shot to my core, sending it throbbing with desire.

She lowered her mouth to my breast, teasing my nipple with her cool tongue. My core clenched, my nipple harden-ing. "Mmm. That feels good."

Roz raised her head, picked up the ice cube and circled it around my nipples and then both of my breasts, leaving a trail of cool water and goosebumps in its wake. A delicious shiver spread over my chest, my breasts tightening. She looked at me, her gaze heavy. "Is this too much?"

"No. I like it."

"Excellent." She lowered herself down so she was inches from me, her hair flopping on my forehead. "Now, close your eyes." Her voice was commanding.

"But I want to see you!" I protested.

"I know. But there will be plenty of time for that later."

I let my eyelids fall. Roz and the flowers disappeared, replaced with darkness. Her body shifted against mine. What was she up to? I waited, anticipation building.

An ice-cold sensation hit my neck, slowly gliding down my collar bone and over my breasts. Soft warmth followed, trailing behind the ice. *Her mouth, lapping up the cool water left by the ice.* The contrast between cold and warm sent my nerve endings tingling. Roz continued, ice followed by the heat of her mouth slowly making its way down my body to the sensitive skin of my stomach. Desire pulsed through me, getting stronger with every stroke of the ice cube and caress of Roz's mouth.

"That feels amazing," I murmured, reaching out a hand until it came in contact with Roz's hair. I gripped it tight.

Roz groaned into my body, her mouth gently vibrating on my stomach.

The ice skimmed lower, tracing around my hip bone and down my inner thigh. My body buzzed, the throbbing in my clit almost unbearable. I eased my legs wider as the cold and warm sensations swirled around my inner thigh and pubic bone, through my curls, dipping close to my outer lips and then away again.

I moaned, fisting Roz's hair tighter, my hips squirming. Roz kept going, teasing me, and then the ice vanished. I stopped breathing. *What's next?*

A cool, wet sensation pressed against my entrance, sending another ripple of desire through me and I exhaled. It slowly moved up to my clit, swirling around, and then back again. *Roz's tongue. She must have ice in her mouth.* She continued to work up and down, every so often opening her mouth so that a swipe of ice grazed my skin.

I began to writhe under her, the pressure building in my core. She stopped again, her body pressing against my thigh for a moment. And then her tongue, cooler than ever, circled my clit and a hard, icy object pressed against my entrance.

I bit my lip. The glass toy.

"Is that okay?" Roz murmured, her voice slightly muffled.

I groaned. "God, yes."

Roz turned her attention back to my clit, swirling her cool tongue against it. When I thought I couldn't take it anymore, she slid the toy slowly in. I moaned again. *This is incredible.* The ice-cold toy glided in and out, in time with the slow, sensual twirls of her tongue. She gradually picked up the pace, angling the toy so it hit my G-spot with each thrust, sending a bolt of pleasure through me. Her tongue and the glass warmed with the friction against my body. I was so close. And then the orgasm slammed into me, my hips arching as I rode the waves of ecstasy that flooded my body. I gasped. Oh. My. God. The waves kept coming, intense pleasure overwhelming my system, sending my legs trembling and my breathing labored. Despite all the ice, my body was on fire, in the best possible way.

The orgasm gradually subsided, leaving my body feeling like jelly. My eyes fluttered open.

Roz grinned from between my legs, her hair tousled. "You liked it?"

"Amazing," I said, still catching my breath.

Roz pulled herself up and lay down next to me.

I gazed into her eyes. "Is your mouth okay? It doesn't have frostbite or anything? It would be a travesty if anything happened to that tongue of yours."

Roz chuckled. "My mouth and tongue are in excellent condition, but thank you for your concern."

I smiled. "The concern wasn't completely selfless. But let me just confirm for myself that everything is in good working order." I leaned in, giving her a long, lingering kiss and then pulled back, running my hand through Roz's silky hair. "What do you feel like? Heat, ice or normal Olivia temperature?"

Roz grinned. "Let's heat things up a bit."

My chest buzzed with nervous energy. While I'd done a lot of research into wax play as part of creating the candles, I'd never done anything like this before. *We have a safe word. Roz will tell me if she doesn't like it.*

I took a deep breath, trying to channel confidence. "Roll over."

Roz raised her eyebrows but rolled onto her stomach without protest. My eyes lingered on her slim muscular back as I straddled her waist. I ran my hands over her shoulder blades and the evenly spaced bumps of her rib cage, down to where her waist tapered in and back again, applying a firm pressure.

"That feels nice," Roz mumbled through the pillow.

I kept going, massaging her smooth back with my hands, until I felt her relax fully into the bed. I leaned down to her cheek. "Are you ready?"

"Yes."

I rolled off the bed, picked up the vulva candle and lit it again before clambering back onto Roz. The flame flickered, the wax around the wick slowly beginning to melt. The scent of cedar and sandalwood filled the air. I ran my free hand over Roz's back again. Biting my lip, I tipped the vulva to one side, positioning it over one of Roz's shoulder blades. Three drips fell, hitting Roz's skin and slowly transforming from hazy clear to white dots.

Roz gave a sharp intake of breath, hands gripping the side of the pillow.

"Was that okay?" I murmured.

"Yes," Roz said. "Intense, but good."

More melted wax was collecting in the candle, so I carefully angled it again, letting it drip onto Roz's upper back and down the curve of her spine. A trail of white raised bumps appeared on her skin as the wax set. My free hand traced over them. Okay, this was hot—in all senses of the word. The fact that Roz was willing to put her trust in me, let me literally play with fire over her naked body, warmed me to my core.

I swung my right leg off Roz, so I was kneeling next to her on the bed. I dripped the hot wax lower on her back, down to her gorgeous round butt. I let a single drop fall on her ass, testing her reaction. Roz turned her head to the side, so I could see her face, one cheek pressed against the pillow. She was biting her lip, but there was no sign of any distress.

I skimmed my free hand over her perfect butt and down across her inner thighs as I slowly let tiny beads of wax drip on to the skin of her lower back and butt.

Roz moaned as my fingers skated up her inner thighs, closer and closer to her entrance. She shifted her body, opening her legs slightly.

I let her wait another minute, continuing to twirl my fingers around her inner thighs and drip the wax on her skin, and then I slid my fingers across her opening. I breathed in sharply as my fingers were covered in her slick. *Damn, this was hot.*

"You're so wet," I murmured. I moved my hand higher, my fingers gliding up to her clit and circling it.

Roz shuddered. "That feels incredible."

I kept my hand there, two fingers attending to her clit while I pressed my thumb to her entrance. With my other hand, I slowly let the wax continue dripping onto Roz's back. Thank god I'd had two weeks of practice sleeping with Roz before I tried this, because it was taking all of my focus to stay in tune with Roz's body, keeping my left hand steady to ensure the wax didn't fall too fast and making sure the pressure and rhythm of my right hand was giving her what she needed. I kept going, slowly increasing the speed and pressure of my fingers as her clit hardened.

"Fuck!" she breathed, her hands gripping the pillow, knuckles white. She gazed over her shoulder at me, her cheeks flushed and her pupils dilated.

"Faster," she gasped. "And more wax."

I obeyed, tilting the candle to let a steady drip of wax trail over her ass, while my fingers worked harder and faster. I pushed my thumb deeper inside her.

Roz groaned, writhing under me, and a rush of exhilaration washed over me. *What a high.* Her walls clenched around my thumb and then spasmed. It took all my concentration to keep my fingers moving and the candle still.

"That's enough! Moo!" She laughed, twisting her hips to extricate them from my hand.

I pulled my hand away, blowing out the candle and placing it on the side table. Then I knelt beside her, running my hand over her back, which was now covered in white bumps. Her cheeks were pink, her breathing heavy.

Roz smiled up at me. "That was amazing, Liv."

I grinned, lowering my head to kiss her on the back of her neck. "It's not over yet. Now I get to peel it all off," I murmured in her ear.

I kissed her neck again, and then slowly worked my way down her back, carefully peeling off the white wax and placing it in a small pile. It was surprisingly satisfying and gave me yet another excuse to drink in Roz's body.

Once it was all gone, I rubbed my hands up and down her back a few more times, then lowered myself next to her, looking forward to snuggling into her warm body.

Cold wet sheets met my skin. I bolted upright. "Shit! Your bed is soaked."

Roz pushed her body up and stared at the large wet patch on the sheet next to her. She laughed. "Whoops. I really should have put a towel down. Things I didn't think of." She shuffled over to the other side of the bed and patted the sheet where she'd been lying. "Just come over here for now. I've got a mattress protector on so at least it's not soaking into the mattress. We can change the sheets later."

I complied, lying down in the spot that had been pre-warmed by Roz's body, pulling over the duvet and wrapping my arm around Roz's waist. I gazed into her eyes and smiled. "Well, that was fun."

"It was more than fun." Roz ran her fingers through my hair.

We lay there for a few minutes, enjoying the warmth of each other's bodies.

"Hey, if you don't mind me asking, why were you so reluctant to ask your parents for the loan?" I asked softly, trailing my fingers over Roz's smooth stomach. "I get that it's not always a great idea to do business with family. Is that what was going on, or was it something else?"

Roz sighed, staring up at the flowers arching above us.

"There's a bit of history there. Do you remember the college admissions scandal?" She rolled on her side so that she faced me.

My eyes widened. "Um, yes, but no offense, wasn't that quite a bit after your time at college?"

Roz let out a small puff of air. "The one that got discovered was. My parents tried to do something similar for me and Matt, but they didn't get caught—at least, not by the authorities. Just by me."

"Oh shit!" I stared at Roz. "So did they bribe someone or have someone take your tests or something?"

"Bribe," Roz said, her voice flat. "I used to meet Mom at her office after school sometimes. One day, I arrived early and overheard Mom on the phone saying she'd donate a whole lot of money to a very prestigious college in return for me getting a place there. It was to a college she really wanted me to get into—not my first choice, mind you. And the stupid thing was that I was just fine on my own—I ended up getting offers from a couple of Ivy League colleges on my own merit. But Mom had been worried that I might not get in, so she did what she always did—tried to pull strings."

I grimaced. "What did you do?"

Roz frowned. "We had a massive falling out. I was furious. It was the final straw in a long history of them trying to use their money and influence to get me and Matt ahead. They'd been doing it on a smaller scale my entire life— expensive presents to my teachers, a sizable donation to build a new library at my high school. I didn't catch on initially, but some kids at my school did. They used to tease me that my straight As might have more to do with my parents' money than my academic abilities. I brushed it off as my parents just being generous... until I overheard that call. It made me question whether anything I'd achieved was legitimate, or if it was all just an outcome of my parents' money. A whole lot of my identity was tied up in my academic success, and it felt like the rug had been pulled out from under me."

I wrapped my arm around Roz's waist and gave her a squeeze. "I'm sorry. That must have been really tough." It explained a lot. With Roz's parents bribing people behind her back and Sadie love-bombing her, it wasn't surprising she'd put up walls to protect herself from further hurt.

"Yeah." Roz let out a breath. "Needless to say, I turned down the place I'd been offered at the college Mom bribed and went to another college that I'd been accepted at without their assistance. I refused to accept any more of my parents' money. I wasn't eligible for scholarships because of their wealth, so I took out loans and I got a job to pay my living expenses. While I'd considered becoming a lawyer, I decided to go into management consulting instead to make sure my parents' names wouldn't help me get ahead. One of the reasons I was so driven in my job was to prove I could do it without them, as well as make sure I'd never need their help."

I rubbed her back. "You definitely proved that. Putting yourself through college, working your way up the corporate ladder, being in a position where you could quit and buy a farm..."

Roz gave me a small smile. "Thanks. But I'll never be able to escape that a lot of my success is still attributable to them, no matter how hard I work. They sent me to the best schools, got me the best tutors when I was struggling, and funded all those extracurricular activities that looked so good on my college applications."

"It's good you can acknowledge that, but that's not your fault. You can't help what family you're born into."

"I know." Roz brushed my hair from my cheek. "I didn't speak to my parents for a couple of years, but we eventually reconnected. I know deep down that they were motivated by wanting to do what was best for me, but they just went about it in the completely wrong way. But accepting any form of help from them is still very hard for me."

"Well, thank you for asking them then." Given what I'd just heard, it must have taken a lot for Roz to reach out to her parents for the loan.

"I heard what you said. If it had just been my livelihood and money on the line, I wouldn't have done it, but in the end I realized I was putting my pride before you, Dana, Ronnie, and all my other employees, not to mention Lottie and all those other kids and their families who love the farm, and you are all way more important."

I smiled. "Thank god Fred pulled through."

"All thanks to you," Roz murmured, gazing into my eyes. "How are you feeling about telling everyone about us —assuming you want to? It's okay if you want to keep things quiet for a while."

"Oh, I forgot to tell you. I already told everyone that I was into you—well, not my parents yet, but Blake, Jenny, George and Hannah." I grinned.

Roz's eyes widened. "You did?"

"Yes, I told them on Sunday, when I was moping about you."

"What did they say?" Roz ran her hand down my upper arm and then let it fall to my waist.

"They were a little surprised, but all supportive, just as I knew they would be. I told them I'm still figuring out my label." I gently squeezed Roz's hand. "But there's one thing I know for sure."

"Oh? What's that?"

"I find you incredibly sexy." I leaned forward and kissed Roz, reveling in the faintly sweet scent of the dahlias above us mixed with her cedar undertones.

The first chance I got, I'd be deleting that dating app. I wasn't going to need to complete the dating profile after all.

CHAPTER THIRTY-EIGHT

ROZ

"THIS LOOKS GREAT!" Olivia exclaimed, standing back to admire the row of vendor stalls next to the farm stand. "And the weather is perfect, thank god!"

My eyes dipped to her chest, where the words *I wet my plants* were scrawled over a pot of flowers. I chuckled. Olivia had found her t-shirt while rummaging in my drawers this morning and insisted on wearing it.

Red Tractor Farm's inaugural spring festival had only opened twenty minutes ago, but kids were already running around, playing the games we'd set up—tug of war, bean bag toss and giant Jenga—while adults and teenagers browsed the stalls.

We'd nervously monitored the weather forecast for the past two weeks. Thankfully the rain and clouds that had been predicted earlier in the week had failed to materialize. It was a glorious spring day, with a forecasted high of 73 degrees.

The blues band that had been setting up on the wooden stage began to play. I grinned. This was perfect.

Prue, standing behind the Rosedale Estate stall, a large

straw hat covering her short black hair, called out. "Would you ladies like a taste of anything before the rush starts?" She gestured at the wine bottles and tasting glasses set up in front of her.

I laughed. "I'm on hayride-driving duties today, so I'll have to decline."

"And I need to talk intelligibly about flowers today, so I'll pass as well. Thanks though," Olivia replied. She was running an eco-friendly flower-arranging workshop at three o'clock.

More visitors streamed onto the farm. We might need the overflow parking we'd set up after all. I didn't need any of Prue's wine to feel a buzz of excitement.

I spotted Matt through the crowds of people, walking toward me.

"I've asked Mom and Dad to keep an eye on Lottie," he said. I followed his gaze to where Lottie was patiently waiting in line to get her face painted, Mom standing next to her. "I just need to duck out to pick up a surprise for her."

"Okay," I said, narrowing my eyes. What on earth was he picking up now? Maybe some noise-cancelling head-phones to drown out the sound of Lottie's new drum kit? "I'm due to drive the first hayride in ten minutes. If her face painting is finished by then, I'll see if they want to come. It'll be a good way to keep her out of mischief."

"Thanks." Matt grinned. "I'll be back soon!"

He walked off, a definite spring to his step. It was good to see him so happy.

"Hey, Roz, where's the bake sale?" I turned to find George holding two large cake tins, Hannah standing next to her, her arms laden with Tupperware.

"Hello! Wow, you've been busy! It's over there." I pointed to a long trestle table close to the stage, covered in baked goods. Jenny and Blake stood behind it, chatting to an elderly couple. "I'll have to pop over before you're sold out."

Blake spotted us and waved, grinning. She'd been in an excellent mood since our win over The Gran Masters at trivia night last week.

"Thanks!" George said, turning to head over to the table.

"Look at my face!" Lottie squealed behind me.

I turned to find my niece's face adorned with a gigantic red flower.

"Oh no! The roses have learned to walk. I hope they don't stage an uprising," I exclaimed, clutching my chest.

"It's a peony, not a rose," Lottie said, a frown visible through the face paint.

An elbow gently bumped my rib cage. "Jeez Roz, I thought you'd be able to tell your roses from your peonies by now," Olivia teased.

I wrapped my arm around her waist. "Ha ha! Where have you been?"

"I was talking to the mayor about how it would be great to get the bike path extended to Red Tractor Farm and she wholeheartedly agreed." Olivia's eyes flashed with excitement.

My heart flipped. It wasn't humanly possible to be more attracted to anyone than I was to Olivia.

"She's going to take it to the next village board meeting. Do you know what that means?"

I squinted. "No?"

Olivia beamed. "You'll need to buy a bike so we can cycle to get quark and apple cider and hang out with Prue at the vineyard."

"Or we could just drive," I said, my lips twitching.

Olivia elbowed me. "But cycling is so much nicer. And it could be our thing."

"Our thing?" I raised my eyebrows.

"George and Hannah are always going off kayaking together. We could be the couple that cycles everywhere." Olivia opened and shut her eyes in quick succession.

I stared at her, my brow furrowing. "What are you doing?"

"I'm fluttering my eyelashes at you," she replied indignantly.

I chuckled. "Good lord, I thought you were having a stroke."

Olivia rolled her eyes. "Ha ha. But I'm not joking about the bikes. I think it could be nice?"

I wrapped my arm around her waist and pulled her to me. "Okay, babe, you've convinced me. I'll buy a bike."

The alarm I'd set on my phone to remind me to take the first hayride buzzed just as my parents approached. I looked at the small line of people who were already standing near the wagon.

"I'm just about to do the first hayride. Lottie, Mom, Dad —want to hop on board?"

"Is there room for me too?" Olivia asked.

"I think you could squish in the tractor with me or sit in the back if you'd prefer."

"Squish sounds good to me." Olivia smiled.

"We just have to keep it G-rated. This is a family affair," I murmured.

Olivia snorted. "Not to mention you'll be driving a hayride full of kids. Don't worry. I'll be on my best behavior."

"The hayride is about to start!" I yelled as we walked over. The kids cheered, bringing another smile to my face.

Ten minutes later, I was driving a cart load of families past the corn maze, where green stalks as high as my knee rose up, their vibrant leaves unfurling, and then past the pumpkin patch, with small vines beginning to creep over the rich soil. Next was the orchards. We had spotted a few tiny green cherries forming on the cherry trees on Friday and small green apples were already hanging from the Royal Gala apple trees, although it was difficult to see them from the hayride. The white blossoms of the Northern Spy apple trees were still visible. Glimpses of the strawberry fields came into view past the orchard, the rows of dark-green plants studded with bright white flowers. To our left, the flower fields stretched out, a riot of color. I smiled as children exclaimed at the sight. I paused the tractor, twisting around to check on Lottie. She was leaning against Mom, beaming.

Olivia put her arm around my shoulder. "I'm glad I hitched a ride with you. This is lovely."

"It is, isn't it?" I exhaled, resuming the ride. Having Olivia snuggled next to me, driving a cartload of kids and their families—including my own—around the farm, was pure bliss.

On the way back, we passed the cows' field. "Wave hello to Thelma and Louise!" I yelled for my passengers' benefit.

"Don't sneeze," Olivia said. "We don't want a stampede at the festival."

I rolled my eyes. "Are you ever going to let me forget that?"

"Umm," Olivia replied, as if she was actually considering my request. "No."

As I slowed the wagon to a grinding halt, Olivia waved

at someone. I pulled on the parking brake and followed Olivia's gaze. Fred.

I jumped out of the tractor and helped all the passengers get down from the hayride. Lottie, Mom and Dad headed toward the petting zoo, where Ronnie's talk on chickens was about to start. Thankfully, Mom had become quite attached to the Mercedes-Benz they had tried to gift me, so they were no longer pushing it on me at every available opportunity.

"Should we say hi to Fred?" Olivia asked once the cart was emptied.

"Yes. I've been meaning to ask if he needs the van for his move," I said, closing the gate to the cart.

"Roz, Olivia!" Fred said as we approached, holding out his hand. "I was just talking about you yesterday, Roz... I ran into an old friend who works at Saunders & Company. It sounds like James's appointment as global managing partner has been fairly rocky so far, and there's been some internal rumblings about potentially trying to replace him. Your name has been flying about." Fred raised an eyebrow. "Any interest?"

I didn't even need to think about it. "Hard pass, thanks."

Lottie came sprinting over, my parents in a slow jog a few feet behind her. "Did you know chickens do their poop and wee at the same time? It just all comes out together!"

"I did not know that," I said. "And I'm not sure I wanted to."

Fred chuckled. "On that note, I might go check out what wines Prue has to offer."

"Enjoy," I said. As he walked off, I realized I'd forgotten to ask him if he wanted the van. I was just about to run after him when I noticed Lottie was staring at something behind my shoulder, her jaw open.

"Mom!!!" she squealed as she sprinted past me.

I turned, my confused frown transforming into a wide grin.

Mel enveloped her daughter in a huge bear hug, lifting Lottie off her feet, tears streaming down her face.

Olivia and I walked over to Matt, who was looking teary himself.

"Does she have to go back again?" I asked.

"Nope," he said, his smile wide. "She's home for good now."

Once Mel and Lottie had finished their exciting reunion, Mel walked over to where we were standing and we hugged.

"It's so good to see you." My voice was muffled by her hair.

"It's great to be back."

"This is my girlfriend, Olivia," I said, disentangling myself from her arms and remembering my manners.

"Lovely to meet you. I've heard so much about you." Mel grinned, and I wondered what exactly Matt and Lottie had said to her.

Lottie bounced up and down, tugging Mel's hand. "Mom, can I show you Thelma and Louise?"

Mel's eyebrows shot up. "Thelma and Louise?"

"They're the cows," Matt muttered.

"Ah. Yes, please!" Mel said, letting Lottie grab her hand and tug her toward their field.

That evening, after the last of the visitors had returned home, Olivia and I sat on the back deck, enjoying the quiet. The sky was fading from orange and yellow to black. The silence was punctuated by the occasional goat bleating and moos from Thelma and Louise.

"What a day," I said, taking Olivia's hand.

"It was great," Olivia said, leaning her shoulder on mine. "I officially pronounce the inaugural Red Tractor Farm Spring Festival a success. Prue sold so much wine she had to call the vineyard to bring over extra supplies."

I grinned. "That's wonderful." I'd heard similar stories from other vendors. "It looks like we may have broken the record for the number of visitors in one day to the farm too."

"No way!"

"It went better than my wildest dreams. I loved that so many local businesses participated. And of course, seeing Lottie and Mel reunited was amazing too." I wrapped my arm around her shoulder. "And, at the risk of sounding corny, another massive highlight was getting to share it all with you."

"Awww." Olivia squeezed my hand.

"I loved it." I swallowed, clearing my throat and turning toward Olivia. "And I love you."

Maybe it was too soon to be saying those words, and a year ago I would never have imagined I'd say them after only two months of dating, one of which was fake, but it felt so right.

Olivia blinked. "What did you say?"

"I love you, you goof. I love your passion for flowers, sustainability and the farm, the way you don't give up, even in the face of adversity, your kindness and your insistence that we become a couple who cycles. I love you, Olivia Mitchell."

Olivia stared at me, eyes wide. I swallowed. Shit. She wasn't saying anything.

"I know it's early on, so don't feel like you need to say anything back, but I just wanted to let you know."

Olivia laughed, cupping her hand to my jaw and running her thumb down my cheek.

"I love you too," she murmured, looking deep into my eyes. "I've been holding back saying anything in case it stressed you out. I thought it might be too soon because of what happened with Sadie. But I love your deafening sneezes, the way you cycle a million miles an hour, how sexy you look in your farmer clothes, your newfound love of flowers and cows, your devotion to Lottie and the way you look after your employees."

I leaned in and kissed her softly. "Way to keep a woman hanging. Now it's my turn to make you wait." I trailed kisses and nibbles down her neck, until she let out a moan. "Just a taste of things to come tonight."

As we sat there, listening to the evening song of the cardinals, it dawned on me that while I'd wanted to buy Red Tractor Farm to ensure the happy memories of generations of children, I'd also created new, very special memories for myself too. Of falling in love with the woman beside me. And, hopefully, making new memories together for the rest of our lives.

THE END

Thank you so much for reading **The Floral Arrangement**.

If you enjoyed it, I would really appreciate if you could leave a review on Amazon, Goodreads or share your thoughts on social media.

If you'd like to receive a **bonus scene** for **The Floral Arrangement** (when it's written!) and hear when future books in the Sapphire Springs series are published, please sign up to my newsletter: https://elizabethluly.com/news letter-sign-up.

If you haven't read Jenny and Blake's love story yet (**Not Just Gal Pals**) you can find it here: https://mybook. to/NotJustGalPals and you can find George and Hannah's romance (**Novel Problems**) here: https://mybook.to/ NovelProblems.

Thanks again,
Liz

ACKNOWLEDGMENTS

Many thanks to my family for their ongoing support and encouragement, in particular my wife and Mum!

An enormous thank you to Kathryn Harris for your insightful feedback and really getting in the trenches with me and Jenn Lockwood for your excellent proofreading (any typos that slipped through are almost certainly due to me making some last-minute changes after Jenn's review!). Huge thanks also to Lauren Clarke for your helpful comments and encouragement.

A big thank you to Holly Brunnbauer (whose debut novel *What Did I Miss* is out July 2025!) and Cherie (@bookshelvesandtealeaves) for naming Thelma and Louise!

Thank you to the sapphic reader, author and bookstagrammer community—I love you all! A special shout out to @sterling_sapphic_reads, @sapphic_book_club and @bookshelvesandtealeaves—your support means so much to me.

A huge thank you to Sam at Ink & Laurel for bringing Olivia and Roz to life through your fantastic cover design and Cath at Cath Grace Designs for the awesome maps at the start of this book (if you missed them, go back and take a look!).

Thank you to the flower farmers and shops who generously answered my questions, including Marina Michahelles at Shoving Leopard Farm and Samantha Ritter at Sea Change Farm and Flower.

Thanks also to the friendly staff at my local café for keeping me caffeinated throughout this process and for providing me with such a welcoming and cozy environment to work in, especially Will and Nikki.

And to everyone else who provided feedback and support along the way, thank you.

ABOUT THE AUTHOR

Elizabeth Luly lived in Canberra and New York before settling in Melbourne with her gardening-obsessed wife, two cheeky sons and highly strung Schnoodle. When she's not writing happy love stories featuring queer women or working in her day job, she can be found singing loudly along to her latest pop obsession, drinking too much coffee at her local cafe or dancing with her kids.

Sign up for her newsletter and stay up to date on her book news: www.elizabethluly.com.

And find her here:

Website: www.elizabethluly.com
Facebook: www.facebook.com/elizabethlulyauthor
Instagram: www.instagram.com/elizabethlulyauthor
Goodreads: https://www.goodreads.com/author/show/22986218.Elizabeth_Luly

SAPPHIRE SPRINGS SERIES

Not Just Gal Pals (Book 1)

A grumpy/sunshine sapphic fall romance featuring Blake, Sapphire Spring's local doctor, and Jenny, an influencer fleeing a social media scandal.

Novel Problems (Book 2)

A feel-good sapphic summer romance between George, the golden retriever owner of the cafe-bookstore Novel Gossip, and Hannah, a secretive fantasy author who has a lot of novel problems.

The Floral Arrangement (Book 3)

An age-gap, fake-dating, enemies-to-lovers spring rom com between an ice queen businesswoman and a bubbly florist.

OTHER

From LA to London, With Love

A Koru-award winning M/F celebrity romance set in London, featuring Sophie Shah, a bisexual single-mom-by-choice, Chris Trent, a humiliated movie star, and a cast of queer characters.